More praise for Liam Jackson and

OFFSPRING

"An awesome tale…an adrenaline-pumping story line."
—Alternative-Worlds.com

"A meticulously crafted chess game of supernatural suspense, a page-turner of the highest order."
—Jay Bonansinga, author of *Shattered*

"An engrossing plot…nightmarish, gory, and riveting."
—*VOYA*

"Readers are rewarded with fast-paced action that's great to the end."
—*Romantic Times BOOKreviews*

"Jackson's classic good-versus-evil story takes us through an exciting biblical battle between angels and demons. An intense, violent, and suspenseful adventure set against a landscape of stark possibilities and doom… A thrilling read to the end!"
—Raymond K. Wong,
author of *The Pacific Between*

D0650930

St. Martin's Paperbacks Titles
by Liam Jackson

Offspring
The Keys of Solomon

THE KEYS OF SOLOMON

Liam Jackson

St. Martin's Paperbacks

THE KEYS OF SOLOMON

Copyright © 2009 by Liam Jackson.

All rights reserved.

For information address St. Martin's Press, 175 Fifth Avenue, New York, NY 10010.

ISBN: 0-312-36742-2
EAN: 978-0-312-36742-8

Printed in the United States of America

St. Martin's Paperbacks edition / May 2009

St. Martin's Paperbacks are published by St. Martin's Press, 175 Fifth Avenue, New York, NY 10010.

10 9 8 7 6 5 4 3 2 1

For Jo, Tabitha, and Tiffany

acknowledgments

I would like to extend my eternal gratitude to friend and mentor Lou Aronica, super-agent Peter Miller, my editor, Lorrie McCann, and publisher Thomas Dunne.

And I thank you, gentle reader. Without you there is no story.

Angels in their various roles have long been focal points of theological debate and biblical interpretation. Conclusions, as one might surmise, are myriad and highly diverse. In writing Offspring, *I have attempted to remain true to mainstream theology as it pertains to the Host of Heaven. The Hierarchy, as identified in* Offspring, *can be found below.*

Divinity: Uncreated Energy
Creation: Created Energy

THE NINE CHOIRS OF ANGELS

Angels of Pure Contemplation
Govern All Creation

1. Seraphim
2. Cherubim
3. Thrones

(Archangels are also associated with the First Choir, in their capacity as War Leaders, i.e. Michael and the First War in Heaven)

Angels of the Cosmos
Govern All the Cosmos

4. Dominions
5. Powers
6. Virtues

Angels of the World
Govern All the World

7. Principalities
8. Archangels (also included in the First Choir, serving as War Leaders)
9. Angels (Heralds)

Hierarchy of Angels
Tiers (ranks) from lowest order (Heralds) to highest (Seraphim)

Heralds: Sharaiel
Virtues
Principalities: Azazeal
Thrones: Joriel
Authorities
Powers: Nathaniel
Dominations: Kiel, Axthiel
Archangels
Cherubim: Baraniel, Theoneal
Seraphim

Nephilim: Title (or class of angel) given to the most powerful of Fallen Angels, according to some versions of the Old Testament

Hierarchy of Sitra Akhra (Demons)
(from lowest order to highest)

Minor Demons
Commonly called "beasts" or "soldiers" (over a dozen sub-types of minor demons, collectively referred to as Legion)

Greater Demon types
Incubus
Succubus
Fane
Wraith
Djinn
Fury: Drammach
Hell Knight

Demon Lords
Nytemare
Wamphyri
Wyrm

Nine Princes of Sitra Akhra
Abbadon, Baphomet, Baal-Peor, Beelzebub, Leviathan, Lix Tetrax (also called Blight), Mastema, Melchiresa, Malach-bel (also called Dread Moloch)

Emperor
Nemesis

"The work of the devil will infiltrate even into the Church in such a way that one will see cardinals opposing cardinals, bishops against bishops. The priests who venerate me will be scorned and opposed by their confreres...churches and altars sacked; the Church will be full of those who accept compromises and the demons will press many priests and consecrated souls..."

—Sister Agnes, Our Lady of Akita Catholic Church, prophesying for the Virgin Mary, 1973

"And the angels, terrible and without pity, carry savage weapons, and their torture is unmerciful."

—The Ascension of Enoch from The Book of the Jews

chapter 1

East St. Louis, Missouri

The building reeked of the enemy. The odor of sulfur and cat urine was stale, perhaps days or weeks old, but it was there nonetheless. Thomas Falco wrinkled his hypersensitive nose and looked around the dimly lit interior of the motel. Beneath the façade of new plaster and fresh paint, potentially lethal black mold festered on the walls and floors, spreading the length of the lobby. Falco grimaced at the metaphorical significance. He moved to the front desk and set his bags upon the dirty tiled floor.

The desk clerk blocked a yawn with the back of his hand, then said, "'Sup, man? What brings you to the murder capital of the western hemisphere?"

Without looking up from the desk, Falco said, "I thought Gary, Indiana, held that distinction."

"Bullshit," replied the young man between more yawns. "Gary's got nothing but a bunch of poseurs and wannabe playas. Eastside is the real deal."

Falco completed the motel registration card and slid it across the desk to the scruffily dressed clerk. The young man had the sleepy eyes and broad, idiot grin of the terminally stoned, and Falco immediately both resented and pitied him. He wanted to snatch the fool by the back of his scrawny neck and shake some sense into him. Instead, Falco thought, *You really don't want to know why I'm here. So do yourself a favor, kid, and invest in another quarter-bag of whatever shit you're smoking. Trust me on this one.*

"I'm just in town to visit an old friend and maybe do some sightseeing."

The word *sightseeing* seemed to trigger something in the stoner's hazy mind. He gave Falco a goofy, exaggerated nod, and a knowing wink. "Ah, sightseeing. Right. I'm tracking with you now. Well, here's a tip for you, my man. Don't let looks deceive you, know what I'm saying? We might be in the low-rent district, but we know how to show our guests a good time. Know what I'm sayin'? You need anything, anything at all, you let me know." Another exaggerated wink. "So, how long you staying?"

"I'm not sure. A couple of days, maybe. I'll let you know."

The clerk gave Falco a third wink followed by another lazy grin, and dropped a plastic door card onto the sticky countertop.

"That's cool, dude, that's cool. Room 112. As you walk out the front door, turn, umm, right. Yeah, right. Last room at the end of the walk."

Falco nodded, picked up the key and his suitcase, and started away from the desk. Over his shoulder, he called out, "No maids, no disturbances. Know what I'm sayin'?"

Once outside, Falco crossed the parking lot to the rental car and retrieved the rest of his luggage. On the way to the room, he chose a leisurely pace, taking care to thoroughly check his surroundings. *Run-down strip mall to the left, mega truck stop to the right. Elementary school across the highway. Not much traffic. Nothing out of the ordinary. Not yet.*

Satisfied, he kicked the snow from his boots and entered the motel room. The place smelled of cigarette smoke, sour beer, and more cat piss. The furnishings were sparse and in poor condition. Against the far wall, a swayback mattress lay atop a warped, metal frame. A funky little neo-modernist lamp leaned crazily atop a three-legged bedside table. A pair of ugly, vinyl-covered chairs flanked a rickety desk in front of the room's single window. Falco was certain the decorator had been a fan of Pleistocene-era art nouveau, a dinosaur best left dead and in the ground.

A shrill bell sounded across the street, and the shouts of young children penetrated the thin walls of the room. *It's not time for school to let out. I can't be running that far behind.* Falco glanced at his watch. It was 1:45 P.M. *Good. Just an afternoon recess. I'm not too far off schedule.*

He stepped to the window and looked out on the busy grade-school playground across the street. A pair of marked police cars were parked along the shoulder of the highway, at opposite ends of the school property. Falco was certain more cruisers were similarly situated on the back side of the grounds. Prudent considering current events, he thought.

Prudent, but futile. You can't stop them, Mr. Policeman, sir. You and a thousand more just like you can't stop them. Legion comes. Falco drew the curtains together and returned to the bed. It was time to prepare.

He opened his suitcase and carefully removed his clothing and equipment and arranged the items in neat, separate piles on the bed. First, he inspected the night-vision monocular, a small cylindrical device that allowed him to see thermal imprints in total darkness. A quick self-test indicated that the battery was hot and the instrument was working properly.

Next, he removed a sound suppressor from its protective pouch and inspected the screw threads. Dry. He took a tube of waxy lip balm from his pocket, removed the cap, and squeezed a liberal amount of the balm inside the threaded connector. He worked the greasy paste into the threads, then reexamined his handiwork. *Much better.* He laid the suppressor aside and opened a small polymer case.

Inside the case, surrounded by thick foam, was another primary tool of his trade, a Glock model 29, chambered in powerful 10 millimeter. Falco inspected the weapon, then threaded the suppressor onto the barrel extension. Then he checked the ammunition and spare magazines. He tapped each magazine against the heel of his hand to seat the shells, ensuring a proper feed into the semi-automatic handgun.

Finally, he checked his combat knife, a legacy item and constant reminder of his former life. The knife slid easily from the oiled sheath. Thomas thumbed the single edge of the Ka-Bar.

If only men were as strong and reliable as the steel in my blade.

Stifling a yawn, Falco inserted the knife back into the sheath and rubbed his eyes with thick, callused fingers. "So tired." Thomas shook his head. "No. I can be tired when this is over." He resumed his meticulous preparations.

A half-hour later, after each tool had been thoroughly examined and the ammo counted and recounted, it was time to perform the Sacrament of Holy Orders, one of seven such sacraments of the Catholic Church, and a requirement of the codex by which Falco lived and served. This particular ritual was steeped in tradition and far older than the Brotherhood Falco served. Many members within his sect had long argued against using the Sacrament of Holy Orders in favor of some other ritual.

Yet in the end, use of the sacrament was approved for servants of Falco's unique vocation. After all, the Sacrament of Holy Orders was intended to imbue a priest with the voice and authority of Christ in certain instances. How could any other ritual be more pertinent or germane to Falco's mission? Was he not speaking for all of Christendom through his actions?

The sacrament was followed by another process, the Rite of Purification. This ceremony, based on New Testament scripture, had a two-fold purpose. First, it was designed to free the tools of any extraneous contamination. The second purpose, and one of much greater significance for Thomas, was to free the user from sin or guilt associated with using the tools. Thomas had never fully bought into the notion that any ritual could absolve him of his many sins, past, present, or future. However, he faithfully performed the rite before every mission. He decided long ago that in his line of work, it was best to cover all the bases.

Falco removed an ornate, leather-bound box from an inner pocket of his suitcase. From the box he took a centuries-old rosary and laid it aside. Next, he removed a white satin vestment stole, pressed it to his lips, then draped it around his neck and crossed the ends over his chest. Finally, he took the last item from the box, a small bottle made of jeweled cloisonné.

Falco knelt beside the bed and removed the cork stopper from the bottle. He dribbled some of the water into his palm and with his index finger, traced the outline of a cross upon his forehead. In a final act of consecration, he sprinkled droplets onto the grips of the handgun and combat knife. Bowing his head, he intoned the ancient ritual prayer, much as it had been recited some eight hundred years earlier. Minutes later, as he neared the finish, Falco raised his hands toward the ceiling and whispered, "Non Nobis Domine Non Nobis Sed Nomini Tuo Da Gloriam." *Not Unto Us, O Lord, But Unto Thy Name Be Given Glory.*

Monday 11:05 P.M., Room 312

A puzzling and persistent noise nagged at Falco's tired mind from some distant place. He was sure he had heard the bothersome sound before and knew he should recognize it. *Fire alarm? No. Phone? Phone!* Rolling over onto his side, Falco took a moment to readjust the shoulder holster, then picked up his cell phone. He checked the incoming call and recognized the number.

"Hello?"

A hoarse, raspy voice answered, "Thomas?"

The voice was familiar but this was a time for extreme caution. The Enemy was treacherous and deceitful beyond imagination.

"Who's calling?" Falco asked.

There was a slight hesitation on the other end, then, "The First Shield. You sound a bit disoriented. Did I wake you?"

Falco felt none of the inner alarms ringing in his head. Still, he needed confirmation. It was highly unusual for a man of the First Shield's status to call a mere field operative, even if the two men were old acquaintances.

"I'm fine, Your Grace. Just a bit groggy. Guess the miles are catching up with me. That's a long flight out of Boston."

"Understandable, Thomas, quite so. However, you didn't fly out of Boston. It was Miami. And please, 'Your Grace' seems too formal among old friends. If not Nicholas, then Bishop Gilbert will do."

Bishop. Heh. Falco relaxed. "Just checking, Your Gra— Nicholas. I hope you aren't offended by my suspicions."

"No, not at all. In fact, I prefer that you always exercise such caution. We live in very dangerous times, my boy. You know what happened to Cohlin Ridley only a month past."

Falco's jaw muscles twitched at the mention of his former partner. "Yes, I know."

"I—I'm sorry. Of course you do. I know the two of you were very close." Archbishop Gilbert quickly changed the subject. "When do you expect William?"

"I'm scheduled to fly out tomorrow afternoon, and arrive in Phoenix around 9:30 P.M. A freak snowstorm came through the area last night, but it's blown itself out. I doubt there'll be any airport delays."

Once more, there was a hesitation, though Falco could hear the sound of labored breathing. Gilbert's bronchitis was acting up again.

After a long pause, Gilbert said, "Did you receive the packet?"

"Yeah. Lexis personally gave it to me just before I boarded my flight. I'm set unless there have been some last-minute changes."

"No changes," replied Gilbert. "Our orders stand." Again, an extended silence.

After a moment, Falco nodded absently. "I'll be in touch once I'm in the air and en route to Phoenix."

Gilbert coughed, then said, "Did you have a chance to catch the evening news? Depressing but telling. It seems things are heating up very quickly."

Falco was unsure how to answer. *Of course, things are heating up! Why else would I be in St. Louis, preparing to kill . . .*

Instead of wasting sarcasm on his well-intentioned superior, Falco simply said, "Yes, Nicholas, things are certainly heating up. That's why I'm here."

"Of course, of course. I'll let you attend your task, now. God speed, Thomas."

Falco disconnected the call and looked at his watch. *Not yet midnight. I can catch another hour of sleep.* But as soon as the notion of sleep entered his mind, he pushed it aside. Falco knew that there would be no more rest tonight. He dressed in the dark, the mission unfolding, playing out in his mind. Again and again, he mentally traced the route leading to a country estate just north of the city of St. Louis. There he would find his target. He shouldered his nylon pack and headed for the parking lot.

He unlocked the door, then paused for a moment, breathing in the night air. He closed his eyes and extended his senses. He was rewarded by an immediate tug on the fringe of his consciousness, the faint, yet unmistakable presence of his supernatural adversaries. Detecting the Enemy by use of his God-given gift was always unnerving.

While the gift was accurate, it also meant the Enemy would be nearby. What he wouldn't give for a bit more range, say, another three or four miles. This Enemy was prowling the night, thus it was most likely a minor minion. At least Falco could be thankful for that. While minions were likely to kill, they usually claimed single victims before crawling back to the nest. The demon lords were another, far more serious matter. He quickly broke contact with the minion and closed his senses. Falco threw his pack into the passenger seat and folded himself into the compact. Thirty minutes later, he was outside of the city and headed toward the Bedford Country Club.

Falco was familiar with the long stretch of cracked asphalt. Every curve, every dip, every pothole was committed to memory. He exited the county road fourteen miles east of St. Louis and turned left onto a freshly paved roadway. He drove along for several miles before cutting his headlights. Falco preferred to drive the final miles by moonlight and instinct, paying close attention to the odometer. When he drew within a couple of miles of his destination, he pulled the car off the roadway and into the tree line. Killing the motor, he glanced at the luminous dial on his watch. It was *2:55 A.M. Right on time.*

He rechecked the Glock, then donned a black nylon hood and cinched the thin elastic cord around his neck. The material was sheer; it allowed him to breathe and see, yet effectively concealed his face. With his small pack slung over one shoulder, Falco paused and tested the air.

The temperature was much colder out among the trees, away from the city. The air should have been fresher, sweeter. Yet, as he reached out with his senses, the stench slammed into his stomach like a fist. Falco bent forward and waited for the assault on his senses to pass. It took a few minutes longer than usual this time.

My God, he's strong! Just—hang on. It'll pass . . . it'll pass.

A full minute later, the nausea began to fade and Falco relaxed. Taking up his gear, he set out on foot. It took almost half an hour to cover the final distance through the dense underbrush. No wasted motion, no noise of any kind. Falco silently recited the assassin's credo: Quick and silent in, quick and silent out. It sounded good, but he knew all too well that things didn't always work out that way. Nogales had been messy. Buenos Aires had escalated into a full-fledged fire fight.

As he crouched inside a thick patch of weeds and vines, Falco surveyed the area with the monocular. The estate was in reality a compound consisting of a main ranch house, surrounded by several large bungalows. Guard posts surrounded the perimeter of the grounds. A sprawling golf course flanked the southeast edge of the estate. The stables and polo grounds were just to the north and west of the main compound. The target expressed a great love for golf and the outdoors, thus he explained his unusual choice for a vacation spot to his superiors. Falco knew better. The country club, once a weekend hideaway for the Midwestern affluent, was now a haven for the Enemy. A nest.

Falco scanned the rest of the grounds. The largest of the bungalows was situated well away from the others, just beyond the periphery of the brilliant security lights. It was also the farthest removed from the stables. From experience, Falco knew the placement of the bungalows was no accident or coincidence. The horses, if any still remained, would not, could not abide such an abomination in close proximity. He would be surprised if any single animal remained on the premises.

Sweeping the night-vision instrument over the rest of the area, Falco detected two thermal outlines, most likely guards, he thought. Neither figure moved for several minutes, suggesting that both were possibly asleep. If only he could be so lucky, he thought.

Falco kept to the shadows as he crept toward his destination. When he was within twenty yards of the first bodyguard, Falco holstered the Beretta and drew a sleek combat knife. Gripping the knife with the blade held down and along his right forearm, he inched forward. The bodyguards were sitting on opposite sides of the front porch, heads down and breathing deeply.

The rear of the building appeared unguarded, striking Falco as odd and more than a little disturbing. Perhaps there was no backdoor, no exit. His anxiety grew. On the one hand, with only the single front door, Falco could easily cover his escape route. On the other hand, if things went badly, he could find himself blocked in. He glanced up and made a mental note of the rows of heavily barred windows. No help there. In fact, the layout smacked of a trap.

Falco crept to within striking distance of the first guard, a thickly built man with bullish shoulders. Falco willed his own muscles to relax, then exploded forward. With the heel of his left hand, he struck the guard high on the bridge of the nose, snapping back his head and exposing the throat. The knife hissed through the air and opened a gaping wound below the man's double chin. On the backstroke, he buried the blade diagonally in the soft, exposed hollow between collarbone and neck. The double strike had taken less then two full seconds and left nothing to chance. The guard dropped in a disheveled heap, body quivering in the morbid manner of the mortally wounded.

The second guard stirred, becoming alert much more quickly than Falco had anticipated. The man spotted his fallen partner, then Falco. Time froze for an instant. The delay was all Falco needed. He closed the distance between the man and himself in an economical blur of motion, drove the pommel into the man's solar plexus, and was rewarded by an instant gush of putrid air smelling of raw sewage and ammonia.

As the guard doubled over, Falco cupped his hand behind the man's head and pulled down sharply. Knee met face with an audible crack. Falco caught the guard as he pitched forward, and slid the blade into the back of the man's brain, just above the first cervical, or Atlas vertebra. Another threat neutralized.

Falco moved to the door and tested the simple latch. The door was unlocked and swung open on well-oiled hinges. He stepped inside and closed the door behind him. The interior of the bungalow was dark and Falco used the monocular to scan the room. He located a second interior door and moved silently across the room.

Reaching the interior door, Falco paused for a few seconds in order to allow his pulse to drop to an acceptable level. Then he pressed his ear to the cool wood and listened for sounds from within. Nothing.

He drew the Beretta from the holster, thumbed off the safety, opened the bedroom door, and crept inside on the balls of his feet.

The bedroom was dark as pitch. Falco again used the monocular. The spacious room was empty except for the lone figure lying on the canopied bed. He moved to the bed and stood over his target. Despite loathing for both the target and his task, there was no last-minute struggle to reconcile duty with morality. This was war.

He was mildly surprised when his target spoke. The man had a love for pain killers and other barbiturates. He should have been dead to the world. He would be very soon.

"So, you've come for me now, have you?"

Falco had once known this man, studied at his side, and considered him both friend and mentor. Despite his anger, he needed to look into the man's eyes a final time. He raised the flashlight. If there remained any sign of humanity, any possibility of redemption . . .

Bishop Everett Hollingsworth lay partially covered by satin sheets. He was dressed in a silk nightshirt that bore an embossed monogram, the emblem of his office. The bishop's expression was one of weary amusement, his eyes dark, calculating. There was no trace of fear . . . or repentance.

Falco's sense of duty was concrete and unassailable, but the resignation in the target's voice struck him like a slap across the face. Falco struggled to find the words.

"You knew I would. You've made it easy for me."

The priest laughed and said, "Oh, Thomas. Do you not think I have prayed for death on a daily basis? If I've assisted you in your duty in any way, perhaps it is my way of atoning for past mistakes."

Anger surged through Falco like wild bolts of summer lightning and for the first time in many years, his emotions took over.

"Discipulus Daemonism! You casually dismiss your transgressions as a . . . a mistake? We know you aided the Enemy in defiling the Veil outside Knoxville. That's more than adequate reason to kill you. But worse, oh, so very much worse, you've committed the single greatest act of heresy in all creation. You willingly provided a demon with sanctuary and sustenance. You offer up your mind and body as a living vessel for the most corrupt essence in all of Creation. For this, you'll endure an eternity of endless deaths, each far worse than its predecessor."

"Bold words, Thomas, but you forget that I know you. I know what you are and what you've done in the name of your God, the King of Liars. I also know your puppeteers, that pompous house of arrogant and degenerate hypocrites.

"The Church. A haven for murderers, thieves, and molesters of small children! By what right does such an institution pronounce any degree of self-righteous judgment upon me or my masters? You've no right to damn me, murderer!"

Through clinched teeth, Falco said, "By virtue of your betrayal and my oath, it is my right, my duty, to do exactly that!"

"Then to hell with us both!" The bishop's voice grew

raspy, deeper, more forceful. His eyes pulsed in the dark with an ugly yellow aura and Falco fought the urge to step back. Throwing back the sheets, Hollingsworth started to rise from the bed.

Can't let him get to his feet!

Falco shoved the Glock's heavy barrel into the man's face and drove him back onto the pillows. Stout fingers clawed at Falco's eyes and throat, but the priest-turned-assassin brushed them aside. Two silicon-tipped slugs tore through the old man's brain, silencing him forever.

Falco steeled himself for the inevitable aftershock, and nearly fell as the room tilted, and spun violently. The episode, familiar yet always disorienting, was over in seconds. As the vertigo receded, Falco looked down upon the ruined face of the man he had once called Father. He searched Hollingsworth's lifeless hand for the ring, the signet of the office of bishop coadjutor. He tugged the ring free and dropped it into his shirt pocket. Falco paused briefly to genuflect.

"So you know me, know what I am, do you?" he asked softly. "And now you know the wrath of my God. Peace, be still."

chapter 2

Tempe, Arizona

Sam Conner walked across the expansive campus of Arizona State University at Tempe, lugging a backpack the size of a small camelback trunk, contemplating his short life. In fact, life hadn't been especially good the past couple of years. Of course, it wasn't all that bad. Many people had it much worse, Sam knew. It was just that things were so unpredictable, so . . . strange. Or weird. Yeah, that's it. Weird.

His father, a good and decent man, was a much-too-young victim of heart disease. This was a man who had never inhaled anything stronger than smoke from burnt toast, and who jogged with religious zealousness, except when it snowed. And snow was seldom a showstopper in Sun City, Arizona. Allan Theodore Conner. Age forty-one. Dead of a massive coronary. Not a weird man by any stretch of the imagination, but certainly the victim of weirdness.

His mother, God bless her pointed little head, had always been an introvert. She was even more so now. Ever socially withdrawn and moody, she had now joined the ranks of the emotionally missing in action, vacant of both mind and soul. Sam supposed this was to be expected of most people when they lose a soul mate. And Sam's parents had been that if nothing else. Of course, it didn't matter that she had an excuse. Excuses didn't help kids navigate their own myriad problems. Kat needed her mother, more now than ever before.

Katherine "Kat" Conner was Sam's younger sister, and the child grew weirder by the day. Again, Sam figured that was also to be expected. In the first place, she was female. Sam figured that covered a lot of the "weirdness" issue. However, to compound problems, she was also more or less a brand-spanking-new teenager, having reached the venerable age of fourteen less than a week before. Unfortunately, she was also far more mature than any of her friends or peers, and some of her middle school teachers. Wisdom in youth usually creates more problems than it ever solves, or at least that was Sam's take on the matter. When it came to kids, the world just wasn't hardwired to draw distinction between "wise" and "wise-ass." And finally, poor Kat was female, or had Sam already factored that in?

But there was more to Kat's problem than gender-specific hormones, age-defying wisdom, and a rapidly maturing self-awareness. Much more. Always an exceptionally bright kid, that intelligence was now augmented by the manifestation of her special gifts, legacies from her genetic inheritance. Sam knew firsthand that few things in this world or any other could possibly be any weirder than an Offspring first coming into his or her legacy.

Offspring. The descendants of angelic trysts with humans as recorded in the Old Testament and other, older non-Christian texts. There had been a special age during which humanity had coupled with divinity, at least according to those diverse religious belief systems. The result of all that coupling was children, but not just any children. These carried perhaps the most amazing bloodline in all of Creation, a bloodline that resulted in genetic freaks possessing a marvelous supernatural "gift." By virtue of the divine heritage, they were capable of extraordinary feats.

Sam had learned that in this modern era, not all who carried the watered-down bloodline experienced an awakening of the genetic gifts. Thousands of Offspring lived mundane lives and died mundane deaths, never the wiser regarding their angelic heritage, and many who did notice their strengths had no idea what to attribute them to. No such luck for Sam. His gifts manifested at birth, and were still emerging twenty years later. And thanks to those gifts, his life was too weird to even consider he would ever know mundane anything. The same applied to Kat.

Sam could admit to himself that while Kat wasn't nearly as weird as her older brother, she was quickly budding into quite the Offspring debutante.

Sam chuckled at the mental image of an Offspring Ball. "Weird or not, I crack me up sometimes."

Things had been strange for Sam long before he learned of the Offspring connection, his blood legacy, or the supernatural gifts associated with his inheritance. You could ask his paternal grandmother, Nanna, about Sam. She could tell you some stories about weird. If she were alive, that is. Nanna had been gone several years now, "moving on to the happy hunting grounds," she'd said just before she died of cancer. Half Scottish, half Lakota Sioux, she loved to slip in those Hollywood clichés about American Indians when you least expected them. Sam was sure Nanna also had the gifts. People who knew her said she had the "second sight."

Sam's old friend Michael Collier could also tell some great stories about Sam's weirdness, but . . . he was dead too. Or at least, Sam thought so. The big cop was taking his last breath on earth, dying from a massive head wound, when he stepped into the damaged supernatural Veil that separated the myriad planes of existence. Planes that comprised much more than the mere universe, they made up all of Creation. The Multiverse, as Horace liked to say. Michael Collier's sacrifice had bought a little time for the much-maligned human race. Only time would tell if humanity was really worthy of the price.

Of course, not all witnesses to Sam's weirdness were dead. Mark Pierce knew all about Sam. Of course he would. He was also an Offspring. Charlene Hastings, Sam's love of loves, knew he was a little *different*, but she had no idea. No idea. No sense asking her about the weirdness. Maybe you could ask Skinny Henderson, Sam's best friend through middle school. Except that, while Skinny was still very much alive today, he refused to talk to or about Sam Conner. Skinny was scared shitless of Sam.

And then there was Horace, the sometimes rambling old black man, sometimes damn near omnipotent archangel. He occasionally went by the name Uriel, but to his friends he was always Horace. Like Nanna, Michael, and Mark, Horace could tell some stories that are weird with a capital *W,* but he wasn't around much these days. Sam figured the old man would turn back up when the time was right. And as much as he loved Horace, he dreaded seeing him again. His appearance would only mean more weirdness was on the way.

In fact, Sam decided there were only two sources you could check with to fully understand his heightened state of weirdness. You could check with Joriel, the angel with the attitude who sometimes lived in Sam's head. She knew Sam inside and out, literally. Sometimes, Joriel would disappear for long stretches, but she always came back. She had been with him since the moment of his birth. Perhaps even before.

And if you were allergic to heavenly beings, you could check with the opposing side. The demons of Legion knew Sam was weird, all right. And they wanted him dead for it. They were the Enemy, and Sam had drawn first blood.

Weirdness had always been Sam's salvation and his eternal damnation. In the case of demons, being different had saved his life several times. He could see the bastards coming, even when they didn't want to be seen. He could hear them over great distances. Hell, he could smell them! The odor nearly always knocked him to his knees and left him shaking like a drunk in the throes of the DTs.

But Sam didn't want to think about that today. Upon reaching the residence hall, Sam staggered upstairs to his dorm room, nudged open the door with the toe of his sneaker, and stepped inside. He grimaced. The air conditioner was set on high, but it was blowing lukewarm air again. Sam dropped his backpack at the foot of the narrow dorm room bed, and sat down beside it. He didn't want to think about angels or demons, Offspring or gifts, today. Not now. Not anytime soon.

Time for the old Jedi mind trick, Sammy. Use the Force. Push that bullshit out of your mind and concentrate on something else. Anything else. Like, maybe the temperature in this friggin' sweatbox!

While Sam hoped to never, ever again see snow, he did find himself wishing for a cool November rain. He peeled off his soggy T-shirt, paused for a moment to examine the mass of angry-looking scars that crisscrossed his chest, then mopped the perspiration from his forehead and dropped the shirt to the floor. *Thanksgiving is next week and it's 102 degrees outside.*

He glanced at the desk clock and groaned. He had an evening biology lab in exactly two hours and thirty-five minutes, in a building located on the other side of the sprawling Arizona State University campus, and the thought of trudging back across a sweltering campus while carrying a backpack full of textbooks did nothing to lighten his mood.

He considered ditching the lab but reluctantly dismissed the idea. He was already having hell with biology. *Like dissecting piglets is gonna help me land that dream job with Boeing or McDonnell Douglas. Maybe I should've taken that scholarship to U of W at Green Bay,* he thought. *I bet they don't have to put up with 102 kiss-my-melted-ass degrees!*

Sam rolled over onto his side and felt the shift of scar tissue and loose cartilage in his chest and ribcage. Unpleasant memories hovered just beyond the periphery of his consciousness. He tried to block them out, and was largely successful. But he would never be completely free of the nightmarish memories, not as long as he had the scars to serve as a daily reminder. His physical wounds caused little discomfort, thanks in part to the healing touch of old Horace. However, his body would bear vivid reminders of his past for the rest of his life. And now . . . new and disturbing blips on his internal radar only aggravated both the physical and emotional injuries sustained in the battle beneath Abbotsville.

For the past couple of years, Sam had been left alone, free of the demonic presences that had stalked him across half of the United States and nearly killed him in the belly of an abandoned mine shaft located in the heart of Tennessee. Since that time, the entire country had experienced inexplicable and unparalleled violence. Sam's small corner of the world was no exception. The city fathers in Phoenix had already established an evening curfew much like those in Chicago, New York, Los Angeles, and Atlanta.

The National Guard now patrolled the streets in parts of

south Florida, Philadelphia, and a dozen other major cities. Not that it helped much. Or maybe it did, thought Sam. Who knows how high the death count would soar if people were still living unrestricted, normal lifestyles? How many more would disappear without a trace? How many children would be found dead, mutilated beyond recognition?

While Sam occasionally sensed a nearby Enemy, it had been a long time since he felt personally threatened. Most times the telepathic signals were fleeting as the entities seemed to pass through the area, oblivious to Sam's presence. Then, a couple of days ago while sitting in class, Sam felt a chilling tug on the edge of his "internal radar." This signal wasn't just passing through. It was searching. For him.

Sam's "radar" was an intuitive, psychic instrument that had never once been wrong. The source of this particular signal was very strong, indicating a close proximity. Since then, other blips had increased in both frequency and intensity. The sources were moving in a spiral pattern, working their way closer to Sam with each passing day.

Man, I need a cigarette.

Ignoring the crumpled box of Marlboros, Sam reached for a pack of gum on the nightstand and unwrapped three sticks. He stuffed them in his mouth, and chewed vigorously for several seconds. After two years, he had just about kicked the smoking habit. Foolishly, he had taken up smoking in the tenth grade in order to impress Cynthia Gault, a popular and more than a little naughty high school pin-up type. He smiled sheepishly at the memory. As far as he knew the tactic had failed miserably and Cynthia graduated from McArthur High, blissfully ignorant of her scrawny, redheaded admirer. Kat still took pleasure in reminding him of that folly. *Oh well, lessons learned, huh?*

He rolled off the bed and headed for the small dorm refrigerator. Before he made it across the room, his cell phone rang, playing the theme song to the '60's campy comedy series *Get Smart*.

"Sam. Shoot," he answered.

"Hiya, kid! How the hell are you?"

Sam grinned. Only one person ever called him "kid."

"Mark! Man, I'm melting like an ice cube in a microwave. Hotter than hell here. Other than that, I'm doing well. How's things with you? Janet doing okay?"

"We're fine, Sam, just fine. Janet's still writing and researching. The newspaper keeps her busy, and she spends all her free time working on the database."

Sam didn't ask about the database. He already knew far more than he cared to about that subject. Janet Davis, a newspaper reporter and the love of Mark Pierce's life, had made it a personal mission to track the spreading demonic activity through various news wires and agencies across the globe. At last count, Janet had entered more than six thousand questionable—and some not so questionable—incidents into the database.

"Mark, it's really good to hear your voice. So, what's up? You just calling to say hello, or have you got something on your mind?"

"I . . ."

There was a long pause and Sam's stomach rolled. "You're stalling, Mark. Come on with it."

"Maybe it's nothing, Sam. It's . . . for the past couple of weeks, I've had some weird dreams . . . like the old days."

Blips on my radar, and now his old dreams. God, don't do this to me. Not again. . . . Sam tried to swallow, but his mouth was as dry as an Arizona dirt road. "Tell me about them."

"I wish I could, but you know how it is. I can never remember the details after I wake up. All I know is, in this dream we're all together again. You, me, and Michael. Running from something. All night long, just running. We manage to stay a step ahead, but there's always the feeling that it's gaining on us."

· Sam walked to the fridge and took out a bottle of energy drink. He popped the top while waiting for Mark to go on. Mark didn't. Sam took a sip then sat back on the bed. "You would think it has to end sometime, wouldn't you? For Christ's sake, it's been two years, Mark. I used to dream about—about things all the time. Like, every single night. I couldn't even take a nap without finding myself back in that goddamned mineshaft."

Mark's voice sounded strained. "I've had my fair share of dreams about Abbotsville, but most were about the motel. The worst always involved the motel. Lately, when I wake up I have this god-awful feeling in the pit of my stomach that things are about to go south again. I don't know, Sam. Like I said, maybe it's nothing. I . . . I just needed to hear your voice, make sure you're okay."

I can't go through it again. Please, God. Sam closed his eyes and held the phone against his chest for several seconds. Finally, he raised the phone to his ear. Mark was calling his name. After a moment Sam said, "Yeah. I'm still here."

"I'm sorry, Sam. I really am. You know I wouldn't hit you with this if I wasn't concerned."

Sam took a deep breath and exhaled slowly. "Mark, do you still hear the voices?"

Mark paused, then said, "I'm not sure, Sam. Sometimes, maybe, but nothing like before. I hear . . . something, but I can't make out the words. I'm not sure I want to."

Sam nodded to himself. *He's hearing them again, all right, but he doesn't want to admit it. Probably telling the truth about not being able to make out the messages. He isn't as sensitive to them as I am. Maybe . . . No! I'm not going there. Not this time. I won't do it. I can't!* He took a second to gather his composure, and noticed he had a white-knuckle death grip on the cell phone.

"I'm okay, Mark, really. No real problems on this end, at least none that I'm aware of. Unless you count Vertebrate Physiology. That course is kicking my ass." The words rang false to his own ears, and he had no doubt that Mark knew he was lying.

To Sam's relief, Mark didn't call him on the lie. Not yet, anyway. Instead, the man laughed weakly, breaking some of the tension. "Vertebrate what? No, never mind, kid. It just sounds nasty."

Sam laughed. "Look, I'm coming out east to see Charlie over the Christmas break. Why don't you and Janet meet us in Knoxville? I'd offer to drive up to Lexington, but Charlie just started a new job and it might be tough on her to get away for any longer than an overnight trip. What do you say?"

"That sounds like a plan, kid." Mark paused for a moment, then changed gears, catching Sam off guard. "Now that we have that out of the way, maybe it's time you come clean with me. Have you sensed anything out of the norm? And I mean anything. The truth this time."

Sam took a moment to frame his reply. They had been through too much together, and he wouldn't lie, not about this. But he didn't want to place additional stress on his old friend by telling the entire truth, either. He took another deep breath and let it out slowly.

"Mark, if I spend more than a few minutes a day thinking about demons or Abbotsville, I'll go bullet-to-the-brain crazy. I know they're out there. We both know the world is crawling with them now. I catch an occasional blip on the radar. Once in a while, I sense something nearby, but it usually moves on after a few hours or days. Nothing has happened to make me think I'm in any danger. I'd tell you if things were different."

Mark grunted, then said, "Sure you would, kid, just as soon as pigs fly out of my ass. Look, you're a special case, Sam. I don't think you'll ever be completely free from all this, and hiding things from me won't help either of us.

"Listen, do me a favor. If you get one of those feelings, and you know damn well what I'm talking about, you call me. Don't take any chances. Anything out of the ordinary and you call me ASAP, or better yet, just get on a plane and haul your skinny butt to Lexington. I'll even drive out and get you if you want me to. I still remember my way to Arizona. Just don't wait around for something bad to happen. Okay?"

"Yeah, Mark, sure. I promise."

After a slight pause, Mark said, "Good. Just . . . good. So, how's your mom holding up? And Kat. They doing okay?"

Glad for the change in subject, Sam said, "I talked to Mom last Saturday. I think the whole month has been kinda tough for her. All holidays are tough for her since Dad passed. And she still makes too many green bean casseroles. Kat is still Kat. The little heathen hasn't changed a bit since you and Janet visited last summer."

"Aww, you think the world of baby sister and you know it.

Besides, she's the only one who has any chance of keeping you in line. Do me a favor and give her a hug for me, okay?"

Sam grinned. "You bet. And give Janet a hug for me. I—I miss you guys."

"Christmas isn't that far off, kid. Meanwhile, do us both a favor and take care of your skinny ass. We'll see you in December."

"Right," said Sam. "December. See you both then."

"Oh, before I forget, have you heard from Pam Collier?"

"Not since the baby was born," said Sam. "Pam and little Mikey seemed as well as can be expected."

There was a long pause on the other end of the line. Finally, Mark said, "That's good to hear. I owe her a phone call. Guess I'll take care of that today, while I'm in the calling mood. Talk to you later, kid."

After Mark hung up, Sam kicked off his shoes and stretched out on the bed. While he loved Mark and Janet like family, the thought of a new storm brewing had unnerved him. He wanted no part in any continued struggle between the ultimate forces of Good and Evil. It wasn't that he didn't care. He did. Perhaps too much. The problem was that Sam believed his involvement in such a titanic battle of wills would, in the end, amount to less than cigarette smoke in a tornado. Abbotsville had been a different matter.

Sam and other Offspring had responded to the call of the Veil and made the dangerous trip to Abbotsville, Tennessee. *How much did it cost us? How much?* It was a rhetorical question. Sam knew all too well the price each member of his small group had paid in the name of "service to humanity." Michael Collier had paid with his life. Mark Pierce was only alive today because of the enigmatic Horace. The remarkable old man had saved Mark from a life-threatening bullet wound that had turned both of the man's lungs into ruined jelly.

Then again, as things turned out, Horace wasn't your typical old timer, was he?

Sam closed his eyes. *And how close did I come to buying the farm?* Another rhetorical question. Sam had come as close to death as any man could beneath the rocky grounds of Abbotsville's Cannuagh Sanatorium. *And for what?* he wondered bitterly. *Legion is still here and the world has never been a more screwed-up place. And there's not a damn thing I can do about it, so just leave me alone! God, are you listening? I did my part. Horace said so. So leave . . . me . . . alone!*

Sam arose from the bed and walked on rubbery legs to the sink where he washed his face with cool water. He reached for a hand towel and paused to study his trembling hand. It was almost time to leave for the lab and his date with piglet cadavers. "Oh, this is just great. The last thing I need right now is to screw around with a four-inch four-forty stainless-steel scalpel," he muttered. "If my luck holds, I'll probably hack off my own arm."

chapter 3

Catholic Archdiocese, Los Angeles, California

Archbishop Nicholas Gilbert waved his hand through the air, stirring life into thick, lazy clouds of cherry-scented smoke. "Nasty habit, Malcolm. Why don't you take up a less offensive hobby, say, crapping on my table during the dinner hour?"

Malcolm Reading chuckled and tapped the bowl of the pipe against his palm, catching the spent ash. "What? Give up the pipe and deprive you of one your greatest pleasures? You'd have nothing to complain about and no reason to live beyond tomorrow if I stop smoking. You're just edgy, Nicholas. Have a warm brandy and relax."

As Gilbert readied his standard reply to this years-old exchange between friends, a soft knock sounded at the door.

"Enter!"

The door swung open and Father Juan Jimenez walked into the study. He carried a tray bearing a crystal decanter and a pair of brandy snifters. He wrinkled his nose as he walked through a thin haze of smoke and cast an accusatory look toward Malcolm.

"Ah! No fair, Gil. You've summoned reinforcements!" said Malcolm.

All three laughed as Father Jimenez, a man some years Gilbert's junior, crossed the room and set the tray upon a small table near the open window. He drew shut the heavy drapes, but not before pausing to stare intently out into the night sky.

"Something . . . wrong, Juan?" asked the bishop.

"What? Uh, no, Your Grace. I was just looking at the clouds. A storm is coming."

"Nonsense, Juan," said Gilbert. "I watched the Weather Channel this evening. Nothing but sunshine for the rest of the week."

Father Jimenez smiled and bowed his head slightly. "As you say, Your Grace. Will you require anything tonight?"

"No, no, I'm quite all right. Run along now, and enjoy your evening. I'll call if I need anything."

"Very well. If you'll excuse me, I'll be in the library."

After the priest was gone, Reading rose awkwardly from his chair and limped to the window and opened the drapes. He opened the window and allowed a swirling breeze to carry the ash from his pipe out into the night air. Gilbert watched his old friend with a mixture of pride, pity, and admiration. Few people embodied the cause as did Malcolm Reading, and fewer still had given as much of themselves.

"Father Jimenez, he's something of an odd fellow, isn't he?"

"Oh, I don't know, Malcolm. If by odd you mean simple, devoted, and without ambition, I suppose so. I've known Juan for a dozen years now and if I'm any judge of character, he's one we'll never have to worry about."

Malcolm turned from the window and smiled. "I'm sure you're right, Gil. I certainly hope so, for all our sake. I believe I was followed here tonight."

Gilbert frowned. "And you mention it as if it were some minor afterthought. At any rate, you must stay until morning. I'll have your regular accommodations prepared."

Malcolm limped back to his chair and gingerly sat with his right leg extended out in front of him. Gilbert looked at the heavy brace that encased the man's ruined knee. "You're in no condition to outrun them these days."

"I appreciate the offer," said Malcolm, "but I'm afraid I'm catching a red-eye to New Orleans. We've located another of the bastard children living just miles from the Metairie safe house. Right under our noses all this time, and we just now found him."

Gilbert tugged at his collar with a gnarled, arthritic finger and cleared his throat. "As if hunting Legion isn't risk enough, I'm afraid we court additional disaster by actively going after the Offspring now."

"We've been over this a dozen times, Nicholas, and our course is clear. We have to take the offensive. We've followed these abominations for generations, yet we still know so little about them and their abilities. We must continue to question and examine them, expose them for what they truly are. Before it's too late.

"And as for courting disaster, I think not. We're already ahead of the game, Nicholas. The challenge is to stay there." Malcolm gestured toward the open window. "There are demons, then there are *demons*. Now, take the motley bastards that followed me here. Lesser minions, each a hollow fragment of a much greater manifestation, and nearly always found mewling about in small packs. Dangerous? Unquestionably, and particularly so to the unwary or unenlightened. But we, old man, are neither. We are armed to the teeth with knowledge, cloaked in righteousness, and shielded by vigilance. In this jungle, we are the hunter and they, the hunted."

"Hah! We both know that for the poor lie that it is," admonished Gilbert. "How many have they claimed this year, in this city alone? Hundreds? Thousands? How many children remain missing here and across the country? Across the globe? Half the metropolitan areas in the United States are under curfew. At least three western European countries are already under martial law."

"Yes, yes!" Malcolm said with a dismissive wave of his hand. "A pity that, and all the more reason we must step up our efforts. We'll eventually win this war," said Malcolm, "but to do so we'll have to carry the fight to them, hit them were it hurts them most. A thousand lesser minions of Legion are a pimple on the ass of St. Michael when compared to the threat posed by a single greater demon. And I for one include the Offspring among their number. In fact, they may be the most dangerous element of all."

Gilbert ran his fingers through his thinning silver hair. "The greatest minds of our Order have pored over the documents for centuries and never reached a consensus. What if . . . what if you're wrong?"

Malcolm refilled his pipe before answering. Striking a match, he looked at Gilbert from the corner of his good eye and said, "If I am wrong, we have several options. We can ignore them and pray the entire lot slips back into anonymity. Or we can always offer an alliance, bring them into the fight on the side of God. After all, there will soon come a time when all creatures, great and small, will have to make that decision.

"But I ask you, what if I'm right? Gil, you carry a tremendous amount of responsibility, both as overseer of a massive archdiocese, and in your life as a Watcher Lord Protector. But when you appointed me to the position of Third Sword, you passed some of that responsibility to me. It's my duty, my obligation, to coordinate our offensive strategies on this continent. Would you suggest I concentrate on Legion and ignore the Offspring, only to find that we're besieged on two fronts a year from now on?"

Gilbert looked away toward the window, refusing to answer the question. It was an old topic between them. Gilbert represented a small but growing faction of the Watchers that urged caution and an open mind when dealing with the Offspring, while Malcolm and the vocal majority would see the bastard children eradicated and the bloodline extinct. However, despite Gilbert's personal opinions, his first and foremost responsibility was to the preservation of the Order. Not even his papal vows superseded his commitment to the ancient Order of Watchers.

Malcolm softened his tone and said, "This we do know: The Offspring have awakened en masse. Through our agents and collaborators, we have identified more than two hundred around the world. Far too many to ignore. Certainly you can agree with that."

Collaborators my ass, thought Gilbert. *Prisoners of the Order, that's what they are. Bewildered people, newly come into a strange, terrifying legacy, and in search of understanding and succor. Instead they find fear and loathing, followed closely by tranquilizers and false imprisonment. My God, what have we become?*

Malcolm continued. "Whatever the catalyst for this sudden emergence, and regardless of their collective intent, the Offspring are still an abomination. We cannot ignore or abide their potential for aggression. Remember, Gilbert, what we do, we do in the name of God and for the sake of His children, and there is no higher calling under the sun."

Gilbert sighed and allowed the matter to drop for the moment. He had his own suspicions about the Offspring and the ancient scrolls that foretold of their awakening, but he was powerless to act. It would require a decree from the Watcher hierarchy to abate this witch hunt. Gilbert tried to remain objective and knew he could be very, very wrong about the half-breeds. They could be every bit as dangerous as Malcolm maintained. Would they know the truth before it was too late? Unfortunately, time wasn't a dependable ally.

He poured two fingers of brandy into the snifter, then glanced at the mantel clock. If Falco was successful, news of the bishop's assassination would spread like a California brushfire. Local, state, and federal law enforcement would soon be involved and the media would descend on the St. Louis archdiocese by sunup. Boston's Cardinal Parelli would send word, offering his assistance, *tsk*ing in that maddening manner while nosing about for details. The man was entirely too full of himself.

Eventually the Vatican would call, probably before noon, demanding details and explanations. The Watchers had a well-rehearsed cover story and would deliver the doctored account through its well-placed operatives within the St. Louis archdiocese. Gilbert knew how the Vatican would respond to the truth that a coadjutor, a vicar general no less, had surrendered his immortal soul to Legion in exchange for a short time of unlimited wealth and debauchery—and that life on this planet as they knew it was now measured in scant years or months rather than millennium because Legion had gained a niche within the Church, and several equally powerful secular institutions.

Sure, he could tell Rome that an ancient religious order, the

Watchers, had reemerged and formed assassination squads in order to counter the threat posed by Legion. That as we speak, those squads were purging Mother Church of demonic influences. Yes, indeed, wouldn't they just love the truth?

Gilbert finished his brandy, then prepared for the final bit of business with Malcolm. "I believe you wanted to talk to me about Ronni Weiss and her promotion? Since you can't stay the night, Malcolm, let's discuss that issue now. I assume she still has your full support?"

Malcolm nodded. He pulled a handkerchief from his pocket and mopped his brow, then said, "Damned warm for November, don't you think? But in answer to your question, yes.

"She is a bit younger than the selection committee would like, but highly disciplined, intelligent, and resourceful, though not especially diligent in her studies. Having served six years in the Israeli military, she has some of the secular talents of a Thomas Falco or Anthony Johnstone. What's more, she's certainly trainable. While I concede that a person of more experience may prove a better choice for this promotion, I maintain she's the best of the four candidates."

Gilbert stared for a long moment at his longtime friend, searching for signs of resolute conviction in Reading's eyes. The promotion of a woman to Sword team leader wasn't unheard of in other Watcher districts, but it was a rare move for Malcolm.

Finally, Gilbert said, "In some ways, her youth and inexperience may actually serve us well. The other three candidates are older, yes. But because of that, they may not prove as malleable in some regards. Leadership opens the door for new knowledge, and often the newly promoted learn things that challenge most all that they've ever believed true about the Church and the supernatural. An open mind is a prerequisite for both success and survival. However, despite all of that, the fact remains that she's young and untested. So many are, these days. You've built a formidable force in the Americas, old man, but with a few exceptions, the bulk of your Swords haven't been tested by fire. Answer me this, Malcolm."

"If I can," said Malcolm.

Gilbert leaned forward in his chair and locked eyes with the hunter of demons. "During preliminary training, have you ever had call to question the faith of your young charges?"

Malcolm looked into the archbishop's dark gray eyes, eyes of smoke and glass, eyes that could strip away flesh and bone and leave nothing but the exposed soul . . . He flinched involuntarily under the intense scrutiny.

"Come, Malcolm. We've known each other far too long for such a display. I'm merely asking a question."

Malcolm recovered quickly. "Pay no attention to me tonight, Gil. Jet lag has me by the balls. In answer to your question, no. Our instructors and evaluators are always vigilant for any sign of shaken or false faith."

Gilbert nodded. "Good. Has a Sword candidate ever given you cause to question his moral convictions?"

Malcolm seemed puzzled by the question. "Are you asking me if these candidates are brave, or if they're righteous?"

Gilbert walked back to the open window and breathed deeply of the night air. Looking out over the rain-soaked streets he thought he saw a pair of elongated shadows disappear between buildings across the street. Looking over his shoulder at Malcolm, he said, "Both."

Malcolm hesitated before answering. "I don't believe it's possible to ever really know such things until they're put to the test, Gil. However, I stood for every one of these candidates during the selection process. I still do."

Still facing the window, Gilbert muttered, "Good enough . . . for now."

Malcolm waited several seconds, then said, "You mentioned three questions. What is the third?"

Gilbert's expression was stoic and unreadable. "How are the grandchildren, Malcolm? I haven't seen them in a couple of years."

From the uncomfortable expression on Malcolm's face, Gilbert knew this question had taken the old hunter by complete surprise. Just as Gilbert intended.

"They're all fine, but why would you ask about them now?"

Gilbert ignored the question and said, "I imagine Barbara

must be . . . what? If memory serves, a few months shy of seventeen. Am I right? And Raymond . . . why, he has a birthday this month! I almost forgot! Where does the time go, Malcolm? It's such a shame that Elizabeth couldn't have seen her grandchildren grow up."

Malcolm's face blanched at the mention of his deceased wife. These thirty years later, her loss still burned a hole through his soul. Or what little was left of it.

Looking toward the window, Malcolm said, "And your point?"

"Trust, Malcolm! Trust is the point. Without trust, we have nothing and our best efforts mean less than a weak piss into the face of a hurricane." Gilbert turned to his friend, his own expression now hard and cold.

"The Enemy is everywhere, Malcolm. They stalk the streets of New York, Los Angeles, and a *thousand* cities and towns in between. Once, they kept to the shadows, searching for the vulnerable. Now they hunt in broad daylight, taking victims and claiming thralls. They . . . are . . . Legion!

"Hell, man, our Order plods along as if we dictate the terms and conditions of this supernatural war. And under our very noses, the tide turns. We're no longer the hunters, Malcolm. We're the hunted. Make no mistake, the demon lords are intelligent and cunning beyond our greatest capacities for either. They possess intellects that shame our greatest minds, masquerading as revered philosophers, economists, military strategists, teachers, and lawmakers. And all the while, they advance their cause, loosing their minions and thralls on the innocent, sapping man's will and resolve. No, Malcolm. Never, ever assume we are in control of this war. Never."

Gilbert's voice dropped to a level just above a whisper. "And there are so few of us. So few. Malcolm, if mankind is meant to survive this onslaught and endure until the Creator calls us home, we must ask of ourselves . . . no, *demand* of ourselves three things. First, we must have faith in Almighty God, and the belief that what we attempt is possible. Next, we must have courage of a kind not seen since Daniel strolled into that Roman zoo."

Nodding, Malcolm tried to interject, but Gilbert cut him off. "Finally, and you listen well, old friend, we must each of us have absolute trust in our brethren. Implicit trust, without hesitation or reservation. And that is the final question, Malcolm. Would you entrust the lives of your children, your children's children, to this current crop of candidates? Would you?"

Malcolm drained his snifter, then stood. He paused, and Gilbert knew the man was carefully choosing his words. When the hunter finally spoke, his tone was soft but even, and he spoke with conviction.

"Gil, we've been friends a long time. You know me as well as any living man. You know my record of service to the Watchers, and *still* you presume to lecture me. Ordinarily, I'd tell you to go bugger yourself, but tonight I'll humor you. The answer to your question is yes, I do trust all of the Swords under my command."

Gilbert nodded and smiled. "That's good, Malcolm. That's very good. Before this fight is finished, trust and faith in Almighty God and one another will be all the ammunition we possess."

Malcolm was still fuming as he pulled into the airport parking garage. *So, Gilbert presumes to lecture me. Me! He even uses Elizabeth's memory against me! I could kill him for that alone. Trust and faith in Almighty God, he says to me. Me! I had faith in his God once upon a time. And what did I receive for my service? Abandonment and grief! But I serve another now. It's your God against mine, holy man, and may the right of might win out!*

Phoenix, Arizona

Falco closed the door and set the deadbolt. The suite was large and roomy, with a full kitchen, a living room, separate bedrooms, and a bath. He wasn't accustomed to such accommodations while in the field, and found it a pleasant change. Entering the bedroom, he tossed his keys onto the dresser, then took a seat in one of the room's plush armchairs. Across the room and sprawled across one of two identical beds, Falco's newest partner, William Caseman, head-bobbed to a tune playing through the headset of his iPod. Will gave Falco a short, casual salute, then resumed his head-bobbing.

"I don't think I mentioned how much I appreciate your choice of accommodations, Will. This is a nice change from the roach motels I've been sleeping in. How're you going to expense this out?"

Will flashed a quick grin. "No worries, Thomas. My birthday is tomorrow. I figure as long as we have to be in the field, I may as well treat myself. The bosses can't fault a lad for doing it up on his birthday, now can they?"

The stereotype of a British marine, Will had ice and black lager in his veins. Usually a friendly, mischievous sort with a ready smile, he was rock steady and hard as nails when shit hit the proverbial fan. He was also something of an enigma, having recently developed a serious affinity for country music, especially the older stuff.

At the foot of Will's bed lay an assortment of gear, carefully packed in waterproof canvas bags. The former SAS Commander was already locked and loaded for the upcoming mission. Falco checked his watch, then arose from his chair and proceeded to his side of the room. His own gear was also bagged and ready, but Falco bordered on obsessive when it came to preoperational equipment checks.

Kneeling, he pulled a heavy polymer case from beneath the bed and opened it. Inside the case, cushioned by several layers of egg-crate foam, laid a Swedish-made SIG SG 550-1 sniper rifle chambered in the accurate and flat-shooting .223 caliber. While perhaps not the preferred sniper tool of most professionals, the gun and ammunition did have certain advantages. For instance, moving at an astounding 4,200 feet per second, the hand-loaded sixty-nine-grain copper-clad hollow-point bullet delivered an incredible amount of energy to the target while leaving behind little evidence for forensics investigators. Due to the extreme velocity, configuration of the hollow points, and resultant fragmentation, there often wasn't enough of the bullet left for an accurate ballistics test.

Falco gave the weapon a quick inspection, then checked the tripod, scope, and mounts. Usually, he preferred getting intimate with his mission objectives, utilizing assorted close quarter antipersonnel weapons. Handguns and knives were his personal favorites. There was little chance to botch a hit in close quarters, but such tactics also carried some high-risk disadvantages. His current target was a prime example. If the reports were true, and he didn't doubt for a moment that they were, Sam Conner was a very, very dangerous young man.

Falco had little left to do except make a final check of the ammo. While he emptied, checked, and reloaded the magazines, he thought about the boy he would kill later this evening, and the bizarre chain of events that led to the termination order.

A couple of years earlier, Falco and his former partner, Cohlin Ridley, had been part of a large Watcher contingency stationed at specific points around the world to observe and record odd behavior at the Veils. The Veils, or Eyes of God, were scattered across the planet with some situated in remote and nearly inaccessible areas, while others were "hidden" in highly conspicuous places: a tourist park in the northwestern United States, a well-traveled roadway near Berlin, a busy mosque in the heart of Mosul, Iraq, and another just to the north of Mosul, near an obscure Turkish village. The Veils could be found in the most likely and unlikely places imaginable.

Very little was known about the Veils, with most of the information coming from ancient documents recovered by the Knights Templar during the second and third Crusades. Only a few of the scrolls recovered from beneath Solomon's Temple in twelfth-century Jerusalem mentioned the Veils. In fact, the single greatest source of information regarding these mysterious "living instruments" was a journal engraved upon copper sheeting and buried with one of the Temple High Priests.

The document proved difficult to decipher, though the Templars eventually managed to piece together the history and function of the Veils. A kind of doorway constructed before recorded time, they were used by an unknown people to traverse the many planes of existence, including the reputed seven levels of Heaven as described by the Old Testament prophet

Enoch. The journal also related a "divinely inspired prophecy" that connected the Veils to the living descendants of ancient trysts between angels and humans. Neither wholly human nor divine, these descendants were referred to as the Offspring.

According to the few texts that referenced the subjects, both the Veils and the Offspring would come together at some future point, and initiate a cataclysmic series of events referred to as "the End of Days." The authors believed the End of Days would occur just prior to the Christian Rapture, and herald in the Great Tribulation, an unprecedented period of famine, disease, death, and human misery. During this short but catastrophic period, Creation's "ageless Enemy" would infiltrate the Plane of Man, and wipe out four-fifths of the earth's population. According to the dismal prophecy, the number of humans destined to survive the End of Days would depend on their commitment to survival and of course, God's will. The Templars and their various offshoots understood they could do little about the latter, and thus, began formulating plans for the former—to survive.

Other scrolls found inside the temple spoke of the same scenario with far less optimism for the survival of man. But the author of the copper scroll urged mankind to remain vigilant for portents indicating the coming of the Enemy, and to resist that coming with all of its might. Templar scholars took this to mean that the outcome wasn't necessarily preordained, and that mankind could influence its own survivability. Other less detailed documents named Legion as the "ageless Enemy" and foretold of the imminent assault on the world of man, as well as the coming of a modern-day usurper, and "an old war made new" that would threaten the very gates of Heaven.

When the Templars had collected what they believed to be all of the documents alluding to the Veils, they discreetly dispatched teams of knights to search for and record their exact locations. The Templars never succeeded in locating the Veils, as France's King Philip the Fair, in an act of desperate greed and infinite stupidity, outlawed the Order in 1307. Many of the Templars were imprisoned and executed for any number of bogus reasons. Yet large numbers of the Order managed to escape, taking priceless religious artifacts with them. These outlawed knights managed to survive and eventually prosper. It was they and their direct descendants who, years later, gave birth to the Order of Watchers.

Within a span of sixty years, the Watchers had succeeded in locating nine of the purported twelve Veils. The leaders, or Hierarchy, of this ultrasecretive organization held knowledge of the Veils in strictest confidence. Generation after generation of Watchers passed, with each contributing to the search for additional Veils, as well as the constant monitoring of those already found.

While the Watchers understood the nature of the Veils no better than did their Templar predecessors, they realized the immense power required to create and sustain these shimmering, translucent gateways. Surely, they reasoned, such powerful instruments must have some great and perhaps ominous destiny. For the next several centuries, the Watchers maintained discreet vigilance over the Veils, waiting for—something. And in the fall of 1997, it started. Overnight, the once effervescent Veils underwent a startling metamorphosis. They took on a murky, opaque appearance, emitted ghastly odors, and undulated violently in the air. A short time later, the first of the greater demons came through into the world of man. The first was soon followed by more. Only a few at first, but the numbers increased at an alarming rate. Just when it seemed a dire situation could degenerate no further, the Offspring began to emerge, the gifts of their mixed heritage manifesting in alarming ways.

The very fact that Conner and Michael Collier had made their way past a host of demons beneath the grounds of the old sanatorium spoke volumes. That only Conner emerged from that nightmarish tunnel said even more.

Centuries-old Watcher doctrine held that the Offspring would play a major role in the collapse of the world just prior to the End of Days. Some members of the Watcher Hierarchy leaned toward a belief that the Offspring were "tainted blood" out of the angelic Nephalim line, or possibly the human line of the Old Testament's Seth or Cain. While some of the original documents collected from various sources during each of the

Crusades spoke in great detail of these potentially powerful entities, the scrolls failed to mention which side of the final conflict they would support.

Watcher scholars predicted the long-dormant Offspring would emerge at the End of Days and become a pivotal factor in the fate of man and the Christian faith. With that belief in mind, the Watchers had sought out and maintained surveillance on suspected Offspring bloodlines. It wasn't an easy task. Such a labor-intensive effort required decades of man-hours, monotonous genealogical research, and exorbitant funding. The Watchers also had in their possession many other tablets and scrolls of a prophetic nature, many of which had little or nothing to do with the blood relations of angels, and in time, less energy was dedicated to locating the Offspring and greater attention paid to more obvious and no less unsettling events in the Middle East and Eastern Europe.

Things remained in status quo until Abbotsville came to a rapid boil. Afterward, the Watcher leadership believed that Sam Connor *could* have been solely responsible for the deliberate destruction of the Veil in Tennessee, an act that allowed Legion to pass from their sordid plane of existence, Sitra Akhra, into the world of man. While Watchers like Falco kept personal opinions to themselves unless asked, he wasn't so sure about the boy's role in Abbotsville.

But one thing was certain. While Conner may or may not have consciously realized the full consequences of his actions, he surely contributed to the damage of every known Veil on the planet. The Veils were interconnected by some odd juxtaposition, and whatever adversely affected one, affected them all. Through Sam's actions, unwitting or otherwise, the Eyes of God were corrupted beyond repair. A supposedly divine, and therefore indestructible, artifact destroyed by a mere boy. With that kind of unchecked power at his command, the boy was a danger to the entire world. Although the vote was divided, the consensus was clear: The boy could not be allowed to live.

Though the Hierarchy remained divided regarding the Offspring, most were convinced Sam Conner was a clear and present danger. Some objected to the boy's termination and instead advocated his abduction. They insisted that the Offspring be studied, examined, and possibly used as a tool in the war with Legion. They feared the boy's assassination would eventually lead to an all-out effort to exterminate the Offspring bloodline. The majority, however, saw the mission as just another necessary precaution. Demonic or not, the Offspring were still very, very dangerous. For his part, Falco relished the task, seeing it as an opportunity to atone for his many sins.

Along with men and women like Ridley, Harriett Tilden, and William Caseman, Falco would carry out counterstrikes against the ageless Enemy until God chose another path for him. And for three years, Falco had done his duty with deadly efficiency. God willing, he vowed to continue for as long as life remained in his body or the threat posed by the Enemy was neutralized.

He glanced at his watch. It was nearly time to strike another blow in the name of God and humanity.

Falco finished the equipment check, then slid the cases back into their hiding places beneath the beds. Finally, he sat down on the bed and kicked off his shoes. With all the preparations completed, he should have been relaxing, allowing his mind to stand down and rejuvenate. But something was worrying him, nagging at the fringes of his mind. Something was wrong.

Since joining the Order and becoming a consecrated Sword, Falco had carried out twenty-three similar missions. He didn't enjoy killing, but he accepted it as a necessary act in the escalating war between good and evil. Thomas Falco had no trouble reconciling his actions or drawing a clear distinction between murder and killing the Enemy. Still, something troubled him. He'd never felt such apprehension while preparing for a mission.

Time frame wasn't an issue. They still had two hours before proceeding to the ambush point. Nor was lack of equipment or planning a problem. The vehicles and other supplies were ready and pre-positioned, and support teams had already been dispatched and were on standby to assist with emergency extraction. He and Will had gone over the plan a dozen times, memorizing all primary and alternate routes to and from the

campus Biology building. Both men had memorized Sam
Connor's usual routes across campus, his face, body type, and
preferred clothing. They even knew the size of Sam's black-
and-white Converse sneakers. Ten and a half, EE. And the
mission wouldn't end with Sam. They also knew about his
mother and younger sister.

*So what is it? What am I missing? Why does this mission feel
so wrong?* Embarrassed by his doubts, Falco chided himself.
*You're a professional. Act like it! Probably still on edge from St.
Louis. After all, forty-eight hours doesn't allow for much separation. Just take it easy and everything will work out just fine.*

He glanced over at Will and was surprised to find the Brit
staring back. There was a curious expression on the man's
face, one Thomas had never seen before. When the two locked
eyes, Falco saw something else he would have never expected
from Will Caseman. It was the resigned look of a man who
knew he wasn't coming back from a mission. After a moment,
Will looked away and made a show of fidgeting with his iPod.
Falco lay back on the bed, though he continued to study his
partner from the corner of his eye.

On the surface, William Caseman was an unremarkable
fellow. Falco often thought Will was the kind of guy you could
overlook in an elevator, making him the perfect physical spec-
imen for this kind of work. But there was more to Will. Much
more.

Only two years earlier, Will had seemed ready to make a career of military service when he inexplicably resigned his com-
mission and applied to a seminary in Northern Ireland. Another
highly irregular coincidence shared with Thomas Falco.

The Watchers had covert operatives embedded in any number of high government offices across the globe. They were
acutely aware of Will's devout Catholic orphanage upbringing
and his sterling military record. Apparently, they were also
aware of the reasons behind his unexpected resignation from
the military and his sudden and puzzling interest in seminary,
though details had been blacked out inside the dossier.

Before moving to recruit Will, the Watchers exercised customary caution, discreetly observing his behavior for nearly a

year. On the day he was finally contacted, Will handed the recruiter a small notebook containing information on his "covert observers." Information included names and detailed physical descriptions, types of automobiles driven, residential addresses, pubs frequented, churches attended, spouses and mistresses. To say the man possessed a sharp eye for detail was an incredible understatement.

Falco and Will had worked only a couple of missions as a team, but one of those missions had been a ball-breaker. The eradication of a "nest," or small colony, of minor minions in Buenos Aires. After months of observation and preparation, the Watchers moved in for a quick kill. They weren't expecting the appearance of a greater demon, nor were they fully prepared for it. Still, the strike team prevailed. Caseman had performed particularly well and earned Falco's respect for his courage and resourcefulness. Falco also came to respect the man's intuition, and from the look on Will's face today, that intuition was giving off some bad vibes.

So I'm not the only one with some serious heartburn over this mission. What the hell is wrong with us?

"You feel it too?" he asked.

Will looked up from his iPod and said, "Feel what, Thomas?"

Falco shook his head. "Don't start that with me, Will."

Will grinned. "Okay, you got me, mate. Truth is, bugger old Fat Freddie if I know what's up. It's just . . . I've a feeling this is going to be a right assed-up affair."

"So what's the problem? Did we miss something during pre-ops planning?" asked Falco.

"Not that I can think of, Thomas. I just know I'll be bloody well happy to see this job over and done. What about you? Bad mojo?"

Falco nodded. "Yeah, you could say that." He looked at his watch again and sighed. "We've got a window of about an hour forty. What say we get on with it?"

Will grinned. "I thought you'd never ask. Get on your bike, mate. If you're waiting for me, you're already late!"

The two men dressed in silence, each wearing a pair of dark

gray utility coveralls over jeans and Polo pullover shirts. As soon as the mission was completed, they would doff the coveralls and stow them in a trash bin, then walk away from the campus wearing casual attire. As Falco knelt to tie his boots, Will turned on the television. Using the remote, he flashed through the channels, and Falco knew his partner was searching for the Country Music Videos station. *A Dixie Chicks freak. Go figure.*

Falco shook his head but said nothing. He really didn't mind what Will watched or listened to as long as the man didn't watch the evening news. Especially today. A homicide involving a prominent St. Louis bishop would be a huge story, and Falco had no desire to listen to a quorum of talking-heads-for-hire discuss asinine conspiracy theories. And why should he? Falco already new the facts better than any living man.

Through the window sheers, he could see dusk descending over the city. He shouldered a light nylon pack, then picked up the case containing the rifle and Starlight scope. Will stood near the door, holding his own gear.

"Ready, mate?"

Falco nodded despite the growing knot in his stomach. "Yeah. Let's do this."

chapter 4

Phoenix, Arizona

At 5:30 P.M. Sam rolled out of bed and trudged over to the sink. The biology lab would start in less than an hour, and while he had no real desire to attend, Sam knew his grade point average wouldn't thank him for cutting the class. Still, it was hard to focus on anything except the sinking feeling in the pit of his stomach. As much as he loved Mark, he almost wished his friend hadn't called earlier. Hearing Mark speak of "dreams" had been unsettling, and Sam's former feelings of trepidation now took on an ugly form and substance. *God, if you're really listening, make this go away. I can't deal with it again. Please.*

He splashed water on his face and the back of his neck, toweled off, and donned a fresh T-shirt. Glancing at his watch, he hurriedly stuffed a worn leather satchel with a thick spiral notebook, mechanical pencils, and a spare lime-green highlighter. As an afterthought, he added a pack of cigarettes and a spare lighter. Walking toward the door, he checked his watch once more. *Dressed in three minutes. A new record!*

Now that he was ready to leave, it again crossed his mind to ditch the class. *What's the use of going? Something really bad is going to happen. Maybe tonight. Maybe tomorrow. Soon. I can feel it. And when it does, one more stinking "D" on my transcript won't make any difference.*

He stood in the center of the room for several minutes, his anxiety growing by the second. *So, God, what about it? Any help for a skinny red-haired kid? No, I didn't think so. Or*

maybe you still only help those who help themselves. Is that it?
Sam shouldered his satchel and walked outside.

He hurried across the lawn to the parking lot, where he threw his satchel into the back seat of a lime-green Honda Civic, then paused to watch the gathering storm. Thunderstorms were uncommon during the fall in central Arizona, but here it was, bigger than life—a dark, ominous squall line running north to south, stretching nearly as far as the eye could see. The line was still some miles in the distance, but Sam thought he smelled rain in the air. He ducked inside the Honda and set off for the Science building, while worry gnawed at his guts like a pack of starving rats.

A tall, broad-shouldered figure dressed in filthy jeans and a stained denim jacket stood beneath the sprawling limbs of a massive century plant and watched the Honda disappear down the street. Little Stevie wasn't overly concerned that he had narrowly missed the little boy-bitch by a few seconds. Stevie had been chasing the troublesome Offspring for several weeks, studying his schedules, habits, and routes. With Little Stevie's heightened psychic senses, a gift from his master, the fallen angel Axthiel, he would have no trouble following the boy across campus . . . or the country, for that matter. And this time, once he had the boy cornered, the unholy pact with Legion would be fulfilled, and Sam Conner would be little more than a grieving mother's memory.

Little Stevie closed his bloodshot eyes and tested the air with the tip of his black, swollen tongue. His master had passed to him both curse and gift, and now Stevie used both to his advantage. A moment later, his eyes opened wide in surprise, and a slow malicious grin spread across his face, revealing rows of broken and rotting teeth. It appeared Sam Conner wasn't the only Offspring within Stevie's grasp. Two boy-bitches for the price of one. Mumbling a thanks for his good fortune, Stevie loped off at a ground-eating pace in the direction of the Biology building.

* * *

From two blocks away, atop the four-story physical plant, Will Caseman, acting as spotter for Falco, monitored the parking lot adjacent to the campus Biology building through a slender spotter's scope. He tensed as the target vehicle came into view and pulled into an outlined parking space. Through the eight-power monocular, he watched the target exit the car and rummage through a leather satchel.

"The target is alone, Thomas, standing on the driver's side of that fugly green Honda. Five collaterals standing near the front door of the building, twenty meters left. We need to take him at the car. You've got the green light."

As Sam paused beside his car to examine the contents of his satchel, Falco settled the scope's reticles over the boy's head. Falco took a shallow breath and exhaled half, and held. His finger tightened on the double position trigger until he heard the first faint *click*. Two more pounds of finger pressure and Sam Conner would be another casualty in the eternal war between good and evil. Will's words echoed in Falco's head: *Green light. Take him!*

Without warning, Will disappeared from Falco's side, lifted up as if by a strong wind. From somewhere to Falco's left, he heard a terrible crash and the cry of a wounded man. Instinct took over and Falco dropped the rifle onto the makeshift sandbags and reached for his sidearm. His hand never reached the Pachmayr grips.

A heavy boot slammed into Falco's ribs, lifting him several inches from the rooftop. Through a pain-induced haze, Falco saw a second boot flashing toward him and managed to roll to his right and absorb some of the shock. The blow only grazed his forehead. When he finally came to a stop, he drew the Glock and swung the front sight onto his attacker, a huge man with hooded, serpentine eyes. The man was laughing, obviously enjoying the moment. Falco chanced a quick glance to his right and saw Will Caseman lying in a widening pool of blood. The dying man tried to suck air into a badly injured chest as crimson froth spilled from both corners of his mouth. One of his eyes lay against his cheek, dangling by a thin thread of sinew. *Dear God, what the hell did he do to Will?*

From the corner of his eye, Falco saw the tall, freakish attacker take a step forward. He fought off a wave of intense nausea, tightened his finger on the trigger, and shouted, "Stop! Don't take another step!" Falco had no personal reservations about shooting this freak, but the deafening roar of the ten-millimeter handgun would draw attention from campus police, and neither he nor Will were now in any condition to slip away quietly. Being apprehended and questioned by civilian authorities was not an option.

Little Stevie stopped as ordered, but he seemed more amused than concerned. Falco hit the collar mike on his coveralls, sending a signal that would initiate an emergency extraction sequence by a waiting support team. Little Stevie laughed.

"Save your energy, cowboy. Ain't no cavalry comin' to save your pitiful ass. In fact, the boys you left behind in that van had some troubles of their own." Stevie howled at his own joke.

Falco glanced over at Will again. Mercifully, the Brit was dead.

"Who are you?" he asked the smirking giant. Stevie's grin turned quickly into a twisted scowl as he advanced, seemingly oblivious to the powerful handgun pointed at the center of his chest.

"Who am I? Who am I? Motherfucker, I'm a god!" Stevie raised his hands toward the sky and yelled, "I'm Death on a pale horse! I'm Disease, Pestilence, and fucking Famine all rolled into one, bro." He smiled wickedly and added, "But my friends call me Little Stevie." Moving with startling speed, Little Stevie grasped Falco by the front of his coveralls and effortlessly jerked the man to his feet.

Falco squeezed the trigger.

Sam stepped out of the car and casually feigned a search of his satchel. Yet, there was nothing feigned about the pounding of his heart or his skyrocketing blood pressure. Every molecule in his body urged him to run from this place. Just get in the car and go. Don't look back. Not now, not ever. They had finally come for him.

But Sam had the benefit of hard-earned experience and he

knew better than to blindly flee from the Enemy. First he needed to know what he was running from. He had felt the presence of the Enemy on his mental radar screen long before the Biology building came into sight. As he drew nearer the building, his internal alarms screamed out mixed signals indicating the enemy was both in front and behind him. It was an odd signal, yet no more so than the signature of this latest threat. It just didn't feel right. Not like the vibes he got from Drammach, the greater demon he had killed beneath the mountain in Abbotsville. In fact, in some way, the vibe was more like that of Axthiel, the murderous fallen angel who had all but murdered Michael Collier, then sacrificed himself to prevent an even greater evil from entering the plane of man.

Going into the lab suddenly seemed like a very bad idea. Sam had started to climb back into the Honda when his knees buckled. He fell against the side of the car holding his head between his trembling hands. It had been a long time since he last experienced the startling sensation of a reach, but it wasn't something he was likely to forget. Another Offspring was nearby and in serious trouble.

God, please don't make me do this! I'm begging you. I—I can't go through this again.

Sam received an answer to his unspoken plea, though it wasn't the answer he had hoped for. A second *reach* filled with agony and desperation nearly blinded him.

"No, goddamn it! This isn't my fight, not anymore. Uriel said my part was done!"

Peace be still, little brother.

Stunned, he looked about the parking lot and over both shoulders for the source before accepting that the Voice had come from inside his head.

"Joriel? My God! Is—is that really you?"

Yes, my Lucky Sam, but there's no time to explain. The tall building to the south. Physical Plant. Take the stairs to the roof. Hurry.

"Oh, no! You don't just show up after two years and—"

Go! Now!

Sam had grown up with the Voice. She had been his constant

companion from birth, and served as both his best friend, guardian, and mentor. He had little trouble recognizing the sense of urgency in her tone. It was the same tone she had used when urging him toward Abbotsville. Reluctantly, Sam broke into a run.

At the end of the second block, he turned left and slowed to a trot. The university's primary maintenance building was dead ahead. The parking lot adjacent to the building was empty except for a pair of panel trucks. Both vehicles bore the distinctive Arizona State mascot, Sparky the Sun Devil, on the sides. Farther down the block, a white van was parked along the curb. Just looking at the van made him violently ill.

The front door of the maintenance building was open and Sam cautiously stepped inside. The building was dark except for a lighted EXIT sign at the foot of the stairs.

The roof, Sam. Hurry!

Sam took the narrow steps two at a time. As he reached the second floor, he flashed on the night he had first met Mark Pierce and Janet Davis. He had raced along a darkened stairway that night too, arriving just in time to save the pair from the Enemy.

By the time he reached the third story, the muscles in his legs were cramping up. Again his mind flashed back to another desperate sprint in Amarillo, Texas. He couldn't help himself. *Déjà vu all over again, huh, Joriel?* He heard the faint rustling of wind chimes in reply.

At the top of the stairway, Sam paused for a moment to catch his breath. The stairway ended on the fourth floor, a vast, single room illuminated by a pair of dim fluorescent lights. Drafting tables and desks were scattered throughout the room and engineering maps covered large expanses of beige-colored walls. Sam trotted into the center of the room and looked about for some way onto the roof. After a few seconds he decided if such a route existed, it was well camouflaged.

Back wall. Drop-down stairs.

Sam acknowledged the Voice in his head with a loud sigh of relief and ran to the rear of the building where he found a stout cord dangling from the ceiling. He gave the cord a sharp tug, then leaped to one side, barely dodging the descending staircase. The opening in the ceiling was pitch-black and reminiscent of yet another time and place; the "rabbit hole" in Abbotsville. The rabbit hole had led from an old pump house to a subterranean mineshaft and a deadly face-to-face encounter with the greater demon, Drammach. That was one memory Sam refused to dwell on. At the top of the rickety stairs, Sam found himself in a small utility room. An exterior door had been left slightly ajar. Through the crack, Sam could see the dingy yellow glow of the rooftop security lights. He opened the door just wide enough to squeeze through, and stepped out into the night air.

A stiff wind whipped Sam's shoulder-length hair about his face, and fat droplets of rain spattered against his neck and arms. To the west, jagged spears of lightning lanced across an ebony sky, and the throaty rumble of distant thunder lent a surreal quality to the scene before him.

The roof was a maze of massive heating and air units, large wooden spools of heavy gauge wire, and pallets of plastic-covered construction materials. Above the wind, he could hear broken spates of harsh, guttural laughter coming from behind the utility building.

"Oh man, I hate this. I mean, I really, really hate this." This time, Joriel didn't offer a reply. Resigned, Sam crept along the side of the utility room on the balls of his feet. As he turned the corner, all hell broke loose.

To Sam's left, a man lay unmoving in a crumpled heap beside a rusted air-conditioning unit. To his right, a hideous mountain on legs held another man by the throat and appeared ready to deliver the coup de grâce. Helplessly, Sam looked on, certain the first man was dead, with the second soon to follow. That would leave him alone with the mountain on legs, the source of his internal radar blip.

Sam flinched as an explosion, the unmistakable roar of a handgun, ripped apart the night. The Mountain dropped his victim and staggered backward, clutching his heavily muscled chest with both hands. Blood spilled from between bent and twisted fingers, yet the Mountain's face showed no indication of pain or shock. Instead, his puffy lips spread into a broad grin and his eyes were alight with . . . amusement!

Only a few feet from the Mountain, the shooter struggled to one knee, leveled the barrel of the handgun, and fired a second and third round. Orange and white flames jetted from the muzzle, the Mountain's body shook from the impact of the two-hundred-grain semi-jacketed slugs. Sam's eyes widened as the bullets seemed to have no discernable effect. If anything, the Mountain's grin grew wider as he advanced again.

Before the shooter could empty the magazine at point-blank range, the Mountain was on him, pinning him to the roof with a knee to the chest and digging talonlike fingers into the man's exposed throat. The shooter, no small man himself, used the gun as a makeshift hammer and beat at the Mountain's face, wrists, and forearms, struggling in vain to break the chokehold. The Mountain seemed impervious to pain, his only reaction an ever-widening rictus grin. He stood, and held the man by the throat at arms' length.

Smiling, always smiling, the Mountain tightened his grip on the man's throat and shook him as a terrier would a rat. The shooter's head snapped violently back and forth until Sam was certain his neck would break. Within seconds, the blows fell with less authority, and then stopped altogether. Sam knew the fight was all but over, and if the man wasn't already dead, he couldn't be far from it. In the distance, Sam heard the wail of sirens. *Always too little, too late!*

The Mountain dropped the now limp body to the roof. He stood over the fallen man, a booted foot poised to stomp down on his victim's unprotected head. Then, for whatever reason, he hesitated and lowered his foot. He turned and brushed limp strands of dirty ash-colored hair from his eyes. A long string of drool hung from one corner of his mouth, and Sam was sure if any man ever truly resembled a rabid dog, it was the creature before him.

The Mountain looked directly at Sam and his expression turned from puzzlement to one of dawning recognition.

"You!"

Sam knew what it meant to stand frozen by abject terror.

He had been there before. The white Lincoln that tailed him to Abbotsville, the rabbit hole, Drammach and his soldiers, Axthiel . . . each had at one time paralyzed Sam with fear. But when he looked into the Mountain's eyes, he experienced perhaps the greatest terror of all. Within those shallow pools of raw sewage, he saw nothing but cold insanity. Unbridled madness driven by a single purpose: to destroy. Through the sheets of driving rain, Sam watched as the Mountain advanced, clenching and unclenching his massive fists. A web of lightning illuminated the sky, framing the monstrous form of the Mountain against roiling blue-black clouds.

Oh, God. Joriel? Joriel!

Her gentle singsong reply cascaded through Sam's terrified mind. *Sayeth the Father, "Touch not my prophets, nor do my anointed ones harm."*

It wasn't exactly what Sam wanted or needed to hear. He screamed, "Just help me, damn it!"

There wasn't time for another exchange as the Mountain now towered over him.

"My friends didn't say nothing about you showing up, so this is a real bonus!"

Stevie took a step forward. "Oh, I've waited a long time for this, little boy-bitch. My master's gonna be pleased. Maybe . . . maybe he'll let me keep your little sister as a pet. Katherine. Ain't that her name, Sammie?" The Mountain massaged his crotch. "Oh, yeah, after I finish with you, me and little sister gonna have us some fun."

The words jolted Sam. "Kat . . ." Her nickname tumbled from his lips, as her image appeared, unbidden, in his mind. Fear surrendered without a whimper to fury. "Stay away from Kat, you son of a bitch!"

The Mountain laughed, then said, "Or what, Sammie? What you gonna do, huh? What you gonna do when I'm putting the god-meat to little sister? Huh?" Stevie broke into a rough rendition of an old Elvis tune, as he suggestively gyrated his hips. "Little sista, don't you cry! Oh, little sista don't you—"

Sam extended his hand toward the Mountain, palm turned outward, and shouted, "NO!"

The air between Sam and Little Stevie rippled, then sizzled as tendrils of brilliant white light shot out from Sam's palm, streaking across the rooftop toward its intended target. The odor of ozone filled Sam's nostrils, and droplets of rain were vaporized by the stream of supernatural energy.

The light struck Little Stevie in the center of his massive chest, lifted him from his feet, and propelled him through the air. He landed on his back with a dull thud several feet away, acrid smoke rising from smoldering fabric and seared flesh. When he struggled to his feet, Sam saw that the monster's chest was a ruined mess of charred cloth, hair, and skin. Even the remaining metal buttons on the lower portion of his denim jacket were reduced to molten lumps of slag metal. Despite the wounds, Little Stevie glared at Sam, undisguised loathing and hatred emanating from twin orbs the color of burned motor oil.

Holding his wounded chest, Little Stevie said, "You shouldn't have done that, Sammie. You really shouldn't have. I was gonna kill you, quick and clean. Well, maybe not so clean. But now, I'm going to hurt you real . . . fucking . . . bad!"

Sam rose to his feet, and nearly fell again when the bones in his legs turned to quivering jelly. He steadied himself against the wall of the utility shed and stared at the Mountain's damaged face and chest. The display of power had taken him by surprise as much as it had the Mountain, and Sam knew he didn't have the necessary energy for a repeat performance. He was defenseless now, and if the Mountain sensed that . . . It was time to bluff. He raised his hand again and extended it toward the monster. His bluff was rewarded as the Mountain flinched and took a single step back.

"You won't go near my sister. Not now, not ever. Now get the fuck outta here before I torch your ugly ass!"

"Boy, you don't know what you've done. Oh, I *will* go near your sister, just as soon as I find that little whore. And when I do, I'll eat her brains, then take a good long piss in her empty skull. Then I'll be back for you. You're gonna beg me for death!"

Sam had heard more than enough. Renewed anger surged through his body like an electrical current. He walked toward

Little Stevie, too angry to acknowledge his own fear any longer. Wild energy coursed through his body, threatening to burst through his flesh at any moment.

Recognizing the dangerous change in demeanor and having already tasted the boy's incredible power, Little Stevie's courage faltered, then shriveled completely. His eyes darted left and right like some caged animal looking for an avenue of escape. As Sam advanced, Little Stevie backed away until the heels of his boots hung over the roof's precipice. In a sudden and unexpected act, Stevie spat at Sam. Instinctively, Sam raised his arms to protect his face, and the acidic phlegm popped and sizzled against the bare skin of his hands and arms.

"I'll be back, Sammie, and next time I won't come alone! I got friends in low places, boy-bitch!" With that, Little Stevie took a final backward step and disappeared over the edge of the four-story building.

Sam rushed to the edge of the building and looked down at the lawn below. Much as he expected, there was no sign of the Mountain. The sirens were still some distance away, though Sam was no longer sure they were headed in his direction. Sudden heavy downpours in central Arizona often resulted in severe flash flooding and rashes of auto accidents and drownings. Still, he didn't want to be within ten miles of this place when the police finally arrived.

The last of Sam's adrenaline rush faded, and every muscle in his body seemed made of Jell-O. He knelt on the roof and gave his thin legs time to recuperate before tackling the stairs again. Then he would have to call . . . damn, who *would* he call?

The monster had threatened Kat, so he would need to call home first. Maybe he should call Mark, too. Kat and his mom could stay with Mark and Janet for a while, at least until . . . Until what? What could he do to stop that . . . that thing? Dear God! Who or what *was* that thing, anyway? It didn't have the same smell as the demons, but it sure as hell wasn't human. Nor was it quite like Axthiel, but . . . Maybe Mark would have some ideas.

Or Joriel. "Are you still there?" he asked aloud.

Yes, I'm still here, Sam.

"You sound so far away, Joriel. Are you okay? I—I've been worried about you."

Sam heard the familiar gentle ringing of wind chimes, a sign that Joriel was happy, or possibly laughing. God, how he had missed that sound.

I'm fine now, Sam. I'm sorry I was away so long. I . . . I may have to leave again.

"No!" Sam shouted. "You can't do this to me, again."

"Who—who are you talking to?"

Sam whirled about to find the Mountain's last victim struggling to a sitting position. Sam stood and walked cautiously to the man's side.

"Damn, man!" said Sam. "You just scared the shit out of me. I thought both you guys were dead!"

The man turned to look at his partner, wincing in the process and gingerly holding his head between his hands. "Dead? Yeah, my partner is. I only feel like it."

Sam followed his gaze, looking at the man who lay beside the heating and air unit. Lying in a bloody heap, the man's head lay at an odd angle to his shoulders, and Sam realized the man's neck was broken. Sam also realized that both men wore identical coveralls, the kind frequently worn around campus by janitors and maintenance men. Looking around the rooftop at the assorted high-tech equipment, including the guns, *especially the guns,* Sam was certain neither man made a living sweeping floors or turning wrenches.

"Where—where did he go? That Little Stevie character?"

What kind of accent is that? Boston? New York? He sure as hell ain't from around here. He doesn't smell like the Enemy. In fact, he carries the same scent as Mark and Michael Collier . . . and the rest of us.

Sam kicked the handgun to the side just to be safe, and helped the man stand. When the man swayed left to right, Sam lent him a shoulder for support. When the man gratefully shifted his weight, Sam's knees nearly buckled. *Damn, this dude is solid!*

When the man started for the edge of the rooftop, Sam steered him away.

"Don't bother looking over the edge. I already did, and he ain't there. I don't think he's coming back." Sam held his injured arm tight against his side and thought, *At least we can hope that walking acid vat doesn't show back up.*

The man nodded and then bent at the waist, his body quaking with a series of loud retches. With each heave, his face screwed into a mask of agony, and at one point his eyes began to roll back into his head. Sam guided him to a large wooden spool of cable and helped him sit. By the yellowish light of the security lamps, Sam could see the man's eyes were glassy and unfocused. One pupil was definitely dilated. Factoring in the projectile vomiting, Sam was sure the guy had a serious head injury.

"You don't look too good. We need to get you to a hospital. I left my cell phone in the car, but if you can hang on, I'll go call an ambulance."

"No."

"Look, dude. I'm not a doctor, but I have carved up my share of frogs and starfish in biology class. I'm telling you, you need medical help."

"NO! No ambulance and no police. Got that?"

The man's vehemence startled Sam, but he thought perhaps he could understand. Only a couple of years earlier, he had a similar conversation with Charlene Hastings.

"Okay, okay! Take it easy. Look, if you want to avoid the cops, we gotta get you off the roof. Someone besides me heard those gunshots, and the police will show up sooner or later. If it wasn't for the flash flooding, they'd already be here. You have a car nearby?"

The man started to shake his head and nearly fell off of the cable spool. "N-no. My car is parked several blocks away. Can—can you help me?" The man held out his hand and said, "My name is—Falco."

Sam shook the man's hand and silently noted the weak grip. "Sure, dude. I'm Sam. I'll help you get out of here."

Déjà vu all over again said the wise man. "But what about your friend? What do we do about him?"

Thomas turned his head slowly, as if careful not to disturb his fractured equilibrium again, and looked at his fallen partner.

"There's nothing we can do for him now. In the chest pocket of his coveralls, there's a cell phone. Would—would you bring it to me?"

Sam did a double take. "Say what? You want me to loot a dead guy?"

Thomas started a reply, then bent forward and vomited on Sam's sneakers.

After the latest wave of nausea passed, he said, "Sorry, kid. If—if it makes you feel any better . . . the phone is mine. Just bring it to me, then we can get out of here."

Sam looked from Thomas to his dead partner and back again. Then, shaking his head, he muttered, "Dead guys . . . cell phones . . . fucking talking mountains . . . This shit just ain't right."

Potty mouth. I hoped you had outgrown your fascination with foul language.

Sam began a scathing retort, then choked it back. Joriel was right. She was always right, damn it. And she was back! Sam wanted to shout it out to the whole world, his best friend was back. Of course, she had some explaining to do. After all, he reasoned, you don't live in a guy's head for nineteen years, then disappear without so much as an "It's been fun. See ya later!" Now, with Joriel back where she belonged, Sam knew they could figure out a way to protect Kat. As for himself, Sam wanted no part of this fight, or any other. He had done his part. Uriel had said so. Joriel would know what to do. With her at his side, he could handle just about anything—including taking a phone off a dead guy.

Gingerly, he patted down the fallen man's waterlogged clothing until he located the phone in a pocket on the front of the coveralls. On the way back, he retrieved the gun. It was a nasty-looking piece of work with a bore the size of a manhole. *Of course,* thought Sam, *it didn't do Falco or his buddy much good.* When he handed the gun and phone to Thomas, he saw that the man was holding a plastic key card.

Thomas held out the card and said, "Think you can find this place?"

Sam looked at the address. *Upscale joint on East Camelback. This guy must be loaded.* "Once we get you to the car, we can be there in thirty to forty minutes." Sam nodded toward Caseman. But what about your friend? We can't just leave him like that."

"Nothing we can do for him now." Falco flipped open the thin cell phone and hit the speed dial function. He listened for several seconds, then disconnected the call.

"My backup isn't answering and I'm pretty sure I know why. I think . . . I think the police will be along shortly, and we shouldn't be here when they arrive."

chapter 5

Phoenix, Arizona

Sam fell back onto the sofa, both mind and body exhausted, and the burns inflicted by Little Stevie's spittle stinging like hell. Slowed by his own wounds, it had taken Sam nearly half an hour to get the much-heavier Falco to the ground floor of the maintenance building. The mystery man had blacked out twice along the way, once atop the stairs, and again at the bottom. Upon reaching the ground floor, Sam left the man sitting inside the doorway, while he went after the car.

Driving time was prolonged by numerous flooded streets and assorted Street Department barricades. By the time they reached the hotel, Falco was fading in and out of consciousness. Several times Sam started to dial 911 and request an ambulance, afraid the man wouldn't survive the night without medical attention. And each time, he recalled Falco's insistence that Sam not involve a hospital or the police. Sam could relate to the man's concerns. There had been a time when the last person Sam wanted to see was a cop. Nothing against police officers, but they usually asked way too many questions when speed was of paramount importance. Needing some guidance, Sam *reached* for Joriel, but she had again retreated to some faraway place and refused or was unable to answer.

Now that Falco was back in his suite, Sam contemplated his next move. He didn't want any continued involvement with the man, and Joriel had said nothing about helping him beyond this point. Perhaps he should just walk out the door, get in his car, and make for Sun City. At the moment, nothing was as important as protecting his mom and little sister. *I'd better call them and give Kat a heads-up*, he decided.

He pulled his cell phone from his back pocket and started to dial the number when he noticed a missed call. Sam punched in the retrieval code. A mechanical female impersonator answered with that familiar monotone delivery:

You have . . . two . . . new messages. First unheard message

*Hey, Sam! I just wanted to let you know Mom is in Tucson, spending a few days with Aunt Jenna, and I'm staying with a friend until Mom gets back. We'll both be home on Wednesday. See you then. Oh . . . hmm . . . try not to worry. Things are about the same, if you catch my drift. No better, no worse. I'll call if I notice any new funny business. Love ya. *click**

Sam sighed and dropped the phone onto the sofa. "No better, no worse" wasn't especially good news. The phrase carried double meaning. On one hand, it meant Kat hadn't sensed any additional threats posed by the Enemy. On the other hand, the phrase told Sam his mother was still dwelling in the black funk of depression, a deteriorating condition that was rapidly approaching critical mass. Doctors and handfuls of prescription antidepressants and mood elevators had done nothing to bring her out of mourning. Sam tried not to think about the long-term consequences. He had more immediate problems, like tracking down his kid sister.

Who the hell is Kat staying with? Sam tried to recall the names of Kat's closest friends, but it was no use. There were too many possibilities. Kat was popular with her classmates, and her friends' parents loved her.

Actually, maybe it's a good thing she isn't home. Sam shuddered at the mental image of the leering monster Falco had called Little Stevie. *He said he had been following me. Said his master would be pleased. Jesus, what kind of master is looking for me who keeps pets like that? How many of them know about Mom and Kat?* Sam's stomach rolled at the thought. *God, what do we do now? Where do we go? Mark. I have to call Mark.* He started to dial the number, then glanced at his watch. *It's getting late. I'll call him from the road.*

Sam cast a guilty glance toward the bedroom. He hated to leave Falco unattended, but there was little he could do for the guy. Maybe he should call for an ambulance despite the man's objections. After all, what good was it to stay one step ahead of the police if you died in the process?

Sam started for the front door, when he heard a weak voice calling out from the bedroom. *Crap! Why couldn't he stay unconscious for another two minutes?* Sam walked to the bedroom door and peered in. Falco was propped up on an elbow, and leaning over the side of the bed. He had been sick again.

"Look, man, I gotta be going. Are you sure you don't want a doctor?"

Falco looked up at Sam with a dull, glazed expression. "I—I know you. Sam Conner."

The man's speech was slightly slurred, and his eyes were unfocused and vacant. It was a pitiful and disturbing sight. *Jesus Christ. Shades of Michael Collier.*

"Uh, yeah. We met up on the roof. Remember?"

Falco blinked several times, as if trying to clear his vision. "Yeah, I remember. I remember everything, but I didn't realize it was you. My—my eyes weren't working so well after I took that beating. Why . . . why the hell did you help me?"

Sam almost laughed aloud. *Why the hell, indeed? What the hell am I supposed to say to that?*

"I guess it just seemed like the thing to do at the moment. But I gotta be going now. I . . . I hope you feel better soon." *At least until you die of a cerebral hemorrhage. And trust me, I know the symptoms when I see them. Oh God, I feel like an ass for leaving him like this, but Kat . . . Mom . . .* Sam turned and started for the front door again when the man called out.

"*Sam . . . you can't go. Have to stay. Here.*"

Sam answered over his shoulder, "I'm sorry, man, really. But I *have* to go."

Sam opened the front door and started outside when Falco

called out a final time. "If you go now, you and Katherine die tonight!"

Sam slammed the door and ran back into the bedroom. "What did you say? What do you know about my sister?"

Falco couldn't answer. He had lost consciousness.

South side of Phoenix

The storm had finally spent itself, leaving a city of flooded backstreets in its wake. Little Stevie, still clutching his throbbing chest, watched from the shadows of an empty storefront as an older-model station wagon parted fender-high waters before coming to a stop at the intersection traffic light.

With supernatural speed and agility that belied his size, Stevie rushed across the sidewalk and leaped across the flooded lane to the idling car. He yanked the heavy door from its hinges and tossed it aside as if it were made of cardboard. An elderly man sat frozen at the wheel with a yapping terrier at his side. Stevie took the old man by the head and pulled him from the front seat. He gave the head a violent twist before dropping the old man facedown in the brackish water. Little Stevie folded himself into the car, backhanded the dog into the back seat, and drove away as fast as the rising run-off would allow. There was no real hurry, Stevie told himself. He had waited this long to fulfill his master's wishes. Another couple of days wouldn't matter. He told himself that, again and again.

But inwardly, Little Stevie was nearly insane with anger. Not one Offspring, but two! He had had them both within arm's reach, a rare opportunity and not one to be squandered. Yet Stevie had not managed to kill even one. Worse still, the boy-bitch had hurt him with the blue fire. It was a good thing his master was away, he thought. Axthiel didn't abide failure gracefully.

As Little Stevie drove into the heart of South Phoenix, he plotted his next move. It galled him to admit it, but he would need help taking the boy. Axthiel's many thralls kept in contact, as much as circumstances allowed, and several had tried to warn him about Sam Conner. Word of events in Abbotsville had traveled quickly. While it was impossible for a thrall to ignore a directive from its master, many thralls, and no few demons, had deliberately avoided the boy. Instead, they sought out lesser prey. Not so with Little Stevie.

There was a distinct hierarchy among the thralls of the Brethren and Legion alike. In order to climb the ranks, one must possess some great combination of metaphysical or physical prowess, cunning, and treachery. Little Stevie had those attributes, as well as another: ambition.

He reveled in his new life, grateful for the gift of Taint bestowed upon him by Axthiel. He had served his master well for the past couple of years and had reaped the rewards. No carnal pleasure or act of debauchery was denied him. In Axthiel's absence, Little Stevie had acquired high status among his "siblings." Killing Sam Conner would cement his position. And in the event Axthiel never returned . . . Little Stevie smiled. The glorious life of a god was well within his reach.

First he would recruit his allies. Then he would make good on his promises to Sam Conner.

chapter 6

Phoenix, Arizona

It was after midnight when Sam returned to the hotel room. He dropped the plastic grocery sacks onto the kitchen bar, then peeked in on Falco. The man lay motionless beneath a light blanket. Sam couldn't tell if he was unconscious from his head injury or simply resting. At any rate, Sam figured his breathing seemed normal, and that offered some reassurance. He'd half expected to find the man cold and stiff upon his return.

Sam walked back into the kitchen and searched the cabinets until he found a sauce pan and cups. He filled the pan with water and set it on the stove to boil. Next, he rummaged through one of the grocery sacks until he located the box of Swiss Miss. While his conscience—and his need to hear what Falco knew about Kat—might demand he stay with the injured man for now, there was no reason he should deny his addiction to hot chocolate.

A few minutes later, Sam situated himself on the sofa with the double shot of hot chocolate. He checked his watch and started to try Mark's number again, then decided to wait until morning. There was nothing to be gained by dragging Mark out of bed at this hour. In fact, he wasn't at all sure what Mark might be able to do in the morning. No doubt, his old friend would be on the first available flight to Phoenix. Then what?

First I have to find Mom and Kat. Then I'll have to convince them both to go with Mark. That's going to be the tough part. While Kat knew of and understood Sam's friendship with the ex-convict, Sam's mother was another matter. Sam had told her that he met Mark while traveling through Tennessee during a faux "I have to find myself" sojourn. The following year, she met Mark and Janet when the pair came out west to visit Sam. She seemed to like them well enough, but Sam knew she kept a subtle but suspicious eye trained on the pair at all times.

Sam's dad had somehow pieced together much of the connection but said little. Sam was certain the Offspring bloodline ran through his dad's side of the family, and he thought it possible that the middle-aged man had been coming into his own inheritance. At any rate, his dad seemed to understand things Sam never bothered to put into words. But his mom . . . *I'll worry about that when the time comes. For now, I need to decide what to do about Mr. Falco.*

He drained the last of the hot chocolate and looked in on the injured man again. Falco was still asleep. *What's his story? He's gotta be an Offspring, but that doesn't account for him knowing me. One thing about it . . . Little Stevie was dead-set on killing him, and as the old saying goes, the enemy of my enemy is my friend. I hope. So what do I do with him now?*

Sam considered his options and only three came readily to mind. The first, calling 911, was really out of the question. Come hell or high water, he would honor the man's request that Sam not call for an ambulance or the police. That left two obvious and disturbing choices: wait for the man to regain consciousness before cutting out, or simply walk out the door without a backward glance. While neither option appealed to him, the mere thought of the latter left him feeling dirty and, oddly enough, disloyal. *Okay, that settles it. I'm in. Until tomorrow, anyway.* Sam kicked off his shoes and stretched out on the sofa. Despite the evening's traumatic resurrection of old fears, his last thought before sleep was pleasant. *At least I don't have to set the alarm for that 8:15 World Lit class.*

The storm had moved out of the area, and the soft light of morning filtered in through the window sheers. Sam propped up on an elbow and rubbed the sleep from his eyes. When he opened them, Falco was sitting across the room, watching quietly. The coveralls were gone, and he was wearing a tight-fitting T-shirt and jeans. He held a cell phone in his lap.

Sam covered his mouth and yawned, then said, "What time is it?"

"A few minutes past seven."

The man's voice was soft and quiet. It made Sam nervous.

"Good to see you sitting up, Mr. Falco. Before I go, I'd like you to explain what you meant about my sister. You said she was in danger."

In place of an answer, a thin smile appeared on Falco's lips, and Sam felt his inner alarms stirring. He swung his feet off the sofa and reached for his sneakers, while Falco watched intently. When Sam was finished with his shoes, he stood and walked toward the door. *Time to bluff again.*

"I see. You don't know anything about my sister, do you? You just heard that ass-ugly mountain call out her name. Well, it's a bullshit tactic, but I guess I can't blame a guy for trying, huh?"

As Sam turned the doorknob, Falco pointed toward the sofa.

"Oh, I know all about your sister, Sam. I know about your father, your mother, and even about your grandmother, Nanna. And I wasn't stalling when I said Kat was in danger. Now, have a seat and we'll talk."

Falco's words left a queasy feeling in the pit of Sam's stomach. For the man to mention Kat and his parents was one thing. It was quite another to bring his long-deceased Nanna into the conversation.

Cautiously, Sam returned to the sofa, then made a show of checking his watch. "You've got five minutes to explain, pal. After that, I'm outta here."

Falco's eyes narrowed for a brief second, and Sam was certain he had touched a nerve. Perhaps Falco wasn't accustomed to having people talk to him in that manner. *Too fucking bad*, thought Sam. *I've been at this game too long to be intimidated or ordered around by another mystery dude.*

"Fix yourself a cup of hot chocolate, Sam. What I'm about to tell you will go down easier with some Swiss Miss."

Swiss Miss? Sam eyed the plastic sack on the kitchen counter. *Lucky guess or what?* Still, he had four minutes left and Falco's suggestion sounded like a good idea.

Sam mixed two cups of Swiss Miss, then fished a bottle of Tylenol from the plastic sack. He popped the cap, dumped two of the capsules into his palm, and handed them to Falco, along with a cup of the Swiss Miss. "Cheers."

The man popped the pills into his mouth, then looked into the cup, and gave the contents a gentle swirl. "This isn't the kind with the mini-marshmallows?"

The comment took Sam by surprise. *Well ain't that something? Never would have figured him for a Swiss Miss connoisseur.*

"The store was out of the good stuff. Drink up."

Falco nursed the chocolate for a couple of minutes before setting the cup aside. Despite Sam's earlier declaration that he would give the man five minutes, he waited patiently. Finally, Falco spoke.

"Good stuff. Thank you. Now, let's get down to business. I wasn't bluffing, Sam. You can't go after your sister. Not now. If you do, you'll only lead the Enemy to her. And your mother."

"And what enemy is that, Mr. Falco?"

"Don't play me, kid. You know damn well what I'm talking about. In fact, until last night, I thought you were one of them. My superiors still believe you are."

The words cut Sam like a knife. He stood up. "With all due respect, Mr. Falco, fuck you sideways!"

Falco smiled wanly. "Don't take offense, Sam. We've been fighting these bastards a long time, and we've learned to be . . . careful in choosing our friends." The man shifted in his seat.

Sam edged toward the door. "I don't know who you are, or who this 'we' might be, but I can tell you all a little something about fighting the Enemy myself. And funny thing. I don't recall seeing your smug ass lending a hand when—"

"When you fought them beneath the grounds of the sanatorium?" finished Falco. "Oh, we know about that. We know about a great many things. We've observed the Offspring for longer than you can imagine."

"Observed?" The word sounded vulgar and despicable when Sam said it. "Were you *observing* while I ran for my life all the way from Arizona to Tennessee? Or maybe you were *observing* when that little prick of a deputy shot Mark Pierce? Oh, wait! I know! You were *observing* when Michael Collier stepped through that goddamned gate and saved all of our sorry asses! Yeah, that must be it. Well, pal, I'm so sorry I missed out on all that *observing,* dude, but I was too busy staying alive!"

At some point during the rant, Sam had stopped retreating toward the door. Instead he had advanced across the living room and now stood with fists clenched only a few feet from the much bigger man.

Falco's stoic demeanor remained unchanged. "Yes, that, and more. We also observed your showdown with the demon lord and his underlings. That was quite a trick you pulled down there. We had the old tunnel under surveillance for several months prior to your arrival. In fact, I lost a close friend down there. A man who, much like Michael Collier, gave his life in order to gather information."

At that, Sam found his tongue again. "Gather information. Observation. Passive bullshit! You think you can compare *that* to the sacrifice Michael made? Mike saved a goddamned planet!"

Falco's expression softened. "Did he, Sam? Tell me about it. All of it." When Sam didn't reply, Falco added, "I'm going to be straight with you. If for no other reason, because you saved my life. I may have been off my feet, but I watched you stand down Little Stevie, and I heard most of the exchange between you two. Most important, I heard him say he had been hunting you, and that . . . changes things."

"Yeah? And I watched you walk away from your dead buddy like it was just another day at the office. What makes you think I want anything to do with you and your other pals? Who *are* you guys anyway? You can't be government. Maybe you're part of some wacko religious cult. That might explain a lot."

"I'll explain in a moment who 'we' are. And as for abandoning my former partner, if that's the way you feel, why did you bring me down from the rooftop? Why did you stay here last night, knowing that that Little Stevie character could return to finish what he started?"

"That's a damn good question, Mr. Falco, and to tell you the truth, I don't have an answer. Considering the way you left your partner behind, I'm beginning to wonder if you were worth the effort!" He regretted the words as soon as they left his mouth. The other man had been beyond help, and Sam knew it. Sam also knew that his anger had nothing to do with Falco abandoning his friend. It did, however, have everything to do with Sam leaving Michael Collier in the belly of that mountain, two years earlier.

Falco's expression hardened, and for a moment Sam thought the man might actually struggle up from the chair and beat the shit out of him. Looking at the man's bulging muscles beneath the T-shirt, Sam had no doubt that even in a weakened condition Falco could make short work of him. *He's not as tall as Mike, but he's put together like a linebacker on a steady diet of steroids.* Sam noticed something else, as well. The grips of a handgun jutted from the waist of Falco's jeans. Yet Sam refused to blink during the stare-down. *And his eyes. They bore right through you, like a pair of blue drill bits.*

For several protracted seconds, the two glared at each other from across the room. Finally, Falco reached for his cup and took another sip, his eyes never leaving the boy. "Sit down, Sam. I'm going to come clean with you. Tell you everything. In doing so, I'm breaking a sacred confidence and it could very well cost me my life."

More dramatic bullshit. Jesus, why can't people just say something without all the verbal condiments? "Sounds serious, so why take the chance? Why not just let me be on my way?"

"I have a couple of reasons. First and foremost, I owe you. You saved my life last night, at great risk to your own. And that may be one of the all-time great ironies."

Puzzled, Sam asked, "How so?"

Falco finished off the chocolate and set the cup aside. "Because you're the reason I'm in Arizona, boy. I came here to kill you."

Sam stared open-mouthed at Falco for a moment, trying to digest what he had just heard. "Maybe you want to run that by me again. Is that supposed to be some kind of joke? Because—"

Falco cut him off. "No joke, Sam. Let me start from the beginning. First, have you ever heard of the Knights Templar?" Sam answered with a dumb nod of his head. "Good. Now, listen closely and don't interrupt. If you have questions, hold them until I finish. Afterward, I'll try to answer them as best I can. This story goes back several hundred years to the time of the Crusades and I would need a couple of years to tell you the entire history of my Order. For now, we'll stick to the abbreviated version.

"During one of the Crusades, a Knight by the name of Hugues de Payens requested permission to establish an order of warrior monks in Jerusalem. He would call this group The Poor Knights of Christ and of the Temple of Solomon. He would task them with guarding the pilgrim's way from Europe into Jerusalem. Permission was granted, and eventually de Payens and his small band of brethren were given space inside Jerusalem's al-Aqs â Mosque for use as headquarters."

"Crusades, knights, and mosques. Fascinating stuff, Mr. Falco, but what's this got to do—"

"Patience, Sam. It won't take long for the picture to come into focus. Many contemporary historians and religious scholars believe that temple is also the fabled Temple of Solomon, and that at the time of the Crusades, it sat atop a vast storehouse of treasures and religious antiquities."

"Yeah, yeah, I read *The Da Vinci Code*. What's your point?"

"Only this: Those historians and scholars weren't all wrong. By following documents and maps recovered during the First Crusade, de Payens's Templars secretly excavated beneath the mosque, and found the treasure rooms of Solomon. I won't attempt to describe the massive wealth they found except to say entire countries could be bought and sold for less. However, the most important finds had little to do with gold and silver. The Templars recovered a number of scrolls and tablets that contained astounding secrets and revelations. Prophecies, if you will. Not the least of which were the locations of the Veils, or Eyes of God."

Sam held up a hand and said, "Whoa, stop. You said 'Veils' and 'Eyes.' Plural."

Falco nodded. "I'm afraid so. The scrolls led to the discovery of nine such portals, all mirror images of one another. To date, we've located six, scattered all across the globe. We're still searching for another three. What's more, one of the scrolls went on to explain that all of the portals are interconnected, that whatever affects one, affects all."

Sam sat down on the sofa, leaned back, and closed his eyes. He had often wondered how the Veil came to be in such an obscure place as Abbotsville. Or even in the United States for that matter. He had also wondered if there had been other such gates. However, neither Uriel nor Joriel had mentioned the existence of other Veils, and eventually, Sam had dismissed the whole thing. Now, however . . . According to Falco and his ancient documents, this meant there were at least nine such portals. Which also meant the demons had at least that many points of entry into this world. *Dear God.*

"Are—are the other Veils still operational?"

"Sorry, Sam," said Falco, "but I think you understand why I won't answer that. Information regarding the Veils is held in close confidence. The short of it is that the Templars were eventually disbanded and outlawed. Many were executed. Others fled France and established new lives, yet they never forgot the prophecies and portents contained in the scrolls. Several surviving members of the original Templars passed the knowledge down through their bloodlines. Eventually, a new order was founded, the Watchers. Their intent was, and is, to watch for signs of the coming of Legion and the End of Days, a time preceding the Great Tribulation by some few months or years. It is our hope that we can salvage much of humanity before the Rapture and Great Tribulation period."

Sam leaned forward, placing his elbows on his knees. "Religious fanatics! Thought so. But why hunt me? If you and your pals have as much intel as you claim, then you know damn well the Veil in Abbotsville was broken and had to be closed. You know I'm not the bad guy!"

Falco shrugged. "Maybe. My superiors aren't so sure you didn't damage that Veil in the first place. You see, several of the scrolls and older tablets also make mention of a future event that foretells the End of Days. This event is heralded by the damaging of the Veils. In fact, prophecy maintains that the ancestors of angelic entities and humans, or Offspring, play a prominent part in mankind's final downfall."

Sam's eyes betrayed him and Falco smiled.

"Oh, yes. We know you're an Offspring. My order has spent hundreds of years and small fortunes to locate and keep tabs on your . . . lineage. No small feat, considering the scope of the task. And not always successful. I admit the results are, at best, incomplete. We've lost track of numerous bloodlines over the centuries, bloodlines that we'll never find again, or at least, not until the gifts manifest themselves and an Offspring does something that draws our attention.

"But we do know this: You and your kind have been around since the dawn of time. According to the scrolls, the bloodline diminished significantly just prior to the time of Christ, with only a few sporadic instances cropping up from time to time. Then, about three or four years ago, those with the blood reemerged in greater numbers than ever before."

"I don't suppose you can tell me how you know that." It was more statement than question.

Falco shook his head. "I can't. But I will tell you this. The sudden appearance of Offspring coincided with the damage to the Veil and the initial influx of Legion. My superiors believe that the Offspring and Legion are related, and that together, you spell the end of Creation. The only survivors will be the few God Himself spares during the Rapture. The End of Days, according to the scrolls.

"Not all of those who share the bloodline have exhibited what we consider supernatural traits. People like your father and sister. Your paternal grandmother, however, was a great concern to us."

Ha! Always knew Nanna was special! At least they don't know about Kat's gifts.

Falco continued. "We feel Katherine may have the potential, but she hasn't demonstrated the abilities, so she's safe . . . for the moment."

Sam fell back onto the sofa, and covered his face with his hands. He didn't know whether to laugh or cry. *Joriel, are you listening to this maniac? I could really use some help right now!* There was no answer, not that he expected one.

Glancing over at Falco, Sam said, "So you came here to kill me. And possibly my sister . . . maybe my mom. I can't . . . You fucking idiots! You've got no idea what you're doing to this world!"

Falco's eyes narrowed. "Be that as it may, you can't go to your sister. Now that we've located her, a team of operators, people like myself, have her under twenty-four-hour surveillance. They're also watching this hotel, with orders to prevent you from leaving. By shooting you if necessary.

"Katherine is safe, unless you show up unannounced. If you do, my men will know I failed and they'll deal with you and your family appropriately."

"Good God, this can't be happening! Look, you guys have seen demons! You know damn well that my sister and I aren't one of them! Besides, if I was a demon, why would I have saved you? Can't you tell your people what happened up on that roof and call them off?"

"Sam, you're a smart kid, but you're a little short on experience. No, listen to me! How many demons have you actually seen to date? I'm talking about face-to-face encounters. Five? Six? And they were almost all of the same order.

"Sam, we've catalogued nearly one hundred types and classes of demons, from minor imps to the greater demons, or demon lords. Not all of them look like the stereotypical Hollywood monster with bloody claws and fangs dripping acid. I assure you, there are hundreds of them walking around this country right now that look every bit as human as you or I. And the snipers outside this building know that. Sorry, kid, but nothing I say will stop them from carrying out their orders."

Through clenched teeth, Sam said, "At least there's a possible bright side to all this."

Falco frowned and said, "Yeah? What's that?"

"If I'm lucky, Little Stevie will go after my sister and find your buddies instead. And I won't be around to save *those* murdering bastards." *And what's more, Mr. Falco, if your buddies are hunting Offspring, you'd better learn to sleep with one eye open. I can't wait to tell . . .* Sam froze.

CHAPTER 7

Phoenix, Arizona

Falco leaned forward in his chair and said something, but the words were lost. Sam had already withdrawn, all his attention now focused on his unerring mental radar. *Three, four . . . five!* Not since Abbotsville had Sam sensed that many of the Enemy at once. *Maybe it's Little Stevie. Not that his arrival would be good news. Anyway, if it is that ass-ugly man-mountain, he has formed a posse.*

Holding up a hand, he motioned for silence. Sam closed his eyes, and took a deep breath. Exhaling slowly, he projected tentative mental fingers, feeling his way across the ethereal plane until at last, the probe connected with a familiar, sinister consciousness. *Six, maybe seven miles to the south. Moving in short bursts, searching, but uncertain.*

Sam withdrew and shut down his mental radar. He had learned long ago that it never paid to overstay a visit to the Enemy. The entity he had touched was strong, but Sam had felt stronger. That was the good news. The bad news was that there were several of the bastards.

Turning to Falco he said, "We have company."

Faster than Sam could follow, Falco produced the handgun from the waistband of his jeans, and was struggling out of the chair. He made it nearly halfway when his face contorted in pain, and he fell back. Falco laid the gun in his lap and held the back of his head with both hands.

Damn, he's in bad shape. Then, as an afterthought, *Like I really care.*

"Take it easy, man. It's not like they're standing outside the door."

"How—how close?" asked Falco.

Sam shrugged and said, "I've got them pinpointed five, maybe six miles south of us. They don't seem to be moving this way. In fact, they're sort of milling around like cattle."

Still holding his head, Falco looked up and said, "Six miles? Bullshit!"

"What do you mean, 'bullshit'? You asked how far and I told you. If you don't like the answer, don't ask the question."

Falco stood up on shaky legs and walked to the window. He pulled back the sheers and looked out into the hotel's interior garden. "You're serious, aren't you? You really believe you can detect a demon from a distance of six miles."

"I said that I can pinpoint them over that distance. But that Little Stevie character is no demon. I'm not sure what he is, but I know what he isn't, and it's not him I'm picking up."

Falco nodded. "I think you're right. About what he isn't, that is. At first I thought he might be an Offspring, one who had finally surrendered to the demonic influence. But now . . . now I think he's something entirely different, something I've never encountered before. But let's get back to this talent of yours. You may or may not be aware, but the ability to sense demonic presence isn't a talent specific to Offspring. I know of humans who are very sensitive to them. We think of it as a kind of spiritual talent. How do you find them?"

Oh, so now I'm not even human. Sam shook his head and said, "I really don't know how it works. I've been able to sense them for as long as I can remember. It starts with a kind of nausea that builds until I'm ready to puke. Then I smell this really putrid odor. After a few seconds, sometimes longer, the nausea passes and I can sorta zero in on their location."

Falco fell silent. He seemed to be struggling with something, and Sam thought he knew what had the man so confused. *Spiritual talent! He didn't know that locating demons was an Offspring gift and he's starting to put two and two together.*

"Wait a second." Falco left the window and walked into the

kitchen area. He filled the pot with tap water and placed it on the stove. Turning on the burner he said, "So you don't exactly sense them at first. You *smell* demons over a distance."

"Not exactly. It's like my mind picks them up on this kind of radar and associates that sense with a really nasty odor. Sometimes it's so strong it gags me."

"Yeah," said Falco.

Sam smirked. *Yeah, indeed, big guy. You know exactly what I'm talking about, don't you? We're carrying the same blood, aren't we, cuz? Why would you kill your own kind? Murdering hypocrite! Unless . . . unless your bullshit Watchers really have no idea what Offspring are, or what we can and can't do. Jesus, what a screwed-up mess!*

"Sam, listen. If you really can sense them over that distance, you've got a hell of a gift. A gift that could prove very useful to us."

"Oh, give me a break!" Sam stood up and walked to the kitchen counter. "First you guys want to kill me, and now you want to recruit me! Do you really think I give a fuck about your little war?"

"Maybe you don't. And maybe you care a lot more than you let on," said Falco. "But I'm certain you give a very large fuck about your mom and your sister. My superiors are waiting for my report, and if I wait much longer, they're going to get nervous. You and your family don't want my superiors any more nervous than they already are. I can't promise anything, but if you consent to help us hunt down and destroy Legion, I'll do what I can to ensure the safety of your family. What do you say?"

He tore open another packet of hot chocolate mix, poured it into a cup, and added boiling water. He slid the cup across the counter to Sam. "Come on, Sam. It's the best deal you're likely to get today. You help us, we help you. Tit for tat. What do you say?"

Looking into Falco's blue-gray eyes, he saw that one pupil was dilated to a size twice that of the other. The sclerae of both eyes were red from hemorrhage. *Severe concussion.*

Good. I hope he croaks!

"No offense, Mr. Falco, but how about you and your superiors just kiss my left ass cheek, then the right? Tit for tat. What do you say?"

Arching an eyebrow, Falco said, "So you won't consider my offer even if it means you and your family would be free to go about your lives without fear of assassin squads lurking in the shadows? Even if it means you can live in relative safety, free from persecution by us or the Enemy?"

Sam sipped the chocolate. For several seconds neither man spoke, until Sam finally broke the silence. "If you want to know the truth, I think you're both the goddamned enemy." With that, he turned and walked back to the sofa.

Exhausted, Falco closed the bedroom door and stretched out on the bed. The boy had no idea how drained he was, otherwise he would have simply walked out the door without a backward glance. Falco was in no condition to stop him, at least not without using the gun. Fortunately, he wouldn't have to shoot the kid. There were a half dozen seasoned killers surrounding the hotel, each just itching to pull the trigger on Sam Conner.

Falco looked at his watch, but the Roman numerals ran together forming a nauseating blur. He guessed the time at nine A.M.

Give or take a mile, he said. Five or six miles to the south, give or take a mile. My God, what a gift! And I thought I had a knack for detecting the Enemy. Hell, I'm doing good if I can sense them beyond half a mile. Still, our talents do seem similar. It's gottta be the Offspring blood that gives him the added range. The Offspring blood . . .

The last was a disturbing thought. Falco pushed it from his mind and focused on Sam again. If the boy's claims were true, and Falco had no reason to doubt them, Sam would prove a tremendous ally in the war against Legion. Provided, of course, he could be persuaded. And *if* the Shield didn't order the boy's immediate termination. That was a big "if." Falco was certain his superiors were less than thrilled to learn the boy was still alive. He chuckled as he visualized the Hierarchy huddled around a massive conference table, each holding a copy of his report and staring blankly at one another. No doubt they would all be struck deaf, mute, and blind when they learned *why* Sam Conner was still alive.

As he considered the contents of the summary he would file, Falco's mood sobered. Gilbert had expected the report last night, and was no doubt concerned by now. The support team had likewise failed to check in. *Checking in is always a difficult task for dead men.*

If for any reason Falco failed to report in today, Gilbert would dispatch another team to Phoenix and any chance Sam Conner might have at redemption would be snuffed like a candle in a hurricane. The thought saddened Falco and he was uncomfortable with the seldom-experienced emotion.

He owed his life to the boy, and still he had lied to him. Of course, Falco *would* lobby for Sam's life. And though improbable, it *was* possible the Watchers would spare him in exchange for the use of his talents. Several members of the Sword had special abilities, gifts from Almighty God used to locate and combat the plague that was Legion. But none of them could detect demons from beyond a few hundred yards. Sam's amazing ability to detect the Enemy over great distances was beyond anything Falco had ever heard of. No doubt, conservative members of the Hierarchy would accept that as irrefutable proof of Sam's demonic heritage. *Just as they've done with at least two dozen other Offspring, none as gifted as Sam, but gifted just the same. Two dozen men, women, and children, imprisoned for as long—or short—as their natural lives may be.*

Then there was the matter of the boy's other "gift," the extraordinary blue fire that had sprung from his fingertips and pierced Little Stevie like a bolt of neon lightning. Falco had purposely avoided mention of that incident in his conversations with Sam, afraid he would have been unable to hide his awe.

No, there was no way the Watchers would ever allow Sam and his family to live out normal lives in obscurity. The boy was too powerful, too dangerous. If the Hierarchy's worst fears proved out and the blood of demons did in fact flow through Sam Conner's veins . . . *May God have mercy on us all.* Meanwhile, and from this moment on, shadowed assassins would be Sam Conner's constant companions.

Falco rose from the bed and made his way to the desk where Will Caseman had set up the laptop and portable HP printer–fax machine. It was time to file the report.

chapter 8

The aide held the phone close to his chest with one hand. With the other, she flashed two fingers, closed her hand into a fist, and then flashed three fingers.

Enrique DeLorenzo felt the muscles in his jaw tighten. *Twenty-two million, three hundred thousand dollars, US.* Quite an opening bid for a chunk of wood, but still less than he had expected. Then again, this was far more than some dusty antiquity salvaged from another era. Religious scholars believed such relics contained great power. Power that would one day be called upon in the war against Legion.

There would be no letter of authenticity provided to the winner of this by-invitation-only auction. The players had been provided with results of the exhaustive dating analysis. Potential buyers were provided with a detailed history of the piece as it made its way from an obscure hill near ancient Jerusalem to its current home in Austria. They were allowed close inspection of the yard-long shard of timber, and they used the opportunity to subject the piece to intense scrutiny by highly qualified third-party scientific contractors. Iron nail fragments had been recovered from the wood and deemed consistent with the historical period in question.

Still, the only documentation provided by the seller was the results of molecular X-rays and carbon-14 dating, conducted at the seller's expense, and under the watchful eye of not one but three independent laboratories. All evidence pointed to an authentic and highly coveted class-one relic. The estimated selling price might be considered unreasonable though, were it not for one simple fact: The Order needed it.

Enrique considered the bid for only a moment, then nodded to his aide. The young woman acknowledged the nod with one of her own, then spoke quietly into the phone. While awaiting the next bidding round, Enrique swirled two fingers of brandy inside a Baccarat snifter and considered the report he had finished earlier that afternoon. The news from Malcolm hadn't been good. In fact, it bordered on catastrophic.

Thomas Falco had confirmed it in a later report: *Three members of an advance support element dead. One highly skilled Sword dead. Another sorely injured and awaiting extraction.* How could such a thing happen? How? Thank God this all went down in Phoenix, and not in Boston or Los Angeles.

Enrique made a mental note to call his contacts in Phoenix as soon as the auction was over. It wouldn't be easy, but eventually the police would determine Will Caseman's identity. If they ever stumbled across his background, the investigation would be relentless. The Watchers had powerful allies within various high-level law enforcement and judiciary communities, and at times such as this, those friends would prove invaluable. The deaths were tragic, and the loss of Will Caseman would be felt throughout the entire Order. Yet, that wasn't the catastrophe that Gilbert spoke of in his early-morning fax.

Enrique's thoughts were interrupted as his aide flashed another bid.

The price has climbed by thirteen-and-a-half million dollars in less than two minutes. Quite a price for a piece of blood-stained wood. I wonder if Christ ever imagined we would be bidding for the instrument of his earthly demise? Ah, well . . . enough.

Enrique held up five fingers, flashed them three times in rapid succession, and waited until his aide acknowledged the bid from across the room. As soon as she gave him a brief nod, Enrique's thoughts returned to the report. The contents were disturbing on so many levels, the greatest of which was that Sam Conner was still alive.

A seventh-generation Watcher, Enrique was the senior-most member of the Order's intelligence branch in the Americas. Though not a member of the Hierarchy, his was a position of tremendous political power and influence, which he wielded with great finesse. More important, as chief legal counsel for the Boston Archdiocese, he had far-reaching access to sensitive information, some of which originated in the secretive confines of Vatican City. Yet, despite his status, Enrique held little personal ambition. Rather, he saw political influence, financial power, and information as common tools to be used toward an uncommon end, weapons to be wielded against the armies of Legion during the End of Days. This was Enrique DeLorenzo's role, his mission in life, to carry the fight to the Enemy. And now, it would seem God had delivered another weapon to the Watchers for use against the putridity that had seeped into the world of man from the despicable plane of Sitra Akhra. A weapon named Sam Conner. An Offspring.

Provided the Hierarchy would approve such a plan. Many of the elders were convinced Offspring were demon-spawn, while the rest simply didn't know what to believe. Despite the ambiguity of the ancient scrolls, not a single Watcher had risen to champion the Offspring as victims of errant interpretations. *At least, not until now.* According to Malcolm's fax, Thomas Falco had all but accepted the role of advocate. How Enrique dreaded passing *that* bit of information up the Watcher chain of command.

Despite the onset of an early winter, Enrique walked outside and thought the night air felt thick and oppressive. The flow of traffic along Long Island's Seventh Street grated on his nerves, and his favorite meal—roasted Monkfish Tournedo—had seemed flat and tasteless. Not even the auction in which he had secured a highly coveted class-one relic could bolster his spirits. The actual value of such a potent artifact was immeasurable and the Hierarchy was well pleased, but Enrique couldn't bring himself to celebrate the victory. He also knew there was nothing wrong with the food, the traffic, or the encroaching

Canadian cold front. His black mood had everything to do with the situation in Phoenix.

A quick glance at his watch told him it was nearly time for the call. He motioned for a taxi, then changed his mind and waved off the black-and-white as it pulled up the curb. It wouldn't be the first time he had conversed with his superiors while walking along the streets of Long Island. Enrique traveled less than a block before his cell phone vibrated. He activated the phone, and waited for the signal that indicated a secure satellite uplink. After a few seconds, the phone chirped three times in rapid succession. The call was now safely encrypted.

Enrique answered, "DeLorenzo."

"Good evening, Rikki. Have you a moment to talk?"

The speech was thick and slightly slurred, as Enrique knew it would be. "Yes, sir. I have all the time in the world, Lord Protector." Enrique used the honorific title given to the highest-ranking Sword in each country or region, and in this case, the North American continent.

"Ah, so kind of you, my son, but let's dispense with the formalities, shall we? How is your family? Angelina is well? And little Rikki?"

"Yes to both, sir. Thank you for asking. And you? You are well?"

The inquiry was another customary courtesy, for Enrique already knew the answer. The Lord Protector was dying. Nothing short of a miracle would see him through the winter, though only those nearest to him would suspect the truth.

"I'm well enough for an old man with a bad hip and an upstart gall bladder," Gilbert replied.

Not to mention lymphatic cancer, thought Enrique.

"You've read the reports from Malcolm, sir?"

"Yes, I've read them. The business in Phoenix is very, very disturbing. Sir Malcolm was en route back to New Orleans when I learned the mission in Phoenix had failed. I rerouted Malcolm and his team to Phoenix, where he now has Falco's hotel under surveillance. Malcolm is prepared to have Falco on a private plane within two hours' notice. A safe house has been notified and appropriate medical staff is on call to attend Falco upon his arrival.

"I assume you've initiated appropriate damage control measures on your end, Rikki?"

"Yes, sir. Caseman is a nonentity. It's as if he never lived. Covers for the deceased members of the support crew are in place. A replacement support team is already en route."

"Good, good. And what of the Enemy? I understand there's been no further sign of them in Phoenix since the attack on our people?"

Them. If Falco is to be believed, there was no "them." A single monstrous entity cut our people down.

"Our observers report no sign of the Enemy, sir. Although . . ." Enrique cut short his reply. He was entering dangerous territory now. Dangerous for Thomas Falco, at least. However, he didn't need to finish the sentence. The Lord Protector did so for him.

". . . although Falco believes the Enemy has gathered in considerable numbers near Phoenix, is that it? Perhaps a *nest*?"

"Yes, sir," said Enrique, while at the same time, hoping Falco was wrong. Nests were extremely dangerous demonic strongholds, usually led by one or more greater demons, or worse, a lord. "Thomas believes the nest is located south of the city, almost due south of his hotel."

"And he has this on good authority . . . from his guest, young Sam Conner, the Offspring? So, tell me, Rikki! What do you make of Thomas's observations regarding the boy?"

Here we go, straight to the chase. "I believe Thomas feels he owes his life to this boy. If his report is even remotely accurate, Conner possesses extraordinary powers, the likes of which we've yet to observe in other Offspring. Thomas is also convinced there is nothing demonic about the boy's abilities. He says he detects no hint of demonic presence in or about Conner, and we all know of Thomas's gift for sniffing out the Enemy.

"However, by his own admission, Thomas suffered severe trauma and a serious head injury. It's possible his observations are clouded, or the result of trauma-induced hallucinations."

There was brief pause, then, "I believe there is one possibility that you've either dismissed out of hand or simply overlooked."

Enrique's pulse quickened. *Here it comes.*

"I've considered it, sir. There is a chance, however remote, that Thomas is now under the influence of the Enemy. We both know he's questioned his faith before, and as much as I'd like to dismiss the notion of demonic influence, I can't. A moment, sir."

Enrique moved toward the edge of the walk, making way for a giggling couple. As soon as the pair was well out of earshot, he continued.

"But Falco seems so certain, sir. In his report, he—"

"Stop, Rikki. You've repeated Falco's report almost verbatim. I asked what *you* think. If you truly believe Falco may be contaminated, then you know what we must do, and be quick about it. His knowledge of the Order in the hands of the Enemy would be devastating."

"I've left him stranded, injured, and alone, just for that reason, sir. And, frankly, it's wounded my very soul to abandon a trusted Sword like this. I—I'm just not sure what to think, sir. I know this isn't what you wanted to hear, but I can't offer a better answer. Not yet."

"Quite the dilemma isn't it?" said the Lord Protector. "We all know how cunning and treacherous the Enemy can be. It's possible the boy is in fact demonic, and this is a well-contrived ploy to infiltrate the Order. God knows they've infiltrated just about every other institution on the planet. On the other hand, if Thomas is correct, we must find a way to utilize Conner's ability to detect and pinpoint the Enemy. My God, what a talent! Provided, of course, that the Hierarchy will permit such a thing.

"Therefore, this is what you must do. And I say you, because I trust this to no one else, not with so much at stake. You must go to Falco. Interview this Offspring, and see for yourself.

Afterward, we will make our recommendation to the Hierarchy."

Enrique silently thanked God for Thomas Falco's reprieve. An hour ago, he wouldn't have taken fifty-to-one odds on Falco's life expectancy beyond tomorrow.

chapter 9

Inspector Arturo Giannini of the Vatican Corps of Gendarmes made his way through the stunned crowd of onlookers. *So many for this time of night!* At the edge of the lawn surrounding the front of Domus Sanctae Marthae, a pair of nervous-looking security officers stepped aside, giving Arturo a first look at the carnage. In his twenty years as a Vatican law police officer, he'd never seen anything like this. Dio Omnipotente! *God Almighty!*

The brutality suggested a mind wound too tightly that had finally snapped. Or perhaps it was a crime of passion brought on by jealousy. Unlikely, but not unheard of. There was another possibility, one too terrible to entertain, yet it was the very reason Arturo had rushed to the scene. It was his covert mission to ferret out infiltration of the Holy See by the Enemy. Arturo lead two lives: one in which he played the stoic, professional police officer, dedicated to the preservation of the law, and one for which he truly lived, a well-kept secret known only to a very few. Arturo Giannini was the eyes and ears of the Watchers inside the walls of the Vatican, in constant vigilance for signs of the Enemy. The crime scene before him could well be such a sign.

Piero Fini, another Gendarmes senior investigator, stood over the first body and snapped several pictures with a thirty-five-millimeter camera. A pair of junior officers, both looking a little green around the gills, knelt beside the bodies. Each held small, metallic rulers near obvious wounds and other evi-

dence for scale. Arturo doubted the pictures would be of much
use. Piero's hands shook like an old log wagon on a mountain
road. When Piero saw Arturo, he stepped away from the
corpse, seemingly grateful for an opportunity to do so.

Arturo reached inside a coat pocket for a stick of gum.
Peeling the wrapper, he said, "Do we know their identities?"

Piero nodded. "I found identification on the woman, a very
fortunate thing as her face has been carved away. Her name is
Maria Giuseppe, a staffer at the hospice."

"Ah. I knew her." Arturo turned to look at the second
corpse. He had been a tall, thin man bordering on gaunt, mid-
fifties, perhaps a bit older. "And him?"

Piero pulled a handkerchief from the inside pocket of his
coat and mopped sweat from his brow. Then, with a slight nod
of his head, he motioned for Arturo to follow. As they walked
away, Piero called over his shoulder to the two plain clothed officers, "No one touches either body. And get that crowd out of
here!" The two men got to the steps of the hospice, well out the
crowd's hearing.

"The man is Father Raoul Acuna, a resident lecturer at the
university. A brilliant man."

"Oh? You knew the Father?"

Piero nodded. "Not very well, but we had talked on a couple
of occasions. I had the pleasure of attending one of his lectures
last year at the Regina Apostolorum, where he is a member of
the faculty. He developed much of the new course work rele-
vant to exorcisms and the occult."

Arturo arched an eyebrow at this revelation. When the pontiff had decided to resurrect the actual teaching of occult-
oriented material, it had touched off disquieting reverberations
felt throughout the global Catholic community. He began another question, then paused. In the distance, Arturo could hear
the high-pitched wail of sirens. An ambulance, no doubt, and
quite possibly the Rome carabinieri. He would need to work
fast.

"Have you any idea how this went down?"

Piero shook his head. "Only one murder. Acuna's death is
a suicide, I'm certain. The murder weapon is still in his hand.

Besides, we have witnesses who watched Acuna run the knife through his own throat. My God, Arturo, this is unthinkable!"

Not nearly so much as you might think, my friend. The entire world has gone mad.

"And you believe the witnesses are reliable?"

Piero shrugged. "As reliable as any group of nuns might be. Ah, the ambulance just came through the gate. I need to finish the photos, then bag and tag the rest of the physical evidence before they haul these two away. Can you can do me a favor?"

"Sure," replied Arturo. "Name it."

Piero handed him a pair of numbered door keys. "Father Acuna had been assigned a suite inside the hospice, a special consideration for his assistance at the university. Maria was a resident caretaker. We'll need to search both apartments, and have a report ready for the Inspector General by morning, if not sooner. I could use the help."

Excellent! "Say no more, Piero. I'll handle the searches myself and notify you immediately should I find anything of interest."

"I appreciate your help, Arturo," said a grateful Piero, as he started back to the crime scene. "Thank you."

No, thank you, my friend.

Domus Sanctae Marthae, or the House of Saint Martha, was a massive building constructed of beige and tan blocks standing adjacent to the basilica. A former hospice, it was now the most exclusive hotel in the world, featuring 107 suites. It reached full capacity only when the cardinals assembled for a papal conclave. At other times, it served as a temporary residence for visiting ecclesiastical dignitaries like Father Acuna, the occasional diplomatico, and a small cadre of year-round caretakers. What few people were in residence had gathered on the pavement adjacent to the lawn, where they looked on with morbid fascination as Piero's men worked the crime scene.

Arturo understood the onlookers' fascination with this tragic event. This was the first homicide committed inside Vatican City since 1998, when a member of the Swiss Guard, Vice

Corporal Cedric Tornay, allegedly committed a double homicide before taking his own life. The official Vatican line was that Tornay was under the influence of drugs at the time, and perhaps suffered from some undiagnosed mental illness. Tornay's family vigorously protested the findings, suggesting that Tornay had been killed to cover the Vatican-inspired murders of Colonel Alois Estermann and his wife. Arturo knew that there was bad blood between Tornay and Estermann, the result of a reprimand given to Tornay just before the tragedy. Given the brutality of the murders, Arturo had secretly considered that perhaps the young guard had, in fact, been under an influence, though not of drugs or other intoxicants.

It was one thing for a warrior to commit such an atrocity, regardless of the impetus, and Tornay certainly had been a highly skilled warrior. It was quite another when an esteemed member of the clergy, a pontifical university theologian no less, succumbed to murderous rage. Arturo checked the time. He knew others shared his opinion and would soon descend upon Acuna's living quarters in search of answers.

While the Gendarmes were responsible for almost all investigations inside Vatican City, there were other security forces at work within the Holy See. Beyond the initial shock, the Swiss Guard would take little more than a passing interest in the crime. After all, it didn't involve the pontiff's safety—not directly, at least. However, the secretary of state commanded his own elite intelligence agency, and would deploy them as he saw fit. Given the identity of the alleged murderer, Arturo fully expected to see intelligence agents combing the hospice before daylight.

He bypassed Maria's quarters and made straight for the elevators at the end of the vaulted hallway. He would have to make a show of checking her apartment, but in his own time. It was Acuna's suite that interested him most, that held the greatest potential for significant discoveries. Arturo stepped onto the elevator and pressed the second-floor button. A few minutes later, he took one of the keys from his pocket. Disregarding the NON DISTURBAR placard hanging from the doorknob, he unlocked suite 217 and stepped inside.

The smell of feces, rotted food, and stale urine assaulted his senses. *How could the live-in staff not have noticed this?*

Covering his nose and mouth with a handkerchief, Arturo shut and locked the door behind him, then walked across the room to close the drapes. He wanted to move about the apartment undetected from the streets. Of course, both the Gendarmes and the Secretary's intelligence group would know he was rummaging around inside the second-story apartment, but closing the drapes might prevent prying eyes from knowing what, if anything, he might discover. After all, the compound was littered with state-of-the-art surveillance equipment.

He pulled a pair of latex gloves from his coat pocket and donned them. Next, he stood in the middle of the living room and surveyed the immediate area. Arturo wasn't sure what he was looking for, but he hoped to recognize it when he saw it.

Newspapers, soiled clothing, and dishes caked with days-old food were strewn about the living area. In one corner of the main room Acuna had apparently relieved his bowels on more than one occasion. *The man was mad, no question. How had he managed to hide his condition from students and peers?*

Mentally sectioning the room off into a grid, Arturo began his search. A half hour later, he finished the preliminary search of the living room and moved to the expansive bedroom. He began with the dressers, carefully checking the contents of each drawer, then removed the drawers to search inside the cabinet. In the bottom drawer of the second chest, Arturo found something: a book.

The hardcover journal was of a type carried in most bookstores. Nothing remarkable on the covers. However, on the inside, tucked between blank pages, he found a small key. The key was unremarkable and simple in design, meaning it likely fit some cheap, uncomplicated lock. Arturo did recognize one peculiarity about the key: a fine, white, chalky substance caked between the large teeth. He took some of the powder between thumb and forefinger and examined the texture.

Commercial chalk? No. Too coarse. Then, what? Talc? Gypsum, maybe? Yes, Gypsum. Sheetrock! Excited, Arturo began a search of the interior walls. He checked behind every picture and bookcase, and around the light fixtures. Failing to find anything in the bedroom, he moved to a large walk-in closet. The closet contained an inexpensive suit, a couple of clean black cassocks, shirts, and slacks. Several cardboard boxes containing textbooks and other supplies associated with academia were stacked along the walls. Arturo took a book from atop one of the boxes and was flipping through the pages when he heard the familiar *click* of a thermostat, followed by the low hum of a heating fan. A stream of warm air blew across the back of his neck.

Looking up, he saw the source of the air: a small rectangular vent mounted in the ceiling above his head. He also noticed the deep tool marks along one side of the grill. Scratches embedded in Sheetrock.

Arturo ran to the dining room, grabbed a chair, then ran back to the closet. He stood on the chair and used the small key to pry up the edge of the grill, much as he expected Acuna had done. Several precious seconds later, he had the grill removed from the vent. Reaching inside the vent up to his elbow, he probed about blindly until at last his fingers made contact with a slim, metallic box. In another minute, he was sitting in the chair, holding a red metal container, its lid fastened by a simple lock. He fit the key into the lock and gave it a quarter turn. The lid of the container came free, and Arturo found himself looking at a copper scroll and a second journal. Arturo's eyes widened as he recognized the papal library label attached to one end of the thin, rolled copper sheeting. The second, smaller book appeared to be another journal, penned in English and Italian. He took the items out into the bedroom to make use of better lighting.

The lettering stamped on the outside of the copper roll was alien and without meaning. For the moment, Arturo set it aside and turned his attention to the journal.

The early entries were written in a clear, concise hand. Several were dated and signed by Acuna, as if the man intended the passages inside the book to serve as a daily diary. The contents of those passages shocked Arturo.

Acuna described in great detail his devotion to beings he

called "The Nine Princes of Sitra Akhra" or "The Great Ones," and their myriad lieutenants on Earth. He wrote of his forthcoming rewards for faithful service, and how he had led others to serve the Great Ones. If the man was to be believed, he had carefully selected and recruited an entire cell of co-conspirators from among the papal staff, beginning with lowly clerks and security personnel, and later from scholars and caretakers associated with the Vatican Library. Every meticulous step toward the final prize was chronicled.

Arturo noticed something else, as well. At the same time he carried out his plan, Acuna was descending into madness. It was no small wonder, thought Arturo. For whatever reasons he may have had, it was obvious Acuna had surrendered his immortal soul to the Enemy. Enthralled or possessed, the end result was the same. Sanity was ever short-lived in the presence of ultimate evil. One particular passage caught Arturo's attention.

> *The work of the devils will infiltrate even into the Church in such a way that one shall see cardinals opposing cardinals, bishops against bishops. The priests who venerate me will be scorned and opposed by their confreres . . . churches and altars sacked; the Church will be filled with those who accept compromises and demons will press many priests and consecrated souls to abandon the service of the Lord . . .*

Arturo flipped through the first dozen or so pages, each containing multiple, handwritten repetitions of the first paragraph. He was familiar with the passage. It was part of a disturbing prophecy uttered by a Sister Agnes of Our Lady of Akita Church, in 1973, and was said to be a dire message from the Blessed Virgin. The warning was accompanied by several unusual instances including stigmata and the shedding of blood and tears by a stone statue of Mary.

As was customary in such cases, the Vatican had instructed the Prefect of the Congregation of Doctrine and Faith to examine the circumstances involving Sister Agnes and Our Lady of

Akita Church. After years of interviews and examinations of fact, including photographic evidence, the prefect issued a definitive judgment in 1988 that the events at Akita were "reliable and worthy of faith." That prefect was none other than Cardinal Joseph Ratzinger, now known as Pope Benedict XVI.

Yet, the repetitious entry was hardly the most disturbing. As Arturo read on, he found himself mesmerized by the content, curiosity turning to fascination, and then to unmitigated horror. There were names, dates, places, and details of horrible crimes. And finally, he found a direct reference to the copper scroll.

Sweat beaded along his brow as Arturo read the entries associated with the scroll. *My God, can this be true? Did he really smuggle the Keys of Solomon out of the Vatican Library? I must get the book and scroll out of the building at once! They mustn't fall into the wrong hands. The intelligence force must never suspect that I've found anything. Especially, not this— this grimoire!*

He tucked the book and scroll into the waistband of his trousers, secured beneath his coat in the small of his back, then walked back into the closet. It took several minutes to secure the vent grill to his satisfaction. Minutes later, Arturo Giannini left the hospice without giving Maria's apartment a second glance. It was time to contact the Watchers.

Enrique arose at daybreak, nibbled at a tasteless breakfast, then packed a single bag for his flight to Phoenix. He suspected the meeting with Falco and Conner would take less than an hour, two at the most. Depending on the outcome of that meeting, he would either coerce the boy into serving the Order, or sanction the immediate termination of both Falco and Sam Conner. The latter would be most unfortunate, but with so much at stake, there could be no compromise.

He set his bag by the door and walked into his study for a final check of both fax machines and e-mail. A quick scroll of his incoming mail revealed nothing out of the ordinary had come in overnight. His business fax showed no transmissions. The second machine, however, encrypted and dedicated to Watcher business, had received two sets of documents.

He scoped the dozen or so sheets of paper from the catch tray and looked at the first cover sheet. The transmission had come from the Lord Protector. Enrique sat down at his desk and quickly read through the report. Then he read it a second time. And a third. Each time, the knot in his stomach grew exponentially. *My God. This can't be true. It can't.*

A murder inside the Holy See was shocking enough. And worse, oh, so very much worse, the "deep cover" Watcher operative, assigned to the Vatican and working for the Gendarmes, had discovered a journal inside the apartments of the killer. The contents of that journal would cast doubt and raise suspicion across the planet. . . . *turning cardinal against cardinal, bishop against bishop* . . . Public discovery of this journal would be catastrophic, destroying the faith of millions and undoing the work of centuries.

It could result in the eventual fall of the world's largest and most influential religious institution, undoing fragile, centuries-old political alliances. Social upheaval and economic collapse of Church-supported third-world causes and agendas were all critical, though secondary, concerns. The greatest devastation would result from the disaffected masses. Protestant and Catholic alike, numbering in the hundreds of millions, lost in a spiritual tempest without a rudder. A world suddenly dominated by a faithless humanity was surely hell on earth. New religious denominations would appear overnight, offering renewed hope. A perfect opportunity for the Enemy to claim the hearts, minds, and souls of a disenfranchised people. The final stage for the emergence of the Antichrist.

A lone tear formed in the corner of Enrique's eye and trailed down his check before dropping on the pages in his hand. He flipped open his cell phone and hit the speed dial function. After a couple of rings, a recording politely informed him the party he sought was unavailable. Enrique tried a second number, and this time, he was rewarded by the sound of a tired and familiar voice.

"Hello?"

"Your Grace? Enrique DeLorenzo. I'm sorry to disturb you at this hour."

"Nonsense, Enrique," said Bishop Gilbert. "I haven't been to bed yet. In fact, I thought you might be Malcolm Reading calling about the situation in Phoenix, or the fax from this morning. I still can't . . ." The voice trailed off.

"I understand, Your Grace. It's quite a shock. And that's the reason I'm calling. I'll be catching a plane in a couple of hours and won't have an opportunity to speak with Malcolm until I reach Phoenix. I assumed he would be in contact with you this morning. Do you think you might give him a message for me? I wouldn't impose, but it's urgent that he receives my instructions."

The old man sighed into the receiver. "Everything is urgent these days, and more so by the hour, it seems. Yes, of course, I'll relay your message. You know he's likely conducting surveillance on the hotel, so it may take some time to track him down. I keep telling him to let the younger operatives do the grunt work, but do you think that old fool listens to me? Now, what would you have me tell Malcolm?"

Enrique smiled despite the desperate circumstances. It was impossible not to love Bishop Gilbert. "I need Malcolm's team to pick up a package for me in Sun City, Arizona. It's imperative that we have the package in our possession no later than this afternoon. Do you have a pen and paper? Ah, good. Now, the package is named Kathleen Conner."

Two hours and twenty minutes later, Enrique boarded a plane for Arizona.

chapter 10

Mississippi Delta, a forest near Sanctuary

Kiel, one of the most powerful angels in all of Creation, watched from the shade-covered banks of the bayou as a red fox busied himself with tearing small chunks of flesh from a plump, freshly killed swamp rabbit. After the rabbit was neatly sectioned, the fox made several trips around its den in a wide arc, burying the pieces beneath bark, twigs, and leaves. Once the task was complete, the fox approached its den and yipped softly to his young.

A chubby kit tentatively poked her head out of the hollowed cypress. Upon seeing her sire, the kit bounced out into the open, followed closely by a pair of slightly larger sibling males.

Kiel chuckled softly at the adult fox as it lay on its stomach and allowed the kits to maul him in playful greeting. After several minutes, the fox shook the kits from his back and began the day's lesson, that of foraging for food. Before long, the kits were sniffing out the hidden meals of fresh rabbit while the sire fed his mate, then took a well-earned rest.

Kiel extended his arms toward the heavens and closed his eyes. *Thank you, Father, for this day and this gift. I do so love this world Your hands have made.* Still smiling, he slipped away from the bank beneath the cover of late afternoon shadows. As he made the short trip back to the old monastery, he wished Nathan had come with him to watch the foxes. Nathan, moody during the best of times, had been depressed since the loss of Baraniel, two years earlier.

Baraniel, one of the few remaining Cherubim on earth, had

long been a bastion of strength and inspiration, rallying the earthbound Host time and again against the combined armies of fallen angels and Legion.

Two years ago, the wretched Theo, second only to Lucifer among the Brethren, had threatened to loose his thralls and the demons of Legion upon an unsuspecting church congregation in Philadelphia unless Baraniel appeared. The Cherubim answered the challenge, knowing Theo had stacked the odds. Unwilling to risk more of the Host, Baraniel came to the church alone, and confronted the Enemy. The outcome was inevitable, and Baraniel's death dealt a terrible blow to the already decimated numbers of the Host. Since then, the war between the Host and the Brethren had escalated, and additional losses in recent months had driven Nathan deeper into despondency.

The loss had also affected Kiel, but in a different manner. Although the two angels shared several commonalities, their coping mechanisms were vastly different. Whereas Nathan grew moody and introspective at the loss of another Host, Kiel's grief manifested in the form of uncharacteristic anger that flashed like webbed lightning, and subsided just as quickly.

Arriving at the ancient, lichen-covered monastery, Kiel removed his muddy boots, left them beside the door, and entered. Centuries earlier, the three-story building, made of native stone, had provided sanctuary for the descendants of an outlaw Templar society, the Order of Watchers. Established in the early 1200s, and comprised of survivors of the Third Crusade, the Watchers were a small, select sect devoted to the preservation of the Templar ideals, those of the Christian warrior monk.

After a greedy King Philip IV, goaded by an equally greedy Pope Clement V, finally outlawed the Templars, he also ordered the Watchers and other Templar-supported sects to stand trial for bogus offenses against the crown and Church. Dozens of knights were taken into custody, stripped of titles and lands, and forced into confessions or renunciations. Those who refused were most often executed.

However, a great many managed to purchase safe passage out of France, seeking refuge in distant lands. While many of the warrior monk sects faded from memory, the Watchers managed to survive centuries of persecution. Eventually, members could be found on nearly every continent, including America. Of course, the French monarchy had a long memory, and an even longer reach. As France expanded its holdings in the Caribbean and costal regions of the New World, it was only a matter of time before authorities discovered small numbers of Watchers already entrenched. Such was the case in this very monastery. Though both King Philip and Pope Clement had long since died, the order to disband and surrender was still very much in effect. In the Year of Our Lord 1588, a French company of soldiers led by a Captain De Moiré attempted to arrest twelve monks, each a direct descendant of members of the original Order. The result was the subject of much lingering discussion among local mystics and romanticists. That the monks benefited from some sort of angelic intervention seemed to be the only point of consensus.

Nathan and Kiel had made a home of the old building, in part because they loved the surreal beauty and quiet solitude of the Mississippi River Delta. It was also their way of honoring the monks who died rather than surrender to a corrupt king and Church.

Kiel found Nathan sitting at the table, sharpening the onyx blade of his Kiv on a fine-grained whetstone. Known as *Kinslayer* in the elder tongue, the Kiv was a terrible weapon in the hands of any angelic warrior. In the hands of one such as Nathaniel, the Kinslayer could wipe stars from the sky. Kiel had prayed that Nathan might find some cause to embrace, some passion that would restore his spirit. Apparently, Nathan had decided upon a cause. *I, above all, should have known to take care in what I pray for.*

Kiel placed his leather pouch of herbs on the table and walked to the hearth where aluminum kettle hung above glowing embers. Though needing neither food nor drink as sustenance, both Kiel and Nathan had developed a fondness for coffee. Nathan fetched two mugs and filled one for Nathan, then one for himself. Nathan accepted the mug with a nod but said nothing. His eyes were red, the color of misery, and both cheeks glistened with tears. Stroke after long stroke, he pulled the stone against the razor-edge of the Kiv.

"You should've visited the den with me this afternoon," said Kiel. "The old fox is teaching the young to hunt now."

Kiel knew the folly of his comment as soon as the words left his mouth.

Nathan set aside the stone and tested the edge of the Kiv with his thumb. Without looking up, he said, "Hunting is a useful skill, Kiel. Perhaps the most useful of all."

He seeks vengeance with no thought of consequences. "Nathan, you can't do this. I'll beg if I must, but you can't go looking for the Brethren. Not now."

Nathan sheathed the Kiv and looked across the table at Kiel. His skin glowed with a soft purple hue as the intricate sigils that covered his body came to life. "And when would be the right time to hunt them? Tomorrow? Next week? Or perhaps next millennium? Maybe you'd prefer that we sit here in this stinking tomb until they come for us? It wouldn't be the first time predators came sniffing at this door, would it?"

Kiel met his brother's glower with a steady gaze. "I don't know the when, or even the how, Nathan. But I *do* know we don't have the numbers to mount an offensive. Not now. Patience, brother. The Father will give us guidance. He—"

"Hold!" shouted Nathan as he slammed a fist down upon the table. Kiel heard the *pop* of splintered wood above the impact.

"Guidance? What guidance? When was the last time He spoke to you? Or any of us? When, Kiel!?" Nathan stood up and leaned across the table, the massive muscles in his neck and shoulders bulging like steel cables. "Half the Host destroyed, the other half scattered to the four corners of the earth. Tell me what terrible sin we've committed that He abandons us at the hour of our greatest need! And don't tell me that He's busy dealing with the Usurper. The Father could lift this burden from us with a thought! Listen well, little brother, I tell you He has left us to our own!"

Kiel ground his teeth and the fierce light within his eyes flared like sunspots. Nathan's words bordered on blasphemy, an unpardonable offense for those in service to the Creator.

"You forget your station, Nathan! Grief has hardened your heart. Careful that it doesn't become a permanent condition."

Nathan's voice dropped an octave, but the anger was still very much in evidence. "My station. And just what is my station, Kiel? What exactly *is* our purpose? Weren't we placed here to protect humanity, and ultimately, fulfill His will? If that's so, we've failed miserably. Without assistance, the combined numbers of Legion and the Brethren will grind us to dust. Of course, if it's His will that we sacrifice ourselves in a hopeless war, we stand poised for success!"

"Enough, Nathan! You can allow despair and misplaced resentment to destroy your faith if you like, but I won't be witness or party to such blasphemy!"

The indigo sigils covering Nathan's naked torso flared in the dim light of the room. For several long seconds the two angelic entities glared at each other across the fractured table. After a moment, Kiel's anger subsided to a point just below boiling. He started an apology when Nathan abruptly cut him off with a raised hand.

Rising slowly from the table, Nathan's eyes remained trained on the front door as he pulled the Kiv from its sheath. Alarmed, Kiel cast a questioning glance in Nathan's direction, and started up from his chair. His supernatural senses screamed out an alarm, and Kiel knew. *A solitary Brethren, just beyond the clearing*.

"I detect only the one, Nathan. You?"

Nathan nodded. "Just the one. It makes no sense. Not even the Runner would risk a confrontation with both of us. Not on consecrated ground. A trap?"

Before Kiel could respond, a vaguely familiar voice filled his mind.

I'm alone. Will you grant me temporary sanctuary?

Knowing Nathan had also heard the request, Kiel looked at him. Nathan vehemently shook his head from side to side and mouthed the word *trap*. Again the voice entered Kiel's mind, uninvited.

You've checked the area by now, and you know there's no one in hiding. You also know I'm no match for either, much less both, of you. Grant me sanctuary and some of your time, and I'll state my business and leave in peace.

Still suspicious, Nathan called out, "I think you should leave while you still can, Orus. You stand too near consecrated ground. Another step and the stench of seared flesh will ruin my supper."

This time, Orus spoke aloud. "Reconsider, Nathan. Please. I . . . I have information that might be of assistance to the Host."

Of all the possible scenarios that Kiel had envisioned, this was the least likely of them all. Among the Brethren, Orus was perhaps the nearest to the Runner in terms of intellect and cunning. A brilliant strategist, Orus had plotted more than one successful raid against the Host. Though Kiel maintained a healthy respect for the fallen angel's mastery of deception and subterfuge, he also knew the Principality had spoken the truth about one thing: As a warrior, Orus was no match for either Kiel or Nathan.

"Lies. Why would he offer aid?" said Nathan.

Kiel answered with a shrug. "I don't know. Regardless of his intentions, he's taken a great risk in coming here. Perhaps we should hear him out."

Nathan sighed, then slumped his massive shoulders in acquiescence. "Do as you will. I can always kill him later. Grant him sanctuary."

As Kiel performed the rite that would allow a fallen angel access to the sanctified grounds of the monastery, he watched Nathan from the corner of his eye. The celestial warrior smiled wolfishly and thumbed the edge of the Kiv.

Sanctuary. Asylum. Two words seldom, if ever, used in the same breath with *Fallen* or the *Brethren*, titles referring to the same accursed traitors. A little more than one-third of the Heavenly Host, they had been cast down for aiding Lucifer's failed attempt at the ultimate blasphemy, the usurpation of God's throne. Kiel fully expected that number to swell in the very near future as a new usurper had arisen to challenge the Creator for the throne.

As Orus approached the building, Kiel tried to recall another instance in which the Host had granted one of the Brethren permission to tread upon consecrated ground. *The mechanism has always existed*, thought Kiel, *so surely it's been done. Surely*. However, he couldn't recall a single prior instance. *And so history is made*.

Orus, like most of his kind, wore a body that typified physical perfection. He was taller than Kiel by some few inches and more heavily muscled. Yet, both he and Kiel both knew that any physical confrontation between the two would end only in Orus's unmaking.

Orus stepped tentatively through the doorway and paused. When he didn't immediately burst into flames, his apprehension faded a notch and he gave Kiel a slight smile and brief nod of his shaved head. Kiel returned the nod, then led his sworn enemy through the common area of the small keep and into the kitchen. Orus was still smiling when he saw Nathan standing near the table, thumbing the edge of the Kiv. The smile evaporated and Orus took a quick step back. All color drained from his face.

"You guaranteed my safety!" The words were both a plea and an accusation. Nathan chuckled, but the sound was more akin to steel grinding against steel. His eyes, normally the color of quicksilver, were now pools of obsidian, and as cold as the depths of the Great Abyss.

"You would do well not to plant thoughts of treachery in my head, Orus."

Kiel cast a disapproving glance in Nathan's direction, then stepped forward and pressed a mug of dandelion wine into Orus's trembling hands.

"You have our surety for as long as it takes to state your business." Kiel nodded toward a chair on the other side of the table. "Sit."

"Thanks, Kiel. I'm satisfied by your assertions."

As Orus made his way around the table, Kiel nearly laughed aloud. *You despicable cur. You might accept my guarantee of safety, but you certainly keep one eye on Nathan. And maybe that's a prudent attitude.*

Now seated, Orus looked at his surroundings. "I've always been curious about this place. Such stories about the former inhabitants . . . Although, I admit I can't understand why you choose to dwell in such a . . . an isolated location."

"I think 'primitive' is the word you're searching for," said Kiel. "However it's really none of your concern. Besides, I don't think you would understand."

Nathan spoke up, his voice soft but clearly full of venom. "What better home for the Host than ground sanctified by the sacrifices of righteous men? As for why we stay, the land is a haven, free of the taint. Until now."

Emboldened by Kiel's guarantee of safety, Orus smirked. "Your anger does justice to Him. Like Father, like puppet, eh?"

Nathan pushed away from the table and stood. Rising to his full height of nearly seven feet, he towered over Orus. "Sanctuary or no, you will *not* make any reference to Him unless it is from your knees. Unless, of course, you are tired of living. Do you understand me?"

Orus gave Nathan a weak nod, then averted his eyes. Again Kiel suppressed a laugh. As a Domination, he was of a higher angelic Choir than either Nathan or Orus, but it was Nathan that Orus clearly feared. And rightly so. Nathan was an ultimate machine of war, and the Kiv was a nightmarish weapon in the hands of one such as him.

But enough of this. "You said you have information."

"Yeah. And I'm sure you're wondering why I would share it with you when it means I'll be an outcast among outcasts."

Kiel smiled. "The question did cross my mind. After all, such a thing has no precedence. Not once since the Fall has a Brethren approached the Host and offered or requested aid. Why now?"

Orus took a sip of the wine. "Excellent. Extra dry and crisp. I suppose it's the spring water, eh? A subtle hint of blackberry and smoke. You make this?"

Kiel shook his head, then nodded to Nathan. "His handiwork. Now answer my question."

Orus took a second sip, then set the cup to the side. "I'll warn you in advance, you won't believe me. Not that you should, of course, but you're really going to have trouble with what I'm about to tell you."

Nathan smirked and said, "I *can* believe that much. Now talk before I run out of patience."

"Easy, *muer maistirad mac tire.*"

Nathan's eyes narrowed. From the mouth of a Brethren, the ancient Gaelic title was little more than base profanity.

Orus continued as if unaware of Nathan's growing anger. "Great Master of Wolves. Some of the Brethren still refer to you by that name, did you know? But I digress."

Orus turned in his seat and looked at Kiel. "The truth is that I *am* tired of living. And don't mistake me. I have no desire to die by Nathan's hand, though it's clear enough he'd like nothing better. But before I face the Void, I'd like to settle some old scores. By helping you, I help myself."

"The enemy of my enemy is my friend. Is that it?" said Kiel.

Orus seemed to relax for the first time since entering the monastery. "Something like that. You see, unlike my Brethren, I freely admit that I made a grave mistake. My resentment of man got the best of me. Still, I've managed to carve out a nice niche for myself, given the circumstances. I'm not exactly contented, but for the most part life has been decent. Live and let live, that's not a bad creed for my kind."

"A lie," said Nathan. "Another and I'll remove your head from your body."

"Oh, I don't deny that on occasion I've been instrumental in attacks against the Host. But I did only what I needed to in order to survive. The Runner is a severe taskmaster, as you might well imagine. I wasn't ready to ignore his orders and incur his wrath."

"So what's changed?" asked Nathan. "You expect us to believe that after all these millennia you've only now developed a conscience? Or maybe you've finally discovered a backbone within that human form, and you're no longer afraid of your lord. Is that it?"

"My lord? No, he was never that. He was, however, by far the most formidable of our number. I assume you know that he was directly responsible for the pact with the Nine Princes of Sitra Akhra and Legion? It was his idea to flood this world with demonic entities. He sold us on the idea by using the premise that he could break the will of these hairless monkeys and finally subjugate them."

"Of course we knew," said Kiel. "Only the Runner had the power and motive necessary to broker such a deal."

It was true. The world of Sitra Akhra existed on a plane so far removed from God's grace, love and righteousness were unknown concepts. The malevolent creatures that dwelled upon that plane, collectively known as Legion, were ruled by the Nine Princes, horrific demons of incalculable power. Only another supernatural entity of similar power, a being such as the Runner, could hope to bargain with the Nine.

Orus continued, "Ah, but what you don't know is why. His arrangement with the Nine went much further than facilitating an invasion of minor demons. In reality, he gave up on the notion of subjugation of mankind long ago. It was never his intention to simply alter the Veils. He wanted them destroyed, giving the Nine unfettered entrance into this world."

Nathan leaned back in his chair and placed his hands behind his head. Kiel noticed that at some point during the exchange, Nathan had sheathed the Kiv.

"Ridiculous," said Kiel. "He knows that should even one of the Nine cross over into the world of man, the universe and everything in it would unravel. Only Heaven itself would survive. It would be suicide and the Runner loves himself far too much.

Nathan paused and looked out through an open window for a moment. When he turned back to Orus, his ebony eyes were glassy and his tone was subdued. "It breaks my heart to admit this, especially to you, but I'm not so sure any of us can survive Legion, as it is. Too many have crossed over. While the

Host and Fallen kill one another off, the demons embed themselves in the planet like some lethal parasite."

Kiel flashed a warning glance, but Nathan ignored him and continued on. "The ranks of lesser demons, once numbering a few hundred, have now swelled to the thousands. Hundreds more, powerful lieutenants and Greater Demons, are organizing, gathering small armies of lesser minions and human thralls. As it is, we barely manage stalemate. Had even another hundred crossed over before the Offspring closed the Veil . . . No, the Runner has always been bent on the conquest and rule of humanity. Why should he now decide to turn the planet into a charred ember and take his own life in the process? The notion is insane!"

Orus shrugged. "We asked ourselves that very question. Believe or not as you like, but none of the Brethren, including Theoneal, had any idea of the Runner's real intentions. Not until it was nearly too late. Our conclusions match yours. The Runner *is* insane. Nuttier than a sack full of drunken monkeys, as the old saying goes. In his insanity, he betrayed us all."

The answer was too simple, too convenient. *And that's why it nearly worked*, thought Kiel, as reality dawned. *Orus is telling the truth. How close did we come to losing all? Had it not been for the Offspring . . .* "Where is the Runner, now?"

Orus laughed. "I suspect he's still running. Some of the Brethren are a little put out with him, as you might imagine. Many of his former disciples now pursue him day and night, but no luck yet, I'm afraid. Frankly, I'm not so sure they really want to catch up with him. We all know what he becomes once the blood lust takes him over. I think only a few really hunt him in earnest."

"When they're not hunting us, you mean," countered Nathan.

"You've got me there," admitted Orus. "But keep in mind, we were at war long before the Runner surrendered to madness."

"Fine," said Nathan. "You can't—or won't—tell us where he is. In fact, you haven't told us anything useful to this point. Knowing the Runner is crazy doesn't exactly aid our cause. We were already looking for him, as you well know."

Orus grinned. "So don't be so eager to find him, Nathan. Don't take this personally, but you aren't his match. But I digress.

"Perhaps you'll consider this of some value. The Brethren are divided. Violent conflicts are a daily occurrence, and more than one of my ill-destined kin now dwell in the Void as a result. Some of us understand the consequences. Had the Runner's scheme succeeded, it would have meant the end of us all.

"Of course, some of the Brethren are still persuaded the Runner never intended to destroy Earth, and that he only intended to use Legion in order to subjugate humanity. They still honor the alliance brokered by the Runner with Legion, and work to break mankind's will. This rift that divides the Brethren grows wider with each passing day."

Kiel considered this for a moment, nodding to himself. Maybe this was useful information, after all. He would pass it on to the rest of the Host as soon as this meeting ended.

"This is good news!" said Nathan. "With his own forces divided, the Runner wouldn't chance another attack on the Veils."

"You would think so, wouldn't you? Even though I adamantly oppose the alliance with Legion, I've gone along like the good little conspirator. I've committed terrible atrocities in order to gather this information. Think of me what you will, but remember that I brought the information to you of my own free will. If and when I'm discovered, my life is forfeit, and trust me when I say that I actually look forward to the day."

"So very noble of you," said Nathan in a dry tone. "Get on with it, Orus, and then we'll judge the value, if any, of your sacrifice."

Orus paused for a moment, and Kiel thought the haughty fallen angel was posturing for effect. He almost said as much when Orus continued, "The threat to this world is much greater than you think. The Runner still intends to destroy mankind, and despite the rift among the Brethren, you may believe he may well have the ability to do so."

Orus had his full attention now. "Tell us," said Kiel.

Orus reached for his cup. "Legion has stolen the Lesser Keys of Solomon."

Stunned, Kiel looked at Nathan, then back at Orus. "How? How could this happen?"

The Keys of Solomon, or the *Goetia*, was a text of near mythical proportion, though Kiel knew all too well that the book existed. The biblical King Solomon, son of the legendary David, had used the "keys" or rituals within the book to bind a host of greater demons to his service as a demonstration of the Creator's dominance over Legion. Later, Solomon imprisoned those same demons beneath Mount Moriah. In a very real sense, the Goetia represented the keys to hell on earth.

Orus shrugged. "It would seem Legion has allies in the damnedest places, if you'll excuse the poor pun, gentlemen. I also suspect the Runner played some significant role in the theft of the scroll. Only he would dare to orchestrate such a daring act of heresy on consecrated ground. Seems one of his, a highly placed priest within the Church, used his considerable influence to gain access to the Vatican library, where he managed to secrete away the Lesser Keys. Even now, the scroll is awaiting transfer to Legion. Who knows? Legion may possess the scroll even now, and we all know what this means, don't we?"

Nathan looked from Kiel to Orus, then said, "You can't be serious!"

"Oh, but I am! They intend to use the Keys in order to break the seals that bind the seventy-two greater demons imprisoned by Solomon."

"What could possibly be of any greater importance?" asked Kiel, in a quiet, somber voice.

"I'll give you a hint," said Orus, grinning sardonically. "Where are the Seventy-two imprisoned?"

"The Abyss, beneath the Holy of Holies. But . . ."

Orus sighed. "I'll make this easy for you. Both the Runner and Legion still want to destroy the world. That's a given. Once the Seventy-two are released, the Runner will possess an army to rival any on earth, including that of the Host and Brethren, combined. He'll also have access to the treasures long buried beneath the Temple. Terrible weapons of incalculable strength. And a Veil. Do you begin to see the picture?

"Again I remind you, no demon or Brethren could have entered the vault in which the Keys were kept. That leaves only a couple of possibilities, but at this point, it doesn't really matter, does it? It's done, and that's that."

Orus refilled his wine cup, while Nathan and Kiel sat in silence. When Nathan finally found his voice, he whispered, *"La fine dei giorni." The End of Days.*

chapter 11

Phoenix, Arizona

The coffee tasted burnt. *How the hell do you burn coffee?* It was a rhetorical question. As a long-time Watcher field operative, Elliott had endured his share of long stakeouts and bad coffee. From the corner of his eye, he watched his partner as she sipped a diet soft drink through a straw.

"How can you drink that crap? Don't you know diet sodas cause cancer in laboratory animals?" Elliott rolled down the window of the van and dropped the foam cup onto the street. His partner gave him a disapproving look. "It's against the law to litter."

A ready smile revealed a mouthful of expensive, flawless crown work. "Lighten up, sweetheart. Street sweepers make good money. You want me to deprive them of a living?"

"Heaven forbid," she replied. "Why don't you torch the car parked in front of us while you're at it? After all, fire fighters need to eat too. Then maybe you could shoot—"

"Okay, okay. I get it." He cracked open the driver's-side door, leaned out, retrieved the cup, then tossed it into the back seat.

"Better?"

"Much. You get a merit badge for . . ." The sentence trailed away as Ronni's attention was diverted to the front of the hotel. "Check the man standing in front of the revolving doors. He's wearing khakis and a blue polo shirt. Is it Falco?" As she spoke, she scooted down in the bucket seat by a couple of inches and reached behind her back to caress the grips of the compact .45-caliber Glock.

Elliott turned and looked toward the hotel entrance. The windows of the van were tinted to a shade just above illegal, and he knew he could observe the man with impunity. Unless of course, it really was Falco. In that case, it was even money that the former marine-turned-priest-turned-assassin had already made the van and its occupants. Elliott immediately picked out the man Ronni had spotted. He was the right age. Dark hair and fair complexion were both matches. Elliott thought the man *could* have been Falco—provided he grew another five inches in height and put on an extra thirty pounds of muscle.

"Relax. It's not him." Although Elliott didn't care for his new charge, he didn't chide her for mistaking the man for the near-legendary Sword. Only three members of Malcolm Reading's personal eight-member team had ever crossed paths with the organization's most effective assassin, and Ronni wasn't one of them. She depended on verbal descriptions, which were generally as useless as teats on a bull, and a standard eight-by-eleven black-and-white mug shot for identification.

Elliott, on the other hand, knew Falco very well. While he would never admit it to Ronni, he secretly hoped very much that Thomas Falco would make the fatal mistake of stepping outside the hotel.

After the botched Conner assassination, Malcolm's team had been flown in and given the unenviable task of holding Thomas Falco and the boy in place until a superior, namely Enrique DeLorenzo, arrived on scene. Neither Conner nor Falco were allowed to leave the hotel without prior permission and at least a pair of armed escorts. If at any time Falco or Conner took it upon themselves to disobey instructions, they would be terminated with extreme prejudice. Falco received those instructions just last night, though Elliott wasn't sure how much the priest understood. Falco had sounded confused and disoriented at times during the conversation. Not that it really mattered to Elliott. He wanted an excuse to kill the man.

Elliott had often wondered about the many rumors regarding

Falco's exploits. He suspected many of the alleged deeds were nothing more than pathetic attempts at legend-building, exaggerating one's achievements in order to rise in rank and stature. In his opinion, there was no other answer. No operative could be half as good as Thomas Falco was reputed to be . . . with the notable exception of Elliott, himself.

He had taken out his fair share of targets over the past couple of years, though not a quarter as many as Falco, if you believed all the bullshit hype. Someday he would call Falco out and confront him about the ridiculous war stories and embellished exploits. How the hell did someone go from Force Recon to the pulpit, anyway?

Elliott also knew he would jeopardize his career if he didn't handle Falco in just the right manner. People loved their legends, even those who were more talk than action, and Falco had powerful friends within the organization. Of course, Elliott wasn't worried. He knew things would work out in due time. Elliott had an ace. No, she was more than that. She was power made manifest, and Elliott's personal benefactor.

Falco would make a mistake, and when he did, Elliott would show them all who was truly the better man. He would kill the legendary Falco graveyard fucking dead. At least Malcolm Reading recognized real talent when he saw it. Hadn't he personally recruited Elliott into his private inner circle? The status carried certain perks, but at times, it also meant he would have his share of distasteful duties. Like now, when Malcolm had him playing nursemaid to a new, untested Sword, and a goddamned wet-behind-the-ears kid, at that. For some unfathomable reason, Malcolm had taken an acute interest in the girl.

Glancing at Ronni from the corner of his eye, he noticed she was busy making additional entries into the surveillance log. While she was distracted, Elliott gave his new partner a bold appraisal. *What the fuck is the world coming to, allowing chicks into the Order as Swords? Israeli commando, my ass. Not with tits like that. Yeah, that's got to be it. She must be greasing the old man's pole. Maybe she brings him warm milk at night. Wouldn't that be a goddamned sight? Old Hugues de Payens is probably turning over in his fucking grave.*

Elliott checked his watch and sighed. He muttered, "Another four hours of this bullshit."

"It's not so bad, you know," said Ronni. "After all, you've got me for company."

Groaning, Elliott sunk down in the seat. "Oh, God. I wish someone would just shoot me and end the misery."

"Easy there," said Ronni. "You know, my grandmother always said we should be careful what we wish for. You never know when you just might get it."

"Yeah? Well, I wish your grandmother would just go fuck herself. When does *that* wish come true?"

Reading studied the fax transmittal for several minutes, reading and rereading each paragraph. The instructions were explicit. And extremely disturbing. Malcolm had very personal reasons for waging war on the Offspring, and under most circumstances, he would have welcomed additional resources. Though "bold" and "daring" were the adjectives most often used by peers to describe Reading's exploits, Malcolm operated by using data to carefully analyze events and take calculated risks. He believed in moving with deliberate caution. The Lord Protector's orders violated every rule of covert operations. *Why the urgency? What's happened? How much does the old fool suspect?*

A knock came at the door that separated the two suites.

"Come in, Brian."

Malcolm watched as the youngish-looking Brian King stepped into the room and locked the door behind him. King, a former Australian paratrooper, had served admirably as Malcolm's unofficial number two in recent months. While perhaps not as physically adept as an Elliott Glenn or a Thomas Falco, Malcolm considered King a great deal more reliable. Falco's current situation seemed to bear that out.

"Sir, you called for me?"

"Yes, yes. Come in, Brian, and shut the door." Malcolm nodded toward the sofa. "Sit down, please. I've received new orders that require immediate attention."

After King was situated, Malcolm handed him a manila

folder. "Two items of business, and you may assume that both are critical. First, Enrique DeLorenzo is en route to Phoenix. He's going to meet with Falco and the Conner boy. I want additional personnel posted around the hotel in case the meeting goes badly. Once inside Falco's room, Enrique will contact us on the hour. If he fails to check in, we are to assume the worst and terminate Falco and the boy. We all know of Thomas's skills, and we've heard several firsthand accounts of Conner's . . . unique talents. If either Falco or Conner emerges from that hotel without Enrique first clearing it by phone, he dies standing up. No exceptions to the rule. Make sure all operators are informed. Understood?"

King's face was expressionless as he nodded. "Understood, sir."

"Fine. Next, I want you to select three operators and leave for Sun City immediately. Use members of the support element for the additional manpower. That folder contains maps of the route, maps of the city, and satellite imagery of the residence. Allow an hour for the drive. Unless you encounter unforeseen trouble, you should arrive thirty minutes after sunset. Half moon tonight, so dress accordingly. You are to enter the house and take two females, Amanda and Katherine Conner, into custody. Physical descriptions and recent photos are also in the folder. If they give you trouble, inform them that we have Sam Conner, and any resistance will endanger his well-being. If they still refuse to cooperate, sedate them. Otherwise, take care that neither is harmed, or at least not overly much. Take special care with the child, Katherine. We don't know that she's exhibited any of her brother's special talents, but she *is* a full sister. That alone gives us cause for concern."

"And after we have them?"

Malcolm paused to fill and light his pipe, then said, "You'll find instructions in the packet. However the short answer is that you'll escort them to an old private airfield once owned by the Asarco Corporation, to the southeast of Casa Grande. It's been closed for years but it can still handle light twin-engine planes like our Piper Chieftain. Primary and secondary routes are clearly marked on your map. Avoid using the secondary route unless you encounter some dire emergency. It'll take you a good thirty miles out of the way and cost precious time.

"A Shield will meet you at the field and fly our guests to the New Orleans safe house. Two of your operators are to accompany them, and wait in New Orleans for further instructions. The remaining two will return here for additional orders. If you encounter any problems, call me at once using the encrypted channel. Have you any questions?"

"A couple, sir. First, what's my window for this mission?"

Malcolm drew on the pipe, then sent a blue-black cloud of smoke spiraling toward the ceiling. "You are to depart Phoenix no later than five P.M. You should conclude your business in Sun City and meet the plane in Casa Grande at nine P.M. Not a second later."

King checked his watch. "And if there are additional actors at the residence?"

Although it wasn't a common occurrence, the Watchers weren't new to the business of abduction, and every operative understood the protocol regarding potential witnesses. Brian King was a seasoned operator and knew the rules of engagement by rote. Still, he was no cold-blooded killer. He needed to hear the orders from a superior.

"This mission has Strike priority. Elliott is currently on post at Falco's hotel. Have him relieved from surveillance duty, and take him and Ronni Weiss with you. Once you reach the scene, he'll assume control of tactical operations." Reading studied the man's expression and saw that he understood. Perhaps Brian King was no cold-blooded killer, but Elliott Glenn was.

After King left the room, Malcolm packed his pipe and struck a match on the windowsill. He touched flame to tobacco, drew hard on the pipe stem, and blew a smoke ring out through the open window. The Runner wanted the Conner boy dead, and it looked as if Malcolm would have a perfect opportunity to fulfill his master's wishes. Malcolm didn't understand the arrangement the Runner had brokered with Legion, and it was just as well. The turncoat Watcher had given over his heart and soul to the Runner, in return for a chance to punish the Creator and his sheep. Whatever sinister designs Malcolm's new master held for the world was fine by him. More than fine, in fact.

Yes, it was going to be a good day. A very good day!

Falco reached for the doorknob, hesitated, then pressed his ear to the door. He could hear Sam rummaging around in the kitchen, slamming cabinet doors in frustration. *He's probably more pissed than hungry. Can't say I blame him.* Falco made it back onto the bed just as the recurring headache reasserted itself. A blinding pain generated at the base of his skull and arced through both temples before finally settling behind his right eye. He seized his head between both hands and curled into a fetal position, and with his remaining strength, willed the nausea away.

When the pain finally subsided, Falco realized he was drenched in perspiration. Every muscle in his upper body ached with fatigue, as if he had just finished a marathon. He wondered if he had lost consciousness. It was an unsettling thought, especially with Enrique DeLorenzo on the way, and Little Stevie unaccounted for.

Falco struggled to a standing position and made his way to the bathroom. As he washed his face, he could hear Sam through the walls, slamming kitchen cabinet doors and muttering loudly. *Yep, the kid's pissed.* Falco also knew the worst was yet to come. He had told the boy of Enrique's impending visit, but not the why. *When he finds out, this suite's going to be very crowded.*

Falco toweled off his face and made it back to the bed without another attack. As his head continued to clear, he considered the upcoming meeting. Enrique was playing mind games by saying he only wanted to meet and assess the Conner kid in person before deciding the boy's fate. It was a half-truth at best. Enrique wasn't an operations supervisor. In fact, he had never served a single day as a strategist or tactical operator. While it might be true that Enrique wanted to meet the boy, Falco knew it hadn't been his idea to fly into Phoenix.

Aside from the obvious—a face-to-face meeting with

Sam—there was another reason for Enrique's visit. Falco had been given explicit orders to terminate Sam, and those orders did not allow him to exercise personal discretion. When Falco reported that Sam was still alive, it had sent a major ripple through the ranks. The Hierarchy was forced to ask if the boy had really saved Falco's life, or if perhaps Falco was now in thrall to the undeniably powerful Offspring.

The Hierarchy needed a trusted Shield to make the final determination. Falco also knew a full complement of experienced killers were now within striking distance of the hotel. If Enrique decided Falco was enthralled, neither he nor Sam would live through the evening. On the other hand, if Enrique gave him the benefit of the doubt and the interview with Sam went well, Falco would live and the boy would be conscripted into service to the organization. Either way, from the moment Sam Conner arrived on the roof of the university maintenance building, his life would never, ever be the same. *Wait a minute. I never asked him* why *he was on that roof. I . . . I remember asking him why he helped me, but not how he knew I was up there. How did he know?*

A quick rap on the door interrupted Falco's thoughts. "Come in."

Sam opened the door and stepped into the bedroom. The boy's eyes were red and swollen. "I need some air. I'm going outside."

Falco shook his head gingerly. "That's not a very good idea, kid."

"Save it, dude," said Sam. "If I intended to cut out on you, I'd already be in Sun City. Or, the way you were snoring, halfway to Mexico City. Now, I'm gonna buy some cigarettes, then take a walk up to the parking deck. If your chickenshit snipers wanna pop a cap in me, now's the time, big shot. But I'm not spending another goddamned second in this suite."

"Kid, if I thought you were going to run, I'd kill you myself. Count on it. The only way you can prove you're not one of the bad guys is to sit tight."

Sam's eyes widened in surprise. "After I . . . you . . . forget it! I'll be back in a little while!" Without waiting for an answer, he did an about-face and left the bedroom, slamming the door behind him.

Jesus! Falco grabbed his cell phone from the bedside table and entered the contact number for the surveillance team. A few seconds later, an unfamiliar voice answered.

"Hello, Mr. Falco."

A woman? Female operators weren't unheard of, but they were extremely rare. Falco checked the digital display to make sure he had dialed correctly. He had.

"Hello?"

"Yeah, I'm here. Listen, the Conner kid is headed to the parking deck to walk off a case of nerves. Tell the shooters to back off the cross-hairs and give him some space."

There was a slight hesitation on the other end, then, "You know he's not allowed out of your suite. The consequences have been explained to him?"

"Oh, I told him, all right. Now I'm telling you. Leave the fucking kid alone. We both know someone is flying in to interview the boy, and that someone won't like it if he finds a cold corpse instead of a living, breathing skinny-ass kid. Besides, if Sam Conner really wanted to escape, I'm not sure your entire team could stop him."

"But . . . but—"

"Look, he should be coming out onto the deck in another couple of minutes. So if I were you, I'd stop with the dumb fucking questions and get the word out to the rest of your team. Unless, of course, you want to explain the bullet holes to some highly placed Shield."

Falco grinned when he heard an abrupt *click. Not so much as a "goodbye" or a "kiss my ass." Well, whoever she is, she isn't stupid.*

The elevator was filled with tourist types, people dressed for the spa or the golf course. Sam made his way through the throng to the rear, ignoring hesitant nods and forced smiles. Perhaps it was something in his eyes or the expression on his face. Or maybe it was his grimy jeans or torn Godsmack 2003

T-shirt. Whatever the reason, the crowd gave Sam plenty of room on his way down to the lobby. It was a sharp contrast to the way people usually reacted to him. Not that he cared. He was in no mood for small talk with strangers.

Once in the lobby, Sam fished in his pockets for cash. He had spent most of his money buying supplies for the suite, and it didn't take long to calculate his meager net worth.

Stuffing the small wad of bills back into his pocket, he pulled a debit card from his wallet. When he finally located the ATM, he hesitated. He knew his bank account was precariously low and would remain that way until new grant money was awarded in January. He could always transfer some money over from savings, but . . . *Ah, screw it. With demons and assassins hunting for me, it's not likely I'll be around for the spring semester anyway.*

Sam withdrew the balance of his account in fifty-dollar increments and shoved the money into his wallet. With cash already on hand, that brought his total to $784.72. Not a fortune, but hell, he'd traversed middle America on far less. When it came time for him to make his break, he'd head straight for his mom and Kat. Once they were together, Sam was sure he could get them all safely to Mark and Janet.

And I'll do it with or without Joriel's help. There. It was out. All the other factors surrounding Sam's current predicament combined didn't bother him as much as the sudden reappearance and equally sudden disappearance of Joriel.

From Sam's earliest memories a presence had been with him, providing constant companionship, protection, and mentoring. For much of his life Sam had simply called the ghost in his head *the Voice*. Then, two years ago, as Sam hid inside an abandoned factory in Knoxville, Tennessee, the Voice finally provided a name: Joriel.

It was then that Sam first learned about the existence of guardian angels, and his own remarkable heritage. Not that it really mattered to Sam. Joriel could have been a figment of his imagination, an alien from Mars, or a talking hamster. He didn't care. The Voice had been a part of his life since birth and was largely responsible for shaping him into the kind of person he was—and the kind of person he would become. He and Joriel were inseparable, or so he thought. That same night in Knoxville, Joriel disappeared. She resurfaced briefly a couple of days later while Sam and Michael fought to close the Veil, but disappeared again after only a few seconds. No "good-bye" or "I'll be back soon." Just . . . gone. More than two years without a word.

The crushing sense of loss was, at times, more than Sam believed he could bear. Then, just over twenty-four hours ago, while standing in a driving rain and facing a psychotic human mountain, Sam heard the familiar, sweet ring of wind chimes. Joriel! He nearly fell to his knees and gave thanks for the answer to his countless prayers. And now, when he perhaps needed her more than at any other time in his life, she was gone, again.

That's cool. I don't need her! I'll get Mom and Kat to Mark's place if I have to carry them on my friggin' back! From Mark's place we can . . . can . . . well, we'll worry about that when the time comes.

For the next several minutes, Sam wandered aimlessly about the massive lobby. In the center of the floor, a lush jungle of palms, ferns, and exotic flowering plants surrounded a sculpted waterfall. In the pool beneath the fall, koi and ornamental carp swam in lazy circles, occasionally breaking the pattern to chase a floating piece of popcorn or corn chip. On the far side of the lobby, he located the courtesy shop.

The clerk behind the counter, a cute Hispanic girl near his own age, gave him a wide, cheerful smile, and the world seemed a couple of shades brighter.

"Hi! What can I do for you?"

Sam leaned on the desk and looked up at the menu display and nearly choked as he read the list of exorbitant prices. *Three dollars for a lousy Mountain Dew, two bucks for a small bag of chips . . . Holy crap! Six bucks for a pack of cigarettes!*

The clerk tapped him lightly on the back of his hand and whispered, "Other customers are waiting. Can I help you find something?"

Sam mumbled an apology and stepped to the side. "Sorry, but no thanks. I think I just gave up smoking. Again."

As he headed for the front of the building, Sam pulled the last bent Marlboro from the crumpled pack and tucked the cigarette behind his ear. When he told the girl he was giving up the habit, he wasn't kidding. Since returning from Tennessee, he'd gradually cut back on smoking, going from more than a pack a day to perhaps a pack per week. He'd been doing well with it, and now seemed like the perfect opportunity to go cold turkey. Pulling a disposable lighter from his pocket, Sam muttered, "Time to play 'Taps' and bury the last soldier."

Outside, afternoon shadows crept across the face of the building. One of the doormen waved a polite greeting and Sam realized he recognized the man. He had been on duty the night Sam and Falco staggered out of the Honda, both drenched to the bone and looking more dead than alive. The man had given the pair a peculiar look but asked no questions. Instead, he offered to assist Sam and his "drunk uncle." When Sam declined the offer, the doorman smiled and gave him a wink, then called for a valet to move Sam's car to the parking deck. *Parking deck! I left my laptop in the car!* He took off at a jog for the elevators.

Several minutes later, Sam sat behind the wheel of the Honda and lit his last cigarette. Everything, including the computer, was exactly as he had left it; a disarrayed mess, but all present and accounted for, nonetheless.

The car was parked on the third tier of the deck, which offered a spectacular view of the valley. In the distance, a halo-shrouded sun settled on the horizon just to the west of Squaw Mountain, a towering peak that overlooked south Phoenix. There was something about the mountain that Sam had always loved, a sense of tranquility, and quiet, ancient wisdom. Sam had the same feeling whenever he visited the Superstition Mountains, or the Salt River Canyon. It was possible, he supposed, that his affinity for those special places came from the stories his grandmother, Nanna, used to tell. However, Sam wanted desperately to believe that magic still existed in the world. A benevolent god had made it so, according to Nanna. Now, Sam only needed evidence that one existed.

God, I miss Nanna. She always made me feel . . . normal. Sam looked down at the logo on his T-shirt. No, the elevator passengers hadn't shied away because of his dress, or even the scowl on his pale, freckled face. They moved away because they instinctively knew he wasn't one of them. He was different, out of his element, and alone. It was a remarkable paradox. Sam could attract perfect strangers to come to his aid with a subconscious thought, yet he couldn't make friends except under the most freakish of circumstances. He could count his true friends on one hand and have several digits to spare. Of course, things were decidedly different now, and none of them had changed for the better. In the past people only shunned him because he was different. Now they wanted to kill him.

Sam stepped out of the car and walked over to the retaining wall. He took a drag on the cigarette, blew a smoke ring, and watched it spiral out over the street below. Traffic was heavy along Marriott Drive as the unsuspecting masses went about their business, oblivious to the horrors now loose on earth. Ordinary people living out mundane lives in a world that's anything but ordinary or mundane. And somewhere out there along the street, men waited patiently to put a bullet in his skinny ass. *Are they hunting Mark, too? Paul Young? Michael Collier's baby?*

Sam took another drag on his cigarette. *Maybe I should just cut back instead of quitting cold. If I'm real lucky, cancer will get me before some sniper. . . .*

He didn't finish the thought. A hostile mental blast slammed hard into Sam, and sent him staggering away from the concrete wall. A sudden rush of vertigo sent the world tilting on its axis, and Sam reached out blindly for the hood of his car. For several seconds, it was all he could do to stay on his feet. It had been a long time since he'd felt a probe this strong, and he knew this wasn't a case of some malevolent entity simply passing through the area. This was no random search.

As the disorienting fog receded from his mind, Sam opened

his mental radar and checked the virtual screen. Nothing. *Impossible! It's got to be there. Anything that hits that hard has to leave a signature.* Sam widened the search grid, pushing out some five miles. Still nothing. *This just isn't possible. Is the son of a bitch hiding? Maybe it's found a way around my radar!* Just the thought of such a possibility sent a hard shiver through his body. It had long been his greatest fear, that somehow the Enemy would find a way past Sam's early-warning system.

Unwilling to accept that dismal prospect, Sam took a couple of deep breaths and focused his will. Probing and *reaching* were two very different actions. The former was subtle, an extension of his mental radar, and carried minimal risks of detection. *Reaching*, however, provided a much greater chance for catastrophe. A probe was little different from ringing someone's telephone, long distance. A *reach* carried over extremely long distances, but it also left a distinctive path back to the sender. Something like an ethereal neon vapor trail, it was highly visible to the Enemy and marked the sender with a kind of psychic irradiation. The Enemy would have little trouble identifying Sam as that sender, and even less trouble following the trail back to its source. This particular Enemy was very powerful and had already pinpointed Sam's general position. Thanks to the gunmen watching the hotel, running wasn't an option. Therefore, Sam needed additional information on this latest threat if he wanted to survive. A probe was the safest option.

He sat down inside the Honda and locked the doors. Next, he reclined the seat and made himself as comfortable as possible under the circumstances. His heart still racing, Sam tried to relax, willing his pulse to slow. Thoughts of his mom and Kat only heightened his anxiety. He took another route, turning all of his attention to Charlie Hastings. His mind's eye captured every delicate feature of her face, the scent of her hair and skin, the warmth in her eyes and in her heart. Charlie. The love of his life.

After a couple of minutes, Sam was ready. Closing his eyes, he pulled up the psychic signature of the Enemy: a miasma of

nauseating waves, ripples, and distortions in the fabric of time
and space. Next, he drew upon his memories of that terrible
odor, of rotten eggs, wormy meat, and stale cat piss. After a
moment, the odor took form and he added that to the signature.
A "picture" took form in his mind, a living portrait of filth, disease, decay, and death . . . every vulgarity known to man, and
many that weren't, were firmly entrenched in his mind. Sam
pushed the probe to the south in a tight cone.

Moving tentatively over the broad landscape, Sam's tendrils of focused mental energy briefly touched, then bypassed
dozens of psychic imprints, some far stronger than others, yet
nearly all of them human. He paused as his probe touched one
particular signature that felt disturbingly familiar. Sam had
found Little Stevie.

A little shaken by finding the murderous man-mountain in
the company of demons, Sam paused to collect his composure.
Little Stevie wasn't human, nor was he a demon. Yet, there was
a sense of familiarity. Something about Little Stevie reminded
Sam of another monster, a crazed long-dead killer named Pe-
tey Scanlon. There was a connection between the two men,
Sam was sure of it, but what that connection was eluded him.

When Sam resumed his search a few minutes later, he detected the demons he had first sensed from back in the suite.
The small gathering hadn't moved from the spot where he had
found them earlier, and their numbers hadn't changed. Sam
ignored them and pushed on. After several minutes with still
no signature he could match to the Enemy's probe, Sam grew
worried. Maybe, he thought, they *had* found a way to block
him. If that's so, the demons could come at him from any direction, at any time. He would be defenseless.

*No. I'm just not looking hard enough, that's all. Got to keep
looking.* Sam took another deep breath, then slowly exhaled.
The image of the Enemy signature was still firmly entrenched
in his mind, and he pressed forward, first narrowing the scope
of the search by several degrees, so that the probe no longer resembled an ethereal cone, but rather a wide, psychic fan. If he
was going to locate the source, it would have to be soon. Past
searches had come easily, and without a great deal of conscious

effort. He was now searching well beyond any distance he had ever attempted. Perspiration beaded along his forehead and trickled into his eyes. Breathing was difficult, as if a heavy weight rested upon his chest, crushing the air from his chest. And for a brief moment, he had it! An incredibly powerful signature of the Enemy radiating from a point some forty miles to the south.

So many . . . so damned many of them!

The tremendous effort required to maintain such a contact drained the rest of his already shaky physical and mental reserves. Finally, frustrated and afraid, Sam released contact, shut down his radar, and leaned back in the car seat. It was a sickening thought, but he had to face the obvious. Either it was a single entity and the most powerful he had ever contacted, or there was a gathering of creatures, similar to that back in Abbotsville. Regardless of the scenario, it spelled extremely bad news for someone.

Sam opened the car door. For the moment, there was little to do except wait for Falco and his superiors to make the next move. It was time to go back to the apartment and deal with Falco. Sam reached into the back seat for his laptop, but his hand stopped short of the black nylon carry case. A thick manila envelope lay atop the case and large block letters in red ink left no doubt as to the intended recipient. FOR LUCKY SAM.

Stunned, Sam stared at the envelope, afraid to pick it up. He had thoroughly searched the car upon reaching the parking deck. There was no way he could have missed this. No way . . .

FOR LUCKY SAM.

Only two people had ever called him that, and one of them had been dead for nearly a decade. Sam picked up the envelope, and hefted it in his hand. *Thick but not too heavy. About the size of a . . . No. No way.* He tore open one end and dumped the contents into his lap. It was a dog-eared Rand McNally Road Atlas. The same one he had used during his trip to Tennessee.

chapter 12

Phoenix, Arizona

Sam tossed the atlas onto the coffee table and took a seat on the sofa. For several minutes he stared at the thick, tattered book of state maps. There was no doubt in his mind it was the same road atlas. He knew every smudge, tear, and stain. Two years earlier, he had traveled nearly thirty-eight hundred miles with that atlas stuffed into his duffel bag. The last time he had seen it, it had been tucked away in a dresser drawer in his bedroom back in Sun City. He had considered more than once tossing it out with the garbage, but each time he tried, something had stopped him. Back then, he attributed his hesitancy to some kind of warped nostalgia. Now, he wasn't so certain.

This is crazy, just plain friggin' crazy. Someone goes to my house in Sun City, steals the atlas, brings it to Phoenix, and plants it in my car while I'm standing less than ten feet away. As ridiculous as the scenario sounded, Sam had learned long ago to avoid the word *impossible*. He had seen too much, experienced too much, to ever again believe anything was truly beyond the realm of possibility. He also knew there really was an explanation, and it began with the hand-lettered words on the face of the envelope: LUCKY SAM. *Horace left it. But why?*

He reached for the book, then stopped. *Man, I really don't want to look at it. I really, really don't.* As soon as the thought entered his mind, he pushed it aside and chided himself. *Pick up the damn book, Conner! Hell, after Abbotsville, everything else is a piece o' cake. Right?* He picked up the atlas and thumbed through the pages. When he reached the back cover, he realized he had been holding his breath, as if half-expecting the boogeyman to jump from the pages and tear out his throat. He flipped through the pages again, looking for a specific map: the state of Tennessee. When he finally located the page, he stared at the red circle someone, probably Horace, had drawn around the tiny hamlet of Abbotsville more than two years earlier. The rest of the page seemed unchanged, and Sam exhaled in relief. He had no reason or desire to visit the Veil again. *So, why bring the book to me now? Wait . . .*

Flipping back to the front, Sam located the map of Arizona. He had missed it on the first pass, but now it leaped off the page and slapped him across the face. Someone had drawn a bright red circle around the city of Casa Grande, a small city just off the interstate that connected Phoenix and Tucson. The word AIRPORT was written in neat, block letters.

Casa Grande has an airport? A nice little town, but nothing special. Of course, Abbotsville had probably been a nice little town at one time.

Casa Grande was a little less than an hour's drive from Phoenix, and from what Sam could recall, it was an unremarkable community. Unlike Abbotsville, it had no history of mass lunacy. In fact, the community's major claim to fame was an ancient ruin left behind by early Native Americans, aptly called Casa Grande, or "large house." It was this adobe settlement that gave the city its name. Other than that, the only other local landmarks were the abandoned open pit copper mines and nearby Florence State Prison, some twenty miles to the east. *Why . . . Oh, shit!*

Casa Grande was nearly due south from southwest Phoenix, the same general direction Sam had probed. It was a stretch, but was this Horace's way of telling Sam the Enemy that had zeroed in on him earlier was in Casa Grande? Was he now supposed to go there and confront the monster much as he had done in Tennessee? He didn't have nearly enough power to pinpoint the Enemy over that distance. Determining the general location was one thing, but in order to get a hard fix on them, he would have to throw caution out the door and *reach*.

He could have an answer within seconds by *reaching*, and

determine not only the precise location but also the number of Enemy. Both Joriel and Horace had repeatedly cautioned Sam against using the power to *reach* unless it was a dire emergency. Maybe this was the type of emergency Joriel meant. *Only one way to find out.* Sam took a deep breath and exhaled slowly. Clearing his mind as best he could under the circumstances, he started to *reach* for his angelic companion, the Voice.

Not long ago, Sam's attempts at *reaching* would have amounted to little more than a mental scream, heard over hundreds of miles by anyone or anything with the "gift." During the past couple of years, his inherited supernatural abilities had increased exponentially, though his control over some of those abilities was still shaky at best. However, *reaching* for Joriel was unlike a general call for help. He supposed it was a result of his lifelong bond with her, or perhaps she had always been near enough that he hadn't needed to "scream" in order for her to hear the *reach*. Regardless, he was growing desperate.

"You look like a young man deep in thought."

Surprised by the unexpected interruption, Sam released his mental focus. When he opened his eyes, he saw Falco standing in the bedroom doorway. Sam thought the man still seemed a little unsteady, but his eyes appeared clear and there was some color in his cheeks for the first time since the battle atop the university maintenance building. Falco gave Sam a short wave as he slowly made his way through the living room and into the kitchen area. Seconds later, Sam heard the man rummaging through drawers and overhead cabinets.

"What are you looking for?" asked Sam.

"Coffee. I don't suppose you came across any while you were . . . never mind. Found it. What time is it, anyway?"

Sam checked his watch. "A little after five."

Falco grunted. "Anytime now," he added in a quiet voice.

"Any time for what? What's that supposed to mean?" asked Sam.

"Just thinking that it's about time for the evening news," replied Falco. "Mind turning on the television? MSNBC or CNN, please."

Sam didn't believe for a moment that Falco's former remark had anything to do with the news, but he did as he was asked. Turning on the set, he surfed through the channels until he found CNN. The current story was about a massive train derailment in Spain. A haggard-looking on-scene reporter soberly explained that a dozen terrorist groups had come forward claiming credit for the disaster as a camera panned to take in the body-strewn wreckage. *I guess demons come in a lot of different shapes and sizes these days,* Sam thought.

The next story caused Sam to sit up on the edge of the sofa. A caption at the bottom of the screen read, "Vatican Murder-Suicide."

"Man, that's something you don't hear every day," said Sam. He started to turn up the sound when a sharp knock came at the front door of the suite. Startled, Sam turned off the set and came to his feet just as Falco entered the living room. Sam backed away from the front door, inching toward the sliding glass doors that led to the balcony and the fire escape.

Damn, I'm jumpy.

"Take it easy, Sam. There's nothing to be afraid of." Falco unlocked the deadbolt and opened the door. "Come in, Enrique."

Sam held his ground near the glass doors as Falco stood aside and allowed the visitor to enter.

So this is Enrique. Shit's about to get interesting.

The man was younger than Sam had expected, and handsome as any movie star. Dressed for the cover of *GQ*, Enrique set down his suitcase and gave Falco an affectionate hug, as if greeting a favorite relative. Falco returned the hug, though a bit reluctantly, thought Sam. Afterward, Falco limped to the kitchen. Enrique turned to Sam.

"And you must be Sam Conner," he said in a silky smooth voice. "I've heard a lot about you. My name is Enrique De-Lorenzo." He picked up his suitcase and walked across the floor, his hand extended. "I'm pleased to finally meet you, Sam. Please accept my sincere gratitude for the aid and care you've rendered Thomas."

Sam managed a wooden nod and shook Enrique's hand. "No worries. He needed help and I just happened to be in the neighborhood."

"Oh, I think we both know there's more to the story than that, Sam. I'm anxious to hear the details. All of them." Enrique took a seat near the end of the sofa, leaving Sam as the last man standing. Feeling awkward, Sam sat down in a nearby armchair directly across from the newcomer. As they waited for Falco to return from the kitchen, Sam studied Enrique from the corner of his eye. *Stylish, but not flashy. Definitely not flashy. Confident, but not cocky. Sophisticated. Yeah, that's a good word. And he's loaded. You don't wear those kinds of suits on a bean counter's salary. This guy carries authority, and a lot of it. So what the hell does he want with me?*

Finally, Falco made his way back to the recliner carrying a steaming mug. "There's fresh coffee in the kitchen. Would you care for some?"

"No thanks, Thomas. Perhaps later."

Falco nodded and sipped from the mug. Grimacing, he said, "Tastes like paint thinner. So, Enrique . . . how was your flight?"

It was a standard question asked of travelers, but Sam thought he detected an edge in Falco's voice, a subtle change in tone. He was sure the seemingly innocuous query carried some hidden significance. Had either man expected trouble during DeLorenzo's trip? Perhaps they had anticipated more Little Stevie–type encounters. The notion sent a slight chill along the nape of Sam's neck.

"The flight was uneventful," said Enrique. "I only wish I could say the same for last night. I'm afraid I have some disturbing news." Turning to Sam, Enrique said, "But that can wait until I've had an opportunity to visit with our new friend, young Mr. Conner."

The two locked eyes and in an instant, and in a flash of clarity, Sam knew. While he wasn't the Enemy, Enrique DeLorenzo could well prove just as deadly. The purpose of his visit wasn't to check on the welfare of Thomas Falco. No, this man was here to determine if Sam Conner would live to see another day.

Sun City, Arizona

The sun had long since disappeared behind the horizon, leaving in its wake a dark crimson sky and the occasional wispy line of clouds. Evenly spaced, ornate street lights flickered with re-newed life, casting a pale amber light over the concrete streets of the subdivision, an upper-middle-class neighborhood filled with new families and retirees alike. This particular street ended in a cul-de-sac featuring a large two-story brick and stucco af-fair. Henri knew the house and its occupants very well.

Pulling a cigarette from a new pack, Henri spoke a Word and the tip of the cigarette smoldered, then ignited. He took a deep drag on the filter, and blew a stream of smoke from his nostrils. *Won't be long now.* He took another drag on the cigarette and looked through the window sheers as a pair of silhouettes moved about in the living room. One of them, Henri knew, was now acutely aware of his presence. He could have shielded himself from her just as he could have shielded himself from her brother two years earlier. But what was the fun in that?

I wonder what she's thinking at this very moment? Is she afraid? It was a rhetorical question. He knew damn well she was afraid. *Maybe she's called her brother. And what would he say to her? Would he come running to the rescue?* Another rhetorical question. He knew Sam would come to his sister's aid if called. He wouldn't be able to stop himself. *That's the kind of person he is: heroic and foolish with only the very best intentions. The graveyards are full of his kind, all dead long before their time. I hope she doesn't call him. His arrival would complicate things. Besides, I really don't want to kill him. Not unless the boy refuses to cooperate.*

Henri cocked an ear toward the east. Smiling, he dropped the cigarette to the ground and smashed it beneath the heel of his silver-toed boots. "About damn time," he said just as a pair of headlights came into view from the main road. He watched as the vehicle turned onto the dead-end street and drove slowly toward the cul-de-sac. The sleek Escalade parked in the driveway of the two-story house and a man and woman, both dressed in business attire, got out and strolled casually to the front door. Seconds later another pair dressed in dark clothing came out of the back seat and quickly disappeared around the side of the house. Sticking close to the privacy fence, they were headed directly for Henri.

Amateurs. I would have expected better. He whispered another Word and a split second later, a wisp of blue-gray smoke drifted across the backyard toward the patio. As the black-clad operators passed through the smoke on the way to the rear entrance of the house, one of them, a tall, slender female, raised her hand, signaling a halt. Her accomplice, a heavily muscled bulldog of a man, moved to her side and whispered, "What? What's wrong?"

The woman paused for a moment and shook her head. "Nothing. I just thought I . . . never mind. Let's go."

The man muttered a string of curses, then said, "We haven't got time for this shit. Move!"

Had the wisp of smoke possessed a mouth and vocal cords, it would have said, "The clock is ticking. Hurry before this entire affair turns into a goddamned train wreck."

The smoke followed lazily as the black-clad pair crossed the short distance from the fence to the patio. Bulldog Man knelt beside the backdoor, holding his pistol in a two-fisted combat shooting grip. He and the female Watcher were now positioned, waiting to deal with anyone who tried to escape the house through the backdoor. Several seconds passed and still no sign of the other two Watchers. *Damn it, be quick,* thought Henri. *You've got company coming!*

The smoke that had been Henri Charpak drifted to the patio and hovered just behind the woman's shoulder. By now, the first pair of Watchers was inside the house, holding the two Conner females at gunpoint. They would allow the mother and her daughter to gather a few belongings, then walk them through the house, out through the backdoor, and into the waiting Escalade. The plan was sloppy, and took far too much time.

If they didn't hurry, other visitors would arrive and derail the kidnap operation as well as Henri's own much grander scheme. He wouldn't allow that.

The four inside the house were coming down the stairs now, and would be at the backdoor within seconds. Henri turned his supernatural senses to the south, and sent out a weak probe. There was no need for a stronger search. The Enemy was less than a mile away and closing fast.

The backdoor opened and the four Watchers herded their female victims into the backyard and toward the SUV. The younger of the two, a teenager with auburn hair, proved obstinate and dug her heels into the damp grass, forcing her gun-toting shepherds to physically propel her forward.

"She's burning precious time," muttered Henri beneath his breath. He closed his eyes and exhaled softly. The young girl turned toward the shadows and Henri's hiding place. She gave the fence line a quick, worried glance, then hurried to the awaiting vehicle. Henri smiled. He knew revealing his presence would speed her along. *Too late. The* other *bad guys will pick up her trail.* He laughed at his weak joke. *Oh well. I've nothing better to do than run interference for a fourteen-year-old.*

Seconds later the Escalade pulled out of the drive and sped away toward the interstate. Soon after, a long white older-model Lincoln driven by Henri followed at a distance.

chapter 13

Rome

Investigator Arturo Giannini zigged in and out of traffic along the narrow thoroughfare, his bleary, bloodshot eyes darting to the rearview mirror and back to the rain-slicked road ahead. There was no sign now of the gray BMW four-door sedan that had tailed him for the better part of ten kilometers, since leaving the Vatican. Arturo was well versed in the art of following vehicles in heavy traffic, and he knew the work of an expert. In fact, had he not been so afraid, he might have admired the other driver's deft and tenacious driving. But he *was* afraid. Very much so.

He hadn't recognized the expensive car, and the windows were heavily tinted. Yet each time the car appeared in his rearview or side mirrors, Arturo's stomach rolled violently. There was something ominous, *dangerous*, about the automobile and its occupants. Of that Arturo was certain. He was also certain the occupants of the BMW were involved in the incident back at the Holy See, and more specifically, with the journal and scroll Arturo had recovered from the apartments of Father Raoul Acuna. He had drafted a report before leaving the Vatican and e-mailed the encrypted file to his contact within the Watchers. Other members of the Gendarmes had interrupted him before he could destroy the original file. That file was now contained within a passworded file on the notebook computer sitting in the passenger seat. The encoded information should be safe enough, he reasoned. The file was unrecoverable by anyone short of Interpol or some other top-shelf intelligence agency. Still, something nagged at him to erase his notes at the earliest opportunity. The appearance of this mysterious pursuer only reinforced the thought. Everything about his current situation spelled extreme danger.

He turned onto a busy avenue, his apartment now just blocks ahead. As he neared an intersection, an old man dressed in a floppy rain hat and heavy overcoat stumbled into the pedestrian crosswalk and shuffled out to the middle of the street. Arturo braked to a stop and waited impatiently for the old timer to make his way across the double lanes. Arturo reached for a pack of chewing gum stashed above the visor when the old man stopped in the center of the lane and slowly turned to face Arturo. With a palsied hand, the old man pushed the brim of the hat away from his face and grinned wickedly.

Arturo's heart skipped a beat, then threatened to explode from his chest. The old man now standing scant inches from the front bumper of Arturo's car was none other than Father Raoul Acuna, his face a bloodless, sallow gray, and the mocking smile forever frozen in place by rigor mortis. Thin, bluish lips moved, trying in vain to form words, but lifeless muscles in the nightmarish face refused to cooperate. Arturo shook his head side to side in an attempt to dislodge the horrid image from his mind, but the dead man remained, leering obscenely.

Arturo squeezed his eyes tightly shut, then stomped on the accelerator. The Fiat's tiny engine buzzed like an angry nest of hornets as it lurched forward. Horns blared as cars entering the intersection swerved to avoid the Fiat, and Arturo braced himself for the impact. Yet, there was none. Not with any of the approaching cars, and not with the ghoulish form of the dead Father Acuna.

As Arturo cleared the intersection, he checked the rearview mirror, but the street was empty except for a tangle of traffic. Stunned, Arturo turned back around in the seat and for the second time in as many minutes, his heart threatened to exit his heaving chest. The distorted face of Father Acuna pressed against the windshield as boney fingers sought purchase on the slick hood of the car. Fat droplets of blood fell from the gaping maw in the man's throat and spattered on the glass. *Jesus!*

The Fiat swerved hard to the right as Arturo jerked on the steering wheel. The small car jumped the curb, traveled a short distance along the narrow sidewalk before striking a utility pole. The impact threw Arturo forward, slamming him hard into the steering wheel. As the car came to rest, he managed to open the door and fall out into the street. His hand snaked inside his jacket and trembling fingers closed around the comforting grips of his handgun. Rising from the street, Arturo made his way around to the front of the car, his gun drawn and held at the ready. Steam hissed through the Fiat's ruptured radiator and obscured his vision, as he moved cautiously forward. A quick glance at the windshield confirmed this hadn't been some hallucination brought on by sleep deprivation. Thin rivulets of blood ran from the center of the cracked glass down to the crumpled hood. As he stepped around to the front of the car, he prayed to the Father, the Son, Mary, and all the saints that he wouldn't find the reanimated corpse of Father Acuna. He didn't. However, pinned between the crushed bumper of the car and the broken utility pole, he did find a floppy rain hat.

Arturo recovered the laptop from the car and broke into a run.

Arturo jogged three flights of stairs leading to the seldom-used apartment. As he approached each landing, his hand strayed to the butt of the handgun hanging from the shoulder holster inside his suit coat. Each time the landing proved deserted and Arturo uttered a quick prayer of thanks.

Upon reaching the last landing, he ran the length of the hallway leading to his apartment. He pulled the keys from his pocket, dropped them onto the carpet, and swore loudly. He picked them up, nearly dropping them again in the process, and finally managed to unlock his apartment door. Once safely inside, he locked the door behind him, locked a second deadbolt, and moved to the living room's double windows. He peered through a narrow seam separating the heavy curtains and looked out over the rain-slick streets below. Traffic was light, and there were no obvious signs of pursuit or of the dead priest.

Holy Mother of God. Arturo pulled the curtains together

and leaned against the wall to catch his breath. An occasional social drinker, he now felt the need for a very large, very stiff drink. A quick inventory of his kitchen cabinets revealed a near-empty pint bottle of Chivas, barely enough liquor to remove the bitter taste of bile from his mouth. He took a bottle of chilled chardonnay from the refrigerator and filled a wineglass to the rim.

Events of the past sixteen hours had sapped his considerable reserves of energy, and nothing had prepared him for the encounter with Acuna. Furthermore, Arturo was afraid this was just the beginning. For years, Arturo had taken tremendous satisfaction in his double identity, serving God and man through both of his chosen vocations, first as a law enforcement officer for the Vatican, and from his more secretive involvement with the Watchers. However, after events of this afternoon he was ready for a career change.

He had managed to smuggle the journal out of Vatican City just minutes before he was called back to the office of the Vatican Corps of Gendarmes. It was now safely in the hands of his Watcher contact, and on the way out of the country. And not a moment too soon.

Understandably, the Vatican was in shock over the murder-suicide and had launched a full-scale investigation. Arturo went through the motions, writing reports that covered his arrival on the scene and his offer to assist Piero with the search of Acuna's apartment. Of course, Arturo avoided any mention of the journal. That information was for the Watchers alone. *And such information!* If the entries were credible, and Arturo now harbored no doubt that they were, the Holy See was already under attack by demonic influences from within. It was an unthinkable, horrific situation, but there it was: Through possession and enthrallment, Legion had contaminated the Church from both without and within.

Arturo carried the bottle and wineglass into the living room and sat down hard upon the sofa. He kicked off his loafers, drained his glass, and refilled it. He closed his eyes and silently recited the prophecy uttered a little more than three decades earlier, in a small church in Akita, Japan, in 1973. The prophecy was well known to all of his brethren within the Watchers, and almost all of the hierarchy of Vatican City.

The work of the devil will infiltrate even into the Church in such a way that one will see cardinals opposing cardinals, bishops against bishops. The priests who venerate me will be scorned and opposed by their confreres . . . churches and altars sacked; the Church will be full of those who accept compromises and the demons will press many priests and consecrated souls . . .

The Watchers had known of this prophecy long before events in Akita. A very similar warning had been found carefully stamped into a thin sheet of copper and left in the belly of Solomon's Temple centuries before. That scroll, together with others also found and secreted away by the original Templars, pointed to this day, the time in which Legion would infiltrate the Church and pave the way toward the most catastrophic event in human history, the End of Days.

Murders inside the Holy See. People stalking me. Dead men riding on the hood of my car . . . Sweet Mother of God!

Reconciling experience with faith was sometimes an impossibility and this was one of those instances. Nothing would convince Arturo that he hadn't seen, with his own eyes, a dead murderer glaring at him from atop the hood of his car. Nor could anything destroy his faith in his Christian belief that dead men do not walk again except by the power and authority of God Almighty. Arturo was also convinced that God had nothing to do with the reanimated corpse of one Father Raoul Acuna. Thus, as a career law enforcement officer and natural investigator with a highly intuitive and analytical mind, Arturo reasoned that there must be a new set of factors at play. Factors that did not adhere to the laws of God. But was that not contradictory to the Christian belief that nothing existed without God? Given the seemingly impossible occurrences and circumstances, Arturo arrived at a single, staggering conclusion: *The End of Days are upon us.*

Arturo finished his wine and made his way into the bedroom. For now, there was little else to do but remain on his guard while he awaited further instructions from his superior within the Watchers. Those instructions would likely come before the evening was out, and no doubt, he would be very busy over the next few days. It was even possible that he would be ordered to abandon his post at the Vatican and travel to Belgium, or perhaps the States, in order to take a more direct role in the upcoming supernatural war. *If I'm lucky.*

Arturo yawned and rubbed his eyes. He must report the incident with Acuna, but it would have to wait. Regardless of what lay ahead, his overtaxed mind needed rest and separation from the unholy events he had witnessed earlier. After today, he might not get another chance to rest for several days. Rising from the sofa, he set the wineglass on the kitchen table. He retrieved his keys, then made his way to the bedroom with the laptop under his arm.

Night was still a couple of hours away, but as a cop who had worked the midnight shift for nearly a decade, Arturo knew the secret to sleeping during daylight hours. The bedroom windows were covered with thick sheets of aluminum foil and heavy drapes. He turned on a lamp. Nothing looked disturbed or out of place. A steel four-drawer filing cabinet occupied one corner of the room. Arturo deposited the laptop in the bottom drawer and locked the cabinet with the inset key, then with a hasp and heavy padlock. As soon as the padlock was in place, he breathed a little easier. It wasn't as if the cabinet couldn't be breeched, but he felt confident that it would require a hell of an effort. *I'll delete all the files after I get some sleep. Please, God, let me sleep!*

Arturo undressed in silence and placed his suit on a hanger inside the closet. As was his custom, he shut the closet door, then closed the bedroom door and locked it. Finally, he laid the semi-automatic handgun in its customary position near the telephone on his bedside table. After all the preparations were complete, he collapsed upon the bed.

For several minutes, he lay in the dark as grotesque visions of a dead Father Acuna drifted through his tired mind. Arturo pushed the images away, and focused on the steady *thrum* of the apartment's central air unit. As his mind and body slowly surrendered to fatigue, he thought, *What becomes of us now? Dear God, what becomes of us now?*

"Arturo. Help meeee, Arturo."

Still groggy, Arturo propped up on an elbow and wiped the sleep from his eyes. The temperature had dropped several degrees and he shivered beneath the light blanket. A glance at the luminous dial of the bedside clock showed the time: 7 P.M. He had slept less than two hours, a deeply disturbed sleep filled with ominous dreams and a disembodied voice pleading for sanctuary. Again and again, the choked, gurgling voice of a drowning man begged for Arturo to save him. *Help meeee, Arturo. Pleasssse, help meeee!* Though it was a call for assistance, the words seemed *wrong*, insincere, perhaps even taunting. *But that's crazy. Makes no sense,* he thought. Then Arturo reminded himself that most dreams made no sense. He stretched to relieve the kinks from the stiff muscles in his shoulders and neck, then lay back on the stack of pillows.

The short rest, filled with an unceasing kaleidoscope of disturbing dream images, had done nothing to refresh his mind or body. *Need more sleep.* He rolled over onto his side and pulled the blankets up to his chin. *Damn. It's colder than a witch's tit in a brass brassiere.*

"Arturo, why won't you help meeee?"

Arturo froze. The horrendous voice that had invaded his dreams now invaded his bedroom.

Careful to remain silent for fear of giving away his precise location, Arturo inched his hand toward the nightstand. Trembling fingers brushed against the handgun, then found the base of the lamp. He clicked the switch and picked up the gun in a single, fluid motion. Shielding his eyes against the brilliant one-hundred-watt bulb with his free hand, he swung the gun around to cover the rest of the bedroom. Nothing. He was alone.

The voice had come from less than a dozen feet away. *I'm awake, so I know it's not a dream. Am I hallucinating or is this more of the same from this afternoon?* Silently, he prayed that it was a hallucination. *Mother of God, I need a drink. Or a valium. Or both.*

He climbed out of bed and flinched as his bare feet made contact with the icy vinyl floor tiles. It was then that he noticed the frosty puffs of his breath as they drifted in the air. He padded across the cold floor to the bathroom and checked the wall-mounted thermostat. *Seventy-eight degrees! Impossible!* Overhead, he could hear the rumble of the central heating unit. He held a hand to the face of the outlet vent. The heating unit and blower seemed fine, as a strong, steady stream of warm air entered the room. *This makes no sense!*

Shaking his head in frustration, Arturo opened the medicine cabinet and reached for the bottle of valium. He dropped two of the pink heart-shaped pills into his hand, hesitated, then placed one of the tablets back into the bottle. One tablet would encourage restful sleep, while two might knock him out for several hours. He couldn't afford to sleep too deeply and miss an important call from his Watcher contact. As he swallowed the pills, he heard a distinctive *click* from the bedroom. Whirling about, he saw the room was now dark. Someone had turned off the bedside lamp.

"No, no. I'm imagining things again. The lamp blew a bulb, nothing more. . . ."

"Arturo, help meeee. Pretty Arturo! Pleasssse."

Arturo's hand moved instinctively to his side where the shoulder holster normally hung. This time, there was no holster and no gun. He had left both on the nightstand. He dropped into a crouch and pressed his back to the bathroom wall. Fluorescent light from the bathroom illuminated the bedroom, all but the far corner just beyond the closet. *The closet!* The door was now standing open.

I know damn well I shut that door. I never leave it open!

"Come, lovely Arturo. Help me." The same terrible voice now called to him from deep inside the closet, mocking him. Cold. Malevolent. Dripping with scorn and contempt. This was no hallucination, though he desperately wished otherwise. He thought of his handgun still lying on the nightstand and mentally estimated the distance across the floor and around the king-size bed. It was a long way across the expansive bedroom, but what choice did he have? As Arturo crept forward through the doorway, the bathroom light flickered twice, then died with a distinctive *pop*. The acrid odor of a fried fluorescent ballast filled his nostrils.

Now he stood in total darkness without so much as a sliver of light penetrating the heavy drapes and foil-covered windows. There was only one thing he could do. Knees bent and head down, he ran across the hardwood floor toward the bed. After a half dozen steps, his shin connected painfully with the bed's iron railing. Arturo pitched forward onto the mattress and rolled. As he reached the head of the bed, he groped for the handgun until he located it on the nightstand. Once the gun was in his grasp, he rolled off the bed and onto the floor.

The thing in the closet laughed. A low chuckle at first, rising to a malicious, gleeful howl. Though Arturo was virtually blind in the darkness, he had lived in the apartment for years and knew the precise layout of the bedroom. He trained the gun on the closet and fought to control his breathing. Instinct told him his adversary was in its element and that as long as he remained in the darkened room, it held every advantage. He decided to make a run for the living room, and if the lights were out in there as well, he would move outside into the hall.

As he rose from his position behind the bed, the laughter subsided and the voice called out to him. However, this time it didn't call to him from the closet. Now it was closer. Much closer.

"You cannot leave, pretty Arturo. Come to me." The words came at him from every direction, as if it now somehow surrounded the room or . . . as if the one had become many.

Arturo turned for the bedroom door, then shrieked as a hand snaked out from beneath the bed and grabbed his ankle. He landed hard on the floor, the gun flying from his hand and sliding out of reach. "NO!"

Something pierced, then peeled away the tender flesh of his calf muscle, then embedded deep within the bone. Arturo screamed again. His assailant, speaking with a grotesque cacophony of discordant voices, pulled him toward the bed.

"Sweet Arturo. Pretty Arturo. Bad Arturo! Give us the book! The book!" Arturo's legs disappeared beneath the bed, and he screamed again as skin and hunks of flesh were torn from both legs.

With his last reserves of will and resolve, Arturo dug his fingernails into the hardwood planks, and prayed aloud. He was no longer fighting for his life for he knew that was forfeit. Now he was fighting for his soul. Through broken sobs, he intoned "Holy . . . Mary, Mother of God . . . oh, my God! P-pray for us sinners . . . now and at . . . the hour of our death."

"The book, bad Arturo! Give it back to us!" The voices were no longer filled with scorn and mockery. Now every word dripped with the venom of rage and hatred.

As Arturo's shoulders and head disappeared beneath the king-size bed, he closed his eyes a final time. An unexpected, overwhelming feeling of peace and solace welled up within his chest, its supernatural warmth spreading throughout his broken, tortured body.

"Amen." With a word, Arturo Giannini's final burden on this earth was lifted.

chapter 14

Sam walked back to the sofa and claimed his former seat. It wasn't so much that he preferred the overstuffed couch to one of the chairs, but he needed an excuse to ensure that the road atlas was well out of sight. He didn't want to explain its presence in the hotel room or the similar markings on the Arizona and Tennessee maps.

Enrique took the chair near the windows and opened his briefcase while Falco returned to the recliner. Though the seating arrangements seemed random and informal, Sam knew better. The two men had chosen vantage points that allowed unobstructed views of the front door. *They think they're so friggin' smart! If they knew what I knew about the Enemy, they'd be keeping an eye on all the doors, the windows, the ceiling, and the toilet drain.*

Enrique sat smiling for a moment, looking from Sam to Falco and back to Sam again. Falco's expression was unreadable, though Sam thought he detected tension in the man's posture. He gave the pretense of settling comfortably in the large armchair when in reality, he was poised to move at the slightest provocation. Sam wondered if Enrique noticed this as well. After several seconds, Sam decided to throw all caution to the wind. It wasn't likely that he would make a winning case for himself by keeping his mouth shut. He took a deep breath and exhaled slowly. For a microsecond, Enrique dropped the cool demeanor and flashed Sam an appraising look. *What's wrong with this guy? He gets jumpy when I breathe! Does he really believe I'm a demon?*

Sam started to speak, and Enrique opened his briefcase and passed a small stack of papers to Falco. "A copy of your report should you need to reference anything."

Falco accepted the papers but seemed less than pleased. "Do you really think I'll need to refresh my memory? I just wrote this yesterday."

Enrique hesitated. Falco's directness had caught him off guard. *A chink in the Armani armor,* thought Sam. *Time to press the attack.*

"As my grandmother used to say, we're wasting daylight. We all know why you're here and it's not to check on Mr. Falco's physical well-being." For the second time, Enrique seemed taken aback. From the corner of his eye, Sam thought he saw Falco flash a quick grin but it came and went so quickly, he couldn't be sure. He turned his full attention back to Enrique.

"You're here to decide if I'm a threat to you, your people, and all God's children. I know you sent Mr. Falco and his playmates to kill me. And *you* know what happened when he tried. If it wasn't for me, Mr. Falco would be sporting the latest in toe-tag fashions down at the local morgue. Now, I don't know about your level of experience with demons, Mr. . . . DeLorenzo, is it? Yeah, DeLorenzo. So, as I was saying, I don't know how much or how little you know about demons. But I do know they aren't in the habit of saving the people who try to kill them. In fact, it's my experience that trying to kill them just really—and I mean *really*—pisses them off."

Enrique started to interrupt, but Sam cut him off. "You'll get your turn, but let me finish. What's your beef with me and my sister? And those like us? What have we really done to deserve being hunted down like dogs by professional hit men? I mean, if I've offended your little club in any way, just let me know and I'll apologize. But you know something, Mr. DeLorenzo? I don't think we've done a damn thing to you or your fellow Cub Scouts . . . except save their sorry murdering asses."

Falco winced at the last remark, but Sam was well past

caring. His temper hovered just above the boiling point. Meanwhile, Enrique's face had taken on the hue of an over-ripe tomato. When he spoke, it was through clenched teeth.

"You're quite a smart-ass, Mr. Conner. No offense, of course."

"None taken. Of course," said Sam. "And now while we're on the subject, maybe you can tell me why I should be polite to some slicked-up Ken doll who tried to have me murdered. Better yet, skip that and just tell me what you need from this meeting in order to get the fuck out of my life and stay out. I've got finals coming up." To his right, Falco burst out laughing but Sam's eyes never left Enrique's.

Enrique's eyes were dark and menacing, the muscles in his jaws spasming violently, and he struggled to maintain a sem-blance of poise. "If you're waiting for an apology, Sam, don't hold your breath. Even if we erred by targeting you, and I'm not saying I believe it was an error, it's of little consequence when factored into the bigger picture."

Now it was Sam who sat in stunned silence. *Of little consequence my ass! The nerve of this bastard!*

Enrique continued. "Notice I didn't say such a mistake wouldn't be unfortunate. We don't callously take innocent lives regardless of what you may think. Tell me, how much do you really know about our organization?"

A helluva lot more than I want to. "Only what little Mr. Falco told me—that the Watchers have been around for cen-turies, chasing Veils and hunting demons. He also said that you believe Offspring are demons, and that we're a danger to the world. He said a lot, but I pretty much stopped listening after the Offspring-are-demons bullshit."

Enrique nodded, his face once more a stoic mask. "And what did you say to Thomas?"

"What did I say? You had observers at the goddamn mine in Abbotsville. You know about the Veil, what it was . . . and what it became after it was corrupted. And you damn well know what it cost us to close it! So what do you *think* I said to Mr. Falco?"

Enrique glanced at Falco, who only shrugged in return.

Looking back to Sam, he said, "Did Thomas also tell you many within the Watcher leadership believe Offspring are responsible for the corruption of the Veil?"

Sam shook his head, grinning. "No, but he didn't have to. I figured you guys suspected us. But you're dead wrong. We don't have the power to alter something like the Veil. It takes . . ."

Sam halted in midsentence. To this point he had never mentioned the word "angels" outside of conversations with Mark and Janet. Falco had never broached the subject, although he had been free enough with the mention of demons. Was it possible the Watchers knew nothing about Horace, Joriel, and their kind? How could that be? If Sam was correct in his suspicions, then more than one of the Watchers carried the Offspring bloodline. He was certain Falco did. Surely, Falco and others like him had heard the Voices during the crisis at the Veil.

Sam sighed and leaned back into the sofa cushions. He didn't want to speak of the angels, not to these mercenary bastards, but he didn't see how he could avoid the subject. His life might well depend on how much he was willing to divulge. His mind made up, he took another deep breath.

"Offspring can close a Veil, that much is true. But only one power on earth can corrupt the Veils, and it's not Offspring or the Enemy . . . I mean, demons. Well, there are two powers if you count God, but I'm not sure He's around much these days."

Enrique stiffened in his chair and again his jaws twitched. "Careful, boy. I won't tolerate blasphemy."

"Yeah, okay," replied Sam. "I guess that was a little snarky on my part. Anyway, the only power that can corrupt a Veil is an angel."

"Angel?" said Enrique. "You expect us to believe an *angel* broke the Veil? Boy, if this is your idea of a joke?"

"What? You don't believe in angels?"

"Of course we believe in angels! That's not the point! It's just that . . . that . . . no one has seen an angel since the time of Christ!"

"Says you," said Sam. "So let me get this straight. You have no problem believing that supernatural Offspring and demons walk around the planet, but angels are out of the question. Is that it?"

"Of course not. I believe anything is possible through Almighty God. But where is your evidence? And furthermore, why would an angel desire harm for one of God's greatest creations? Angels are incapable of such sacrilege!"

"Ah, so that's it. An angel would never harm the Veils or take an innocent life. Just making sure I understand all this," said Sam, straight-faced.

"All angels are servants of the Almighty and subject to His authority," explained Enrique as if he were speaking to a simpleton. "They could never act in such a manner, provided they even walk the planet today." He gave Sam a smug little smile that said, *You're out of your league on this subject, boy.*

Sam glanced over at Falco and was surprised to see a thoughtful expression on the man's face.

It's now or never. "Servants of the Big Boss, huh? And that includes the Fallen?"

"What?" said Enrique. "What do you mean?"

"I think most religious texts, including the Old Testament, state that God created all angels as servants or messengers. Even the fallen angels who were thrown out of Heaven. You do believe that account, don't you? You do believe in the biblical accounts, right? Aren't you all Christians?"

"Of course we're Christians! We only exist to serve! As for the Bible, I mean, well, many believe various passages are parables and not meant to be taken literally. I still don't see where any of this is going."

Sam grinned. *I've got you now, Mr. Armani Smart-ass.* "I'll speak slowly. Try to follow me. I asked if God's dominion over angels includes the Fallen. You know, one third of all the angels who rebelled against God and were kicked out of Heaven? They could attempt a coup in Heaven, but they wouldn't dare damage a Veil on Earth, is that what you're saying?"

"Well, I mean, it's possible, but—"

"No 'buts,'" interrupted Sam. "Either it's possible or it isn't."

"The boy has you there, Rikki." Falco turned to Sam and

said, "Like you said before, we're wasting daylight, so just spit it out. Are you saying a fallen angel broke the Veil in Tennessee?"

Sam nodded while trying to gauge Falco's expression. "That's exactly what I'm saying. The fallen angels and Legion have a pact. They're in this thing together, but it was an angel who actually broke the Veil. I think they call him the Runner."

Falco's voice was soft, almost pleading. "How do you know this, Sam? How?"

Sam put on his best two-dollar smile. "An old guy named Horace told me."

Stunned silence was followed by, "I see. And I suppose it's this angelic assistance that allows you to detect demonic entities over several miles. Oh, for Christ's sake! Boy, I've been very patient with you. Some might say I've been more patient than you deserve or circumstances dictate. Yet, you refuse to cooperate. You do understand the consequences, do you not?"

Sam had expected this response and was prepared for it. "Cooperation? I don't owe you any cooperation. I don't owe you anything but contempt, you self-righteous son of a bitch!"

"Sam!" said Falco.

Sam ignored the reprimand. "So I'm supposed to kneel down and kiss your ass because you think you're on a mission from God? Well, I got a news flash for you. You're no better than a few thousand other pissant radical groups scattered across the planet."

"That's enough!" shouted Enrique.

"Enough? Enough, hell! I'm just getting started. You know what separates you guys from all the other gun-toting, dogma-spouting terrorists? They at least have the balls to stand up and take credit for their crimes, and that, by God, is the *only* difference!

"All you've done since you walked in here is threaten me and my family. But your mind was made up before you ever stepped on that plane this morning, wasn't it? You came here to hold mock court and justify a decision to commit another cold-blooded murder.

"You need to get this straight. I never wanted any part of the Veil in the first place! You think I asked for that trip to Abbotsville? You think I wanted to watch a man like Michael Collier sacrifice himself while you sat back on your worthless asses and watched him die? I did it because your God drafted me!"

"Take it easy, kid."

Sam could hear the earnest pleading in Falco's voice but he tuned it out. He wasn't through with Mr. Rolex-fucking-Armani. Not by a long shot.

"Yeah, there are angels working to straighten out this mess before the world is eaten alive by the Enemy. And it doesn't surprise me a damn bit that they aren't exactly on speaking terms with you and your little social club. And neither am I, so shoot me and get it over with, 'cause I'm through taking your crap!"

When Sam finished, the only sound in the room was that of his pounding heart. Enrique's expression was carved out of stone, and unreadable. Falco, however, looked as if he had just witnessed his own execution.

Such language! Do you kiss your mother with that mouth?

The Voice in his head sounded weak and very distant, but it was unmistakable.

Joriel! If I wasn't so glad to hear you, I'd put you on permanent ignore! Where've you been? These guys are going to kill me, then Kat and Mom!

In case you haven't noticed, Sam, there's a war going on and I've been rather busy. But don't worry. These men aren't going to hurt you or your family. We keep close watch over you . . . in spite of your language. Now show them the maps.

Sam wasn't sure whether to laugh or cry. *Watching over me? You call the fight with that Little Stevie character watching over me?*

Sam was distantly aware of someone in the room calling his name, but blocked out the words and concentrated on his link with Joriel. When next she spoke her psychic voice was full of familiar exasperation.

Why must you be so hard-headed? The maps, Sam.

Now it was Sam's turn to feel exasperation, followed closely by frustration and irritation. *No offense, Joriel, but these people have no right looking through my book. I—I've never told you, but . . . look, I know it sounds crazy but that book is more than just a collection of road maps. A lot more. It holds parts of me, Mark, Janet—and Michael. I don't want these people touching any of us, especially not Michael. You were there. You saw through my eyes and you know what he did. You know. These fuckers haven't earned the right or the privilege to know any part of Michael Collier. Can . . . can you understand what I'm saying?*

For the first time in his short life, Sam both felt and heard Joriel's nonverbal response, and it wasn't the familiar tinkling of wind chimes. It was the sound of swaying treetops, and of cold and lonely winds kissing the branches of ancient and majestic oaks. It was the sound of great personal loss and bleak mourning. It was the sound of sorrow and of tribute. The sound of angel tears.

He glanced down at his feet and saw the corner of the book sticking out from beneath the sofa. Then he recalled the tiny circle drawn around the city of Casa Grande.

Does this have anything to do with a Veil? said Sam. *I mean, if it does, I really don't want anything to do with it. Please, Joriel. Please . . .*

Joriel's answer was slow in coming. When she finally spoke, her tone was calm yet distant, as if she was still lost in the memory of Michael Collier's final seconds on this earth.

No, this doesn't involve a Veil, Sam. It involves something of much greater importance.

"More important than a friggin' Veil? You're kidding, right?" Sam didn't realize he had spoken aloud until both Falco and Enrique turned to stare at him.

Joriel continued and Sam thought she now sounded hurried and farther away. *When it's time for you to go, take these men with you. They'll help you reach Katherine and your mother. They'll not harm you, Sam, you have my word. Events are moving very quickly now, and you're wasting time. Show them the map. Please.*

The room spun as it often did whenever Joriel withdrew abruptly from his mind. As the vertigo passed, he heard Falco calling his name. The man's voice was stern and filled with genuine concern. Enrique said nothing as he looked on, though Sam was certain he, too, was concerned, though not for the same reasons as Falco.

The bastard is just waiting for me to turn into the bogeyman.

"I'm fine. Just low blood sugar or something."

Enrique stood up and glanced at his watch. "Is there anything else you'd like to say? Something besides 'You murdering bastards'?"

Sam bent over and retrieved the atlas from beneath the sofa. "While you're deciding whether or not to have me shot or thrown off a bridge, you may want to look at this." Sam reached across the coffee table and passed the book to Enrique.

Enrique examined the front and back covers, then thumbed through the pages. "I assume there's something special about this atlas?"

Sam nodded. "Very special. The maps in that book led me halfway across the country, all the way to Abbotsville."

Enrique held up the book, showing the cover to Falco. "Have you seen this?"

Falco shook his head. "Not until now. I didn't know it was in the suite."

"Okay, Sam," said Enrique. "It's a road atlas. Lots of people use maps when they travel across the country. What's so special about this one?"

"Turn to the map of Tennessee and tell me what you see," said Sam.

Enrique did as Sam instructed and studied the map for several seconds. "I see some handwriting in red marker. The writing is smudged as if it's been wet. Can't make it out. I also see where you traced your route from Knoxville with a highlighter and . . . and the circle you drew around the town of Abbotsville."

Sam slowly shook his head from side to side. "I didn't trace the route, or draw the circle. The marks and notations were already there when I found the book inside my bedroom, a little more than two years ago. At first I didn't understand, so I laid it aside and tried to forget about it. But I . . . I couldn't. It was on my mind from the time I woke up until I went to bed at night. After a while I even started dreaming about it. It's like I was being pulled and pushed to a place I'd never heard of before I found the atlas. Finally, I couldn't stand it anymore. I figured I was either already crazy or heading in that direction in a hurry. Not much to lose when those are your only options, so I packed a duffel bag and headed out. I never found out who marked the route to Abbotsville. I have a hunch, but you'll have to wait for that story. You're not ready to hear it, and I'm not ready to tell it.

"So, after—after I got home from Tennessee, I left the book in my bedroom, in the bottom drawer of my dresser. It was still there months later when I moved into the dorm in Tempe. It turned up in the back seat of my car today. I found it laying on top of my laptop case in the back seat."

Enrique studied the map of Tennessee in silence for a moment and his wry grin said it all. When he finally spoke, he sounded less than impressed. "All very interesting, Sam. Maybe it was there all along and you just forgot about it. I'm sure there's a plausible explanation, *if* you're even telling the truth."

"*If* my ass! If you're half as smart as *you* think you are, you know goddamn well I'm telling the truth. But if you want further proof, turn to the map of Arizona."

Enrique sighed and shook his head, now clearly exasperated. "What's the point, Sam? It won't prove anything about what you are—or aren't—or what you did or didn't do. In fact, I think I already have most of that already figured out."

"Then looking at the map of Arizona won't hurt anything, will it?" Sam shot back.

"Just do it, Rikki."

Sam and Enrique both shot startled glances at Falco. The big man had been quiet for much of the exchange, and Sam had almost forgotten he was in the room.

After a moment, Enrique shrugged and turned to the front of the atlas and searched until he found the map of Arizona. It took only a few seconds for the surprise to register on his face.

"See the circle around Casa Grande? I didn't draw it, just like I didn't draw that circle around Abbotsville. Does it mean anything to you?" As Sam waited, he sent a message to Joriel, *From the look on his face, it means* something *to him. Now, would you mind letting me in on—*

"How did you know about Casa Grande?" demanded Enrique. "Who told you?" He turned to Falco. "You? You told him? Wait . . ." Enrique paused as his anger gave way to puzzlement. "No, you couldn't have told him anything, could you, Thomas? You knew we would make the extraction, but you knew nothing about the airport."

"Wait a minute," said Sam. "What extraction?"

Falco's disgust was evident in his tone. "You know better than to suggest that I would tell the boy anything about an ongoing mission, Rikki. If I haven't earned your trust by now, then fuck you and the organization."

"Now wait, Thom—"

"There's no wait. I don't even discuss missions with other Swords unless they're directly involved, and I resent the hell out of your suspicion. But we'll come back to this issue in a moment. We *are* talking about relocating his sister, aren't we?"

"My sister? Relocate?" said Sam, standing up. "Whaddaya mean, 'relocate'?"

Enrique turned in his chair and locked eyes with Falco. "I'm sorry, Thomas. I wanted to bring you up to speed before now and give you the details, but . . . well, until I had a chance to speak with you and Sam, I couldn't chance it. I was under orders to divulge nothing until I had an opportunity to assess the situation here. I trust you understand."

"So make *me* understand, goddamn it!" shouted Sam. "What the hell does this extraction thing have to do with my sister? And where's my mom?"

His eyes never leaving Falco, Enrique said, "Your sister and mother are fine, Sam. A team is moving them to a safe location. In fact, at this very moment they're en route—"

"To the goddamn airfield in Casa Grande," Sam finished. "You stupid . . . ! Get dressed, Thomas. We've got to hurry!"

Enrique motioned for Sam to take a seat on the sofa. "Just hold on, boy. You aren't going anywhere. Not yet. I told you Katherine and your mother are safe. The escort team is very competent."

"Safe? Competent? I've seen your idea of competent, in case you've already forgotten about Falco's buddy. Man, you've got no idea what you're up against! Thomas, do you remember earlier when I said we had company?"

Falco, already up from his chair and moving toward the bedroom, called back over his shoulder, "Yeah, I remember. You said they were five or six miles away."

"Yeah, well those were just the advance scouts or whatever you wanna call them. The real threat is a little farther south. In Casa Grande."

Falco emerged from the bedroom with his shoulder holster and a fresh shirt, but stopped in his tracks. "You've got to be kidding. That's a good thirty miles from here! You said you couldn't detect them beyond five or six miles."

Enrique stood up and faced Falco. "Now, wait a damn minute. I read your report, Thomas, but do you really believe this boy can sense demonic entities over five or six miles?"

This time it was Sam's turn to ignore Enrique. "First of all, Casa Grande is closer to forty miles, Falco, and what I said is that I can *pinpoint* the Enemy out to five or six miles. At that distance I can tell you exactly what shithole they're hiding in, and what—or who—they ate for breakfast. But I can sense their general presence over a much longer distance, and I'm telling you, you've sent your team and my family straight into a nest!"

Enrique looked at Falco and said, "I can't fix what's been done, but maybe I can give you a hand in Casa Grande."

Falco studied Enrique for a long moment. "I'm not sure I'm buying your sudden reversal, but if it's legit, I'm thankful. But as for going to Casa Grande, you're out of your mind, Rikki. I can't allow that. You're too valuable to the organization, and there's no guarantee anyone's coming back from this trip."

"It isn't for you to decide, Thomas. I can read a map just as well as you can, so we may as well ride together. Have you got a spare gun?"

Falco laid a polymer gun case containing a compact .40-caliber Glock on the coffee table, along with four loaded magazines.

"This was William's spare. He also left a twelve-gauge riot gun under his bed, and a mixed case of sabot slugs and 00 buckshot. You do remember how to shoot, don't you?"

Enrique gave him a "Go to hell" look and Falco laughed. "Since you're determined to give us a hand, you might want to notify the surveillance team that we'll be leaving the hotel in a few minutes."

Enrique stared at Will's handgun for several seconds, then reached for the cell phone on his belt. As he dialed Malcolm Reading's secure line, he said, "We'll take my rental car." Looking over his shoulder at Sam, he added, "While we're on the road, maybe you can tell me how the hell you do . . . whatever it is you do."

"Do exactly as you're told, when you're told, and we'll all get along just fine. Do you understand?" The woman at the wheel spoke in a calm manner but something in her tone clearly said *Obey or pay.*

Kat and her mother both mumbled acknowledgments. One of the men in the front seat, thickly built and menacing even without the gun, looked over his shoulder and snickered.

He has a mean, mean spirit, thought Kat. *The others are almost robots, cold and indifferent. But that one . . . Mr. Snickers, he's just mean.*

Her mother kept her eyes focused straight ahead as she and Kat had been instructed, but Kat didn't need to look into Amanda Conner's eyes to see the woman was afraid. The odor of fear mingled with those of confusion and anger made the confines of the vehicle extremely uncomfortable for Kat. Her supernatural senses were choking on the raw emotions pouring from her mother.

Amanda Conner had never been a strong person, and since the death of her husband she had demonstrated time and again her inability to function in the midst of a full-blown crisis, even with the aid of those tiny, pink, heart-shaped pills. And if ever an event qualified as a full-blown crisis, Kat figured this was surely it. Not that Kat wasn't also afraid. But she knew the burden of acting like the adult was, at least for the moment, squarely upon her fourteen-year-old shoulders.

Her own fear, however, wasn't so much for their dire predicament as it was for its root cause. Kat somehow knew the bizarre abduction had something, perhaps everything, to do with Sam and the events in Abbotsville. She also sensed that the kidnappers, highly efficient and well organized, were acting on orders from some higher authority. Katherine and Amanda Conner were little more than bait or barter material. Of course, that also meant they were of value, for now anyway. No, they wouldn't be harmed, unless . . . *That Mr. Snickers has a real mean spirit.*

As for the others, they were merely following orders. Behind the steering wheel of the Escalade sat the young blonde who, with her partner, had come to the Conner front door posing as canvassers for a local church. Kat noted she didn't seem so friendly now. However, to her credit, the woman had glared across the front seat at Mr. Snickers when he laughed at the hostages, then cast a quick glance at Kat via the rearview mirror. A "Pay that idiot no mind, kid" kind of glance.

Kat and her mother were seat-belted into the back seat of the large SUV and pinned between a woman dressed all in black and the man who had come to the front door with the driver. Neither of them spoke or paid any attention to their prisoners. Instead, they maintained a constant vigil through the rear windshield and side glass. Kat knew they were both watching for signs of pursuit, and that was probably a very good thing. She could feel that pursuit was gaining ground.

While Kat didn't have Sam's ability to detect the Enemy at long distances, she did possess her own set of unique gifts, some of which she kept hidden even from Sam. It wasn't that she didn't trust her brother. On the contrary, he was the lone person in her life whom she trusted implicitly. However, she had always figured some secrets just weren't meant to be shared, not even with an older brother. Perhaps especially an older brother.

As the SUV weaved in and out of mid-evening interstate traffic, Kat felt the arrival of a familiar travel companion: carsickness. *I don't have time for this! Not now!*

Riding in the back seat always made her carsick, but tonight, an upset stomach was the very least of her problems. Her supernatural senses detected the sickening presence of the Enemy. However, this was more than a mere presence. The SUV was surrounded, the Enemy converging on the Escalade from every direction.

She squirmed closer to her mother. Amanda Conner made a valiant effort to hide her fear, but the uncontrollable trembling of her slender shoulders was a dead giveaway. *Don't worry, Mama. Sam's coming. He'll find us and . . . What? What will happen when Sam comes? What can he possibly do?* The men and women who abducted them at gunpoint were scary enough, but tonight they were the lesser of numerous evils. Except for the man. Kat was unsure of him. She didn't have Sam's gifts for spotting the Enemy, but something was wrong with the man in black. Very wrong. And then there was the matter of the white Lincoln.

That loathsome entity paced them from a short distance, neither gaining nor losing ground. Kat had recognized the presence of the Lincoln as her masked captors led her from the house to the waiting SUV. The sudden realization was a punch to the stomach that nearly buckled her knees, and then sent her running for the waiting vehicle. When the SUV reached the interstate, Kat felt another presence, or rather, a collective presence. The sensation was similar to that caused by the Lincoln, but it was stronger and more malevolent. The collective Enemy wasn't content with pacing. They were making every effort to overtake the SUV, and Kat had no doubt what the outcome would be should that happen. *They're gaining on us. Won't be long now. Oh, God, it won't be long now.*

While the car terrified her, she intuitively understood the new threat was far more dangerous. For the first time she thought perhaps she could understand a tiny portion of the horror Sam had experienced two years earlier when he had descended into the bowels of the mountain in search of the Veil. The knowledge nearly broke her heart.

She squeezed her mother's hand and cried silently, not for her own situation, but for the terrible emotional toll that had been exacted on her brother in the tiny hamlet of Abbotsville.

Kat whispered a silent prayer. *Please, God, keep Sam away from here.*

chapter 15

Mississippi Delta

A stiff wind whistled through the open shutters as evening descended over the secluded glen and the old stone and mud-brick monastery. Inside the building, the three Immortals—Kiel, Nathan, and Orus—sat quietly at an ancient wooden table. Perhaps *Immortal* wasn't entirely accurate. While the three were immune to the ravages of age and disease, they could be destroyed by catastrophic injury.

Of course, with angels, death is both subjective and relative. In the truest sense, angels cannot die. They are unmade. Cosmic and supernatural forces that bind together ethereal energies and flesh and blood molecules unravel, left to float across the infinite planes of time and space until they wink out of existence. Among the Immortals, this is called "entering the Void," a condition to evade at any cost, as there is no coming back. Still, even in the Void, an angel's remnants may dwell in perpetuity in the presence of the Creator.

Thus, not even the Void represented an angel's greatest fear. True death comes not from physical destruction, but rather from spiritual isolation. The ultimate form of death results from an eternal separation from the sight and mind of the Creator. Unmade versus eternal separation from God; ask any angel which is worse. The answer is always the same.

As the three sat around the table in silence, Kiel studied Orus, a fallen angel of prodigious intellect and cunning. Orus claimed that after eons of banishment from God, thoughts of being unmade and the Void meant little. His only real concern, or so he said, is that he might live long enough to take his vengeance upon the Runner. Kiel almost laughed when he considered the latter. Given the news Orus brought, it seemed unlikely anyone would live to see the Runner's fall.

Nathan cleared his throat and reached for the ceramic jug of dandelion wine. "The End of Days," he repeated to himself. As he filled his cup, he glanced at Orus from the corner of his eye. "You've come with important news, my fine fanged brother of serpents, I'll grant you that. Now I have some questions for you."

"Ask away, Nathan," said Orus. "I've nothing to hide. Afterward, I may have a question for you and Kiel."

"Fair enough. First, how did the Enemy acquire the Keys? Secondly, how does Legion propose to use them? The Enemy may not enter the Holy of Holies unless they are commanded to do so by one of the Host, or the Creator Himself. The Brethren have no such authority."

Orus smiled, but Kiel thought the fallen angel looked extremely nervous. It was clear he didn't want to answer the question. Still . . .

"I don't know who or what hatched the plan to acquire the Goetia, and free the Seventy-two. If I didn't know better, I'd suspect the Runner, but as you say, he doesn't have the power to walk into the Temple. Finding the Goetia was no simple matter, but it wasn't the most difficult of tasks, either. The Brethren have known its location for centuries."

This came as a major surprise to both Nathan and Kiel. Not even they had known of the book's exact location. "I'll tell you, but you're not going to like the answer worth a shit. Legion has always been drawn to places of power, or places of fear and despair. Greater demons are crawling all over the Middle East. Even in Jerusalem. Someone with the authority granted Legion permission to enter the Temple. Someone who knows the exact location of the hidden icons and artifacts."

"You're lying," said Nathan. "Why?"

"Oh, come off it, Nathan! Think about it. Why would I risk walking in here just to tell you some bullshit story?"

"I don't know, Orus. Perhaps you intend to commit suicide by angel."

Orus grinned. "Ordinarily, I'd applaud your wit, Nate. But not today. Hell, you both have the power of discernment. You know I'm not lying!"

"Not entirely, no," said Kiel. "I believe you when you say the Enemy now holds the Lesser Keys of Solomon. I can even believe the Enemy plots to release the Seventy-two. However, I do *not* believe they have the means to accomplish this."

"You don't believe because you don't *want* to believe, Kiel. Nathan said it himself. There's only one way Legion can enter the Temple. Someone with the spiritual authority must command or invite them inside. Now, if the Brethren don't have that authority—and we don't—that only leaves . . ." Orus cast a nervous glance at Nathan before finishing the sentence. "That only leaves the Creator and the Host. It's a safe bet that God hasn't done such a thing. That means it must be . . ."

"The Host," said Nathan. "Impossible!"

"I said you wouldn't like the answer, but there is no one else, Nathan. That brings us to a single, conceivable conclusion: One of the Host intends to grant Legion access to the Temple."

"How can you know this?" asked Nathan. "Why are you so sure?"

Orus sighed, then massaged the muscles in his neck. "Why have you two always been so hardheaded? I know Legion has the Keys because I saw the book with my own eyes, damn it! I know they intend to infiltrate the Temple and release the Seventy-two because I overheard a conversation between a council of greater demons and a pair of Brethren—Mulciber and Azazeal."

Nathan's right hand dropped to the wire-wrapped handle of the Kiv, and Orus fell off the bench and scuttled on hands and knees to the far wall. Kiel smiled and sipped his watered wine. He knew the fallen angel wasn't in any immediate danger. Nathan had merely reacted to one of the names. Azazeal had played a significant role in the death of Baraniel, and Nathan had vowed vengeance for the fallen Cherubim.

"Peace, Orus. Nathan will not harm you. Now, what's this about a council of greater demons?"

Orus made his way back to the bench, though his eyes never

strayed from Nathan or the Kiv. "I thought that might get your attention. As—as I said, it was a council. Six, perhaps seven greater demons, each attended by several lieutenants. Mulciber and . . . you-know-who represented the Brethren. I was also there, along with Nilaihah and Olivier.

"Mulciber is crazy. He actually believes the Runner controls Legion and intends to rule over them once the subjugation of humanity is complete. In fact, it was Mulciber who discovered the hiding place of the Lesser Keys and gave that information to Legion. He thinks the Runner will reward him. Idiot."

Kiel studied Orus with a thoughtful expression, then said, "Where did this meeting take place?"

"The first meeting was held at an island palace located on the Aegean Sea. I think it once belonged to another raving lunatic, Axthiel. I may be mistaken, but I believe Nathaniel knows him intimately. Didn't you two have a minor skirmish a couple of years ago?"

Nathan growled under his breath and glared at Orus.

Orus looked away, unwilling to lock eyes with the huge power. To Kiel, he said, "Aza . . . I mean, you-know-who, claims the place now. It was he who first suggested one of the Host could be counted on to grant Legion access to the Holy of Holies. We held a second meeting a week later, in the Sudan. I was afraid we might not escape the place alive. There was a lot of infighting as the demon lords jockeyed for leadership. Worse than a damned pack of rabid wolverines.

"Mulciber reminded them of where we were and they quieted down. A depressing little cave with multiple underground levels. It once served as the principal temple to the greater demon, Nazzikim. Remember him?"

Kiel nodded absently. He remembered Nazzikim very well, and knew Orus was wrong about one thing: Nazzikim was no greater demon. He was a demon lord, but a few steps removed from the Nine Princes in terms of power and status. He was a terrible foe and now one of the imprisoned Seventy-two.

As if reading Kiel's thoughts, Nathan said, "Do you see some significance in the choice of meeting places?"

Kiel shrugged. "I can't say. I'm not sure why they chose Axthiel's former home, unless it was simply Aza . . . I mean, *him* showing off his new acquisition. The use of Nazzikim's old temple disturbs me on several levels. However, I think the greatest cause for concern is that the greater demons are now working in concert. Their proximity to Jerusalem is another troubling issue."

Nathan released his grip on the Kiv and stood up from the table. He walked to a nearby window and threw open the shutters. The air was thick, and a chill wind carried the promise of rain. High above swaying treetops to the west, a streak of lightning lanced the sky. As banks of clouds clashed high overhead, a powerful storm gathered momentum. Nathan knew a storm of another kind now gained momentum on earth. While he could alter the former, the latter was far beyond his power to control.

When next Nathan spoke, his natural tone, a brassy bass baritone, was subdued, reduced to little more than a raspy whisper. "Who is the traitor, Orus? Who would grant Legion access to the Temple?"

Kiel held his breath, awaiting the answer. He wanted to know. *Had* to know. At the same time, he silently prayed for the Creator to strike him deaf and blind, that he may never know the name of the betrayer.

"I—I don't know, Nathan. I would tell you even should it cost me my life here and now, but I don't know. I can only tell you that I believe the Runner intends to pass the Keys to a demon lord named Fuzan. In fact, Fuzan may already have them. You must move swiftly if you're to recover them before Legion makes its move."

Nathan turned away from the window and looked at Orus. His face was expressionless. "It would make sense that he pass the Keys to Legion. Were the Runner to attempt to enter the Holy of Holies, he would be unmade in an instant.

"You say you've had this information for a week and yet you just now come to us. Is this some cruel sport? Do you taunt us with our own impotence? What do you gain from this?"

"What kind of foolish question is that?" said Orus. "Look,

I have one chance, albeit a slim one, to repay the Runner for his treachery. He's too powerful for a direct confrontation. I know him better than he knows himself, and I tell you this plan has his signature all over it. If you find some way to defeat this scheme, then you've defeated the Runner. I believe this is a last, desperate gamble. If his plan fails, Legion will turn on him. Not even the Runner can defeat the combined might of Legion and half the Brethren!"

Kiel leaned his elbows on the table and stared intently at Orus. "As you've already noted, I do have the power of discernment. And that power says you're lying. At least, in part."

Orus pushed back from the table and protested. "I swear all I've said today is true! If Legion frees the Seventy-two and gains control of the Holy of Holies, then the End of Days are upon us. The world ends and so does any chance I ever had for revenge."

Kiel shook his head from side to side, a thin smile playing along his lips. "The lie isn't in what you've told us, Orus. It's in what you've purposely omitted. There is another reason you've come to us. Can you not speak the simple truth and be done with it?"

For several seconds, screeching wind, creaking roof timbers, and distant thunder were the only sounds within the monastery. Nathan, looking from Orus to Kiel, stood with his back to the open window, enjoying the feel of fat rain droplets upon his bare torso. Orus lowered his gaze, and stared at the toes of his boots, while Kiel waited patiently. Kiel already knew the answer to his question. But it was worthless unless Orus made the admission of his own free will.

Come, Orus. Speak the words. It may not exonerate you of blasphemy, but it cannot hurt, either. Speak the words.

Orus's shoulders began to quiver and his head bobbed slightly. Kiel was stunned. He had heard the Brethren had lost any capacity for tears long ago. After several minutes, Orus raised his head. A single glistening tear trickled down his smooth cheek and fell to the table top as an uncut diamond.

"Nathan is right. I chose sides eons ago. Any chance I may have had for redemption was lost when I followed Lucifer into the throne room. I forfeited my right to petition Him for all time.

"How ironic is that, Kiel? A human loses some petty job, turns an ankle, or experiences some other trifling misfortune and curses God for the inconvenience. Yet, in the twinkling of an eye, that man may be forgiven by uttering a simple prayer and demonstrating an ounce of faith. We, however, are dismissed from His sight and forgotten, without any hope of redemption."

"No man ever stormed the throne room of God with a sword in his hand," said Nathan. "As to the matter of redemption, how would you know? Has any Fallen ever dropped to his knees, confessed his transgressions, and begged forgiveness? Have you? No need to confirm or deny. It was a rhetorical question and I already know the answer. You've never once expressed remorse for your actions, so don't talk to me of an existence without any possibility of redemption, Orus. Until you crawl before the Throne of God and beg forgiveness, you don't have that right."

Orus looked at Nathan for a long moment. "If I thought . . . You know, not all of the Brethren sought power. Most of us only wanted His favor, to be loved above man. All we ever wanted . . ." His voice trailed off as he walked toward the common area and the front door.

For a moment, Kiel had thought Orus might actually fall upon the cobbled floor, prostrate himself and cry out to the Creator for mercy and forgiveness. The moment came and went, quickly. In the end, Orus's remorse retreated in the face of pride, fear of rejection, or some other equally damning barrier.

Perhaps another day, Orus. I'll pray for you.

Kiel and Nathan followed Orus into the common room. At the door, Orus turned and extended his hand toward the pair, palm turned out, thumb, index, and middle fingers extended. The sign of peace and the Holy Trinity; the Father, Son, and Holy Spirit. It wasn't a sign Kiel ever expected to see from a Brethren.

"I'll try to learn the name of the traitor and get back to you as soon as I can. Meanwhile, I suggest you closely guard the contents of this conversation. We don't want the traitor knowing we're closing in on his or her identity. Suspicions run high these days and I can't risk *reaching* for you, so I'll need to return here with any new information. Is that acceptable?"

"Provided you come alone, you'll be fine. But remember this, Orus. I don't like you, nor do I trust you. If you give me reason to suspect a betrayal, you won't have to worry about the Brethren any longer."

"Understood."

As Orus stepped outside, Kiel called out. "Wait a moment. Earlier you said you may have a question for us."

Orus paused, thought for a moment, then smiled. "Oh, yeah. Well, it's nothing really, but it's puzzled me for a long time. One of those nagging things that keeps nipping at your ass, know what I mean?"

"Get to the point, Orus," said Nathan. "What would you like to know?"

"Very well. Bear in mind, I mean no offense, but . . . Why? Why do you throw away your lives for the humans? We were there in the beginning. We sacrificed and endured for His sake and He elevates these hairless monkeys above us. Above you! What has mankind ever done except work in concert to destroy paradise on earth? So why? Why do you fight . . . and die for them?"

Kiel didn't have to ponder the question. The answer was engraved in his heart. He saw that Nathan was smiling. Apparently at some point during the discussion with Orus, he had remembered why they fought and died for a species that was so much less—and so much more—than the Choruses of Heaven.

"Orus," said Kiel, "I mean no disrespect when I say there's no answer I can give that you could accept or understand. Perhaps that's always been our problem: our limited capacity for understanding, and our inability to believe in things unseen. Once, it was enough that we served the will of the Creator. Such servitude requires only obedience. Man has the benefit of faith.

"Humanity is a living monument to the Creator. Name any virtue and it may be found within the human race. Honor, courage, faith, charity, hope—all are evident in abundance despite man's weaknesses and imperfections. Most of all, I sincerely admire man's ability to seek and find God. That's no small thing when you consider many of us lived beneath His roof and still managed to lose sight of Him."

Orus looked at Kiel for a long, solemn moment before nodding. "Maybe you're right. I don't know much of anything these days. Recovering the Keys won't cleanse me of my transgressions, but perhaps it will make some small amends. On the other hand, should you not recover the Keys before the Seventy-two are released, well, I'll join you all in the Void."

Turning, Orus stepped through the doorway. Over his shoulder, he called back, "I was just curious. No harm in asking, right? You know, this is the first time I've talked to either of you outside of a friggin' dogfight. And speaking of dogfights, watch your backs. Both of you are well marked by the Brethren. I'll be in touch soon."

Kiel watched as Orus walked across the yard to the edge of the clearing. Ordinarily, angels move across great distances at the speed of thought by assuming ethereal form. However, the monastery was consecrated ground, and in such places, the rules were vastly different.

Orus reached the southern edge of the clearing, and the boundary of sanctuary. He turned and raised a hand into the air, bidding Kiel and Nathan safe journeys in the customary manner of the Host.

Nathan frowned at the farewell salute and walked back into the monastery. He had no intention of parting company with the fallen angel on amiable terms. Kiel hesitated, then returned the gesture. *Another historic moment,* he thought. His hand was still raised when he felt the tell-tale electrical charge course through his body, a sure and familiar sign that an enemy was near.

Orus was still smiling when the first jagged finger of brilliant green fire sizzled through the air and exploded in his face.

Istanbul, Turkey

Such an easy matter to destroy one feeble old man. The temptation held such sweet allure. Killing the living symbol of the Church would be delicious, fostering additional chaos and confusion in a world already rife with turmoil. In another age, killing a Pope would have set the human race on a path toward a regional, or with luck, world war. Global conflicts had been started over far more trivial matters. The Runner knew this fact all too well. He had been present for every one of them. Oh, those were the days! But that was then, and this was now, and new triumphs awaited. The Runner strolled casually along the broad walk like any other tourist. This could well be the last time he would pass this way. Who knew?

He took the pedestrian route that ran past the Cathedral of the Holy Spirit. The sidewalks were teeming with camera-wielding tourists and local faithful, all hoping for a glimpse of Pope Benedict as he exited the church. While the Ecumenical patriarch, Bartholomew I, was officially the head of the Orthodox movement, and though Istanbul was his official seat of power, Benedict's position as head of the Catholic Church in Rome established him as a religious icon of unparalleled status. His influence rivaled that of many and exceeded that of most.

Once more, as it had done many times over the course of history, the office of Pope had flexed its considerable muscle, coming to Istanbul to treat with the head of the Orthodox sect. Recent, unprecedented violence throughout the world had created a state of panic among the people. Turkey and other Mediterranean nations, because of their geographical proximity to Rome, and because of Rome's long and storied history with the region, were targeted early on for assistance from the Vatican. The Catholic Church was reaching out to help stabilize an already volatile region, an ironic departure, thought some, from the Church's position in the third and fourth centuries. As was the case throughout history, there were those who viewed any Vatican overture with suspicion. The Runner took great pride in his many contributions in furthering that suspicion, though there were times when he thought he'd not done enough. Of course, that was all about to change. And what better place to correct that oversight? And what better target?

Istanbul's Catholic community was small by European and Western standards, but Benedict had not traveled to Turkey especially for their benefit. He had presided over the Eucharistic liturgy in the Cathedral of the Holy Spirit, with Bartholomew I and the Armenian Patriarch, Mesrob II, at his side. During Mass, Benedict told the tiny congregation, and more important, Bartholomew and Mesrob, that "the Church wishes to impose nothing on anyone, and merely asks to live in freedom, in order to reveal the One whom she cannot hide: Christ Jesus." The message seemed well received. Benedict, long considered a Catholic hardliner, was fast demonstrating an unexpected ability to bridge gaps between denominations and ideologies.

Already, more than one billion Catholics and millions of Protestants considered the man beneath the papal tiara the ultimate symbol of grace, obedience, and "faith made manifest." Additionally, the position, if not the man, held the power to galvanize much of humanity in the face of overwhelming adversity. That was reason enough to kill the man, but there were other more compelling reasons.

Killing Benedict would temporarily expose the Runner's whereabouts to an angry mob of Brethren and the ever persistent Host of Heaven, unwilling allies in the hunt for the Runner's head. The notion was almost laughable. The very thought of fallen angels and God's stalwart servants working toward a common cause was just to the left of ridiculous. Yes, both sides would descend on Istanbul with all the fury of the just and unjust. The diversion would provide Legion with the opportunity to strike unopposed at the real target in Jerusalem, the Temple Mount, without opposition. The Seventy-two would be released upon a world already seething in turmoil. It would be the beginning of the end. *The End of Days.*

The Runner made his way through the throng of sightseers and pilgrims to a nearby bench, taking great care to stay well away from the cathedral proper. He pulled a small bag of caramel popcorn from his jacket pocket and opened it.

I won't miss many things about this pitiful swirling ball of hydrogen, but I think I'll miss popcorn. And the sickly-sweet stench of war . . . cold ocean spray on my face . . . and beer. Yes, I'll miss beer.

A husband and wife passed by the bench, oblivious to the Runner's scrutiny. The woman hung tenaciously to the collar of a rambunctious youngster of perhaps five or six. The Runner smiled.

Ah! The children. I'll miss them most of all. I do so love to educate the young in the ways of the world and nature! But I would gladly give my life today just to see His face when it's all gone, and by my hand!

The Runner munched another handful of popcorn as he watched other wide-eyed people walk slowly through the square in front of the cathedral. Once, he'd dreamed of ruling over these cattle, thus taking his revenge on the Creator. Centuries of thwarted plans and machinations had brought him to the stunning conclusion that it was simply not to be. It had been a bitter pill, but swallowed nonetheless. Thus, he had settled on the best available alternative. A much better alternative, in retrospect. He would, with the aid of Legion, erase mankind from Creation. His first attempt had nearly succeeded.

By altering one of the Veils that connected the finite planes of existence, he had allowed the demon horde of Legion to cross over from the far distant plane of Sitra Akhra. Had the Veil remained open only a few minutes longer, the world of man would have been invaded by the lords of all demons, the Nine Princes. The fabric that held together the reality of this world would have crumbled beneath the presence of those demigods, and the plane of man would have imploded. Creation obliterated. Of course, the destruction would have claimed the lives of every creature on this miserable planet including his Brethren, the fallen angels who'd been cast out of paradise on his heels. A pity, perhaps, but a small price for the ultimate revenge. Oh, what he would have given to see the expression on God's face when mankind was snuffed from existence like some insignificant candle flame!

Now, he was hunted by the Host of Heaven, as well as many of his former followers. Some of the Brethren still clung doggedly to the belief that the Runner never meant to sacrifice them in his bid for revenge against the Creator.

Loyal but misguided fools that they are! I may even miss them. A little.

His supporters argued that the Runner surely harbored some great secret that would allow him to flood the earth with demonic allies, enabling the Brethren to finally slay the remnants of the earthbound Host. Afterward, the Runner would establish his dominion over all of humanity, and then force Legion into a subservient role.

What a circus that would be! Hairless monkeys under my left foot, and the demons of Sitra Akhra under my right.

Only, the meddling of a handful of bastard children from a long-dead age had salvaged the day in the eleventh hour.

How could I have underestimated them so badly? Regrettable, but little more than a delay of the inevitable. In a few days, I'll possess the instrument to seal my bargain with Legion. They will do for me what I cannot do for myself. And Heaven and Earth will be damned!

But this was a new day and a different game. An unknown benefactor, possibly another defector from the Host, had presented him with the means to ultimate victory. The Lesser Keys of Solomon, the rituals that bound the Seventy-two demon lords beneath the Temple Mount, now in the hands of Legion! Once the Seventy-two were freed, the Veils would fall, and all of Sitra Akhra would cross the barrier and lay waste to the plane of man.

I do wonder what the Creator must be thinking today. I wonder if He regrets casting me down to this miserable prison. If not, He soon will.

Finishing the popcorn, he stood up from the bench and looked about for a trash can. The nearest one stood across the walk, at the other end of the cathedral. The Runner considered making his way back through the milling pilgrims, then

changed his mind. He had no desire to pass that close to consecrated ground. Instead, he held the bag at eye level and blew
out a single puff of air. A woman passing by in that instant
screamed as the popcorn bag burst into brilliant green flame.
The Runner gave the startled woman an appraising glance and
a quick wink as he dropped the burning debris to the sidewalk.

"If you think that little trick was special, you should hang
around for my grand finale." Whistling a John Lennon tune,
he stepped into the moving stream of humanity and slipped
away into the heart of Istanbul.

chapter 16

Florence, Arizona

"We're being followed," said Brian King. "Two vehicles. A station wagon and an older-model white four-door. I'm pretty sure the four-door is a Lincoln, but the damn thing is riding the station wagon's rear bumper. Hard to get a good look."

Ronni Weiss checked the rearview and side mirrors. Interstate traffic had picked up, but she had no trouble spotting the two vehicles. All field operatives were given extensive training in defensive driving and vehicle identification. She accelerated and set the cruise control on seventy-five, the maximum speed limit.

"Highway Patrol, maybe? Or some other police agency?"

"Maybe, but I don't think so. And here they come, right up on our ass."

A tiny voice spoke up from the back seat. "It's not the police, and I wouldn't slow down if I were you."

"Okay, Miss Smart-ass, who's trailing us?" said Elliott. "Did you manage to signal someone? Is that it?"

Ronni tried to ignore the commotion and concentrate on matters at hand. This routine extraction, if there was such a thing, was going very badly. No one had seen them leave the Conner house, and the drivers of the station wagon and Lincoln weren't behaving at all like law enforcement. The contingency called for the extraction team to make for the regional airport in Tucson, but under the current circumstances, Ronni thought it was a bad idea. Too many things could go wrong on

the interstate. If the extraction turned into a running gun battle, she much preferred a deserted stretch of country road.

"Holy shit!" Elliott Glenn shouted and drew his handgun, a
powerful 10-mm Glock. He was staring slack-jawed through
the passenger-side window. From the back seat, Brian King
echoed Elliott's remark.

"What? What do you see?" said Ronni.

"I'm not sure," replied Elliott. "A hundred yards at three
o'clock. It looks like a big cat. And I mean big! About the size
of a fucking horse. But it moves funny. Not like a cat at all.
And its head . . . something's wrong with its head."

"Maybe it's one of those mountain lions," said Brian. "Are
there cougars in Arizona?"

"Could be a cougar . . . if cougars ran on two legs, you
fucking idiot. It's a demon! Look, it just dropped down on all
fours. Jesus Christ, look at that thing move!" Looking over his
shoulder into the back seat, Elliott glared at the woman and
her daughter. "One of yours? I swear to God, if I could prove
you summoned that thing, I'd kill you both where you sit!"

"Quit waving that damn hand-cannon around, Elliott, and
shut up," said Ronni. "And check the map and give me an ETA
to the airfield!" Over her shoulder, she said, "Brian, call Reading and apprise him of the situation. Tell him we're making a
run for the airfield. And tell him to advise our people there that
we're coming in hot."

Brian looked at Elliott as if he expected counterorders.
When none were forthcoming, he said, "Gotcha, Ronni," and
pulled the cell phone from his belt. He punched in the security
code and waited. A second later, he had someone on the line.

While Ronni waited for Brian to connect with Reading's
party, she said, "We're coming up on the Florence exit, Elliott.
How much further to the airfield?"

Elliott pulled a folded map from the glove compartment
and tossed it into the back seat. "Check the map, Lexis. I'm not
taking my eyes off of this goddamn cat-horse thing."

The well-dressed woman sitting on Kat Conner's left gave
the back of Elliott's head an icy glare, then turned on the dome

light and unfolded the map. She quickly found the town of Florence, and traced the route from the interstate exit to a small country road just south of Casa Grande.

"Twenty miles, give or take a quarter. It's a state highway, so the road should be in pretty good shape if this turns into a race."

"You can't take the goddamned exit, Ronni!" yelled Elliott. "This horse-cat thing is matching us mile for fucking mile, and it has the angle. It'll hit us about the time we reach the end of the off ramp."

"It's all moot," said Brian. "I got Reading on the first try. He said he already knows about our little convoy, and that we should forget the contingency and head for the original destination. He said we have help in front and behind, and to keep moving."

"I'm the team leader on this mission," said Elliott in a calm voice. "I have tactical command and by God, I'm ordering you, do *not* take that exit."

From the corner of her eye, Ronni noticed that Elliott now held the Glock in his lap with the muzzle pointed at her ribcage.

"Before you shoot me, keep in mind I'm driving along at eighty-five miles per hour. Now pull the trigger or shut the fuck up."

The Escalade was nearly parallel to the exit when Ronni gave the wheel a savage turn and crossed three lanes of traffic. Two drivers in the inside lane locked up their brakes and skidded sideways onto the shoulder of the interstate. A third vehicle, a refrigerated box truck, swerved to the left, narrowly missing the Escalade. The driver overcorrected and fishtailed back to the right, slamming hard into the first pair of cars.

Still driving at a high rate of speed, Ronni called out to the pair of Watchers in the back seat. "Check our 'six' for pursuit. And hold on. We're coming off the ramp, and merging with the state highway!"

Before Lexis or Brian could answer, Elliott yelled, "Fuck the six! The fucking demon is on top of us!" Not bothering to lower the window, he fired his 10-mm through the glass at the catlike monster. A pair of deafening explosions, in rapid succession, filled the interior of the Escalade. They were closely followed by the distinctive *pop, pop, pop* of Brian's 9-mm.

Ronnie wanted to look, but kept her eyes glued to the road-way ahead. She guided the Escalade past a slow-moving four-door sedan, and off the exit ramp, onto the two-lane highway. Just as the Escalade settled into the westbound lane, several voices melded into a disharmonious scream of terror. In that moment, something crashed into the side of the Escalade. The vehicle fishtailed across the asphalt as Ronni fought to maintain control of the steering wheel. She heard Lexis ordering the two Conner females onto the floorboard. Brian screamed out in pain as Elliott emptied his magazine into the creature. A split second later, Ronni heard the dull *pop* of another 9-mm, and let out a yelp of her own as a hot shell casing fell down the back of her black blouse.

The gunfire ceased as if someone had flipped an "off" switch and Ronni knew the battle was over. For several seconds the only sound inside the Escalade was that of labored breathing and a few muffled moans from the back seat. Elliott had reloaded and leaned out of the shattered passenger window, checking the roadway and exit ramp behind them.

"Check in, folks!"

"We shot the bastard up, but I don't think we killed it. Jesus, I've been doing this shit for a long time and I've never seen *anything* like that! It—it tore through the roof and door panels like a can opener!"

Ronni glanced up and noted the five long gashes in the steel rooftop. She white-knuckled the steering wheel to reduce the involuntary shudder that went through her slender body.

From the back seat Lexis said, "I'm good. Our guests are good. Brian is bleeding. Hold on while I . . . dear God. His arm . . ."

"What is it, Lexis? What's wrong with his arm?"

"It's—gone, Ronni. From the shoulder. His arm is gone!"

Jesus, help us! "Take your jacket and roll it up as tightly as you can. Then hold pressure to the wound. We aren't far from the airfield now. Maybe twenty minutes out. They'll have a paramedic on board the plane."

Elliott looked into the back seat, then turned to Ronni. "Hell, Brian doesn't need a paramedic," said Elliott. "He needs last rites. This is your fault, you know. I knew this would happen if you took that exit. I gave you an order, and you disobeyed. When King dies, and he will, you'll be tried by the Order for insubordination to a superior."

"Oh, shut up, Elliott. Before they can try me for that, they'll have to assign me to a superior!"

When Elliott failed to reply, Ronni figured the retort had sailed over his head or he was fuming and scheming on her demise in silence. She figured the latter was a safe bet. While she had never considered him more than an aggravation in the past, Elliott Glenn was now openly hostile. He might be an asshole, but he was a dangerous asshole, and her superior in terms of rank and seniority. Ronni would have to be very, very careful around him from this point forward.

"Oh, Jesus."

"What now, Lexis?"

"Brian's dead, Ronni. I tried. I really did, but he lost so much blood. So much . . ."

"Forget Brian!" said Elliott. "The Ford and Lincoln are still with us."

Ronni's grip on the wheel tightened again. She looked into the rearview mirror and saw the youngest Conner staring back at her. Looking past the girl, Ronni noted a pair of vehicles following at a distance. As she pressed down on the accelerator, she said, "Are you sure it's them?"

"No doubt about it. You can't mistake the headlights and grill work on either model. They closed the gap for a little bit, then dropped back. Shit! Another problem!"

"For Christ's sake, what now?"

"Red and blue flashing lights up on the interstate. Looks like somebody notified the Arizona Highway Patrol."

Her voice devoid of emotion or inflection, Lexis said, "Cell phones: Can't live with 'em, can't live without 'em, huh?"

Ronni cursed under her breath. The last thing they needed was law enforcement intervention. *We've got to shake them.* She quickly calculated the distance to the turn-off that would take them to the airport. Driving off-road would slow them down, but it might also give them an advantage. Ronni had grown up driving in the desert country surrounding Tel Aviv. She knew the hazards of partially hidden sink holes and small rocks that could rip holes in oil pans, break brake fluid lines, or puncture radiators.

The Escalade was equipped with an off-road package that included skid plates to protect the underside of the vehicle, and an over-size radiator. The Ford that followed them might have a similar setup, but it was worth a shot. She knew damn well an older-model low-riding luxury car couldn't keep up in the desert. Besides, the longer she kept to the asphalt, the better chance they had of being spotted by state or local police, and that would mean disaster. Off-road was the only real choice.

"Buckle up if you haven't already," said Ronni. "We're going off-road."

Immediately, Elliott objected, but she ignored him and punched the accelerator. By the time the truck and Lincoln realized the Escalade was pulling away, Ronni had increased her lead by nearly a quarter mile.

"Hang on!" She flipped the kill switch that would deactivate the Escalade's brake and tail lights, then turned off the headlights. She glanced up through the broken windshield and noticed the half moon. While not exactly bright, it would provide more than enough light. She steered the SUV across the eastbound lane and into the shallow ditch that bordered the shoulder of the highway. A hard bump, and the Escalade was off the shoulder of the blacktop and speeding across open desert.

"Well, look at this, will ya?" said Lexis. "The station wagon slowed down. He's watching us from the highway. But the damn Lincoln jumped the median and is coming this way. He just cut his lights and jumped the ditch. In fact, I think he's gaining. This son of a bitch is serious!"

"Let him bring it," said Ronni. And she meant it. The Lincoln had been on their ass since the beginning of the operation. No doubt the driver had been close enough to witness the bizarre cat creature attack the Escalade, and he'd also witnessed the muzzle flashes from at least three handguns. He knew the occupants of the SUV were heavily armed, and still he followed them into the desert.

"Lexis, get Reading on the phone. Tell him we're about fifteen miles out and still coming in hot."

Sam decided there might be more to Enrique DeLorenzo than met the eye. At first, the man had balked when Falco produced a magnetic police-style strobe light from one of the equipment bags. He protested, saying use of the light was illegal and would only call undue attention to them. Falco countered, pointing out the advantages of having police lights in certain emergency situations. *"People tend to move their asses out of the way when they see blue lights."*

"I still think it's too risky, Thomas, and we've got enough trouble with this operation without asking for more. But if you really think—"

Falco said, "Excellent decision, Rikki. Leave everything to me. We won't use the light unless we need a diversion." Falco gave Sam a quick wink before stashing the light into a small equipment bag.

The next surprise came when the three reached the top parking deck and Enrique's rental car turned out to be a sleek Lexus ES350. As they maneuvered through town, the ES350 looked and rode like a luxury executive car. But once they reached Interstate-10, Enrique released the beast within and the car performed like it was made for oval tracks instead of geriatric highway driving. The rich kid from Manhattan handled the car like he'd been road racing all of his life. Weaving in and out of traffic, he reached peak speeds nearing 120 miles per hour. He seemed to possess a sixth sense, knowing when to back off the accelerator, and when to push it. The miles separating Phoenix and Florence melted away.

As they neared the Casa Grande exit, Sam leaned back in his seat and closed his eyes. Mindful of Joriel's long-standing admonition, he was afraid to reach for *Kat*. At the same time, he was afraid not to. There was no doubt in his mind they were all heading into a shit storm and for the sake of his sanity, he had to know if his mom and sister were okay. He also wanted a firm fix on their whereabouts. He wouldn't have time to make a leisurely search of the area once they arrived at the airfield.

According to the phone conversation with Malcolm Reading, the extraction team, provided it was on schedule, left Sun City at the same time Enrique, Falco, and Sam pulled away from the hotel. Using Falco as a go-between, Sam warned Malcolm Reading of a possible ambush and begged Reading to turn the extraction team around and send them back to Phoenix. The man flatly refused, saying he had more than enough personnel to take care of any potential problems at the airfield, "including that punk Conner kid." Falco laughed as he relayed that message to Sam.

"Don't tell me. Reading belongs to the 'All Offspring are demon scum' club."

Falco chuckled again. "Yeah, you could say that. He's a good man to have around in tough spots, and a helluva strategist, but he has his head firmly entrenched in his ass when it comes to the Offspring. This little excursion serves several purposes. You'll have a chance to demonstrate your abilities for Rikki, and possibly save your life in the process. And in doing so, I get to shove it in Reading's face."

Enrique grunted and shot Falco a stern look that said, *Shut up about Reading. Now.* "Let's just get this over with. I've got some important news and I can't dispense it until I'm back in Boston. And that had better be tomorrow afternoon, at the latest."

Falco glanced at his half-brother. "What's the problem, Rikki? If it's the Hierarchy's position toward Sam and the others—"

"No," said Enrique. "This doesn't have much to do with the Offspring. Or maybe it does. At any rate, it's imperative I'm back on the East Coast tomorrow. I'll fill you in then."

"Fair enough," replied Falco. "I just thought that if this concerns Sam, well, if he's going to help us, he needs to know where he stands."

"Hey, I haven't said anything about helping you guys," interjected Sam. "I just said your little merry band of kidnappers is heading straight into a trap, and they're taking my mom and sister with them. I'll help you get everyone clear of the airfield if I can, but after that, you're on your own."

Before Enrique could respond, Falco said, "Looks like they had a little fender-bender up ahead. A bob truck and . . . a car, maybe two. They've got the damn exit blocked."

"There's another exit farther down," said Enrique. "We could take it and backtrack."

"It's ten to twelve miles out of the way," said Sam. "If we don't make this exit, we won't catch your team before they hit the airfield. It—it'll be too late by then."

"No problem, kid." Falco rolled down the passenger window and fixed the magnetic base of the strobe light to the roof. Before Enrique could stop him, Falco then plugged the cord into the dashboard electrical outlet. Immediately, blue light pulsed from atop the car.

"You've got the right of way now, Rikki. Just keep driving and don't look back."

As Enrique made his way through the tangle of vehicles, Sam closed his eyes and tried to push the image of the wreckage from his mind. Kat and his mother were only minutes ahead now. So was the Enemy. The stench of rotted meat and days-old cat urine had grown stronger with each passing mile. He focused on the mental image of his mother, but drew a hazy, distorted image. Shaken and unsure of the meaning, Sam dismissed the picture and focused on Kat. He could sense her presence only a short distance ahead, but her face remained a blur. Again, he breathed in and out, refocused his efforts, and tried again. Instantly, a landscape image, similar to a movie screen appeared in his head. He was looking into the front seat of a moving vehicle. A woman dressed in black battle fatigues sat behind the steering wheel while a man, also dressed in black, occupied the passenger side.

Sam shifted his view, and found himself looking at his mother. Or, rather, he thought it was his mother. Amanda Conner was an ashy shell of a person, unmoving, and unblinking. Startled, Sam realized he was seeing the interior of the kidnap vehicle through Kat's eyes. He immediately dropped the contact. A split second later, he felt a familiar probe, the signature so very similar to his own. However, while he had extended his senses with a deft touch, Kat had sensed his psychic presence and was reaching for him with all the mental energy she possessed. It was all Sam could do to block the psychic plea for help, and it nearly crushed his spirit. Kat had reached out for him, desperately needing assurances that help was on the way. And all Sam could do was shove her aside like some minor afterthought.

He wanted to reach for Kat, to reassure her that he was coming to end this nightmare, but he dared not make contact this close to a nest. It was one thing to draw attention to himself, but if Kat locked onto his psychic sending, or worse . . . if she answered, the Enemy would be all over her within minutes.

Sam wiped a tear from the corner of his eye. *And Mom . . . what's happened to Mom? C'mon, God, answer me! Get in the game, will You? We're about to die out in the middle of a friggin' desert. Nothing but scorpions, tarantulas, and a few mangy coyotes for witnesses. How's this supposed to help humanity? Couldn't You find a better spot to end this crap?*

Why here? Why not in New York? Or Paris or . . . Abbotsville, Tennessee? Maybe Falco lied and there really is a Veil nearby? Naw, couldn't be. I would know if there was. Maybe it's just that the Enemy is everywhere now, crawling over the planet like mutant army ants assaulting a giant picnic basket.

"How much farther, Falco?"

"I have no idea, Sam. I don't know shit about the area or the route. Malcolm's group didn't bother to brief me on the extraction plan. I'm not exactly in good standing these days."

"We've already been over that, Thomas," said Enrique. "As for the airfield, it's not much farther. I know the route."

"Of course you do, Rikki boy. I'd be shocked and amazed if you didn't." Looking over his shoulder at Sam, Falco explained. "Malcolm Reading planned the operation, but Rikki always has final approval. In fact, the Order doesn't make a move on this side of the planet unless our little Rikki knows about it first."

"Yeah, I figured as much," said Sam. "You know, the way you two act, a guy would think you're related or something."

Enrique shot Falco a sharp glance, and Falco chuckled. "I told you he was a sharp kid, Rikki." Over his shoulder he said, "That's because we are, Sam. We're related by creed, oath, and vision. Oh, and Rikki is also my half-brother."

As Sam digested that unexpected revelation, he again felt the mysterious psychic tickle at the periphery of his mental radar. Not enough of a signal to lock onto, but undeniable, all the same. Sam was sure he knew the source. And again, it was gone as quickly as it had appeared.

"Don't you fucking get it?" said Elliott. "They're after the Conner bitches! They've already cost us one man. I say we abort this stinking mission and just throw them both out of the vehicle and head for the plane. It's our only chance!"

The Escalade hit a rock. It wasn't much of a rock, perhaps the size of a football, but at sixty miles per hour such a jolt can shake the fillings from your teeth. Ronni swerved hard to the left to avoid a sink hole, then back to the right as a large patch of knee-high cacti came into view. Ronni kept her eyes focused on the terrain ahead. If she had heard Elliott, she was ignoring him.

"Okay, Weiss! Have it your way. But be ready to explain to Reading how a highly trained, highly motivated professional can screw up a simple extraction this bad. The entire Order will be interested in your explanation. All you had to do was follow the goddamn asphalt, but no, that would have entailed following *orders*! How the *fuck* did I get stuck with you, anyway? The bosses must have been checking out your rack instead of your credentials, huh? That it?"

For ten continuous, nerve-wracking minutes, Ronni had endured Elliott Glenn's caustic insults in silence. After suffering through all the abuse she intended to take, she formed a retort and made ready to fire. However, the usually reserved Lexis beat her to the punch.

"Elliott?"

"Yeah?"

"I'm sitting back here with my dead partner. Brian and I were a team long before you were ever recruited to the Order.

He had my respect and admiration. You are entitled to neither, and I swear before God, if you don't shut up, I'll cap your mouthy ass right here, right now."

"Oh, so now you're going all smart-ass on me, is that—" The words stuck in Elliott's throat at the familiar *schick-schick* of a semi-automatic handgun chambering a round.

"That's a good boy, Elliott," said Lexis. "You may be an egotistical dumbass but you're not entirely stupid, are you? Now, sit there and be very quiet while Ronni gets us out of this mess. Oh, and don't even turn around. If you do, I'll be the last thing you ever see. Got it?"

Ronni caught a glimpse of Elliott from the corner of her eye, and winced inwardly. He held his gun in a two-fisted shooting grip, and his eyes blinked furiously. She recognized the signs and knew Elliott Glenn was on the verge of a killing rage. She also knew that while Elliott had a reputation for a rattlesnake disposition, deadly and quick to strike, he really wasn't crazy. Or rather, he wasn't crazy enough to challenge Lexis as long as she had the muzzle of her own gun pointed at the back of his head. He would bear close scrutiny once they arrived at the airfield. For that matter, so would Lexis.

"Ronni?"

"Yeah, Lexis?"

"The Lincoln."

Ronni looked at Lexis through the rearview mirror. "What about the Lincoln?"

"It's gone. It was there, maybe fifty meters back, and now it's gone."

Finally! I knew the sonofabitch couldn't keep up with us once we went off-road!

"Great news, Lexis. He probably blew out a tire or smashed up his radiator. Stay alert, though. We don't need any surprises. Hey! Speaking of surprises, I can see the airfield beacons! Just above that ridge to the right."

Seconds later, the Escalade topped the ridge, and Ronni had to resist the urge to shout. A mere thirty meters straight ahead was the blacktop highway. Along the shoulder of the road, a sign read ASARCO AIRPORT—6 MILES. *The airfield! We made it!*

Ronni's elation was short-lived as something large and incredibly fast flashed in front of the SUV. Ronni turned on the headlights just in time to watch the fleeting figure disappear into the darkness. For a second, she thought it had been an optical illusion produced by a combination of mental stress and poor lighting.

"Oh, my God, what was that?"

"You saw it too?" said Elliott.

Ronni let up on the accelerator. As the Escalade rolled to an idle, she surveyed the route to the service road just ahead, then the darkness just beyond the range of the dual halogen headlights.

"I saw . . . something. Guys, I don't like this place. Keep your eyes open and your weapons locked and cocked."

For once, Elliott had no snide remark. Instead, his head was on a swivel and he kept watch on the surrounding area.

"Yeah, let's go. Just hurry."

Ronni shifted into reverse, and gunned the engine. The tires whined as they sought traction in the loose sand, and the Escalade moved backward at an agonizing crawl. They were fighting through the sandy loam, inching toward the road when the Conner child screamed.

As Ronni whirled about, she caught another blur of motion as a dark shadow the size of a very tall man ran alongside the Escalade and paused long enough to ram its fist through the remaining driver's-side window. Lexis fired her weapon twice at point-blank range, then watched helplessly as the creature, exhibiting no sign of injury, leaped forward a dozen meters and landed lightly on the road. She fired another three rounds for good measure.

The creature, a ghoulish apparition half as tall as the average man, rose up on long sinewy legs and stepped toward the vehicle. Long gangly arms that nearly dragged on the ground ended with gleaming talons like those of some giant raptor.

Ronni could still hear the screams of the Conner child, but the sound seemed distant, and unimportant. Leaving the vehicle and abandoning the "guests" was out of the question. Even if cowardice won out, to what end? She knew she could never outrun the creature. She also knew the steel and glass that surrounded them may as well have been cardboard for all the protection it afforded.

The thing that now stood directly before the vehicle defied adequate description. No genetic experiment gone awry or fevered nightmare could ever produce such an abomination. The gross, misshapen head vaguely reminded Ronni of that of a jackal. A long, slender neck connected the head to a grotesque, ill-proportioned body, seemingly constructed of nothing but strings of sinew and thick ropes of muscle. The creature grinned at Elliott from outside the van, revealing an impossibly wide maw filled with rows of gleaming teeth.

The creature took another step, crouched, then leaped high into the air, disappearing over the hood and windshield. Ronni crouched low in her seat, expecting to hear a loud thud on the roof at any second. To her right, Elliott blindly fired several shots through the steel-reinforced roof. He was dropping the spent magazine and reaching for another when the cracked windshield imploded, spraying the interior of the van with shards of tempered glass.

Elliott shrieked as slivers of glass peppered his face. He was still screaming as icy talons dug into his shoulder and dragged him forward, toward the jagged hole in the windshield.

Before Ronni could react, Lexis dove over the back of Elliott's seat, and jammed the barrel of her gun into the creature's eye socket. Six rapid rounds drove the creature back. Kneeling on the dented hood, the demon emitted an ear-splitting screech, then rolled onto its side and lay still. A shaken Elliott dropped back into his seat, wiping blood from his face.

Not stopping to drag the carcass from the hood, Ronni shifted the transmission into low and stepped on the gas. Seconds later, the Escalade, complete with its hideous hood ornament, crawled out of the sand, caught traction on the asphalt, and headed for the airfield.

With at least one of the monsters dead and the airfield in sight, Kat gave her mother's hand a gentle squeeze. But Amanda

Conner, the right side of her body covered in Brian King's blood, was unresponsive. She sat motionless, eyes unblinking, staring blankly ahead. The only sign of life was the occasional rise and fall of her thin chest.

Amanda hadn't heard the sounds of battle around her, or feel the gentle touch of her youngest child. It wasn't that she didn't love her children, nor did she want to leave them, especially not the bright and precocious Kat. It was just that she couldn't see or hear them. Not now, not ever again.

Amanda Conner had retreated from reality a final time, and in doing so, severed the delicate threads that once tethered her to an increasingly cruel and insane world. There was no lighthouse in the distance or a trail of bread crumbs that might lead her back to that dark and dismal world, a world with no future beyond a few days or weeks. And she was happy.

chapter 17

Rain from a rare southern California thunderstorm drenched the streets, and fury raged behind jet-black eyes, and sleek, sinewy muscles tensed and relaxed beneath coarse, brindle fur. Days ago, the pair of minor demons had been summoned to this most hated of all earthly places, a place of worship dedicated to He Who Lives Beyond, the entity men called God, or the Creator. Had the demons possessed the will to resist the order, they would have, for even close proximity to such a place was painful, even fatal.

However, they would be well compensated for their discomfort. The great demon lord Vetis had made a pact with one of the human weaklings who dwelled within the sanctuary. How foolish! Only a petty human made any kind of deal with demons and expected fairness in return. Now fully enthralled, the human had granted entry to all who served Vetis. For his faithful service, the human thrall would die a gruesome death. As would others. As would they all.

The demons watched with the patience of supreme predators as a car came down the rain-slick street and stopped in front of the stone and iron gateway that led to the sanctuary. A man stepped out of the car, opened a battered umbrella above his head, and ran the short distance to the sidewalk.

Fortune! The demons knew this man. He was the true object of tonight's hunt. This human didn't carry the bloodline of the hated Offspring. Blood of another sort coursed through his veins. This puny mortal carried the hereditary mark of the

Hunter, the bloodline of men who long dared to track and slay the demons of this world. As did his forefather before him, this man transgressed against the great demon lords. He was old and portly, and age had robbed him of most of his physical strength. And still, he was worthy of caution.

Dangerous. Dangeroussss!

They watched the man lock the tall iron gates behind him, then hurry into the building. The demons loped across the street and crouched beside the stone fence. The largest of the pair peered up into the overcast night sky and tasted the air with its split tongue. Dreaded sunlight was still hours away. Although both demons were capable of hunting by light of day, sunlight robbed them of some of their innate advantages. They preferred the night, a time when men were most sensory-deprived and vulnerable.

The larger demon fell to all fours and trotted away into the night. It sought another route, possibly a rear entrance, where it might not have to share its kills. The smaller of the pair, although by no means small as measured against a normal man, stood up on its hind legs, took hold of the gates, and gave them a violent shake. The gates rattled but refused to budge more than a few inches. The iron bars were too close together and in its natural form, the demon was too broad and muscular to squeeze past. It could shape-shift easily enough, but there was no need. It crouched again, gathering its long, powerful legs beneath it, then in a blur of motion, sprang up and over the eight-foot fence and onto the path beyond.

For several minutes, it stood statue-still, observing the massive structure ahead and testing the air for the scent of men. Instinctively, the demon knew the building ahead had been built long ago as a holy monument, a gathering place for the adopted children of He Who Lives Beyond. However, in all its many years of existence, the building had rarely fulfilled its intended purpose. Instead, it was an ostentatious testament to human vanity, a house of greed, wretchedness, and wanton debauchery; a house in which horrible acts had been carried out for, and by, the very guardians of piety. Vile, self-serving men dressed in black robes and white collars. To be sure, not all of these men were found wanting. But enough. More than enough.

The demon knew little about the priest who had just entered the building, but it could see and smell the aura that clung about him. This man was dangerous; a righteous human and utterly devoted to his Creator.

Dropping down onto all fours, the demon moved along the cobbled path, its senses scanning the building ahead for warding spells or protective talismans. Dependent upon the skill and foresight of the human shaman, blessed artifacts and talismans, combinations of various herbs, or other seemingly mundane items were given limited power over demons. As the demon studied the building, it sensed no such restrictions.

Now, sitting up on the sidewalk that surrounded the building, the demon searched for a suitable entrance. It could easily take down the wooden doors, or even sections of the brick and mortar wall if need be. However the noise would alert the prey and aid his temporary escape.

The demon scanned the second and third stories with keen eyes until it spied a narrow ledge that underscored vaulted windows. Above the ledge, at the rear corner of the building, the tattered edge of a curtain whipped viciously in the wind. Someone had left a window open on the second floor. The demon stood and stretched. It was time to conclude the night's business.

Bishop Gilbert strolled through the sanctuary as he often did when worry plagued his thoughts. He should be resting, conserving his strength for the trials ahead. With the escalation of horrors both home and abroad, the Watcher Hierarchy found themselves on the threshold of a new and terrifying era. The End of Days approached, and it could be many days before he found another opportunity to sleep.

He made his way down the aisle, inspecting the carpet for lint. Such duties were far beneath his station, or so he was often reminded, yet he maintained vigilance over the church like some worrisome grandmother watching over her kitchen.

Stewardship of God's house was a sacred trust, and not to be taken lightly. He frowned as he examined items atop the credence table. The water and wine cruets were out of place, and a thin film of grunge covered the lip of the finger bowl. Well, perhaps not grunge, he admitted, but *something* nonetheless. It was unacceptable, at any rate. He would address this lack of attentiveness with his aides, Fathers Carrington and Jimenez. The two priests would give all involved a stern lecture on cleanliness and the virtues of stewardship.

Gilbert refolded the towel, and placed it between the finger bowl and Communion Paten. He stepped back and examined the table with a critical eye, then smiled. *"Parfait, sans défaut!"*

His spirits lifted, he started for the study, whistling cheerfully. It was time to face that infernal beast, the fax machine. He expected any number of communiqués from his Catholic European counterparts regarding the recent events in Rome. No doubt he would have an equal number of messages from the Watchers and, hopefully, some good news from Malcolm in Phoenix. Good news would be a welcomed change.

So many monsters, so little time.

As Gilbert started out of the nave, he heard a loud *thump* on the second floor, just above his head. He froze, holding his breath, and strained to hear above the shrill wind that whistled outside the church. "Who's there? Come forward, now!"

After several seconds, Gilbert relaxed. The noise hadn't repeated itself, and he told himself such sounds in the old building weren't at all uncommon. The sanctuary was well known for its occasional groans and moans. Or it could have been the wind, he supposed, blowing open a window and toppling some item or other from a table or shelf.

But it had sounded so heavy! I really should summon Father Carrington and have him check out the upper floors.

Gilbert started again for the study and had nearly reached the door when a loud crash overhead shook dust and plaster from the ceiling. *That's damn sure not any wind*, he thought. *Must call the police!*

A sudden noise from the narthex stairwell froze him. When

Gilbert looked up, he was startled to see the outline of a man standing at the far end of the second-floor landing. Partially hidden in deep shadow, the man stood motionless. Watching. Waiting. Something about the man's presence struck Gilbert as terribly wrong, and the hair rose along the nape of his neck.

The bishop moved to his left for a better view, but succeeded only in losing sight of the man. *Impossible! There's nowhere to hide along that walkway, and I would have noticed had he entered one of the rooms. Where is he?*

After several seconds, Gilbert nearly convinced himself that he had imagined the entire incident, but then the man reappeared, standing just behind the second-floor railing. He was dressed in the tattered clothes of a street beggar, and appeared soaked to the bone. He smiled serenely at Gilbert, and something in that smile made the old bishop's skin crawl.

"You there! Come down from there this instant," said Gilbert. "I have already called the police, and they will be here any moment." *Forgive me this lie, dear God, but I'm afraid.*

The beggar turned and walked slowly along the balcony, his dark, feral eyes never leaving Gilbert, the gentle smile never leaving his lips. As the man neared the top of the stairway, Gilbert's blood froze in his veins. Something was terribly wrong with the scene, something he couldn't quite grasp.

As the beggar stared down from the railing, Gilbert recognized the inexplicable contradiction. While the man stood motionless, his elongated shadow writhed and undulated in an obscene fashion, multiple arms flailing in every direction.

Gilbert took a step back and genuflected. "Oh, my God, my Redeemer, behold me here at Thy . . ."

Before he could finish the opening of the prayer, the beggar peered over the railing at the bewildered priest below. The smile disappeared, replaced by an inhuman scowl that contorted and twisted the human features into a grotesque mask. Though the beggar's lips never moved, a snarl not unlike that of a wounded animal tore through the building, and he vaulted over the railing. Too startled to run, Gilbert stared in stunned amazement as the man fell. The laws of time and motion were suspended as the beggar tumbled haltingly through the air frame by broken frame, while his body underwent an impossible metamorphosis—from man to animal, and from animal to monster.

The creature that landed lightly at Bishop Nicholas Gilbert's feet was unlike anything he had ever, *could* ever, imagine. Rising up on long, muscular hind legs, it loomed over Gilbert, its mouth widening into a hideous, gaping grimace.

A familiar voice called down from the balcony above. "Simple. Devout. No ambition. Isn't that what you said of me, old man?"

Gilbert looked up at the smiling figure of Father Juan Jimenez. "What is this, Juan? Dear God, man, what have you done?"

"Done? I've done nothing, old fool. You brought this upon yourself. Did you think the lords of Legion wouldn't find you out? Did you really believe your pathetic pretend knights would be allowed to hunt Legion with impunity? Arrogant fool!"

Gilbert shook his head with profound sadness. "I—I don't understand. What could make men such as you forsake the Most High God? What bargain have you made with Satan?"

"Satan? Satan!" Jimenez began to laugh. He continued until tears streamed down both cheeks. While he enjoyed the grand joke, the demon inched closer to the archbishop.

"Satan is the Great Pretender, Gilbert! No, I serve a greater power, the greatest collective intelligence in all of Creation, old man, and it has nothing to do with Satan and his little band of cosmic brigands. The angels of your God are less than insects before the might of Legion! Does the name Zynth mean anything to you? No? A shame, that. Were you to live another month, you'd hear that name from the lips of all humanity as they petitioned my queen for their pathetic lives.

"But, really Gilbert, how could you know? The Church is your life and damnation. The Vatican took an intelligent, thinking man and turned him into a blind, foolish puppet. Sad. So sad.

"You know, I tried to warn you for years, Gilbert. Oh, yes. I found my way years ago, all the while playing the part of the obedient errand boy. But I did try to warn you, you know. Just last night I told you a storm was coming. Do you remember? You said I was foolish. Foolish! Well, the storm has come and the Hunter stalks his prey! But don't worry about your little operation here. We're going to take good care of Our Lady. The symbolism of the Church is a powerful tool, as you know. Perfect for fattening the sheep just before the slaughter. But as for the Watchers, I'm afraid the outlook isn't as rosy. We're going to destroy them from the inside out, and I assure you, it's going to be a very, very painful experience. Malcolm Reading has proven himself a master of subterfuge and destruction."

A storm is coming and the Hunter hunts ... Malcolm Reading is the Hunter! Merciful God, what have I done?

Filled with the horrible truth, Gilbert turned away, unable to look at his former aide. Instead, he locked eyes with the face of Death. As it advanced, the creature seemed to once again bend time to its will. Gilbert watched helplessly as row upon row of nail-like teeth descended in slow motion. The gaping maw closed over his face. Nose, orbital sockets, and jaw bones all shattered beneath incredible force, and the bishop's screams were garbled deep within the ruins of a once-refined face. As the creature dragged him away in the direction of the basement, Gilbert silently begged God for a quick and merciful death. As the demon fed, Gilbert's last conscious thought was that God, perhaps, no longer listened.

And the Hunter still hunts.

Malcolm reviewed the latest stack of communiqués from Los Angeles, Boston, St. Louis, and Rome. The news, for the most part, was interesting.

According the latest report, Arturo Giannini went missing shortly after transferring the recovered grimoire to his contact. A search of Arturo's premises revealed signs of a horrific struggle, though details were omitted or blacked out in the official report. Both Watcher personnel and the Rome Gendarmes suspected foul play.

I just bet they do, the idiots, thought Malcolm Reading.

Arturo's firearm had been recovered at the scene. It still had a full magazine. Apparently, Giannini had succumbed without firing a shot. Watcher intelligence believed his attackers were after the grimoire Giannini had recovered from the apartment of the recently deceased Father Raoul Acuna. That book, Malcolm knew, was of particular interest to a great many people these days.

Though scribbled by the hand of a madman, the book was a remarkable depository of knowledge: It contained the names and locations of Legion collaborators and thralls, at least six of whom were Watchers. Reading's eyes watered as he mouthed the names, refusing to validate their existence by giving them voice. Other information denoted major cities, minor towns, and other more obscure locations in which Legion maintained centers of power.

It also contained a list of potential targets, men and women, both secular and nonsecular. It came as no surprise to Reading that dozens of Watchers were marked for death, including Nicholas Gilbert. Katherine and Samuel Conner also appeared on the list, well above Gilbert's. In fact, Sam's name was listed very near the top of the "must die" column, sandwiched between a Cardinal in France and an American presidential hopeful. Legion clearly considered Sam Conner a threat.

According to additional reports, several chapters within the grimoire were nearly indecipherable, with meandering lines of confusing text, referencing obscure names such as *Keil*, *Baraniel*, *Seraph*, *Atuesuel*, and *Raziel*. A separate column contained names more familiar to Malcolm. *Buer*, a third-order demon, but one who commanded fifty legions of lesser predatory evil spirits; *Nazzikim*, a demon lord who toppled entire governments with little more than cunning; *Shabriri*, a bestial greater demon, commanding forty-six legions of lesser entities, and capable of both ethereal and physical manifestation; *Furefor*, another demon lord who carried the ancient title of Slayer of Heralds; and finally, at the bottom of the column, *Vetis*, a legendary demon lord of immense power, also called Devourer of Souls in ancient texts and by modern-day worshipers. According to several prophecies, it would be Vetis who corrupts the Holy of Holies and frees the Seventy-two greater demons imprisoned by Solomon. Many modern scholars were in vocal disagreement regarding that prophecy, as according to all known related texts, demons were forbidden entrance to the sacred temple.

Despite numerous disturbing elements of the book, the final pages contained the most curious text of all—the reference to the End of Days in conjunction with the great theft of the Lesser Keys of Solomon buried beneath the Temple Mount in Jerusalem.

Thanks in part to the cache of scrolls and other artifacts recovered from the Temple Mount during the Crusades, the Watchers had long been aware of Legion's ultimate motive: to destroy mankind before the Creator could gather His people. However, having the desire to destroy humanity was one thing. It was quite another to actually possess the tools and opportunity to follow through. The Runner had delivered the Lesser Keys of Solomon into the hands of Legion. It was only a matter of time now.

Reading placed the stack of reports into a ballistic-proof briefcase and spun the combination tumblers. Taking his cell phone from his belt, he punched in a speed-dial code, the number for Brian King. No signal. He dialed a second number and a voice answered almost immediately.

"Carter here."

Malcolm smiled. Edward Carter was a solid operator, if a tad not too bright. The perfect man to assist with the next phase of Malcolm's plan.

"Carter, this is Malcolm Reading. I want support out of here by tomorrow morning with the equipment vans, headed back to the Watcher safe house in New Orleans."

"Expecting trouble, sir?"

"Son, is that supposed to be a rhetorical question or just a plain, old-fashioned dumb-ass question?"

"Uh, n-no, I mean, neither . . . sir."

"Good. Now, after making the travel assignments, book commercial airline reservations for me and the remaining team members. First available flight for New Orleans, tonight."

"I-It's late, sir. There may not be another flight leaving Phoenix tonight."

Reading paused to relight his pipe, then said, "Carter, I don't care if you have to shit a Boeing 767; I better be on a plane, tonight!

Malcolm disconnected the call and resumed packing. He intended to be well away from Arizona by the next morning.

CHAPTER 18

Asarco Airfield, south of Casa Grande, Arizona

As Ronni approached the entrance to the private airfield, she hit the brakes and surveyed the damage in silence. The gate, a heavy-duty apparatus of welded tubular steel and mesh had been all but destroyed. The damage wasn't consistent with that inflicted by vehicular impact. This wasn't damage at all. It was carnage, the kind left in the wake of level-three tornadoes. The massive iron posts that had anchored the gate had been ripped from their concrete foundations and tossed about like twisted pixie sticks. The gate itself resembled a mesh washcloth, wrung dry and laid out upon the ground to dry. The creature that still adorned the wrecked hood of the Escalade was formidable in myriad ways, but Ronni knew even that monstrosity couldn't have dealt out this kind of damage. *What, then? What waited for them inside the airfield?*

"We can't sit here," said Lexis. "Too exposed."

Ronni nodded and took her foot off the brake. As the Escalade started forward at a slow idle, Elliott said, "Wait!"

Before Ronni could bring the SUV to a full stop, Elliott opened the passenger door and jumped out. He ran around to the front of the vehicle. Favoring his injured shoulder, he took hold of the dead creature's foot and dragged it from the hood. It landed on the road with a heavy *thud*. Elliott removed his fatigue jacket and spent a few seconds cleaning his hands. Afterward, he dropped the ruined jacket on top of the creature and climbed back into the vehicle.

"I don't know about you two, but I was getting sick of looking at that motherfucker. What *was* that thing, anyway?"

"I'm not positive," said Lexis, "but it fits the general description of a *demi-wight*, a minor demon associated with service to the demon lord Dagon, first catalogued in the fifteenth century by Sir Edmund Buhler, I believe. There have been increased sightings since 2002 and the corruption of the Abbotsville Veil, but they're still considered rare. *Demi-wights* have supernatural strength, speed, and agility, but no other discernable powers. They are low maintenance and very dangerous with limited intelligence, but excellent tactical skills."

"Well, aren't you just a fucking encyclopedia. And how is that bit of information supposed to help us deal with them?"

"Heh. In your case, I doubt that it will. However, if you'd bother to study the Order's codex, you probably would have recognized it. Most all of the minor demons are listed. You also would have known that *demi-wights* can be killed by small-arms fire."

"Fuck you, Lexis."

"Is your dick as short as your vocabulary?"

"Cunt!"

Lexis cracked a rare smile. "I'll take that as a yes."

"Knock it off, goddamnit!" yelled Ronni. "We don't have time for this!" The words came out louder than she intended, but the situation was desperate. Two demons had already attacked the party within the last half hour, leaving one Watcher dead and another wounded. From the look of the airfield gate, it was likely more waited just ahead. Then there was the small matter of the two vehicles that had followed them from Sun City. The station wagon had decided against following them off-road, but the Lincoln stayed on their ass until finally falling behind less than two miles from the airfield access road. It was probable either—or both—would catch up with them before the party could board the plane.

Once through the gate, Ronni coasted along the road, watchful for signs of the Enemy and the plane that would fly them to safety. Neither Elliott nor Lexis spoke, and the Conner child had ceased with those annoying sobs. Not that Ronni could really blame her. This entire ordeal had to be a nightmare for any kid raised in middle-class America.

At least the mother remained quiet. Not a sound from her since the extraction in Sun City. Odd, now that Ronni thought back on it. Not once did the woman ask who, what, or why. She didn't express any concern for her daughter, not in the way most mothers would, nor did she ever ask about her son. She simply complied with a deadpan expression, staring blankly through those soulless, soft brown eyes. *Maybe she already knew*, thought Ronni. *Maybe she knew and surrendered without a fight. Maybe she doesn't care anymore.*

A mile south of the wrecked chain-link gate, a pair of tall security lights illuminated the grounds around a long Quonset-style metal building. A short distance to the west of the building, a single-propeller Cessna rested on flat tires overgrown by desert brambles near a mobile fuel tanker. *Good God. What holds that plane together? It looks like a rusted-out beer can with wings.*

Ronni nosed the Escalade into a parking slot near the building and shut off the engine. After enduring the near wreck along the interstate, the bone-jarring dash over broken desert terrain, and running gun battles with demons, the sudden quiet was physically and emotionally painful. No sound. Even the chilly desert wind had subsided to a hoarse whisper, then died completely. Gathering clouds blotted out much of the light from the half moon and the darkness, much like the quiet, seemed to possess substance and mass.

Ronni checked her watch: *8:52 P.M. Where's the damn plane?* She checked the magazine in her Glock and made sure a round was chambered and ready to fire. Reaching under the seat, she pulled a flashlight from its charger.

"Lexis, call Reading and let him know we're at the field. And—and tell him about Brian. I'm going to have a look around. Keep a watch over our guests while I check out the building and lean on the horn if anything comes up."

"No good, Ronni. I tried and we can't get a signal out here. I think the clouds are screwing with the satellite."

"Shit! Okay, but keep trying, okay? We need to let someone know we made it this far."

Looking over at Elliott, she added, "You can stay here or come with me. Choice is yours."

"You keep forgetting who's in charge of this mission, Weiss," said Elliott. "We're not splitting up, so sit your ass down."

Ronni shook her head and smiled. "We're not out of the woods yet, Elliott, and I don't like surprises. Stay here if you like, but I'm checking out the place before the plane arrives."

Exasperated, Elliott said, "Look, Weiss, this isn't the Gaza Strip, and you're not Rambo. Just be a good little girl and pull the rig over into those shadows on the back side of the building. We'll just sit here and wait on the damn plane, together."

Ronni shoved the flashlight into a trouser cargo pocket and opened the door. As she stepped out of the Escalade, she said, "You know, you had me right up until the moment you mentioned Gaza and Rambo. Now, if you had said Ariel Sharon . . ." Looking into the back seat, Ronni added, "Kid, I don't suppose I need to tell you to keep quiet. No heroics. Do you understand me?"

Kat nodded and scooted closer to her mother. Ronni thought Amanda Conner seemed more dead than alive.

Ronni pushed the door shut before Elliott could reply. As she started for the building, the front door swung open. Reflex and training took over, and in a fraction of a second, the laser-guided red dot from her Glock, one of three, was planted on the chest of a short, slim young man wearing a goofy grin who was holding a cup of coffee in one hand and a small, plastic flashlight in the other. He wore a much too large powder blue jacket bearing the Asarco Mining Corporation logo on a dirty breast pocket. The name DUKE was stitched across the opposite pocket. Ronni nearly laughed out loud. The guy couldn't weigh any more than John Wayne's left leg.

Like the kid in that movie, Rudy. *Five feet nothing, and weighs a hundred and nothing*.

"Hey, hey! No need to get all gun happy," the man in the overalls called out with his hands raised in the air. "We don't keep any money around here. Just debit vouchers. Only drugs I got are some BC powders and a quart of Colt Malt Liquor in the frig inside." He gave Ronni a quick once over, noting the black fatigues, combat boots, and other assorted gear, before turning his attention to the others in the damaged SUV.

"Say, you folks military? Or police?"

A second red dot had appeared on top of the man's shirt, third button from the top. *Good woman, Lexis,* thought Ronni. For a fleeting second, she wondered what Elliott was doing. The prick probably had his laser pointing at the back of her head. She decided it was probably best not to think about it.

"Joint task force, DEA and ATF," she lied.

"Oh, well hell! That explains it. I heard all that racket a while ago. Thought it might be somebody hunting coyotes. But hell, if you're ATF, that sure 'nuff explains everything. No offense."

"None taken," said Ronni as she holstered her pistol.

The watchman looked past Ronni and seemed to notice the damaged SUV for the first time. He let out a low whistle. He turned the flashlight toward the front grill, though Ronni thought it did damn little good while they stood beneath the powerful floodlights mounted atop the building.

"No offense, girlfriend," said Duke, "but your rig looks like it was rode hard and put away wet. What did you do, roll it off one of them high spots to the east? The company did a lot of open pit mining around those ridges. Damn good thing y'all didn't roll off into one of those holes. Nobody would've ever found you."

Ronni wasn't sure what to make of the man. He had to be the real deal because no one could act that goofy. "No, we didn't roll it. It's a—a training vehicle for field exercises . . . like tonight."

"Well, kiss my ass and say you didn't! That's what y'all are doing out here? Training? Say! I bet you're waiting for that flight that's coming in. Is it a part of the training exercise too?"

"I'm sorry. Somebody should have notified you, but we were told the office was closed this time of night," lied Ronni again. The team had been told no such thing. In fact, they were told the field had been abandoned several years ago by the former owner. "When is the flight due in? Or is there more than one incoming plane tonight?"

The young man took a sip of his coffee and nodded. "Just the one, girlfriend. You know, we don't get many visitors these days. An occasional distress stop, you know, like a type-one FAA emergency. That's sort of my specialty, them type-one snafus. We keep a night crew, a couple of mechanics, and a shop flunky on staff just for those kinds of problems. They're back in the shop now, probably playing poker. The bosses depend on me to keep them on the straight and narrow, if you know what I mean. I'm not just a guard, you know. I'm sorta the ramrod of this outfit." Duke puffed out his anemic chest as he said this.

"Sometimes, some hotshot in a single-engine job needs emergency refueling. That's a little beneath my qualifications, but what the hell. A job's a job, right, girlfriend?"

He pulled a large key ring from his jacket pocket, dangling it in front of Ronni's face. "They have to go through me to get the fuel. Then I get his John Hancock on the old dotted line, and Mr. Hotshot is on his way to Vegas or Cancún. Rest of the time, I just keep the peace out here. You know, discourage poaching on company property, and keep out the trespassers and sightseers.

"Get a load of this! Sometimes, on weekends, I turn on the juice to the electric fence and go hide out near the front gate. Damn kids drive out here to drink all the time. It's funny as hell when one of them pisses on that fence. Seriously, I don't like being such a hard case, girlfriend, but it *is* a private airfield, you understand." Slapping the plastic flashlight holder at his side, he said, "And that's my job. I keep it private, if you know what I mean."

Ronni just nodded her head, unable to speak. The whole conversation was now a study in the juxtaposed worlds of the surreal and macabre. A dead field operative in the back seat of the SUV, another one injured and bleeding, and a pair of kidnapped "guests." And now, this self-important little Barney Fife wannabe, the embodiment of every night watchman joke

she'd ever heard. Ronni figured it was even odds that he carried a single spare battery for that flashlight in the breast
pocket of his shirt. After dueling demons, he was actually a
welcomed relief.

"The pilot is expecting us. It's all a part of the drill, you
know." She gave him a conspiratorial wink, which he promptly
returned. Checking her watch again, Ronni said, "In fact, our
man is running late. Have you heard from him?"

"Oh, we ain't got a radio out here. Well, we do have Oscar's
boom box, but we mainly use it for playing CDs. Dance mix."
Another wink.

Never taking her eyes from Duke, Ronni called out, "Any
luck with a signal yet, Lexis?"

"Not yet. Still trying."

Ronni gave Duke what she hoped would pass for a busi-
nesslike smile. "We're having a little trouble with our cell
phone. I don't suppose you have a phone I could use?"

"Well," drawled Duke, "I don't know. I mean, sure, we have
a land line, but it's for official business and all."

Ronni turned up the wattage on her smile, and Duke melted.
"Oh, hell, what with you being feds and all, we're practically on
the same team! C'mon in, girlfriend. Phone's inside the office,
far end of the building." He turned for the front door and motioned for Ronnie to follow.

"C'mon, now. And don't worry about your friends. Nothing ever comes around here except a jack rabbit or maybe a
skinny wolf."

Ronni started forward, nearly reaching the door when
Lexis called out, "Ronni! It's the . . . I mean, it's Katherine.
She's having a seizure!"

Sam leaned over in the seat and clutched his stomach. Since
exiting the interstate, the nausea seemed to increase with each
passing mile. Now that they were on the service road leading
to the airfield, a fire raged in his upper abdomen and threatened to burn its way through his thin chest.

From his first harsh dry heave, Thomas Falco peppered him
with questions.

"Sam? Sam, listen to me. Are you sick because we're getting closer to the nest? Is that it?" he asked.

Unable to talk, Sam nodded, then folded tighter into a ball with both arms wrapped tightly across his lower chest.

"Sign up ahead," said Enrique. "Six miles to the airfield. We'll be there in a few minutes, Thomas. Can Sam tell us what we're walking into?"

Falco leaned over the back of his seat and shook Sam's arm. "Sam? Listen to me, Sam. Do you know how many there are? I know it's tough. Hell, even I can feel something. Try, Sam. How many are there?"

Sam said, "Three or four lesser entities and at least two greater demons."

The car hit an oily spot on the asphalt and slid. Enrique yelled, "What was that?"

Looking out the passenger-side window, Falco said, "It looks like a *wight* that's been shot all to hell." Looking over his shoulder at Sam, he said, "Stinks like hell, huh?"

Sam nodded as he waited for the nausea to pass.

"Our young friend concurs, Rikki. It looks like your extraction team encountered some early resistance. We don't see many of those things in rural areas. They usually hunt in rundown metro areas, places where serious urban decay—or war—makes detection very difficult. Its usual victims aren't the kind of people one would miss right away. I killed my first in Kosovo after it ate half a United Nations reconnaissance team."

Sam struggled to a sitting position and looked out the rear window. The car was moving too fast and the distance now too great for him to see anything but a lump on the shoulder of the road. However, he didn't need to see the monster. He knew the smell. It was very similar to that of Drammach's soldier demons killed by Michael Conner in the old mine shaft beneath Abbotsville.

"Jesus!" said Enrique. "It looks like Sam was right. We're headed into a hornet's nest. What happens if we run into something we can't kill with a bullet?"

Falco scowled at his half-brother. "I told you this was a bad idea. You should have stayed behind."

"Don't worry," said Sam. "We'll find a way to handle whatever we encounter."

Enrique looked at Sam through the rearview mirror. "You sound pretty sure of yourself."

"Let's just say I'm highly motivated to stay alive," said Sam.

Falco chuckled, but it wasn't a jovial sound. Sam thought it was more akin to the growl of an angry Doberman. "Looks like you're feeling better, kid, and it couldn't come at a better time. We're probably less than four or five miles from the airfield."

"Yeah, I can feel them. The worst of the nausea is passing. I haven't had a signal hit me this hard since . . . I can't tell if we're going to find a dozen like those back there, or two or three of the larger variety. The signatures are all running together. Either scenario sucks, to be honest."

"Headlights in the rearview mirror," said Enrique. "One car, maybe two, trailing us now. They're coming up fast, so stay alert."

Sam turned around in the seat and looked down the long stretch of road. Definitely two vehicles. The first was the station wagon, with its duel headlights on low beam. The driver maintained a steady pace, neither gaining nor losing ground. Sam couldn't make out the second vehicle, but he thought there was something disturbing and familiar about it. *Just one more thing to worry about*, thought Sam. *You know, I really don't want to die today. God? You listening? Joriel? Anyone out there?*

Enrique added, "Lights up ahead, too. A red beacon sandwiched between a pair of bright whites. I think we're coming up on the airfield."

When Ronni reached the Escalade, she crawled into the back seat, where she found Lexis hovered over the petite, violently shaking form of Katherine Conner. The girl's mother, Amanda, hadn't moved from her stiff, upright position, but a single tear trailed down her cheek.

Lexis whispered, "Can you move Brian? It's too crowded back here. No room to work."

Calling for Elliott to give her a hand, Ronni ran around to the other side of the vehicle and opened the rear passenger door. She just managed to catch the limp body of Brian King as he slid out of the seat toward the ground. "Help me get Brian out of the way. We can move him into the back of the Escalade."

Though Brian had been a man of average height and weight, tipping the scales at just over 180 pounds, moving the limp form of a dead person was always a challenge. Fortunately, Elliott was a large man and fit, and Ronni was in excellent shape. Elliott took Brian's upper body and Ronni took his feet. Together, they moved the dead Watcher out of the passenger seat and into the roomy rear cargo compartment.

Night watchman Duke was still standing by the front door of the building, his vision partially obscured by shadows and the vehicle.

"Hey, what's wrong with your friend? He don't look so good. I got a cot inside if he needs to lie down. We got a first-aid kit, too."

That cracked Elliott up. "Not a bad idea you have there, Sheriff. Have you got a spare blanket? Our buddy's a little cold."

Under her breath, Ronni whispered, "You're a sick fuck, do you know that? If you're not careful, Lexis's going to take your head off."

"Nothing to worry about, Duke," Ronni called out. "He ate some bad oysters back in Apache Junction. Just a little sick to his stomach. It'll pass after he lies down for a little while."

Elliott let loose another belly laugh. "Oysters. Apache Junction. You're a real fucking comedienne, aren't you? As for Lexis, well, it ain't my fault she had a thing going with old Brian. Boy must have been hung like a Clydesdale the way she's acting. You might want to tell her to get her head out of her ass real quick, Weiss. We're not out of the shit yet. In fact, if you ask me, none of us are going to live out the night if that plane doesn't hurry up. I mean, we might have a chance if we dump our guests. Hell, you saw how those shit-eating cat-monkeys were acting. It's the Conner bitches they want, not us!"

Ronni shot Elliott a look that spoke volumes and relieved any need for conversation, then hurried back to Lexis and Katherine. When she crawled into the back seat, the girl was still shaking, though the severity of the seizure had lessened.

"How is she, Lexis?"

"I'm fine, Ms. Weiss," whispered Kat. "I'm not really having a seizure."

Surprised, Ronnie looked at Lexis. Lexis shook her head in warning and whispered, "Keep it down. The kid spotted something you need to know about. I'll keep an eye on the watchman while Katherine tells you . . . Hey, what's Elliott doing?"

Over her shoulder, Ronni watched as Elliott engaged Duke in conversation. After a moment, the watchman shook his head and took another sip of his coffee. Elliott reached over and thumped Duke's breast pocket with a finger. Duke seemed surprised, as if he hadn't been aware of the item in his pocket. Laughing, he produced the pack of cigarettes and a cheap lighter and handed them to Elliott.

"He's just bumming a smoke, Lexis." Turning to Kat, she said, "Now, what's this all about, girl? And no games. I'm not in the mood."

"Screw your moods, lady," Kat said in a matter-of-fact manner. Ronni almost slapped the impertinence from the kid's mouth, but Kat continued. "Don't expect any sympathy from me or my mom. If you think you're having a bad day, you should see it from where I'm sitting. And it's about to get worse. Now, do you want to know what I saw or not?"

"Go ahead, kid, and hurry up."

Kat raised her head a fraction, making sure Elliott still had Duke engaged. When she saw that he did, she smiled. Keeping her voice low, she said, "At least Mr. Snickers is good for something."

Ronni started to ask who Kat meant, then realized the girl was talking about Elliott. "That blowhard is no friend of mine, kid."

"Yeah, right. You two looked pretty chummy when you

kidnapped me and my mom. Anyways, don't go in that building with Duke. If you do, you won't be coming back."

"What do you mean?"

"He's been lying to you from the moment you began talking. First off, he told you only rabbits and wolves came around at night. There aren't any wolves in this part of the state—haven't been for years and years. I was born and raised within fifty miles of here, and I should know."

Ronni sighed, "Is that all you got, kid?"

"Not hardly. I heard him say you could use his phone. You need a telephone pole and phone lines to make that work unless you really believe they laid fiber optic cable out to this shack. Now look over at the northeast corner of the building at the telephone pole and tell me what you see."

Ronnie did as Kat suggested. All the lines were disconnected from the building and tied in a tight bundle near the top of the pole. *No phone, no radio.*

"What else, Kat?"

"His flashlight. No batteries in it. I noticed when he made a show of shining his light on us. And just now, he dropped it when he took the cigarettes from his pocket. The flashlight hit the pavement and bounced. Flashlights with batteries in them don't bounce six inches off the ground. What kind of security guard has a flashlight with no batteries?"

Ronni stared at Kat for a couple of seconds, then eased her gun from its holster. Lexis already held her gun in a shooter's grip. "Are you sure you're a kid and not some forty-year-old little person?"

"My name is Kat."

Acting nonchalantly, Ronni looked back toward Duke. Elliott was lighting another pilfered cigarette. *Keep smoking 'em, big guy.*

"Okay, Kat. Anything else I need to know?"

The girl nodded. "Yeah. If you had gone into that building with Mr. Duke, you'd be dead right now too. I probably should have let you go considering the way you and your friends have treated me and my mom. But the way I see it, you're the lesser of two evils. Keep your distance from Duke. If Mr. Snickers isn't careful, Duke will hurt him real bad. And I'm not too sure I really care."

Despite her growing anxiety, Ronni smiled at the thought of the diminutive security guard giving any of the Watcher operators any trouble. "Don't worry about Duke, kid. We can handle Duke and a dozen more just like him."

"Sorry, Ms. Weiss, but you can't. He's one of the Enemy. You *do* know what that means, don't you? They wear human disguises sometimes to trick people. My brother can spot them a mile away. I'm not that good, but I know one when I see one. Duke knows I'm in here and he'll eat you and a dozen more just like you just to get to me. His kind hates my kind, you know." Once again, there was that matter-of-fact directness.

"This place is full of them. The Enemy, I mean. I don't know as much about them as my brother does, but I can feel them when they get this close, and I know this place is crawling with them. Unless my brother finds us very soon, we're all going to die. I don't want to die; do you, Ms. Weiss?"

Before Ronnie could answer, a shrill scream was answered by the sharp report of gunfire.

chapter 19

The airfield

Enrique, Falco, and Sam approached the building just as the first shot rang out from somewhere near the front of the Quonset hut. As they rounded the rear end of the Escalade, they saw a pair of men locked in physical combat near the front door of the building. Actually, only one, the larger of the two combatants, was a man. He wore the black battle dress uniform and gear of a Watcher tactical operator. His opponent, smaller by several inches and nearly a hundred pounds, was both more and less than any man. A particularly cunning species of demon, the Zaxt straddled the prone Watcher and rained blow after heavy blow down upon the man's head.

The man in black thrust the muzzle of his handgun into the creature's face and pulled the trigger several times in rapid succession. Instead of reacting as though he'd just been shot through an eye at point-blank range, the monster stood and pulled the Watcher from the ground. A punch to the chest propelled the Watcher across the lot and through the wooden door of the Quonset hut.

To the left of this one-sided battle, two women, one dressed in similar blacks-ops gear, took up firing positions near the front tire well of the SUV. The woman in black lay across the hood and fired several rounds at the demon in human clothing as it shrugged off the heavy slugs and moved forward.

"That's Lexis!" said Falco.

"Do something fast or your friends and my family are dead!" cried Sam.

There was no moment of hesitation on Enrique's part. The Boston-born-and-bred Ivy League lawyer responded by stomping on the accelerator, turning the Lexus into a two-ton guided missile aimed straight at the greater demon in human disguise.

As the car sped toward the demon, Sam held his breath. Would the demon see the car coming and avoid the collision? Would it rush the women inside the Escalade and kill them all before Enrique and Falco could effect a rescue?

Within the short span of a few seconds, Sam had most of his answers. The demon was tunnel-visioned, its attention focused solely on the prey inside the Escalade. It never saw the Lexus until the moment of impact.

The front bumper struck the demon at the knees and pitched it up and over the car. Enrique came to a tire-squealing halt. Muttering something beneath his breath, Falco kicked open the door and slid from the seat to the pavement like some great jungle cat. Sam marveled at the big man's grace and agility. When Sam opened his door, he heard the steady *pop* of small-arms fire and the shouts of a man calling for help.

The demon arose from the pavement, oozing blood and green pus from a dozen wounds. One of its legs, broken in at least two places, bent in the opposite direction, giving the creature a birdlike gait as it moved toward the Escalade again. A second woman exited the Escalade with a smoking pistol in her hand. She dropped an empty magazine, inserted a spare, and kept firing.

Sam started for the Escalade, then staggered to the side as Falco pushed past him, firing at the wounded demon with measured control and deadly accuracy. From the other side of the Lexus, Enrique came at the monster with a shotgun held high. He fired, and a great gout of flame erupted from the shotgun's muzzle. The slug took the demon high in the chest, just left of center, and spun it around.

From the corner of his eye Sam saw a winged figure leap from the roof of the metal building and slam into Enrique, knocking the shotgun from his hands. The weapon skittered across the pavement and came to rest underneath the Lexus.

Sam ducked beneath another swooping creature and started for the gun.

As he bent down to retrieve the riot gun, Sam realized another vehicle had pulled into the parking lot, and a dual set of high beams was bearing down on him. *Deer in the headlights.* Feet rooted to the asphalt, unable to think or move, the tired old cliché echoed in Sam's mind. For the first time, he understood its meaning with perfect clarity as the oncoming station wagon closed the gap. It wasn't fear. Not exactly. Sam thought it was more like dread coupled with simple resignation, the knowledge that there was no place to run, no place to hide.

As the car bore down on him, an alien voice invaded his head with overwhelming force. *Move, Sam! Now!*

Jarred from his temporary paralysis, Sam leaped back, tripped, and fell hard to the pavement. The oncoming station wagon swerved in a final effort to hit him, but the front bumper missed Sam by inches. A shrill scream of pain erupted from Duke as the car's left front tire crushed the greater demon's remaining good leg. As the station wagon roared past him, Sam had a good look at the driver. Little Stevie had made good on his promise. He had come back, and this time he brought friends.

The station wagon never slowed as it struck the rear end of the Lexus, driving the smaller, lighter car across the parking lot and into the side of the fuel truck. The resulting explosion sucked the oxygen from the air and sent a swirling fireball hundreds of feet into the night sky. A split second later, chunks of metal, tires, and other burning debris rained down on the parking lot, casting a hellish glow over the barren landscape.

"Sam! Sam, over here!"

Sam stood and shielded his eyes from the intense flames with an arm. Through a dense, oily cloud he saw the outline of a small girl waving to him from behind the now smoldering Escalade. She stood dangerously close to the burning wreckage.

"Kat, move back! You're too close to the fire!" *Where's Mom? Why isn't she with Kat?*

Kat yelled again, but most of her words were drowned out

by random gunshots, and the screams of men and monsters. Sam broke into a run, then fell hard to the pavement as his left leg buckled. Acute pain knifed through his knee, and for the first time, he noticed the bright crimson stain that surrounded the jagged tear in his jeans. He struggled up onto his good leg and was limping toward his sister when he noticed a thick plume of smoke rising out of the Escalade's broken windshield. Kat screamed and motioned toward the burning SUV. And Sam understood.

He willed his injured leg to bear his weight as he limped forward. He traveled a single step before falling a second time. From the pavement he watched helplessly as long, slender fingers of flame now sprang up in a dozen places throughout the battered vehicle. Within seconds the interior of the SUV was ablaze from dashboard to the rear cargo area.

Great sobs wracked Sam's body as he grieved for his mother. Kat had called out, begging him to save their mother. And he had failed. Just as he had failed Michael Collier.

"I'm sorry, Kat. I'm so sorry!" he cried. He reached out a hand to her, yelling her name, when something exploded underneath the Escalade. Kat crouched low to the ground, both arms shielding her head. A hulking silhouette appeared at the girl's side and snatched her from the ground. Tucking her beneath a massive arm, the figure retreated behind a curtain of noxious smoke.

"NO! You can't have her!"

Strong arms surrounded his chest and lifted him effortlessly. He heard his name called from some far distant place, but he wasn't interested. His only thoughts were of his younger sister. Nothing else mattered. Nothing. Crazed by grief, he fought the man or monster that held him, almost breaking free until something clipped him hard on the chin, turning his legs to jelly and sending his mind spinning in dizzy circles.

As he felt himself being dragged along, he recognized Falco's familiar voice.

"Sam, we've got enough trouble. Quit fighting me! We've got to find shelter, now!"

"Little Stevie . . . he has Kat!"

"First things first, kid. We regroup, then we get your sister! C'mon."

It wasn't as if Sam had any choice. Falco lifted him with one arm and jogged the short distance to the Quonset hut.

The demons had retreated beyond the glow of the burning wreckage and the security lights. Enrique had somehow reclaimed the shotgun and stood with his back to the front door, covering the debris-littered lot. To his left, a man and woman, both wearing black commando gear, were reloading their handguns. The man, nearly as tall as Falco but thicker through the chest and shoulders, was having trouble feeding ammunition into a magazine. Long, bloody furrows crisscrossed his face and scalp. He hugged his left arm close to his side, an indication of a chest or rib injury.

The black-clad woman wasn't in any better condition, bleeding from at least a dozen places. However, the expression on her face gave no hint that she either knew or cared. The other woman, the one who had exited the now destroyed Escalade with Kat, was nowhere in sight. Maybe they got her, too. *God, I hope so. Serves the bitch right for killing my mother!*

Enrique looked as if he had been run down by a bulldozer, but his eyes were alight with defiance. As Falco and Sam reached the group, Enrique held the door open with his foot and motioned them inside. "Hurry up. I'll hold the door until everyone is inside. Move!" No one argued.

The metal building, easily the length of a football field, was actually a line of connected airplane hangars and smaller room. The office just inside the front door was lit by a single lamp, sans the shade. The rear wall of the room had a doorway but no door. Sam stared into the dimly lit hangar area, as shadows shifted and danced along high, vaulted ceilings and corrugated walls. He was acutely aware of the Enemy's presence. Of all the evil places Sam had ever seen, this building ranked second only to the cavern beneath the well house in Abbotsville. *Why so many? Why here?*

"We have to find my sister, Thomas. Little Stevie took her. We can't stay in here anyway. There's too many of them."

Falco looked out onto the parking lot from the room's single window. He held his pistol as if he expected an assault at any moment. Enrique had taken a position near the door and looked equally alert.

"Did you hear me? I said—"

"Easy, Sam. We'll find her, I promise, but first we've got to regroup. We can't go stumbling around in the dark, kid. Hell, I don't think you can make it to the front door on your own two feet at the moment. When the plane arrives, we'll have some extra hands to search the place, so just sit tight."

"Let him go. Hell's gonna freeze over before I go after him," said Elliott. He sat on the floor against the east wall, well away from any of the room's three openings, counting his ammunition. It didn't take him long.

The woman in black said, "Our mission is to put that girl and her . . . to put her on the plane. I'll be damned if I let those monsters have her."

Elliott laughed. "Weiss, you crack me up. I've got one full magazine and six rounds in another. That's twenty rounds, and I'm betting you and Falco don't have that many combined. I figure there're six, maybe seven rounds in that shotgun. That gives us a grand total of fifty rounds of ammunition between us."

"So, what's your point?" said the woman.

"Damn, you're dumber than a sack full of hammers. My point is we must have shot up half a case of ammo during that clusterfuck, outside. Did you see any dead bogeymen? Did we kill even one of the bastards? No. Now, if we can't knock down a single goddamn demon after shooting up a couple hundred rounds, explain to me how in the hell we're going to survive out there. And if you think I'm going to waste even one shot to save that fucking kid, you're crazy as hell."

Falco looked over his shoulder and said, "You look like shit, Elliott. Maybe you should conserve your energy and shut the fuck up."

"Screw you, Falco," muttered Elliott.

Enrique kicked a broken chair across the floor. "Knock it off, both of you. We've got to work together if we're going to salvage the mission and get out of this alive. Did anyone see what happened to Lexis?"

"I lost sight of her right after that station wagon plowed into your rental car," said Falco.

Enrique shook his head. "We'll have to get a team in here to search for her as soon as the mission is complete."

"Mission?" said Elliott. "What mission? This operation is over! Tell him, Weiss. Tell us all how you and Lexis fucked up this gig."

"I said knock it off, Elliott." Enrique turned to the woman. "I know you through your personnel dossier. I'm Enrique De-Lorenzo." Nodding toward Thomas, he said, "This is Thomas Falco. As the senior operator in this group, he'll take tactical command. I suggest you follow his orders if you want to live to see tomorrow. That goes for you, too, Elliott."

Nodding in Sam's direction, Enrique finished the introductions. "That young man sitting over there in the corner is Sam Conner. I think you both know of Sam."

Sam noticed the woman give Falco a quick, thorough appraisal, one peer to another, and gave him a brusque "you'll do" nod. Yet, when she turned to him, her eyes locked with his, and she stared as if searching for . . . something. After a couple of uncomfortable seconds, she gave him a slight nod, and turned back to Enrique. Sam wasn't sure if she'd found her answer or not.

"It's a pleasure to meet you, Mr. DeLorenzo. My name is Ronni Weiss. I'm attached to the Bravo group. I've heard much about you, and about Mr. Falco. We owe you one. Things were about to get ugly when you showed up." Across the room, Elliott smirked, but Ronni ignored him and continued.

"We were followed almost from the time we left Sun City, so I probably should have known they'd have a welcome committee waiting on us."

"Followed in? Why didn't you follow the contingency plan and make for Tucson?"

"Yeah, smart-ass," said Elliott. "Tell us all why you ignored protocol and drove us into this goddamn ambush."

Ronni turned to Elliott and gave him a cold, crooked smile. "If you address me one more time in any fashion or by any name or title other than 'Weiss,' I'll put a bullet in you." Elliott started to object but dropped it when Ronni turned her attention back to Enrique.

"When we discovered we were being followed, Lexis notified Malcolm. He instructed us to make for the Casa Grande airfield."

"Malcolm knows better than that!" said Enrique. "The contingency plan would have taken longer, but at least we had people on the ground in Tucson."

"Maybe so, but those were the orders. Frankly, at the time I agreed with them. I didn't want an open gun battle on an interstate. You know how cops are about shootings. Everyone in their right mind runs a hundred miles an hour away from gunshots, and cops run twice as fast toward them. We really didn't need to meet any police while we had our guests, so taking the Casa Grande exit seemed like a sound calculated risk.

"Right after we talked to Malcolm, we were jumped as we came off the Casa Grande exit ramp. Never saw anything like it. It jumped on top of the car and smashed the windshield and side glass. That's . . . that's when we lost Brian King. If it hadn't been for Elliott, it probably would have gotten us all, and you've no idea how it pains me to admit that. We were attacked a second time when we reached the airfield access road. Lexis managed to kill that one."

"Any idea where she might have gone during the fight?" said Falco. "I saw her behind the SUV when we first pulled into the lot, but lost sight of her a few seconds later."

Ronni shrugged. "No idea. One minute she was there, and the next . . ."

Sam had heard enough. "Maybe she's dead. Too bad the demons didn't kill you all. None of you deserve to live." He was surprised to hear himself speaking in a calm, clear manner. He felt neither calm nor clear. He felt like crying. Or screaming. Or curling up into a ball on the floor and dying. He felt like cursing God for allowing any of this to happen in the first place. His entire family was gone now. Because of these people, he would live the rest of his life alone. He felt like killing them all.

"You let my mother burn to death. You let a monster take my sister. Modern-day Templars. What a fucking joke! Inept bunch of cold-blooded killers, that's what you are, and I hold you all responsible. You'll pay for what you did to my family. Count on it."

Elliott laughed and started up from the floor. "Mouthy for a punk half-breed, aren't you? If I were you, I'd be careful not to let my alligator mouth overload my hummingbird ass, demon boy."

"And if I were you, I'd be praying he doesn't roast your ignorant ass."

All eyes, including Sam's, turned to Falco as the big man stepped away from the window and took up position in the center of the floor.

Elliott looked at Sam and his lip curled in a sneer. "You're getting soft, Falco. If you had done your goddamned job, the fucking kid would be dead, and we wouldn't be having this conversation!" It was obvious to everyone in the room that while Elliott's words were directed to Falco, they were aimed at Sam.

Falco replied in a calm, cold tone. "Go on, loudmouth, keep pressing your luck. I've seen what the boy can do. In fact, he saved my life. Better yet, just leave him out of this. If you've got any more remarks for the kid, you can just bring them straight to me. You might not like the outcome, but at least you'll probably still be alive when we're done. Probably."

The temperature in the room dropped by several degrees and the only sound was that of the fire raging outside. Elliott glared at Falco for a few seconds, before averting his gaze. He made a show of rechecking his handgun while Enrique and Ronni turned uneasy attention back on the doors and windows.

Sam didn't look at Falco. The man's little speech didn't let him off the hook. After all, Falco had been sent to gun down the Conner family in cold blood. Thanks to Elliott and Ronni

Weiss, at least a third of the mission was now complete. His mother was dead, burned alive only a few short yards from where he now sat. Only thoughts of Kat prevented Sam from experiencing a complete emotional meltdown. Sam knew that with every passing second, Kat's chances for survival diminished exponentially, and he would need these people in order to save her. But then what? The Watchers had their own plans for Katherine Conner. He leaned back against the wall of the tin building and held his face in his hands.

After an awkward silence, the woman in black continued with her report to Enrique.

"We . . . I mean, I decided to cut across the desert, figuring the two tail cars couldn't keep up with the Escalade off-road. Only one of them followed us, an old beat-up Lincoln Continental. The second car, that station wagon, stayed with the highway. That's why it came in late."

The mention of a Lincoln immediately caught Sam's attention. *Lincoln? Couldn't be* that *Lincoln! No way. Could it?*

"Are you sure it was a Lincoln? What color was it?"

Ronni looked at Sam, then back to Enrique. "I—I'm not—"

"It's a simple question, Ms. Weiss. Think," said Sam. "Was it a white Lincoln? A late-seventies model with a bullet-nose aerial on the rear truck deck?"

"It stayed behind us and I was driving," said Ronni. "I never got a good look at the car. But, yeah, I remember Lexis saying it was an older car, white, mid to late seventies. Why do you ask? Do you know the car or the driver?"

"Yeah, kid, let's have it," said Elliott. "Someone you know? A friend of yours maybe?"

Sam shook his head. "I can't believe this is happening. I just can't . . ."

Falco walked over to the corner of the room and knelt beside Sam. He laid a light, tentative hand on the boy's shoulder, as if he fully expected to draw back a bloody nub.

"What's the deal with the Lincoln, Sam?" he asked softly. "Look, if you can tell us anything that might help, anything at all, this would be a damn good time to come out with it."

"Oh, we go way back." Sam leaned back against the tin. This

was the final straw. He was already nearly helpless against the monsters that waited beyond the walls or the monster that had taken Kat. Without Joriel, he had no chance against the driver of the Lincoln. He had always thought of the white Lincoln as Death riding a pale horse, a force too terrible, too destructive to ever defeat. The white Lincoln was a predator. Perhaps it was something less than the angels, though Sam wasn't even sure of that. He *was* sure the driver of the white Lincoln was something far different from any mere demon. It might be possible to out-run him, at least for a short time, but defeating the monster in the machine was beyond Sam's power.

"Yeah, I know the car. I don't know the driver, but I know the car. It followed me every step of the way from Arizona to Tennessee. Somehow it knew where I was going, and the route I would take. It anticipated every move I made. Tried to run me down a couple of times, but I finally shook him in Knoxville. Or maybe he just let me go. I really don't know. Anyway, I haven't seen it since leaving Tennessee. I barely managed to stay alive with Joriel's help. Without her, I'm dead. It's finally going to get me. At least I won't be alone anymore.

"What's a Joriel?" asked Elliott.

Oh, stop that sniveling, cousin.

Startled, Sam looked at Falco. "What did you say?"

Falco shook his head. "You're not going to die on my watch, kid. I promise you that. Are you sure you can't tell us anything else about the Lincoln? Don't dismiss anything as too trivial."

My, my, cousin. The big fellow is persistent, isn't he? Perhaps wound a bit tight about the axle, that one is, but you can trust him. At least as far as you can trust any of your kin. Poor fellow carries the Blood, you know. Of course you do. It's he who has no idea. Think of the marvelous irony, cousin! Oh, the stories I can tell you about our Mr. Falco! But enough of him. Let's you and I have a little chat.

Sam had spent the better part of twenty years with a voice in his head. Rather, sometimes it was a voice. On many occasions, it was the sound of wind chimes, sometimes gentle and many times not. Still, in whatever form it chose, it was the unmistakable sound of Joriel, his guardian angel. But this voice was entirely unlike that of Joriel. Obviously male. Youthful sounding, almost glib, but with a quality that spoke of maturity. Cultured, and with a distinctive accent. British? Welsh? Maybe Scottish without the rolled *R*'s. Most of all, it was the clarity of mind-speak that took Sam by surprise. It was as if someone spoke directly in his ear, rather than in his head. The words carried an unmistakable stench of demons.

You're no cousin of mine, pal. Who are you and what do you want?

The immediate response was the sound of strong, gusting winds over a crashing waterfall. Not harsh exactly, but far different from the delicate tinkle of wind chimes favored by Joriel.

Now, is that any way to speak to a relative, however distant? It may interest you to know that I've created quite a stir by taking an interest in you and your sister. On the other hand, my own kind have no idea regarding my true intentions. I've been told it's unhealthy to carry too many secrets. Drains the spirit and muddles the mind. Yes, I think perhaps it's time to share them with someone. Interested?

Sam looked around the room. Elliott was still sulking against the far wall, while Enrique, Falco, and Ronni discussed strategy and tactics. The words were so clear and distinct, Sam was amazed that no one in the tiny office heard them.

You're one of the bad guys. Why in the hell would I want to talk to you? You've tried to kill me, for Christ's sake. Unless maybe you're offering to bring back my sister. Me for her. Do we have a deal?

Laughter, loud and genuine. *My dear Sam, you are priceless! First, let us straighten out a few misconceptions. Yes, I suppose I'm technically your enemy, that's true. But I'm not the Enemy. Besides, our differences are more the result of birth. After all, one cannot choose one's parents.*

Parentage aside, I mean you and your sister no harm. Not now nor in the foreseeable future. We won't discuss the past. What's done is done, and we'll both be better off if you don't hold a grudge. Let bygones be bygones, that's my motto.

Sam fumed at the man's audacity. *Okay. I'll let it slide . . . when pigs fly out my ass!*

The ghost ignored the comment. *As for Katherine, I don't have her, Sam, and if I did, I'd return her to you, no strings attached. I want you together and unharmed. In fact, I've known you much longer than these so-called servants of God you keep company with, and I've done you and your family far less harm. Care to debate that last point?*

Look, I don't know who or what you are, replied Sam. *For all I know, you're the fucking devil incarnate and you're responsible for this whole goddamn mess.*

More laughter. *Me? The cause of all this? You flatter me, cousin! You may be reasonably sure of four things in this life: First, the Devil is real, and second, I'm not him. Third, you may also believe me when I say that cretin, the Devil as you call him, is largely responsible for this current impending catastrophe. And it is a catastrophe, Sam, of a magnitude beyond your comprehension.*

I don't know what you're talking about, dude, so feel free to elaborate. I can comprehend a hell of a lot. But we could debate that all night, so I'll concede for the sake of expediency, said Sam. *You've named three. What's the fourth thing I can be sure of?*

That I'm neither man nor God. Nor am I an angel, demon, or Offspring. That doesn't leave many choices, does it? You're a bright lad, Sam. I'm sure you'll figure it out before our association is finished. And please, call me Henri. With an i."

A demon by any other name still smells the same, said Sam. *Call yourself anything you like, Henri with an i, but my radar is never wrong, and right now it says you're a bad guy. I'm going to ask you one more time. What do you want, and where is my sister?*

Such impatience, Sam! But then, you're young. Still, I would think the angelic genes would have tempered your human abruptness.

Now it was Sam who laughed. Aloud. Seeing the puzzled looks from Falco, Weiss, and Enrique, he shrugged. "Inside joke, folks. Sorry."

To the new ghost in his head, he said, *You haven't met many angels if you think they're down with the patience thing. And I don't have time to enlighten you. Now get the fuck out of my head while I go look for my sister.*

Sam, you really should clean up your language. Profanity is the crutch of the uncouth and uncultured, and you're neither. A little rough around the edges, perhaps, but nothing that can't be corrected with a little time, effort, and the proper influences.

Now stand up and make your way to the door. I'll be there in less than a minute, and we'll go get your sister. Katherine isn't far. In fact, the worm you call Little Stevie has her at the far end of the hangar. He also has some of his associates with him, and they're waiting for you. She's just the bait. You're the real target.

If you want to survive this, you must be careful and follow my lead. Afterward, we'll discuss how you can repay me. Hurry, now. The sooner we're done with this little inconvenience, the better. More important matters require our attention. And do let her know we're coming, cousin. There's no harm in that now, and she needs the reassurance.

That was all Sam needed to hear. He knew he shouldn't trust the ghost in his head, this Henri with an *i*, but the situation left him little choice. He was speaking to the one being he had long feared more than any other, but if there was any chance to rescue Kat, any at all, Sam was willing to take the risk.

Using the wall for support, Sam stood and tested his injured leg. He bit through his bottom lip as incredible pain shot through the wounded joint, but the knee supported his weight. He limped toward the door, nudging past Enrique. He expected Falco to stop him at the door, but the big man watched him with a passive expression. As Sam stood in the doorway, he exhaled and emptied his mind, then quickly refilled it with a mental image of Kat. He took a deep breath, exhaled again, and *reached*.

Kat? He felt her presence and knew she'd felt his *reach*, yet she couldn't or wouldn't respond. He tried again.

Kat. Answer me! I know where you are and we're coming to get you.

S-Sam. Mom is dead. The short, despondent reply tore at Sam's heart. The words were spoken in a wooden monotone, dead, devoid of either hope or emotion.

Hang on, Kat. We're coming. Just hang on.

Don't come here, Sam. Go away. Just . . . go away and never come back.

Sam cursed beneath his breath, and opened the front door. He started through when Falco caught him by the upper arm. "We've been through this, Sam. You know you can't go out there. It's not . . ."

Perhaps it was the look in Sam's eyes, or the expression on his face. Whatever the reason, Falco halted in midsentence and released his hold.

"You know where she is, don't you?"

Sam nodded. "Yeah. They're holding her in a room at the far end of the building. The thing that killed your partner has her, and he's waiting for me. If you want to help, wait until you hear the commotion, then come through the hangar, all the way to the end. If you don't want to help, stay out of my way, Mr. Falco. I won't be responsible for anything that happens if you try to stop me."

"You can't be serious, Sam," said Enrique. "Even if you know her exact location, you can't possibly believe we can get to her without additional help. Hell, I'm betting it's you they want, and if I'm right, you're playing right into their hands. Please. Be patient. The plane is overdue now. It can't be much longer. I swear, Sam, if you'll just wait a few more minutes, we'll figure out a way to get everyone out of here, including Kat."

Sam shook his head. "Mr. DeLorenzo, I don't give a damn about the rest of you. You people are the reason we're in this mess. I'm going after my sister and if you're half as smart as you think you are, you'll stay out of my way."

Outside, the wreckage of four vehicles burned, casting an eerie orange glow over the bleak desert landscape. Glass cracked and shattered from the intense heat, and expanding metal popped glowing rivets. The station wagon, now little more than a burned-out hull, exploded anew as the crankcase caught fire, and a geyser of orange flame exploded through the floorboard and out through a jagged hole in the partially melted roof. The fire in the Escalade was dying out, and its smoldering remains sent black smoke curling up into the night sky. *A funeral pyre. Nanna, Dad, and now Mom, all gone. It's just me and Kat.*

When he reached the corner of the building, Sam paused for a moment to get his emotions under control, then sent out a weak mental probe. It didn't require much effort to confirm the mysterious Henri's assertions that the demons waited for him at the end of the hangars. There weren't as many as he first thought. Three or four at most. Despite Elliott's long-winded contention that bullets had little effect, at least two demons nursed serious, perhaps fatal wounds.

Sam also sensed the alien presence of the monster who called himself Little Stevie. Stevie's psychic signature was unlike those of his allies. Whatever he was, he wasn't a demon, and he sure as hell wasn't human. Sam thought he might have encountered such an entity once before, but the time and place wouldn't come to him.

As he tried to remember, a pair of headlights appeared at the far end of the runway, sandwiched between two rows of bright blue landing lights. The driver revved the engine and Sam recognized the throaty rumble of heavy horsepower. Two years earlier, the roar of that engine was usually followed by the sound of squealing tires, Sam's racing heart, and the frantic pounding of Sam's sneakers on pavement. Even now, the sound aroused long-buried fears, and every instinct demanded he run. Run far and run fast, and never, ever look back. But the time for running had passed.

Hold steady, cousin, I'm on the way. Oh, and you may want to tell your knights errant their aeroplane is very near. Three to four minutes out. The pilot encountered some rather radical weather over New Mexico.

"Now, how the hell does he know *that*?" muttered Sam. While the notion seemed ridiculous, Sam had an odd feeling Henri knew what he was talking about. He banged against the tin wall of the building with his fist and a second later Falco's upper body leaned out through the window, his handgun held in a two-handed shooting grip.

"What's wrong, kid? You okay?"

"I can hear a plane," lied Sam. "It's still a few minutes out, but it's coming in fast. If we time this right, we can grab Kat and get the hell out of here before the Enemy knows what hit 'em. If you want to help, wait for my move."

Falco cocked his head to the side and winced, apparently still feeling the effects of the concussion. After a moment he said, "Kid, I don't hear—" He stopped in midsentence when he saw headlights speeding across the runway and bearing down on the building.

"Sam, run! Get back inside!" Falco raised the handgun, placed the laser dot on the driver's side of the windshield, and slowly squeezed the trigger.

Sam knew in an instant. "Don't shoot! It's Henri!"

Falco pulled his shot at the last possible moment and fired just above the tinted glass. Before he could say anything, the white Lincoln Continental roared into the front parking lot. The driver braked hard and spun the steering wheel. The car turned broadside and yawed toward the building before finally coming to rest, the passenger-side door scant inches from Sam.

As Sam opened the door and started inside, he called out, "Just be ready to move when you hear my signal!"

"Wait, kid! What are you going to do? What signal?"

Sam started to answer, then paused and ducked his head inside the car. He said something to the driver, then stood up and yelled out over the roof of the car to Falco. "I already told you, I'm going after my sister. As for the signal . . . I'll get back to you on that. Just be ready!"

chapter 20

Sanctuary

The attack was well coordinated, swift, and sure. Orus screamed once before a second ball of green *quickfire* struck him in the back, lifting him from his feet and slamming him into a nearby live oak. Kiel *reached* for Nathan as he scanned the tree line surrounding the glade with supernatural senses. *Assassins! Three. Maybe more. They're trying to block me.*

Nathan's response was short and direct. *Coming!*

Across the glade, Orus knelt at the base of the tree, holding both hands to his ruined face. His clothing had been burned away and much of his once pale, flawless body was now the color of ashy charcoal.

For Kiel, there was but one course of action. He charged across the clearing, determined to save his sworn enemy–turned–unlikely ally. Orus had come to Sanctuary of his own free will, without promises of redemption or coercion. He brought with him an offer of aid at a time when the Host was in dire need. Of course, any use Orus may have had as an informant was now over and done. His second great act of treachery had been discovered and his life was forfeit. That, however, did not negate the fact that he had tried to help the Host. That alone was worth some measure of consideration. More important, Orus had been granted safe conduct and now he lay dying. True, he was some feet beyond the boundary of Sanctuary, but in Kiel's mind, that was a minor detail. Another Fallen dared bring death to this consecrated place, an ancient shrine to the faith, courage, and valor of humanity. It was an intolerable transgression.

From somewhere to Kiel's right, another ball of *quickfire* hissed through the air, vaporizing trace molecules of water in its path. This time, however, Orus was safe. Kiel was the intended target. He somersaulted at the last possible second, narrowly avoiding the mass of molten cosmic dust. The back of his shirt burst into flame and he grunted in pain as the skin of his back sizzled like bacon over an open flame. Behind him, a magnificent cypress tree exploded as *quickfire* struck wood and superheated the sap within.

The boundary of the Sanctuary was only yards away, and Orus but a few steps farther. Orus was kneeling now and waving Kiel away. His eyes had melted in their sockets from the first attack. However, to celestial beings, eyes and other external features were little more than aesthetics. Sight and other senses were supernatural in nature and not subject to physical injury.

"Stay close to the ground, Orus! I'm nearly . . ." Kiel stopped in midsentence. The air behind Orus shimmered, then parted, revealing Kokabel, a fallen Domination possessing considerable war prowess. Powerful, but no match for Kiel in a duel. Of course, dueling wasn't Kokabel's intent. An instant later, he was joined by Mulciber. Mulciber carried a short sword of green fire, a terrible weapon in the hands of any angel. And Mulciber wasn't just any angel.

"Stand down, Kiel," said Kokabel. "We came for the traitor. Our quarrel can wait for another day."

Kiel smiled. "You know I can't do that. I gave Orus my surety of safety for as long as he remains in the glade." Kiel looked around for the remaining assailants. He knew there were more. The air was thick with the taint of the Fallen.

Orus, still holding his hands to his face, rolled onto his back and groaned. His lips and tongue were charred, rendering him incapable of speech. Like all of his kind, Orus could heal his wounds . . . eventually. Given the nature and extent of the damage, Kiel figured it would take a couple of days, perhaps longer. Orus had come very close to being unmade, the angelic equivalent of death everlasting.

Using the gift of mind-speak, Orus said, *Let them . . . take me, Kiel. I would rather die than endure this agony a moment longer.*

"You should listen to him, Kiel," said Kokabel, clearly enjoying the moment. "You don't have the advantage of consecrated ground now. You really should pay more attention to your own boundaries." He nodded his head toward Orus. "The Brethren have some questions for that one, and he'd better have some answers. You know, he isn't half as smart as he likes to believe. We've known for some time that he's been playing both ends against the middle. It was just a matter of waiting for him to contact one of the Host. I don't know what he's told you, but it really doesn't matter at this point. We'll know soon enough, once he's back among the Brethren.

"You and Nathan are quite a team, but there are only the two of you and five of us. Outnumbered again, as usual."

Kiel knew it was no bluff. The *quickfire* attacks had come from both the left and the right of the glade. There were at least three hidden Brethren watching him from cover at this very moment.

Two.

Kokabel's smile disappeared. "Tell Nathaniel to stop that, or we'll be forced to rescind our offer to let you live."

Kiel chuckled. Nathan's new tally couldn't have come at a better time. "Oh, be serious! You know Nathan as well as any of the Brethren. Do you really think he'll listen to me at a time like this? I suggest you leave now, and live to hunt another day."

Mulciber took a step forward, his eyes darting back and forth from Kiel to Orus. "Enough, Kokabel. Let's just kill this little fuck and be done. And Kiel, I really hope you try to stop me. I've been waiting to kill you for a long, long time."

One.

"Damn you, Nathaniel!" yelled Kokabel.

That's what you get for bringing Heralds to do a Power's work. Sort of like bringing a knife to a swordfight. Idiot.

Kiel burst out laughing. He wanted to stop, he really did. Laughter would only infuriate Mulciber and that was never a good idea, but Kiel couldn't help himself. Nathan had eliminated two of the assassins in less than a couple of minutes. Now it was two against three. Still poor odds, especially considering Mulciber was one of the three. The fallen Domination was an extremely dangerous adversary. He also had a reputation for taking human servants—men, women, and children enthralled by supernatural means. Kiel's contempt for Mulciber bordered on pure hatred.

Kokabel and Mulciber exchanged glances, and Kiel knew the standoff was drawing to a close. It was time to spell out the situation in terms that even a berserker like Mulciber would understand.

"So, here we are and it comes to this. If either of you so much as twitches an eyelid, I will kill you, Kokabel. And make no mistake, I *will* kill you. Of course, that gives Mulciber or the coward in hiding a free shot at me. Which will give Nathan a free shot in return. Regardless, you won't be around to see the outcome. Leave now or I will be the last thing you ever see in this world."

"Suits me, Kiel," said Mulciber. "Kill him and let's get on with it. Hell, I never liked Kokabel, anyway, and I absolutely detest you. After you're both dead, I get to kill the traitor and Nathaniel. Or should I call him *Nathan*? He's even adopted the human version of his name. He has no pride. No shame! And neither do you, you little cocksucker, else you wouldn't be guarding a planet filled by fucking semiliterate monkeys!"

Kiel tensed for the coming attack. Kokabel was ready to cut his loses and run, but Mulciber's eyes were glazing over, and his face was flushed. He was working himself into a battle rage, succumbing to the blood lust. There was no turning back.

Kiel whispered an ancient prayer. "May God not weaken my hand." As Kiel uttered the last syllable, the ground shuddered beneath his feet and he stumbled forward until he stood astraddle of the prostrate Orus.

Bewildered, he thought, *Earthquake? Here?*

Nathan's voice, a rich, deep bass filled with triumph and

jubilation, boomed across the glade. "And then there were none!"

Kiel smiled.

Nathan emerged from the northern tree line, covered in liquid gold, the life blood of angels. Much of the blood was his. All three of the fights had been in close quarters, chest to chest. Two of the assassins, a Herald and a Throne, had been badly overmatched and died quickly, felled by swift thrusts of Nathan's deadly onyx blade. The third assassin-in-hiding was far more formidable—a Dominion and seasoned warrior named Procell.

While Nathan was a warrior by design, created to protect humanity against the likes of Legion and the Fallen, Procell was a killer by choice. In the early years of exile, she had discovered the thrill of murder. She also realized she was very, very good at it. The Runner often used her to stalk and kill certain troublesome members of the Host. Procell seldom failed.

After finishing the Throne, Nathan crouched in the thick honeysuckle that lined the banks of the bayou and scanned the area with supernatural senses. It was a dangerous tactic, one that could lead an adversary directly to him. In fact, Nathan was counting on that very thing. The remaining assassin was skilled in stealth and hiding. While Nathan was a consummate warrior, his tracking skills weren't nearly as refined. His only option was to draw the Enemy to him.

It worked.

Homing in on Nathan's scan, Procell followed the signal back to him by assuming ethereal form. Now she stood scant feet away from the thicket, dressed in her customary outfit of black boots, slacks, and turtleneck. She held a curved kris knife in her left hand. Nathan recognized the weapon. Its blade was made of obsidian, green-and-black–banded glass, formed millions of years earlier when volcanic magma bled into some nameless sea. The knife glowed with a sickly yellow aura, concrete evidence that it had been imbued with the poisonous taint of the Fallen.

Taint was a physical manifestation of a fallen angel's spiritual corruption, vile and toxic in the extreme to the just and righteous. Only a handful of weapons in all of Creation could inflict mortal wounds upon the Host, regardless of the wielder. A blade imbued with the taint was just as deadly in the hands of a human child as it was when carried by one of the Fallen. Procell's tainted kris was such a weapon.

Few of the fallen angels ever attempted to create a tainted weapon, as the process involved surrendering a measure of their life essence, a portion that could never be regained. Procell had decided long ago that such an added advantage in battle was worth the sacrifice.

Nathan stood up and stepped out of the tangle of vines to Procell's right. He could have rushed her from behind and possibly scored a fatal blow, but that wasn't his style. He preferred that the Fallen know who it was that sent them to the Void. Especially this Fallen.

"Hello, Procell. You're looking very well today. Well, except for the cheap turtleneck. Although the color does match your teeth."

Procell *tsk*ed and said, "Heh. And I thought petty insults were beneath the Host."

The muscles in her jaws twitched as she self-consciously ran her tongue across her discolored teeth. Over vast eons, many angels had sampled debauchery and other human vices. Although angels were immune to the physical requirements of humans—food, water, sleep—they weren't above partaking in certain pleasurable experiences of the flesh. It was widely rumored that Procell had cultivated a taste for milk of the poppy in any form, but with a preference for raw opium and heroin.

Nathan smiled. In preparation for the duel, she had unconsciously dropped the illusion of physical perfection, and the manifestations of daily drug use were all too obvious. Procell was vain to an extreme, as were most of the Fallen. Yet her voracious appetite for opium had exacted a heavy toll on her appearance, and she knew it. Nathan's sophomoric joke about her teeth had scored.

Procell quickly recovered from the wound to her pride.

"I'm glad to see your sense of humor is intact, Nathaniel, considering these will be your last few seconds among the living. Will you *reach* for assistance, or do you have the courage to duel me?"

Nathan smirked. He had no intention of *reaching* out to other members of the Host. For all he knew, an army of Fallen and Legion were waiting for a similar summons from Procell. Neither Nathan nor Kiel would risk the lives of the Host by summoning them to a potential ambush. Of course, Nathan would never admit such a fear to Procell or any of the Fallen.

"It doesn't require any courage to crush the life from a cockroach, Procell."

"Very well. Any last words before you join the ranks of the unmade?"

"Go ahead, Procell. You won't be the first among the Fallen to die by my hand today, and you'll likely not be the last. You might, however, be the most inconsequential."

The final goad was a lie. Nathan knew the unmaking of Procell would be a considerable victory for the Host. It was also one goad too many for the ill-tempered Procell. Snarling like some great feral cat, she launched herself across the narrow distance that separated the two. No foreplay. No testing of defenses or probing for weaknesses. Her tainted kris was poised for a killing strike.

Nathan was stronger than Procell by a wide margin, but she was quicker. He couldn't hope to fence with her and survive the duel. The air around Nathan shimmered as he slipped into ethereal form. Using the mind-gate, he moved several feet to his left and reappeared in physical form. All angels, the Host or otherwise, had the ability to mind-gate. However, as with all "gifts," it came with a cost. The change from flesh to ethereal form and back again would drain some of his strength and speed for a short time. Nathan had once described the negative effects of mind-gating as "melting here and reforming there, all in the same instant." The maneuver was always risky when performed in the heat of combat and this instance was no exception. The transformation had occurred at the speed of thought. Yet, however fast, Procell's agility proved its equal.

The moment Nathan reverted to his physical form, Procell's kris stabbed toward his eyes. He twisted his upper torso and felt the flat of the poisoned blade brush past his nose. Procell reversed the stroke, aiming for his throat, looking for a critical strike that would end the fight quickly. She nearly succeeded.

Nathan anticipated the move and ducked beneath the singing blade as it sliced through the air millimeters above his head. From a crouched position, he delivered a thunderous palm heel blow to her midsection with his free hand. The Kiv snaked forward, aimed at the point where the crown of Procell's head should be. The strike missed badly. Instead of folding over from the blow to her midsection and exposing her head for a swift, clean kill, the impact from Nathan's open palm lifted Procell from her feet. She landed several yards away, temporarily out of range of the Kiv.

Now the battle shifted from tactical to strategic. They circled each other warily, looking for minuscule openings in the opposing defenses. Nathan had won hundreds of duels by engaging enemies in battles of attrition, absorbing moderate damage in order to inflict critical blows in return. That tactic wouldn't work against Procell. While Nathan held an advantage in terms of strength and stamina, she neutralized those attributes with unparalleled agility. Nathan carried the Kiv, a weapon made of radioactive cosmic dust capable of shoring through granite. Procell used the tainted kris, a more than adequate equalizer. The poison within the blade could turn a scratch into a potentially mortal wound, festering and melting supernatural flesh from bone. Rarely did an angel survive an encounter with a tainted weapon. Today, the overall advantage went to Procell.

Procell made her move as Nathan shuffled to his right, catching him in midstep. She darted forward and jabbed the kris at Nathan's groin. Nathan shifted the Kiv to intercept and deflect her thrust, but the onyx blade found nothing but air. He realized his mistake too late.

Procell reversed the blade and delivered an arcing blow to Nathan's throat. He twisted away from the blade, bending his back into a near impossible position until his vertebrae threatened to snap. The kris sang as it sliced through the air. Nathan returned the stroke with one of his own, missing the intended mark by a wide margin. Procell was no longer in front of him. Now she stood across the small clearing. Smiling. Nathan thought he had never seen a more awful expression. And he knew what it meant.

Regaining his balance, he looked at the tainted blade in Procell's hand. One edge of the weapon glowed with liquid gold, the life's blood of angels. Nathan raised a hand to the side of his neck. When he drew his hand away, his fingers were slick with molten gold.

Procell wore a broad smile. "It's only a matter of time now. That hulking body will weaken rapidly. Your reflexes will diminish, then fail you completely. The legendary strength and stamina of Nathaniel will surrender without a whimper to the taint.

"You know, had you taken the wound on the arm or leg you might have survived another day, provided, of course, you lived through the duel. But now . . . well, I suppose it's all rather academic." Procell shrugged. "I'd say you have a couple of hours, maybe less. Certainly no more. A couple of very painful hours, at that."

Nathan took a step forward, but Procell sprang back, well out of his reach. She giggled and said, "Now, now. Reconcile yourself, Nathaniel. You lasted a good deal longer than most, but the duel is over. You've lost. Be a good sport, won't you? Tell you what. We both know how painful death by taint is for the Host. I mean, it hurts like a bitch!

"If you like, I'll grant you a clean, quick death. Oh, it'll still hurt like a bitch, but only for a moment. Think of it as my way of saying, '*Adios*, motherfucker, and thanks for the memories.' "

Nathan gave no appearance that he'd heard Procell's offer. He simply stared ahead, silent and unmoving, as if he was focused on something miles beyond the tiny clearing.

Procell frowned. "Final offer, Nathaniel. Just toss the Kiv over here at my feet and kneel, or I gate away and leave you to your unmaking."

Nathan tilted his head as if listening to some faraway

sound. He nodded slowly, mechanically, and looked at Procell as if again aware of her presence. "A long, painful unmaking, or a quick death. That's your offer."

"Yeah, and it's the best offer you'll get from me. Hell, I couldn't stop the taint from coursing through your body if I wanted to. And I don't. Want to, that is. But the clock's ticking. You've got three seconds to surrender the Kiv and take your medicine. Otherwise, I'll come back tomorrow, after your body rots from the inside out."

"You want the Kiv badly, don't you?"

"One . . ."

Nathan forced a weak grin. "I suppose it really doesn't matter anymore. I mean, what use will I have for a Kiv in the Void?"

"Two . . ."

"Why the hurry? Here. Take the damn thing. Better you than Theoneal or Azazeal."

Procell hesitated, her eyes alight with hunger as they locked onto the blade in Nathan's outstretched hand. Once she imbued the Kiv with taint, she would be invincible. A goddess.

"Toss it at my feet. Gently."

Nathan had counted on such a reaction. Avarice and excess had always been Procell's failing. Today it would lead to her unmaking. Nathan took a slow, cautious step forward, extending the Kiv toward procell.

"Stop!"

Nathan froze in midstride, one foot suspended in the air. He winced and staggered to his right. "What is it now? Don't you want it? Take it. Hurry. I can't stand here all day."

"I told you to toss it on the ground at my feet," said Procell. "You're either very deaf or very stupid. Now, stand still and do as I say or I'll leave you alone to deal with the taint."

Nathan wobbled on unsteady legs, and Procell giggled again.

"From the looks of things, you'll be dead in an hour anyway. I could just leave now and come back later for the blade."

"Procell, we both know you won't leave the Kiv behind. Mulciber would find it before you could return. Can you imag-

ine that berserker with a Kiv? I'd rather it pass to a real warrior. Like you."

Procell smiled. Not a sneer or smirk as before, but a genuine smile. Flattery always worked on the vain. She lowered
the point of the kris and took a small step forward. "You surprise me, Nathan. That's very gracious of—"

Nathan set his foot on the ground. Hard. Very hard.

Nathan's physical strength *was* legendary among the Host
and Fallen alike, and for good reason. The ancient Gaels had
told tales of him, the deity they called *maistirad mac tire*—
Master of Wolves. In one such tale, a tribal shaman swore he
stood witness as Nathan buried a seven-headed demon lord
beneath a mountain—a mountain Nathan had ripped from the
earth. Some tribal legends contain more truth than fiction.

Nathan summoned every ounce of power within his massive body, then borrowed still more from another willing
source—a source so distant it existed not only in another place,
but another time as well. He focused it on the ground beneath
him. Soft loam drew minerals from the very dirt and surrounding plant life. Trees and shrubs were bleached slate gray as
Nathan bled them of still more trace minerals. As the minerals
flowed into him, he channeled the material back to the ground
beneath his feet, converting fresh earth into super-hardened
bedrock. His foot slammed into the rock and sent a shockwave
through the ground that toppled nearby trees and flung water
from the bayou up and over its steep, eight-foot bank.

Procell's eyes widened as the ground quaked beneath her
and she lost her footing. Her fabled agility had never failed
her. Not once since the Great Fall had she been knocked from
her feet during combat. Not once, until today. As her back
struck the ground, the kris flew from her hand and landed in
the thick tangle of honeysuckle.

In panic over the loss of the weapon that had helped make
her the quintessential assassin, she kipped up from the
ground—and onto the point of Nathan's waiting Kiv. Nathan
drove the Kiv through her breastbone and gave the wire-bound
hilt a savage twist, grinding heart and lung into gory pulp. As
the tip of the blade exited Procell's back, it severed her spinal

column. The bones in her legs melted and she sagged back onto the ground-turned-rock.

Nathan leaned over her. He wiped the liquid gold from his fingers and held the hand in front of her face. For the first time, Procell saw the self-inflicted cut that marred Nathan's palm. He then turned his head to the side, showing his neck was clean and uncut.

"Sorry to disappoint you, Procell, but you never touched me. Don't you just hate when that happens?"

Her bloodless lips formed a silent O and the light faded from her eyes. Her corporeal body erupted in a tall column of flame. Seconds later, a pile of ash the color of coal dust was the only evidence that Procell ever existed on Earth.

And then there were none!

And then there were none!

Nathan's triumph clearly caught Kokabel and Mulciber by surprise. Neither thought the Power had any real chance of taking out all the hidden Brethren. Kiel seized the moment and leaped forward, twisting in midair and launching a savage spinning kick at Mulciber's chest. The tactic caught the sword-wielding Dominion off guard. Both of the Brethren had figured Kiel would make good on his threat and go for Kokabel first.

Kiel's heel connected and the impact rumbled through the Mississippi low land like thunder. He felt Mulciber's sternum give way beneath his heel. However there was no time for self-congratulations. The injury was severe and would hamper the Dominion's mobility and sap his stamina, but it wouldn't take him out of the fight. And there was still Kokabel to consider.

As he dropped back onto his feet, Kiel thrust out his hand and shouted a Word of Power. A lance of blue fire aimed at Kokabel's head leaped from his fingertips, but Kiel never saw the result. Kokabel had already recovered from his initial surprise and launched his own attack. Emerald-colored chain lightning crackled across the small clearing, engulfing Kiel and dropping him to his knees. His hair burst into flame, and smoke poured from his mouth and nostrils. Skin fell from his exposed flesh in long, blackened strips. He hadn't expected the power or ferocity of Kokabel's lightning strike.

His slender body contorted by excruciating pain, Kiel tried to scream but the sound stuck in his throat. In his many eons on Earth, Kiel had fought countless battles against the Fallen and endured his share of wounds inflicted by Words of Power. But he'd never felt anything like this. Never like this. Through scorched eyes, he watched as Mulciber advanced. The berserker carried the flaming sword.

Father, help your servant!

Nearly blind, Kiel glanced at the spot where Kokabel had stood and saw nothing but trees, the bark blistered and peeled away from their scarred trunks. His line of sight was interrupted by the looming form of Mulciber. The fallen angel advanced, grinning, his eyes gleaming with madness brought on by battle lust.

"Say good-bye, Nathaniel."

Mulciber raised the sword high overhead in a two-handed grip.

I'm coming, Kiel!

Too late, my brother. Too . . .

Mulciber froze with the sword still poised above his head. His maniacal grin disappeared and he looked at Kiel with a puzzled expression. His lips moved but no words came out. Instead, golden froth bubbled from his mouth. He shook his head from side to side as if in denial that such a thing could happen. Not to him, not to the scourge of the Host, the great and mighty Mulciber. His body shuddered once before falling facedown upon the ground.

Nathan shoved the Kiv into the ground to clean the taint from its blade, then stepped over the fallen Dominion and knelt beside Kiel.

"You're a mess, brother. I'll get you back to Sanctuary and we'll tend to this nasty sunburn."

Kiel winced, then chuckled through gritted teeth. "You're in a fine humor, all things con—considered. Tend to Orus first, then come back for me."

"I'm afraid there's nothing left of Orus to tend. He dwells

in the Void now." Nathan gathered Kiel to his chest and stood up. "Let's go home. I've some long overdue news for you."

With Kiel cradled in his powerful arms, Nathan made the short walk across the glade to the monastery. In minutes, Kiel lay upon a bed inside the same bedroom where he had tended to the near-fatal wounds of the Offspring Paul Young. Young had suffered the grave misfortune of encountering Axthiel in a roadside motel. The treacherous Axthiel, one of the most powerful of all the Fallen, had entered into a pact with Legion. He would seek out and eradicate the Offspring in exchange for a place of prominence in a newly made world—a world in which humans, what few might remain, would be kept as cattle.

Nathan had heard the injured Offspring's *reach* and responded, along with another member of the Host, Sharaiel. They arrived in time to save Young, though Sharaiel lost her life during the rescue. After Axthiel killed Sharaiel, he turned his wrath on Nathan. The battle leveled eleven rooms and destroyed a dozen vehicles in the motel parking lot. Axthiel fled when it seemed Nathan would gain the upper hand.

After the battle, Nathan brought Young to Sanctuary where Kiel could best utilize his prowess in the healing arts. The man's recovery was no less than a miracle of divine intervention, an act that lay beyond even Kiel's mastery. Today, as Nathan examined the horrific burns that covered much of Kiel's body, he hoped the Creator might see fit to intervene again. Otherwise, he feared his brother might not survive the night. If, by the grace of God, Kiel lived until morning, the healing rays of the sun would facilitate his return to health.

After removing Kiel's charred clothing and loose strips of fire-blackened skin, Nathan applied an herbal salve to the worst of the burns, then held his hands several inches above Kiel's ruined body. He drew healing energies from his own body and the surrounding land, then channeled those energies into Kiel. A soft glow of golden light filled the room and surrounded the bed. Nathan sank to his knees, and speaking in a near-dead language not heard on Earth for thousands of years, he uttered a prayer on Kiel's behalf. Kiel was conscious throughout the ordeal, and twice, Nathan paused in his ministrations to listen as Kiel mumbled his own simple prayer. He didn't ask that his life be spared or that his misery be lessened. Instead, he praised the Creator's name, and asked that His will be done. The earnest request shamed Nathan.

Not two hours earlier, I stood in this very spot and cursed my sorry lot. Yet Kiel endures the kiss of quickfire, *and gives thanks to the Creator! I'm not worthy to stand in his company.*

After Kiel finished his prayers, Nathan leaned low over the bed. "Don't try to speak. Just listen. While I battled Procell, God spoke to me. The Usurper's vanguard is broken, and the war for the Throne of the Host nears its climax. Very soon, a new band of traitors will fall from Heaven's Grace. When I first heard this news, I despaired. Forgive me my weakness, Kiel, but I nearly surrendered the fight against Procell.

"But then, I heard the clarion call of victory as it rang across the multiverse. I heard the rallying cries of the Earth-bound Host, a clamor that rose up with one voice and shouted its defiance at Legion, Lucifer, and their collective minions. In that instant, the Creator touched my mind and body and I understood, Kiel. I understood! As long as we are willing to carry the fight, we may not lose. Humanity can survive this trial provided they find the courage and the will to endure. We must help them, Kiel. This is our destiny.

"And first, we must find Sam Conner."

chapter 21

Casa Grande

"Buckle up, cousin!"

Living in a state of "scared spitless" was fast becoming a habit Sam could do without, but there was damn little he could do about it at the moment. He tried to stare straight ahead, afraid if he ever looked at the driver of the white Lincoln, his heart would stop on the spot. The Lincoln accelerated with surprising speed, and Sam placed both hands on the dash to prevent himself from rolling into the driver's lap.

The driver. Henri. With an *i*. Sam's nemesis from two years past, now come back to help him rescue Kat, for an as of yet unnamed price. A kaleidoscope of thoughts, jumbled and nearly incoherent, raced through Sam's mind as he summoned up his courage and looked to his left at the boy who'd tried to kill him on so many occasions.

Though sitting behind an oversize steering wheel, Sam figured the boy was three or four inches short of his own six feet. Slim, with fine facial features framed by jet-black hair, and stylish wire-rimmed glasses sitting upon an aquiline nose, he looked nothing like the bogeyman Sam had imagined, nothing like the monster that had stalked his nightmares for two long, nerve-wracking years. Sam also knew looks could be deceiving.

It was true that Henri carried the stench of demons. In fact, his psychic signature was among the strongest Sam had ever encountered. However, there was something else, another element to that signature. Sam couldn't quite place it, but it was very familiar.

At the corner of the Quonset hut, Henri veered away from the building, and took them out toward the landing strip.

"W-where are we going? My sister is back there!"

"Relax, cousin. I'm just getting into position. We're going to make a strafing run. As your friend Mr. Falco would say, the far end of that building is a target-rich environment. In lay-man's terms, it's saturated with bad guys. We'll make a pass and take out as many as we can. That should cause sufficient confusion among their ranks. When we double back again, I'll let you out at the last hangar. You'll have to go after Katherine on foot, but I shouldn't think you'll have any difficulty locat-ing her. Her aura burns like a small nova. Now roll down the passenger window and make ready with that nasty *quickfire* you use so well. When we—"

"Wait! Please slow down. Do you know exactly where they're holding Kat? And what's *quickfire*? I've never heard of it."

Henri *tsked*. "Your education is woefully inadequate. I ex-pected more from Joriel. *Quickfire* is—"

"Get outta town! You know about Joriel?"

"Cousin, everyone who is anyone knows of the sublime Joriel, just as we all know of Uriel, or if you prefer, Horace. I try to avoid that one, but it's not easy. He does get around, and af-ter all, this *is* a small world." Henri spun the steering wheel, whipping the Lincoln into a 180-degree turn, and throwing Sam into the passenger-side door.

Henri shifted into "park" and revved the engine. Sam wasn't a car expert by any stretch, but the Lincoln sounded more like a Hemi-powered muscle car than a tired old mid-seventies luxury sedan. Like most everything in Sam's life over the past couple of years, there was more to Henri and the Lincoln than met the eye.

"Now, about *quickfire*. I know you've used it on at least two occasions. You melted Drammach with it in Abbotsville, which is no small feat. The fire doesn't usually work that way. I attribute the dramatic results to your emotional state at the time. Then, a couple of days ago, you used it again to send Axthiel's man-child packing."

Sam's head snapped up with a start. "You know Axthiel, too?"

"Oh, I knew him very well, cousin. Another one I avoided whenever possible. But I'm referring to his nasty boy-toy, that Little Stevie character. Axthiel, haughty highbrow that he was, took great delight in his human slaves. He sent Little Stevie after you weeks before you reached the Veil.

"Enthralling humans is such bad form. But I digress. You nearly burned a hole through that soulless brute with *quickfire*. He hasn't forgotten, either. That's why he brought so much help this time."

Sam's mind was reeling. So many twists and turns. Nothing was ever simple. Who or what was Henri that he could casually mention Joriel and Axthiel in conversation? Or Horace? Especially Horace! Did Henri really know them or was he still playing mind games? And if he did know them, why hadn't either of them mentioned Henri by name while Sam was running for his life from the Lincoln across a half dozen states? Joriel and Horace had both warned him that the white Lincoln wanted him dead.

Henri shifted the car back into "drive" and allowed it to coast forward at a fast idle.

"The two instances of *quickfire* share a common denominator, you know. Care to hazard a guess before we begin our run?"

Sam thought back to the fight beneath the Cannuagh Sanatorium and the encounter with Little Stevie, two very different sets of circumstances. *Common denominator? How the hell am I supposed to know? I've never even heard of* quickfire *before now.*

"Yes, yes. You've already indicated that your training has been less than satisfactory."

Startled, Sam looked at Henri. "How do you know what I'm thinking? Look, dude, don't screw around in my head uninvited. Not now, not ever. You got that?"

Laughing, Henri stomped on the accelerator. The Lincoln lurched forward, leaving behind a thick cloud of white smoke and the smell of burning rubber. As the car sped toward the distant row of hangars, Henri said, "Bravo, cousin! You've discovered the common denominator. I always knew you were a quick study."

"I don't know what you're talking about," said Sam.

"Think, cousin! Both times, you were angry. Very, very angry. The human side of your dual nature unleashed the divine! Now, prepare yourself. We're almost there, and you would do well to get angry again."

"Damn it, Falco, why didn't you shoot the little son of a bitch?"

"Why would I do that? He's not going anywhere. Not as long as his sister is still somewhere in the area." *God, I hope I'm right.*

Elliott shook his head in disgust. "Oh, so you're a fucking mind reader now. I suppose the kid told you he'd be right back with pizzas and a six-pack. Jesus H. Christ, Falco! How the hell do you know he won't bail out now that he has a way out of here? You know, it seems to me you're damned friendly with Conner. I bet Reading's going to find your relationship very, very interesting."

Eyes blazing, Falco turned away from the door and started toward Elliott when Enrique grabbed his arm. "Let it go, Thomas. We've got more important things to worry about. Besides, Elliott has a point."

Falco shook Enrique's hand from his arm, and turned on his half-brother. His voice was low and carried a dangerous edge. "You might want to explain that remark, Rikki."

Despite his gentle manner and white-collar exterior, Enrique DeLorenzo was no coward. Nor was he a fool. He was treading on dangerous ground with Falco and he knew it.

"A poor choice of words, Thomas. I only meant that we'll have to explain how we managed to lose the boy *and* his sister. Malcolm is in charge of all Sword operations in the United States. As such, the Hierarchy will demand an explanation.

We'll have to provide that explanation. Frankly, this has all happened so fast, I'm not sure what to say.

Falco knew Enrique was right. Malcolm Reading was a stern taskmaster, a man with zero tolerance for failure, and the Hierarchy was even more demanding of its field operatives. It was the only way such a group could operate undetected over the centuries. Now the entire organization risked exposure. Sam Conner knew too much about the Watchers, and it was Falco's fault.

What would he and Enrique tell Reading? What *could* they tell him? Falco had lost control of the mission the moment Little Stevie appeared on that rooftop. From that moment, Falco was swept along by currents he had never before known existed.

Who, or what, exactly was this Little Stevie? Neither demon nor Offspring, he damn sure wasn't human. Why was the monster drawn to Sam Conner? The boy had said something about fallen angels. Was it possible?

No, reasoned Falco, Sam would have said something if that were the case. Were there others like this mysterious Stevie, watching, waiting for the perfect opportunity to strike? Another question nagged at Falco, but he hadn't dared to confront the issue. Little Stevie had attacked the Watchers atop the maintenance building before Sam arrived. But when Sam appeared, Stevie was instantly drawn to the boy. Why? Was there some connection between the Watchers and Sam Conner? More important, were the Watchers and Offspring somehow united in some hidden cause? Falco had dozens of questions and damn few answers. Some answers, he thought, were perhaps best unexplored for the time being.

There was one thing Falco *did* know. "Sam didn't run out on us, Rikki. Don't ask me how I know, but I know. He said the demons were holding his sister at the far end of the hangar, and that he would send a signal when it was time to make a move. He also said the plane was only a few minutes out, so we need to be ready to move fast."

Elliott laughed. "And Thomas Falco, demon hunter extraordinaire, believes this . . . this Offspring! Goddamn it, Enrique, the entire Hierarchy believes those freaks *are* demonic, and Falco acts like Conner is his new best friend! Hell, man, we've terminated entire generations for less than that! Not that it fucking matters. We're all going to die, tonight."

Looking over at Falco, Elliott added, "But you already know that, don't you, tough guy?"

Enrique stared intently at his half-brother for several seconds. By the dim light of the single lamp, he thought he saw a pleading in Falco's eyes, an expression Enrique had seldom if ever seen before tonight. Enrique knew Falco wasn't pleading for himself. He was seeking pardon for Sam Conner, and perhaps all the other Offspring who were being hunted and persecuted across the globe.

Softly, Enrique said, "No, Elliott. Not every member of the Hierarchy believes the Offspring are demonic. And neither do I. Now check your weapons and ammo. We need to be ready when Sam gives us the signal."

Turning to Falco and leaning in close, Enrique whispered, "You'd better hope to God you're right. Our lives depend on it."

The Lincoln rounded the corner of the building, tires squealing and engine roaring. As the car bore down on the building, Sam braced for the impact, certain Henri had lost his mind and intended to crash through the bay door.

At the last possible moment, Henri spun the steering wheel to the right, narrowly missing the building by mere inches. As the car sped past the building, Sam caught a fleeting glimpse of a dark, formless shape as it swooped down from the rooftop.

"A pair of imps were waiting to ambush you. They won't like that we've drawn them out and ruined the surprise."

Henri gave the steering wheel another sharp turn. Sam, afraid he might be flung from the car, gripped the dashboard until his hands cramped. The Lincoln was now pointed toward the building again, and Henri stomped the accelerator. After a final hard turn to the left, Henri stomped on the brakes, bringing the Lincoln to an abrupt halt in front of the bay door and sending Sam head-first into the windshield.

Henri shifted into "park" and opened the driver's-side door.

"Sorry about that, cousin. Now get out, but stay near the car until I call for you. If we're lucky they'll target me. I'll keep them occupied while you work your magic."

"Uh? What magic?" said Sam as he fumbled with the door handle.

"*Quickfire,* cousin! Damn, but I'll have to re-school you once we're away from here." Henri didn't wait for a response. He sprinted to a spot directly in front of the overhead door, some twenty steps from the building. Facing the building, he called out something in an unintelligible language. Standing at the rear of the Lincoln, Sam tried to catch the words, but they slipped from his mind almost as soon as his ears registered the sound.

As soon as Sam stepped out onto the pavement, a familiar wave of nausea slammed into him, and for a moment the world seemed to tilt off its axis and spin out of control. *T-too many of them. Too many! God, if you can hear me . . .*

Henri stood with his arms folded across his chest and yelled out again. While Sam couldn't catch the words, he knew Henri was shouting out a challenge.

When no immediate response came, Sam thought, *Maybe he's wrong. Maybe Kat isn't in—*

The black shape Sam had seen on the first pass flittered slowly down from the tin roof and made a lazy circle around Henri.

"Be gone, imp!" said Henri. "I've no time for the sorry likes of you. Fetch your master and be quick!"

Though Henri had already demonstrated a penchant for theatrics, his voice was full of contempt and loathing, and Sam wasn't so sure it was an act. The shape writhed angrily in the air, made another pass just above Henri's head, then floated back to the building and passed through the steel-paneled bay door.

Henri called over his shoulder, "It goes to deliver my message. Won't be long now. Can you feel Katherine? They've hurt her, Sam. We must be quick."

Sam stared at Henri, then at the bay door that separated him from his sister. He knew it was possible that Henri added the last as fuel for anger. If so, it worked. Sam could feel the pent-up heat escaping from every pore of his skin.

Come out and fight! Come out or I'm coming in! He needed a target, to lash out before his anger and the *quickfire* consumed him.

"Steady, cousin," said Henri. "They come. This is a good time to fetch your friend, Mr. Falco. Tell him to make his way through the building to the last hangar, and be quick. He'll find Katherine on the floor against the back wall."

Exasperated, Sam yelled, "How the hell am I supposed to contact Falco?"

"Oh, come now, cousin! You're killing me! We both know who and what he is, so *reaching* for him shouldn't be a problem for you. Ah, here we go. The demon lord comes. Hurry!"

So Henri also knows Falco is an Offspring. Sam had thought it from the moment he felt Falco's frantic *reach* from atop the maintenance building in Tempe.

Okay, here goes. Let's hope the dude isn't big on denial. Sam closed his eyes and formed a detailed mental image of the Watcher. Once the picture was complete, Sam *reached.* Contact was almost immediate. The sense of surprise and shock was staggering.

From birth, Joriel, Sam's lifelong companion and guardian angel, had used vivid mental imagery to speak to him. Messages and emotions were transmitted through colors, sounds, and geometric shapes. She didn't use words until Sam was well into his teens, though that never hindered her ability to effectively communicate. Falco had no such mental or emotional preparation for Sam's *reach.*

Wha . . .

Easy, Falco. This is Sam.

H-how are . . . Where are you?

Sam could feel Falco's confusion and fear through the psychic connection. For a second he took guilty pleasure in the Watcher's mental turmoil.

Calm down and listen. Henri and I are at the far end of the hangar row. Henri says you should make your way through the building now. We'll keep the bad guys busy while you rescue

Kat. When you have her, get away from that hangar. Regroup back at the office.

But—

Sam cut him off. There wasn't time for explanations. *No time for buts, Falco! Just do it! I'll explain everything after Kat is safe.*

If Falco responded, Sam missed it. The bay door of the small hangar exploded off the tracks, spraying twisted steel panels over the parking lot. A large jagged shard slammed into the side of the Lincoln, forcing Sam to duck for cover.

Christ! What the hell . . . Henri!

Sam peered over the trunk of the car, certain he would find the ruined body of Henri Charpak buried beneath an avalanche of shredded steel and aluminum. Instead, he found Henri standing unscathed and defiant. A slim figure stepped through the broken doorway of the hangar, and moved out onto the pavement. As the figure drew near, Sam saw that it was a female. The most beautiful woman he'd ever seen. No, not just beautiful. This woman was lust made manifest. She was draped in sheer silvery material that could have been spun moonlight. High, firm breasts, nipples hard and erect. Long, slender legs that seemed to go on forever until they culminated in a pair of exquisite hips that swayed seductively, inviting pleasure and promising it tenfold in return. Long, flowing hair of pale blond . . . no, wait. Dark, cascading curls that fell to her bare shoulders. She could have been twenty or forty or whatever age one desired. And her face . . . If it was true that Helen of Troy possessed the face that launched a thousand ships, then this woman had surely moved galaxies.

She looked at Henri and smiled. She didn't speak. The pink tip of her tongue caressed full, inviting lips. Sam took a step forward, but a hand caught his arm and held fast. Looking away from Henri, she seemed to see Sam for the first time. She crouched, her hands held before her as if warding off a blow. A rumble started deep in her chest, building, gaining volume until she threw back her head and loosed a feral, high-pitched cry. The ideal of female perfection melted away before Sam's eyes.

Within seconds, the woman was gone, replaced by a hideous harpy out of myth and legend.

"Easy, Sam," whispered Henri. "Follow my lead."

Sam was too stunned to reply. In many ways, the monster resembled Drammach, the greater demon Sam had killed beneath the grounds of the sanatorium in Abbotsville. Both had the jackal-like snout and almond-shaped eyes the color of milk. However, Drammach had been shorter than Sam's own 6'0", and thickly built with a powerful chest and shoulders. This creature was neck and shoulders taller than Sam. A gaunt frame gave the monster a ghoulish appearance, its leathery slate-gray skin stretched taut over sharp, angular bones. Heavy, pendulous breasts swung obscenely from a narrow, sunken chest. The creature walked to within a few feet of Henri and stopped.

Loud laughter came from inside the darkened hangar, followed by a familiar voice. "Hey, boy-bitch! I told you we'd meet again. So, how do you like my friends? Huh? What'sa matter, Sammie? Cat got your tongue?"

Henri defiantly stood his ground with arms folded across his chest. In that moment Sam decided the mysterious young man was either extremely sure of himself or extremely stupid. Or both.

Henri called out, "Sam, meet Zynth. She's a demon lord of some reputation. Among Legion, the title of lord isn't gender-specific, you understand.

"She most often appears in a decidedly more appealing shape. After all, she's a succubus. Wouldn't do for her to come to your bed in her present form, now would it? It's a rare event for a human to see Zynth in her corporeal form, and when it does happen, she's usually the last thing that human ever sees in this lifetime."

Sam's mind reeled. The confrontation back in Abbotsville had been a shock, but this was worse. So much worse. The area of Sam's brain that controlled the "fight or flight" mechanism was in denial and unresponsive, crippled by the sight of the demon.

That thing isn't real. None of this is real. I'm either dreaming or I'm laid up in some Phoenix psych ward, chugging a Thorazine cocktail through an IV.

On the off chance the world had gone crazier than a sack full of cranked-up ferrets and the monster standing before him *was* real, Sam whispered, "Come on, Henri. You're on a first-name basis with that, that *thing*?"

"Why do you always ask me that when I've already said as much? But yes, Zynth and I are old acquaintances. She's dwelled upon this plane long before man received the Divine spark and crawled out of the sea. Perhaps a gentleman shouldn't kiss and tell, but for a time, she and I were lovers."

Lovers? With that*? No way! He's pulling my chain.*

"Oh, I know what you're thinking, Sam. But really, you have to see her in the right light to fully appreciate her considerable assets."

"T-tell it, I mean tell *her*, that we want my sister. Now."

Zynth's head snapped up, her eyes locking onto Sam. Jaws snapping, the demon took a menacing step in his direction. Henri stepped in quickly, moving to block her path, and to Sam's surprise, she stopped her advance.

"You don't want to do this, Zynth," said Henri. "He comes for his sister and I think he means to have her. Quit this place and take the others with you while you still may."

The demon waved her spindly arms in the air and emitted a series of high-pitched chirps and whistles. Henri listened intently as the demon ranted. When the odd noises subsided, he called back to Sam.

"Well, cousin, I tried. She says she must kill you and Katherine. Sorry." Henri stepped to the side, offering the demon a clear path to the Lincoln and Sam.

Bewildered and enraged, Sam stepped out from behind the car. "Sorry? You're *sorry*? You backstabbing son of a bitch!"

The demon kicked aside a crumpled door panel made of plate steel as if it a wadded sheet of newspaper, and lumbered toward Sam. Long strings of smoldering pea green drool dropped to the pavement as Zynth snapped powerful jaws at empty air.

"I'm sorry, Sam, I really am. But she seems rather determined. And while I don't necessarily approve, I do understand her position. After all, Legion has been at war with the Offspring since . . . well, since Offspring first appeared on this planet. Homicidal hatred for your kind is a natural state of being for Legion. It's engrained in their DNA. Can't really fault them for poor genetics, now can you?"

Henri rambled on while Zynth advanced. As Sam backed toward the car, one of the formless imps swooped down from the roof and slammed into him, raking all too real claws across his head and face. The force of the unexpected blow staggered him, and blood trickled into his eyes from a wide gash across his forehead. The black, fluttering shape soared up into the night sky, made a wide, arcing turn, and came at him again with an unexpected burst of speed. There was no time to seek cover.

Instinctively, Sam thrust out his hand and shouted a single word.

"Burn!"

Living tendrils of brilliant white light lanced out from his fingertips, engulfing the imp in a web of lightning. In an instant, the imp was gone, its smoldering ashes borne aloft by a steady breeze. Sam's celebration was short-lived, interrupted by Zynth's shrill cry.

He whirled about to find the succubus had called for reinforcements. A short, squat man with exceptionally long arms had taken up a position to her left. At least, Sam thought it was a man until he noticed the feral glow of yellow eyes. An imp had landed to Zynth's right and assumed a more substantial form. Sam thought the minor demon looked something like a tall, gangly stork sporting a human head.

More laughter spilled from the hangar. "Hey, Sammie! Looks like you're about to be Zynth's guest for dinner! But don't you worry none about little sista. We're getting along real good!"

Sam tried to push Stevie's taunts from his mind. Before he could help Kat he would have to survive Zynth. The succubus, followed closely by the imp, looped around the front end of the Lincoln, while the manlike demon came at Sam from the left. All three of the monsters appeared cautious, perhaps out of respect for the *quickfire*. Sam also knew that in a few more seconds, it wouldn't matter. Cautious or not, they would cut him off from both the car and the building, leaving him no place to run or hide in the expansive parking lot.

And then, over the pounding of his heart, Sam heard the steady thrum of a low-flying aircraft as it approached the airfield. Desperate, he *reached*.

Where are you, Falco? The plane is landing!

The answer was loud and immediate. *Almost there, Sam. Hang on!*

Sam knew that even with the extra firepower, Falco and company would have a difficult time with Little Stevie. Even if they managed to defeat the man-mountain, the Watchers would still have to fight their way past Zynth in order to reach the plane.

Falco, I'm going to draw the rest of them away from the hangar. Get Kat out there and head for the run—"

A shotgun roared from inside the hangar, joined a fraction of a second later by a sustained volley of small-arms fire. Sam broke into a sprint to the south, toward open desert, when he caught a flash of white sail over the hood of the Lincoln. And then, all hell broke loose.

No fire alarm or wailing police siren ever reached the decibel level of Zynth's outcry of pain and outrage. Looking over his shoulder, Sam saw that Henri had launched a preemptive strike. The young man had somehow leaped onto the top of the Lincoln, and then onto Zynth's back, abandoning any pretense of his former genteel demeanor. Stroke after savage stroke, he plunged a long metal blade into the succubus's neck. Smoke poured from multiple gaping wounds as Zynth thrashed about in an attempt to dislodge her diminutive attacker.

Sam cried out a warning as the imp, dissolving once more into a swirling airborne miasma the color of burned motor oil, took flight and dove at Henri's head. Henri either didn't hear the shout or ignored it. The imp darted in, struck Henri's head a glancing blow, then turned skyward. As Henri listed to the left to avoid the worst of the next blow, Zynth caught him by the back of the neck and flung him to the pavement. Henri landed hard on his back, but came to his feet with surprising quickness. He still held on to the odd blade, a fact not unnoticed by Zynth. She advanced with caution.

Sam wanted to help Henri, but he had his own troubles. The man-demon had stopped for a moment, watching Zynth's life-and-death struggle with mild interest, then turned his attention back to Sam. He came forward, one slow, wooden step after another, those impossibly long arms reaching, beckoning.

Sam thrust forth his hand a second time and yelled, "Burn!" Nothing.

Ohshitohshitoh . . . shit!

"I said, burn!" Again, nothing. Not so much as a spark or flicker of flame. Behind him, the plane touched down and coasted along the runway toward the hangars, its powerful spotlights washing over the surreal battleground.

Sam's eyes darted to the plane and back to the man-demon. *I don't have time for this!* He backpedaled, took a deep breath, then broke into an awkward run that took him a wide loop around the startled demon. Gritting his teeth against the pain in his injured knee, he rushed past the struggling Zynth and Henri, surprised to see the succubus now limp upon the asphalt. Henri hadn't escaped the battle unscathed. Remnants of a once white shirt hung in shreds from the young man's thin shoulders, and long rivulets of blood streamed down one side of his pale, smooth face.

Just as Sam reached the hangar entrance, Falco and Ronni emerged side by side. Both looked as if they'd been run through a gigantic meat grinder. Twice. Falco grabbed Sam by the shoulders and spun him around.

"Head for the runway! Run!" cried Falco.

"Where's my sister?"

"I've got her," said Enrique as he came through the door. In his arms, he carried the limp, battered form of Katherine Conner. Elliott, gasping for breath and bleeding from a dozen superficial wounds, brought up the rear. As Elliott cleared the door, he turned and emptied the magazine of his handgun into the building. The final round was followed by a bright yellow flash and a small explosion that sent shockwaves rippling through the air.

Sam tried to reach Katherine, but Falco held him fast. "You can't carry her and run. Just get to the plane, Sam! We'll take care of Kat. Now run!"

Sam swallowed the grapefruit-size lump in his throat and nodded. Though badly shaken by Kat's condition, he knew Falco was right. He was spent, wasted, drained of almost all physical and emotional energy. He couldn't have taken ten steps with Kat. In fact, were it not for the desperate need to get Kat to safety, Sam thought he could easily lie down and "give up the ghost." Tired. So tired of everything.

But quitting wasn't an option. Not yet. *Somebody has to pay for this, and I'm the only one left to collect.*

Sam stumbled to his knees as Falco let go of his shoulders. A split second later, Sam smelled the odor of burned hair. Looking up, he saw that the man-demon had stepped out from behind the Lincoln and now loomed above him, poised to strike with those apelike arms. Ronni Weiss appeared at Sam's side, firing the 12-gauge as fast as she could rack the slide and chamber a round. Slug after slug punched large holes in the walking obscenity's upper torso and face. As the demon swayed on unsteady legs and held both hands to its ruined face, Sam tried to roll to his left, out from beneath the demon's reach, but he was a fraction of a second too slow. The monster swung a heavy fist and connected with the side of Sam's face. The boy felt the crunch of bone, then mercifully slipped away into darkness.

chapter 22

Malcolm Reading sipped his brandy and studied the row of snowy egrets perched atop a line of skiffs and john boats moored along the southern edge of Lake Pontchartrain. Occasionally, one of the birds would take flight and dart down to the water's surface, snatching a morning morsel . . . before circling high above the manor and shitting on everything in sight.

Filthy little buggers. God, how I hate those fucking birds!

Despite his aggravation with the egrets, Malcolm usually enjoyed time spent on the balcony. It was the one place on the entire estate where he could enjoy a moment of privacy. It also afforded an excellent view of the lake and surrounding area, if one enjoyed such things. Malcolm Reading did not. Aesthetics had meant little to him in his former life, and decidedly less now.

The Watchers purchased the sprawling property for pennies on the dollar during the aftermath of Hurricane Katrina, and converted the historic French manor into a four-story safe house for field operatives and intelligence personnel. Nicholas Gilbert had christened the massive estate Le Chateau De Molay, so named after the last official grand master of the Knights Templar. Much had transpired since the christening of the manor, to both the Watcher organization and Sir Malcolm Reading.

Malcolm refilled his snifter, then lit his pipe. Despite the calm, peaceful setting, he had one nerve left and someone was standing on it. The tranquility of a chill November morning had been bruised just before dawn with the miraculous arrival of Enrique and his battered party. The situation looked no better by midmorning light. Malcolm hadn't expected to ever see any of them again, and for good reason, yet they had arrived by private plane a half-hour before sunrise. There had been no advance notification from the pilot until just before the plane touched down on the private airfield, east of the estate. During the debriefing, Malcolm learned that Falco had insisted on radio silence while the plane was in the air.

Do Falco or DeLorenzo suspect I set them up for ambush in Casa Grande? If so, why would they still allow the plane to land in Metairie? Malcolm decided he would have to exercise extreme caution when around either man. The sooner they were out of the picture the better, but the safe house was full of Watchers. It was imperative that Malcolm remain above suspicion in the deaths of Falco and Enrique.

Not only had the majority of the ill-fated Watcher party survived the ambush in Casa Grande, they had managed to inflict heavy casualties upon their attackers and extricate both of the Conner children. The girl was in poor condition, but the boy . . . something would have to be done about Sam Conner, and soon.

In the eyes of the Watcher Hierarchy, the Casa Grande extraction had been an unmitigated and expensive disaster. One hostage lost, two operators dead, and a third, Ronni Weiss, seriously injured. The Hierarchy could hardly be faulted for believing the mission to be a complete and utter failure. Only Malcolm and his coconspirators knew the truth—that the extraction had been much more of a success than anyone inside the organization realized.

Vastly outnumbered, the group had survived Casa Grande against all odds. It was inconceivable that anyone lived through the ordeal, especially Thomas Falco and his new pet, Sam Conner. Both had been specifically targeted during the fight, yet only Conner suffered any significant damage. Of course, the jury was still out on Conner's mental well-being. After all, the boy *had* watched his mother burn alive. Now, his sister was a different matter altogether. It was very likely Katherine Conner was now fucked up beyond repair. Literally.

Sam Conner and Falco were the real wildcards; they were volatile and unpredictable with an as yet undefined connection. The relationship between assassin and Offspring had taken an unexpected turn. From Elliott's sketchy account, the Conner boy had organized and directed the unlikely rescue of his sister. DeLorenzo and Falco had followed along meekly like some enthralled lapdogs. Was it possible? Had the boy really possessed the power necessary to enthrall? Malcolm couldn't bring himself to believe it, yet he had no other explanation for Falco's behavior. The man had never been especially compliant or subservient during a crisis, preferring to take charge and assume full responsibility for the outcome.

Bugger the bastard, no man is that lucky! He's got more lives than my sister's mangy fucking cat!

Not all of the operatives shared Falco's luck. Two experienced Swords had died during the operation. Brian King fell during the mad dash to Casa Grande, the unfortunate victim of a *wight*.

A bloody shame, that. The lad was pliable enough, and none too bright. I could have used him a while longer. Now I'll have to find another young, tender rabbit to run my errands.

The other loss was of much more significance to the organization. Alexis Dos Passos, the former Argentinean secret service agent, wasn't officially listed as killed in action. Not yet. She had disappeared early during the battle at the airfield and was presumed dead by Falco, though the others weren't so sure. While Alexis was a relative newcomer to the Watchers, she was a legacy case. A member of her family had served the Watchers without fail or exception since the late sixteenth century.

By all accounts, the young woman was a highly skilled warrior, courageous and resourceful during a crisis, and highly dedicated to the cause. Not exactly the type to run or abandon her comrades during the heat of battle. Then again, battle against the supernatural had broken many a seasoned warrior.

If by some chance Lexis still lived, she was no doubt praying for death with every breath by now. Given her vocation and the unforgiving nature of her captors, it was certainly more comforting for her peers to believe she died during the first few minutes of the fight.

Amanda Conner, the mother of Katherine and Sam Conner, was the third casualty. The entire party, including her children, watched as the disturbed woman slow-roasted in the Ford Escalade. *Too bad she didn't take that snot-nosed pair of aberrations with her!*

Of the remaining members of the group, Elliott Glenn and Ronni Weiss had escaped with minor injuries. Malcolm smiled and sipped at the brandy.

It's fortunate that Elliott survived. His mistress has plans for him, but first, he has work to do on my *behalf.*

"I'm sorry to intrude, Sir Malcolm."

Malcolm turned to find Bruce Purcell, an administrative aid, standing in the doorway. A single glance at the young Shield's face told the tale.

It's about goddamned time I received some good news! Resisting the urge to shout out his joy, Malcolm played out his part.

"Good morning, Bruce. What can I do for you?"

"Sir, I have Brussels on line two. Cardinal Dresselhaus."

Dresselhaus! No mere messenger but a member of the Hierarchy. I do love it so when a plan comes together!

"Oh? Very well, let's not keep the good Cardinal waiting."

Malcolm followed Purcell through the double doors and into the living room of the suite, where he took the call.

"Reading here."

After a slight delay, a heavily accented voice speaking perfect English answered, "Malcolm, this is Jon. Have you seen any of the news programs this morning?"

It was all Malcolm could do to contain his glee. "And a good morning to you, too, Jon. As for the news, no, I haven't had a chance to check phone messages this morning." *I don't need to check the messages, you fool! I know damn well why you're calling.* "Forgive me for saying so, but you sound terrible, old man! Is something wrong?"

Again, a short pause, then, "First, tell me, how are our new guests? Have you had any trouble with the Conner children?"

"None that I'm aware of, Jon. Our medical staff have done all they can for the girl but her injuries are severe. In addition to her physical injuries, Dr. Haskins says she's suffering from shock and severe emotional trauma. He's doubtful she'll live out the week, and frankly, I say good riddance. The boy's wounds are less severe. He's under guard along with the others. We've got quite a collection of these abominations, you know. Nine of the bloody bastards housed in the security wing. I trust you've read my recommendation?"

"I have, Mal. However, the Hierarchy prefers to postpone any decision regarding the Offspring until we've had an opportunity to thoroughly analyze reports from the survivors of the Arizona strike team. Speaking of which, I realize we lost some very good people during that operation. You have both our condolences and our gratitude. As for your guests, keep them comfortable and isolated. I'll be in touch with additional instructions soon.

"Now, to other matters. I'd rather tell you in person, Malcolm, but it can't be helped. It's about Nicholas Gilbert. I'm afraid . . . Nicholas is dead."

Malcolm stifled a chuckle and waited, counting silently to three before answering.

"Malcolm, are you still on the line?"

"I'm here, Jon, and I should say this is a damn poor joke, old man. Bad form. Very bad."

"I wish it was a joke, Mal. Or a bad dream. Members of the Diocese staff found him inside the vestibule around seven A.M., Pacific time. I don't have all the details, but apparently he'd been horribly mauled. The local authorities suspect it's the work of some deranged drug addict, but our man insists the sheer brutality of the murder points to the Enemy. You, of course, understand the implication; that Legion has found a way to breach consecrated ground. It's unthinkable, Malcolm, but there you have it. We are now under siege in God's own temples.

"According to our contact inside the LA Coroner's Office,

the authorities made a positive identification less than an hour ago. I know you and Nicholas were very close. Again, you have my deepest condolences."

Malcolm covered his face with an open hand to hide a wide smile. "A moment, Jon."

"Of course, Malcolm. I can call back in a while if you need time. . . ."

"No, no. I just need a moment." Turning to the waiting Purcell, Malcolm said, "Bruce, inform all personnel on the premises that we will assemble in the conference room in one hour. No exceptions, no excuses." Purcell nodded once and left the room.

"I apologize for the interruption, Jon. As you no doubt heard, I've called a staff meeting in order to apprise everyone of the situation. Unless you feel we should wait, of course . . ."

"There's no need to postpone the news, Malcolm. The End of Days are upon us, and I ask that you speak candidly with those in your charge. You've lost a great friend this day, and the organization has lost a true champion. The Hierarchy would prefer to postpone filling Nicholas's position until we'd had a chance to influence the Vatican's appointment to the Los Angeles Diocese, but I'm afraid we won't have that luxury."

Malcolm nearly laughed aloud at the obvious statement. The Watchers were highly efficient at grooming and placing hand-selected candidates in prominent positions within the Church, with the Vatican none the wiser. But such political maneuvering required time, finesse, and no meager amount of good fortune. Neither time nor fortune was in great abundance these days. All the better for Malcolm.

As archbishop, Nicholas had wielded tremendous religious, social, and political influence. However, his real power resided in the covert role of Lord Protector, the highest ranking Sword in the Americas and the Watcher's bulwark against the advance of Legion in the Western hemisphere. Malcolm couldn't match Gilbert's influence or status inside the Church. In fact, except for a few close acquaintances, he had no influence at all.

However, he had something neither Gilbert nor any other member of the Watchers could claim. First of all, Malcolm was a noted demon hunter with more than twenty kills to his credit, a record matched only by an elite few. And most of his victories occurred "back in the day," before the Veil was damaged, thus spanning the ethereal gap between Sitra Akhra and the world of men.

Malcolm was also a legacy case, his ancestry dating back to the thirteenth-century house of a notable Templar, James of Plany. The Watchers placed great stock in family legacies, tradition, and longevity of service to the Order. Few could match Malcolm's heritage, and that heritage placed him in esteemed company within the organization.

As the sole heir to the Reading-Redwall South India Trading conglomerate, Malcolm was also wealthy, and wealth bought contacts, information, and valuable resources. Wealth, lineage, courage, and audacity; Malcolm Reading was the total package, which made him a valuable ally or formidable opponent. Of course, the same could be said of others within the organization. However, Malcolm held a trump card. He possessed one advantage none of the others could claim, the most important advantage of all.

"Mal, it would be better for all if the Church waits until an appropriate period of mourning passes to appoint Gilbert's replacement, but these aren't ordinary times, and we're certain the Vatican will move before we have an opportunity to influence the appointment."

"I understand, Jon. Do you have any further instructions before I go?"

"Only one last item, Malcolm. The Hierarchy has already decided on Gilbert's replacement as Lord Protector."

It's about damned time! I didn't think the meandering old bastard would ever get around to it.

"Time is critical. I would ask that you make the announcement to all satellites in the Americas. You can start with your staff meeting. Enrique DeLorenzo will assume the mantle."

The blood drained from Malcolm's cheeks. "What . . . did you say?"

"I said the Hierarchy has selected Rikki DeLorenzo as Gilbert's successor. He's perhaps a bit young and lacking

Gilbert's raw grit, but the boy has proven extremely capable under some very trying conditions. In fact, it was my pleasure to place his name in nomination before the council."

The supernatural entity who shared Malcolm Reading's mind and soul raged silently. *This is most disturbing, Malcolm. How could you allow this to happen? The End of Days has come and yet, you fail me at the most critical juncture.*

A few simple requests, that is all I asked. That you find the means to gain control of the office of Lord Protector, yet the Church even now names another. That you ensure the death of the Offspring, Sam Conner, and instead he finds a champion among your former brethren! I cannot kill the boy myself without drawing a . . . crowd. At this time, it's imperative that I maintain a low profile, thus I relied on you. A poor choice, it would seem. Ah, dear Malcolm, you do know the penalty for failure.

The still-lucid portion of Malcolm's mind cringed. Yes, he knew the punishment for servants who failed the master. *Give me another opportunity to serve, Lord! I won't fail a second time!*

Hmmm . . . perhaps there is a way for you to redeem your pitiful life. If, for any reason, this gambit should fail, there may still be a use for you. Therefore, you will flee forthwith to my haven in the Sudan and wait there for my instructions. Do you understand?

Malcolm nodded meekly.

Excellent. And now I must pay another visit to our faithful lapdog, Elliott.

chapter 23

Elliott Glenn didn't feel the empty bottle slide from his hand or hear when it landed on the plush carpet beside the bed in his apartment inside the Watcher compound. He slept the shallow, troubled sleep of the afflicted. Not that there was anything wrong with Elliott's body. But his mind and soul were corrupt, fouled by the touch of Legion. To be sure, Elliott was no victim. He leaned willingly to the darker side of human nature. He embraced his lack of faith in a higher cause like a badge of honor. He was an antihero in some grand motion picture epic, railing against a false morality. He had decided early on that the only higher cause worth serving was his own. He had trusted others in the past, and the result was pain and heartbreak. Such scars were slow to heal. Some never did.

He had little immediate family and none were close. No friends to speak of save one, and Elliott couldn't speak of him without facing charges of heresy and collusion with the Enemy. Besides, who would he tell? What could he say? One night he simply fell asleep and he was there. Tall with piercing dark blue eyes and a face chiseled from alabaster, he never gave his name, and Elliott never asked. It was enough that they had come together in this dream world. From the beginning, theirs was a relationship that defied rational explanation. He saw what Elliott saw, felt what Elliott felt, and knew what Elliott knew. Elliott's mind and soul were laid bare before this remarkable dream-man.

On the second nocturnal visit, or perhaps the third, the

dream-man had reached out and caressed Elliott's face with a tenderness that suggested more. Yet Elliott turned away. Despite their obvious and undeniable mental and emotional connection, Elliott couldn't surrender himself to another man, not even in a dream.

Unwounded by rejection, the man had smiled and waved his hand in front of Elliott's eyes, instantly mesmerizing the assassin. When Elliott emerged from the stupor minutes later, the dream-man was gone, and in his place stood the most beautiful woman Elliott Glenn had ever seen. Of course, Elliott knew instinctively that this was the same person now draped in a different physical shell. Yet the new physical form melted away all of Elliott's former inhibitions. This time, when the dream man-turned-woman reached out to caress Elliott's cheek, Elliott didn't turn away.

The lovemaking was at once brutal and sensuous. Her appetites were diverse and insatiable. Elliott knew some might scoff at the notion of metaphysical sex, but whatever the term, it often left him exhausted throughout his waking hours and anxious for a return to the dream state. If she really was a dream, Elliott hoped he never awoke.

Tonight she came to him, just as she had every other night over the past three months. She floated across the dreamscape, smiling at him, sucking seductively on a finger, then using that finger to tease her bare nipples to erection. The dream shifted into a swirling miasma of color—soft pastels, then warm earth tones, and finally harsh angry hues of red, blue, and purple. Elliott found himself kneeling naked upon cool, crisp sheets. His dream mate lay beneath him and large tears welled in the corners of her almond-shaped eyes. Elliott was puzzled. He'd never seen her cry.

"What's wrong? Why are you crying?"

She sniffed and said, "I'm so very sad, my love. This may be our last night together."

"Don't say that! Not ever! We'll always be together. Nothing can come between us."

"Something can. Or rather, someone. And it's your fault. You brought them here and now they want to hurt me."

Stunned, Elliott sat upright on the bed. "I brought them here? Who? What are you talking about?"

The woman reached up and stroked Elliott's face. The touch was both electric and hypnotic. "The boy and girl. You were supposed to kill them. Instead, you brought them here, and now they're going to hurt me. They'll send me away from you. Forever. Why did you do this? Wasn't I good to you? Didn't I please you?"

The Conner brats! But how could they hurt her? She's a dream. My dream, goddamnit! Maybe it's got something to do with the Offspring bloodline. I've seen more than enough to know there's something to it. Yeah, that's got to be it!

"Don't worry, baby. Nobody's going to hurt you. Nobody! I won't let them."

She looked up from the bed, her golden eyes bright with hope. "You mean that? You won't let them hurt me? Even if it means you must kill them both? I mean, I could show you how, if—if you really mean it. It would be very easy for someone with a gun."

"I'll take care of you even if it means I have to kill every son of a bitch in this whole goddamn complex, baby! Just tell me what I need to do."

And she did.

Where . . . am I? His eyes searched for the light. Nothing but cold, infinite darkness. *Am I dead?* His mind pushed back against a growing swell of claustrophobia. Something, perhaps a thick bandage, he thought, covered his face and obscured his vision. There was nothing wrong with his hearing, though. A series of soft beeps, unfamiliar, yet oddly reassuring, sounded near his head. *Dead people don't hear sounds, do they?* he wondered.

He sniffed loudly, as the sharp odor of raw chemicals irritated his nose. *Rubbing alcohol, maybe? And iodine. Hospital? Yeah, that's it. I'm in a hospital. But why?*

He tried to blink but a firm pressure rested against his eyelids. With tentative fingers, he probed his face and head and decided his earlier assessment was indeed correct. *Thick bandages . . . several layers of gauze. Burns? Sutures? Both?* Maybe neither if the absence of pain was any indication, he decided.

So why the elaborate headgear?

He tried to remember how he'd come to be in this place, but his memories were full of spiraling black holes. What few remained were jagged fragments. He took a deep breath.

His arms and legs tingled as if awaking from a long sleep. *No pain in my chest or shoulders. Lungs seem free of congestion, so I haven't been lying here prone for very long. A day? A week? And where the hell is* here *anyway?*

He flexed the muscles in his back and arms, then tested his legs. No pain, they were just a little shaky. He somehow knew the slight tremors would pass soon.

As he rolled onto his side, he was struck by a horrific headache and an intense bout of nausea. Lying still, he struggled to regulate his breathing. The sickness would pass. It always did.

How do I know that? Have I got some disease that causes me to lose my lunch every time I roll over? No, not a disease, but it is a permanent condition, and it means . . . means . . . Damn, I can't remember! But whatever it is, it's bad. Real bad. I know that much.

As the nausea subsided, he also felt a sharp sting in the hollow of his right elbow. There wasn't much he could do about the headache so he turned his attention to the arm. Probing with tentative fingers, he located the cause of his discomfort, the business end of an IV. Throwing the crisp sheets aside, he swung his legs from the bed to the floor and felt cold tile beneath his feet.

Good nerve conduction. Legs working fine. Now let's get a look at this place.

He searched for and found the thin strips of tape that held one end of the gauze in place. Carefully, he began removing the bandages. Minutes later, a large pile of discarded cloth lay at his feet and he felt cool air against the naked skin of his face. He ran his hands over the light stubble growing on his cheeks and chin.

He took a moment to survey his surroundings. The room was spacious, though furnishings were nearly nonexistent. Other than the old hospital bed, a single retro-style chair and a worn chest of drawers represented the only furniture. The walls, painted a depressing shade of beige, were barren. Not so much as a cheap print from Wal-Mart. And no windows. What kind of hospital room had no windows?

The room was windowless, though a thick rectangle of opaque glass passed for a window in the room's only door. He could see thick mesh wire embedded in the glass, an added security feature. *Where the hell am I? I'm . . . I'm . . . Wait a minute.*

"*Who* the hell am I?"

His mind wasn't a total blank. Broken pieces of memory floated around in his head, but nothing that indicated who he was, where he was, or how he'd gotten here.

Sam glanced at the chrome IV pole that stood beside the bed. A digital medication dispenser was mounted on the pole. He read the label on the medication cartridge. Morphine 4mg Auto-Injector. The cartridge was half-full, but someone had clamped off the line.

Sam grasped the pole with both hands and rose from the bed on shaky legs. Cautiously, he made his way across the room to a stainless-steel sink. Above the basin, a small mirror made of highly polished metal was bolted to the wall. He stooped slightly and looked at his rippled reflection. He found himself looking into the battered face of a stranger. He supposed he should have been shocked, or at the very least, surprised. He was neither. He had always heard that amnesia was an extremely traumatic experience. Hadn't he always heard that? Regardless, he felt no panic, no fear. There was only a nagging irritation.

Sam dismissed the matter for the moment and surveyed his face, scalp, and neck. A wide strip of white tape covered the bridge of his nose. The left side of his face was a mass of purplish black, and his eye was swollen shut. He'd seen worse in his time. A damn sight worse. He couldn't remember when or where, but he knew it was so.

Looks like I'll live. Live. Live . . .

A broad-brush image flashed in Sam's mind. A mental picture of a woman, his mother, trapped inside a blazing coffin. Black, oily smoke clung to earth and sky. Explosions followed by tufts of ash and chunks of burning debris borne aloft by a suffocating desert wind. Men and women engaged in a desperate battle against an onslaught of horrific creatures filled with nightmarish malevolence. His sister taken by the monster known as Little Stevie . . .

The Enemy! Here! The realization slammed into Sam with the force of a runaway truck.

"Kat! I've got to find Kat."

Sam stood up and stretched, his stiff muscles already gaining strength. Looking at the crook of his arm, he frowned. He pulled the IV needle out and left it dangling from the end of the IV tubing. With the hem of his hospital gown, he applied pressure to the tiny puncture in his arm.

Feeling a draft as he lifted the gown, he said, "Need clothes." Sam took a firm grip on the IV pole and steered it across the floor to the chest of drawers. Before he could reach the chest, the room's only door swung open. A broad figure silhouetted against the bright hallway light.

After a moment, a nurse stepped into the room. At least, Sam was fairly certain she was a nurse. He also conceded it could perhaps be a massive, bi-pedal bulldog in a white dress. At the sight of him, the woman's eyes narrowed, then widened with alarm.

"Uh, hello. I need clothes. Now."

"Wha—what have you done with the bandages? And what are you doing out of that bed?" she demanded. Even her voice reminded Sam of his neighbor's Staffordshire terrier, back in Sun City. *If it looks like a bulldog, and it barks like a bulldog . . . ,* he thought. And this bulldog is immune to the old Conner two-dollar smile.

"Oh! And why is that IV? . . . Oh, this is highly irregular! You've no business walking around in your condition. Now, be a good boy and get back into bed this instant!"

Sam shook his head and again started for the chest. "Sorry. Can't do that. I've got to find my sister. Where are my clothes?"

As Sam searched the drawers, he could hear the woman's indignant grunting and stuttering. He couldn't be sure, but if her muffled sounds were any indication, he figured her blood pressure was approaching critical mass. Abruptly, the door slammed and Nurse Fido was gone. Sam sighed, then finished his search of the chest. All the drawers were empty.

Well, ain't this a bitch!

Based on Nurse Fido's hasty retreat, Sam figured there were a couple of possible outcomes. First, someone might have the good sense to page a doctor, who would then come post-haste and explain why Sam was in a hospital, then take him to Kat. The second possibility was that Nurse Fido would summon some muscle, most likely a pair of ex–high school jocks–turned–hospital orderlies, who would manhandle his near-naked skinny ass back into bed.

Before Sam could finish the thought, the solid oak door swung back with sufficient force to loosen the hinges. *Ah, lucky me. Possibility number two just arrived.*

Sam turned toward the door and saw a pair of husky thugs, both dressed in hospital greens and smiling with sadistic anticipation. Nurse Fido stood in the hallway behind them, her facial expression alternating between a scowl and a smirk. Sam spread his hands wide in supplication.

"Guys, I just want to find my sister. Back off."

The largest of the orderlies, a barrel-chested, no-necked behemoth, came through the doorway with the only slightly smaller man on his flank. Sam backed up to the bed.

"C'mon, fellas, you really don't want to do this."

"Then don't make us do anything you'll regret," said the largest of the orderlies. "Climb back into bed and let Nurse Sheppard do her job. If you don't, we'll have to put the leather restraints on you."

"Can't do that, man. Like I told you, I've got to find my sister."

The second orderly smiled and said, "Don't say we didn't

warn you, Mr. Conner, but we've got our orders." Nurse Fido had stepped into the room and stood behind the orderlies. She was wearing a smug smile.

Sam grabbed the IV pole and held it in a two-handed grip like a chromed spear as he backed up to the bed. "Don't try it, man. I ain't in the mood!"

A familiar voice boomed from out in the hallway, "Stop!"

The orderlies froze and exchanged worried glances. A second later, Thomas Falco stepped into the room and pushed past the two men. Enrique DeLorenzo was close behind.

Sam expected the two men to try talking him into submitting to the orderlies. He was surprised when Falco took a position between Sam and the door, then turned to face the orderlies.

Falco said, "You're dismissed, gentlemen. Leave. Now."

"Who in hell do you think you are?" said the nurse. "This is *my* infirmary and you've no authority down here."

The orderlies looked uncertainly at each other. The larger of the two men turned to Falco, swallowed hard, and said, "We've got our orders." As an afterthought, he added a hasty "sir." Apparently, the goons in white knew Thomas Falco.

"Boys, I won't tell you again. Get the fuck outta here while you can still walk. And take Lassie with you."

The nurse humphed loudly and spun on her heel quicker than Sam would have believed possible. Her pet orderlies almost beat her through the door.

Falco paused to allow the trio time to reach the end of the hall, then shut the door. Afterward, he walked across the room and took a seat on the edge of the bed. Sam noticed the man walked with a slight limp, no doubt picked up during the battle back in Casa Grande. Other than the limp, Falco seemed in good shape. Today he wore a tight black T-shirt and black jeans. The T-shirt's short sleeves also revealed a large US Marine Corps tattoo on Falco's left bicep, a pair of crossed combat knives underscored by the words *Semper Fi*.

Realizing he was still holding the IV pole, Sam set it on the floor and took a seat on the bed beside Falco. All of a sudden, he wasn't feeling so well. His face hurt like a bitch.

"You look like you've been run over by a truck, kid. How ya feeling? Are you hungry? I can have some food brought down."

"Not hungry. As for how I feel, I feel pretty much like I look, but why would you care? You brought us to the Enemy! That was your game all along, wasn't it? Man, you almost had me fooled. Where's my sister? I want to see her. Now!"

"Easy, Sam. Kat's room is across the hall, but she needs rest. Maybe—"

"Maybe my ass!" Sam stood up, but had to hold onto the IV pole as a wave of vertigo set the world spinning from north to south. "Listen to me. I don't know where we are, but the Enemy is nearby. I—I've got to find Kat."

Falco exchanged looks with Enrique, then whispered, "Keep your voice down, kid, and take it easy. You couldn't make it across the room by yourself right now. You've got a small crack in your left orbital socket and a broken nose. If the blow had landed a half centimeter lower, you'd have lost the eye."

Falco nodded at the drip machine. "Pulling out the IV wasn't the smartest thing you've done. You were getting a couple of grains of morphine every four hours. Just enough to take the edge off the pain without really fucking up your head. Sorry, but I clamped off the line until I was sure you were getting meds and not . . . something else."

Sam gave Falco a puzzled look.

"We already know the Enemy is on the grounds, Sam, but I swear to you, this was never a part of any plan. I'm ashamed to admit it, but it caught me by surprise. For the moment, there's not a lot we can do. Enrique and I have taken certain steps to ensure your medication and food aren't tampered with. There can't be more than a couple of bad guys on the property. Otherwise I'd know. My talent at spotting the Enemy isn't as sharp as yours, but it works well enough over short distances."

"Now sit down before you fall down!"

Falco's voice softened as he added, "Please. We've got to talk. Later, I'll take you to see Katherine. I promise."

Sam surrendered reluctantly. He didn't want to admit it, but Falco was right; Sam couldn't make it across the room without help. Not now. But later Falco would take him to Kat or else.

Or else . . . what a fucking laugh. The guy could probably kill me with an eyelash. He swung his feet from the floor and back beneath the thin sheets. Gingerly, he lay back. Even the overstuffed foam pillow felt uncomfortable against his aching head.

"How did you talk to me, Sam . . . you know, in my head? You were on the other end of the building, but I heard you clearly in my mind. How did you do that?"

"I've already told you about *reaching*. It's one of my gifts. It's just a way of communicating across distances. I guess you could consider it a kind of mental telepathy." Sam almost added that *reaching* was only possible between two or more entities who shared the gift, but he wasn't sure Falco was ready for that. He changed the subject.

"Okay, I answered a question for you. It's my turn. What happened to Henri?"

"Who?"

"The guy in the white Lincoln. His name is Henri. He had his hands full the last time I saw him."

Falco shook his head. "Don't know. The last time I saw the Lincoln, you were climbing in the passenger seat. Never saw him again. In fact, I was going to ask you about him."

"I don't get it," said Sam. "He was a dozen steps from me when you came out of the building. He was fighting that, that *thing*. But . . . come to think of it, I don't recall seeing him again, after Enrique came outside with Kat. I'll tell you everything I know about him, which isn't much, a little later," said Sam. "Okay, next question. Where are we?"

"This is a Watcher safe house, a few minutes east of New Orleans. The estate is fully self-sufficient, with supplies and staff enough for six months. At the moment, we're standing in the lowest level, two stories underground."

Trapped two stories below sea level with demons!

"Safe house? Safe for who? I'm telling you . . ." Sam dropped his voice to a whisper. "The Enemy is close! The stench is so strong, I can almost taste it. Where is Kat? We've got to get out of here!"

Falco sighed. "Ronni Weiss is taking care of Katherine . . . and the exits are guarded. We can't get you out of here. Not yet. Now tell me, how much do you remember about Casa Grande? Or the flight out of there?"

"Remember? Where do you want me to start? Never mind. I've got it. I remember that your buddies left my mother to burn alive. I remember they let Little Stevie take my sister. Oh yeah, I remember that much."

"Okay," said Falco. "We've got that much coming to us. I know it won't help, but I'm sorry. Very, very sorry."

"You're right. It doesn't help."

"It's not going to get any easier, either. Little Stevie . . . he did something to Katherine."

Sam sat up in the bed, his eyes narrowed. "What do you mean he *did* something to her?"

Falco looked down at the floor for a moment. When he looked up again, his face was ashen. "Kat was beaten, then . . . she was abused, Sam. She was catatonic and bleeding badly when we reached the hangar. That's why I wouldn't let you near her. I didn't want you to see her in that condition."

"You're lying. I want to see her, goddamn it!"

Falco shook his head slowly. "I wish to God I was, Sam. I wish I was."

Sam closed his eyes. He'd failed her, the last surviving member of his immediate family. His baby sister. Pesky, too-smart-for-her-own-damn-good Katherine. Innocent little Katherine. Raped-by-a-fucking-monster Katherine. With a pang of guilt that seared his soul, Sam recalled Kat's last words to him. Words sent via the *reach*.

Don't come here, Sam. Go away. Just . . . go away and never come back.

"Physically, she'll mend," said Falco. "We've got the finest trauma facility and medical staff this side of Johns Hopkins, but the doctors can't gauge the extent of her emotional or psychological damage. It'll be a while before they know anything.

Her recovery could take days, months, or a lifetime. God only knows what she endured in that place."

Sam began to cry, a pitiful muffled whimper that slowly gained momentum and culminated with hard, wracking cries of anguish, shame, and uncontrolled rage. Only merciful sleep helped dull the crushing pain in his heart.

When Sam awoke, the room was dark except for a dim fluorescent light above the bed. The pain in his face had subsided, and though his mind was clear, perhaps too clear, he felt a little off-center. He tried to sit up and noticed that at some point, Nurse Fido had restarted the IV, and the morphine drip was doing its thing. A covered tray sat atop a bedside table. Sam rose to a sitting position and removed the metal lid. The food was standard hospital fare and Sam thought nothing had ever looked so good. He pulled the small table near to the bed and ate in silence.

After he finished the meal and strong coffee, Sam found a plastic urinal beneath the bed and answered the call of nature. Afterward, he tested his legs by leaning on the roll-around drip machine and navigating the short distance from the bed to the door. So far, so good. Time to find Kat.

As he reached for the door, it swung open, revealing a startled Thomas Falco and Enrique DeLorenzo. Enrique stood behind a wheelchair.

"Sorry, gentlemen, but I was just on my way out."

"You'll need a guide," said Falco. "A guy could get lost down here for weeks."

"We thought you might be ready to look in on Katherine," added Enrique. He nodded toward the wheelchair. "Have a seat and I'll play chauffeur."

Sam didn't want the escort. Neither Falco nor Enrique had any right to go near his sister. After all, they were the reason she was here in the first place. Weren't they? Still, he knew he had no choice. He wasn't in any shape to stop them, and any verbal protest would just be a waste of breath.

"Yeah, sure." Sam sat down in the wheelchair. "Lead the way, but don't talk to me while I'm with her. Not a fucking word, got it?"

Falco and Enrique exchanged glances, and Falco nodded. "Sure kid, we got it."

Falco removed the portable morphine pump from the IV pole and attached it to a second, smaller pole fixed to the back of the wheelchair.

"Turn that thing off, would ya?" said Sam. "I think I've had enough for a while."

"No dice, tough guy. Doc Stone says you'll probably need a little juice of the poppy to get you through the next couple of days. In fact, it's probably the only reason you're still vertical. But let the nurses know if you start seeing little green men or circus ponies in the room. Morphine, even in moderate doses, is notorious for inducing audio and visual hallucinations. The doctor can reduce the dosage and the hallucinations should clear up within a couple of hours."

"Yeah, sure. Now take me to Kat."

Enrique piloted the wheelchair out into the hallway and paused. Sam, having grown somewhat accustomed to the relative cramped confines of his room, was immediately struck by the enormity of the building. To his left, the hallway, illuminated by bright fluorescent lights and dotted by dozens of doors identical to Sam's own, seemed to run forever before disappearing over a distant, artificial horizon. An optical illusion, he suspected, but damned disturbing, nonetheless. To his right, the hall extended for a good thirty to forty yards, before ending in front of an imposing set of metal double doors.

"When you said this was a safe house, I pictured, well . . . a *house*. Just how big is this place?"

Falco chuckled, then said, "Not all that large in terms of floors. Two stories below, five above. But you're right, it's a massive structure. Much larger than the fifteenth-century French keep it's patterned after. Anyone unfamiliar with the layout could wander around for a day and never see the same room twice. Reaching an exit without a guide would prove daunting, at best."

The message wasn't lost on Sam. An easy escape was out of the question. Not that Sam had notions of leaving. Not without Kat, anyway.

"A couple of things before we go inside, Sam," said Enrique. "Her doctor asked me to tell you Kat won't know you're here. She won't see you or speak. She's under heavy sedation in order to give her mind and body a chance to recover without the added stress of conscious thought. You don't have to do this now, you know. It won't hurt to wait a couple of days, until you're stronger."

When Sam spoke, his voice was just above a whisper. "Take me to my sister."

Seconds later, Sam sat next to Kat's bed, staring in horror at the tortured look on the unconscious girl's once angelic face. Despite the heavy medication, Kat's expression was that of a trapped and wounded animal, her jaws snapping at the air again and again. Only a molded plastic mouthpiece prevented her jagged, broken teeth from chewing through an already ravaged bottom lip. Not even eighteen hundred miles and a drug-induced coma were enough to keep Little Stevie at bay.

Once back in his room, Sam allowed Falco to help him out of the chair and onto the bed. He wanted to cry, but his tears had been long since exhausted. He wanted to scream but couldn't summon the energy or his voice. He wanted to lash out at everything, and everyone, to punish those responsible for his mother's death and Kat's condition. *All in good time*, he told himself. *All in good time.*

Nurse Sheppard stepped inside the room but kept her distance until Sam was beneath the sheets. Falco and Enrique stepped aside and watched as Sheppard started a new IV line, and reset the morphine drip. After she adjusted the flow rate, she produced a syringe from one of the deep pockets of her smock, removed the cap and inserted the needle into the IV line.

"What's that?" asked Sam.

"Dr. Stone ordered a round of antibiotics. You're to stay on them while your injuries heal."

He knew she was lying. The syringe may have held a course of antibiotics, but it held something else, as well. Or perhaps the doctor had loaded the syringe and the nurse really didn't realize what she was giving him. But Sam knew. It was a sedative, and a rather strong one at that. The Watchers didn't want any trouble from an Offspring wildcard while they decided what to do with him. It was just as well. Seeing Kat in her condition had sapped Sam's remaining energy. He wanted nothing more than to fall asleep and never wake up.

The sedative did its job and within a few minutes, Sam teetered on the precipice of unconsciousness. Calm and relaxed for the first time in days. He looked across the room at Falco and Enrique. The two men had their heads together, talking in muted whispers.

Here it comes. They think my resistance is down, and the interrogation begins.

Sam decided to beat them to the punch. "So, Tommy boy, how many people does it take to run this operation, anyway?"

Enrique's head snapped up and he stared at Sam for a long moment. He then glanced at his watch, before whispering something to Falco. Falco seemed amused. He scooted one of the chairs closer to Sam's bed and took a seat.

"The safe house employs about sixty full-time personnel. Communications and administrative specialists, physical security, medical, and housekeeping. We've got a dozen similar operations scattered across the Americas."

"Thomas!" said Enrique. "That's a little more than Sam wants or needs to know."

Sam laughed, then grew somber. "You'd be surprised at just how much I want and need to know, Mr. DeLorenzo. And I will know. I'll know more about your little group than they know about themselves. Count on it."

"And why is that, Sam? Have you decided to help us? Or maybe you've got revenge on your mind. Preparing to claim your pound of flesh. Is that it?"

"I'd say the latter is accurate. See, it's like this; my mother and sister aren't in any position to repay the Watchers for your kindness. That leaves me."

"Yeah, I figured as much. I can understand your need to strike back, but you're targeting the wrong side. Of course, I can probably understand that, too," said Falco.

"Man, don't even go there," said Sam. "*Understand?* You don't understand shit!"

"Tell him," said Enrique in a small voice.

"We don't have time for this, Rikki. We've got to figure some way to get you out of the compound. Save the story for another day. Right now, we've got to get you and the kids back to Boston in one piece."

Sam was intrigued by Falco's tone. "What story? C'mon, Falco, you owe me that much."

Falco studied the tops of his shoes for several seconds, then looked at Sam and nodded. "Yeah, I owe you, kid. Okay, here's my story, but you'll have to be satisfied with the abbreviated version."

"Wait a minute," said Enrique. He pulled something from his pocket, a small electronic device not much larger than a cigarette pack. He flipped a small switch and the instrument answered with a chirp. Holding a finger to his lips to indicate silence, Enrique walked around the room, sliding the instrument along walls, furniture, and finally, the IV and automated drug dispenser. As he moved the odd instrument over the pole, he was rewarded by a high-pitched whine. Enrique looked over at Falco and nodded. The two men examined the pole from base to top before Falco found the object of their search: a small, metallic button sporting a pair of tiny wire antennas. Sam started to ask about the item, but Enrique shook his head and again held his finger to his lips. Neither man spoke as Falco twisted the miniature antennae from the button, then carefully replaced the hollowed section of the IV pole.

After he was finished, Enrique looked at his watch and said, "We've got maybe fifteen minutes to wrap this up before maintenance arrives. Once they discover the bug is on the blink, they'll make some excuse about a routine inspection, then remove this pole and replace it with another that has a functioning listening device."

Puzzled, Sam said, "But why—"

"Standard procedure any time we have Offspring on the premises. And no, you aren't the first, not by a long shot."

Sam laughed. "Man, you guys don't trust anyone. Not even each other!"

"With good reason, Sam, but I don't have time to explain." Turning to Falco, Enrique said, "Please continue."

Falco nodded. "I was raised by my mother, Sam. Didn't meet my father until I was twenty-three. My mother never said much about him. She told me not to hate him, that what he did for a living was far more important than taking care of a small family. Of course, she never explained what he did.

"Meanwhile, my mother supported us by working at a crosstown hospital as a nurse's aide. Not a very lucrative occupation, but she was always working extra shifts, or so I thought. Even at minimum wage, she always had more than enough money to pay the bills. In fact, I didn't realize it until I was older, but we lived in a large house in an upscale neighborhood. Certainly not the sort of place a single mom working for minimum wage could afford.

"I used to bug her about going to see where she worked, but she always had an excuse. I—I didn't see much of her for the last ten years of her life. I didn't know my father, so she was the only immediate family I had. My mother was the center of my universe, though we seldom really spoke during the last years of her life. Her every waking moment was dedicated to her work at the hospital. At least, that's what I was told. Conversation around home dried up, except for the cursory 'Hi, how's school?' 'Fine, how's work?' Oh, I loved her, and she loved me. But we didn't know each other for those last few years. Not really."

"Wait a minute," interrupted a drowsy Sam. "I thought you and DeLorenzo were brothers."

"Half-brothers. And I'm getting to that, so take it easy. So, I turn seventeen and decide I want to join the Marines. My mother wouldn't hear of it. Wouldn't even discuss it. I didn't want to go against her wishes, but my mind was made up. Figured I'd wait until I turned eighteen, then slip out one night and just disappear. And that's exactly the way it played out. I pulled six years in the Corps.

"My mother wasn't much of a letter writer and neither was

I, but we managed to stay in touch. Then, during my last year of active duty, I get this letter. She's moving out of the old neighborhood. Leaving New York and moving to the Midwest. The fucking Midwest! Giving up a great house that she owns, and exchanging it for an apartment in the Midwest. Hell, she didn't even know *where* in the Midwest. Said she'd figure it out later.

"I was close to the end of my obligation to Uncle Sam. I decided to get a ten-day furlough and surprise my mother. Help her pack, and maybe even talk her out of leaving the city.

"I arrived early Friday evening. From the sidewalk, I could see the lights were off in the house except for an upstairs bedroom. I checked the front door and it was locked. I didn't have a key, but I knew how to trip the lock on the back door.

"On the way around the house, I heard a crash followed by a muffled scream. The scream was really more of a loud, dying moan."

Sam was surprised to see Falco's eyes were glassy and filled with tears. This wasn't an act. The big man was shaken by the account he shared. Sam started to cut him off, but he couldn't. He didn't want to hear another word, but it was no longer a matter of "want" or "don't want." Sam *needed* to hear Falco's story.

Falco continued. "I knew that sound. Knew it very well. The sound of someone so terrified, they actually begged for death. Anything, *anything* to stop the horror.

"I kicked in the back door and stopped in the kitchen long enough to locate a suitable weapon. I found a butcher knife on the drain board, then headed for my mother's room. I met a shadow man on the stairway."

"Shadow man? Explain, please."

"A powerful demon, Sam," offered Enrique. "Supernatural intelligence with an arsenal of mental and physical weapons at its disposal. They rarely assume a substantial form, preferring to use psychological torture, spiritual possession, and coercion to gather victims. When they enter the three-dimensional realm, very bad things happen."

"And this demon came for your mother?"

Falco nodded. "It did. I won't tell you how she died, but I will say this: Although you've had some remarkable experiences with demons, I can guarantee you've never witnessed anything like that.

"The demon was still in corporeal form and it attacked me. Damn near had me until two men whom I'd never seen before rushed up the stairs and took up the fight. One of those men died saving my life. I later learned it was my father, a Watcher Sword. My mother had also been a Watcher, though I wouldn't learn that until much later.

"The experience left me with some serious emotional baggage and a lot of unanswered questions. No gentle way of putting this, Sam. I was a fucking mental trainwreck. Upon leaving the Corps, I came back to New York and sought out my parish priest and he steered me toward seminary. I had nowhere else to go, so I decided, why not? I began to study to join the priesthood that same year.

"It was only after I was ordained that I learned the truth. The demons were looking for my father. They stumbled across my mother instead, and tried to make her talk. My father was overseas on an extended mission at the time, and that was all the information she had. She couldn't tell the demon what she didn't know, so the shadow man butchered her. I just happened home at the wrong time. My father had returned to the US and learned that Legion was actively hunting him. On a hunch, he decided to look in on my mother and me. That's how he came to be in New York that night.

"But I'm getting ahead of myself. The Watchers contacted me soon after I was ordained. I was a legacy case, a direct descendant of the Watcher line, and it was a given that I'd be recruited into the organization. It's a long-standing custom and practice. Legacies are almost an automatic. We're indoctrinated, trained in primary and secondary skill sets, then reassigned anywhere in the world as various missions dictate.

"But . . . after I learned the truth, that my mother had died because of her involvement with the Watchers, I wanted nothing to do with them. I blamed the organization for everything.

"A short time after that, I also learned why I saw so little of my father growing up. My father and mother were never married, though he apparently cared deeply for her. Despite his work and other family, he spent a lot of time with us."

"Other family," said Sam.

Falco nodded toward Enrique. "Yeah. After my mother's death, I learned that he had a legitimate family living in Boston and that I had a half-brother. That's when I first meet Rikki.

"I won't drag this out, Sam. I finally came to understand that no matter how dark and manipulative the Watchers seemed, joining them sure as hell beat the alternatives. Legion had already established a foothold on the planet, and their numbers were about to explode. I had to make a decision: Remain neutral or enter the battle on the side of the Watchers, and more important, on the side of God. In the end, it was an easy decision, and I eventually took up where my father left off and became a field operator for the organization."

"An assassin for the Catholic Church."

Falco nodded. "If the mission required it, then yes, I killed. But for the Catholics? Hardly. The Watchers have operatives inside the Church, and a few of those operatives sit in high positions. But the Church only suspects that we exist. We maintain our covert ties in order to make use of the Vatican's vast resources. Besides, we trust the Vatican about as far as we can throw 'em.

"And I'll share something else, though I doubt you'll believe me. It's true the Hierarchy wants the Offspring taken out of this war. Half the council is afraid of you and the other half hates you. But whatever you may think of us, our greatest concern is in serving the will of God. In doing so, we serve the best interest of mankind. That's all we've ever wanted."

Sam shook his head. "Dude, give me a break! Your God lets you persecute innocent people out of fear or hatred? Man, if that's the case . . . Look, my mother is dead and my sister is a vegetable because of you! That's how your God operates?"

"Maybe, if it served a greater good. But not necessarily," said Falco. "I won't insult your intelligence by reciting the old mantra that God works in mysterious ways, though He certainly does that. But what happened to your mother and sister is the result of our sometimes pathetic attempts to do His will. God might provide the tools and opportunities, but He's not a puppeteer, pulling the strings on a bunch of mindless wooden dolls."

"Thomas is right, Sam. Whatever mistakes were made, they're *our* mistakes, not God's," added Enrique. "We try to do the right thing. Sometimes we succeed and sometimes we fail, but none of us are hardwired for perfection.

"Look at it this way. According to you, Offspring carry the DNA of angels. Yet, during our search, we've found Offspring sitting in jails or prisons, locked away for committing horrible crimes. Others were near death from years of drug or alcohol abuse. Carrying divine blood doesn't prevent your kind from making poor choices or committing mistakes. Even the most favored angel in history was capable of committing the ultimate sin, and he took one-third of Heaven with him. As for us mortals, serving a divine cause damn sure doesn't mean we're incapable of making mistakes."

A tear ran along Sam's cheek before dropping to the pillow. Enrique spoke so casually of "mistakes" that had contributed to the death of his mother. Still, though he hated to admit it, the Watcher made sense.

Over time, Sam had come to believe Horace and Joriel and accept his angelic heritage. It was a wild tale, but Sam had witnessed too much corroborating evidence. However, along with that acceptance came some troubling questions. For starters, how could someone with the blood of angels be so . . . human? From Sam's perspective, he was no better or worse than most other kids his age. He had made more than his share of bad choices and mistakes. He had committed acts that would put him outside the parameters of "goodness" established by most of the major, mainstream religions.

Along with committing a host of minor misdeeds, he knew what it was to hate another human being. He damn well hated the Watchers for the part they played in the death of his mother and Kat's abuse. He knew what it was to hate someone or something so bad, he could kill without remorse. How could he really be the descendant of angels and still lead such a flawed human existence? Unless maybe Enrique had it right. Sam had always tried to do the right thing. Most of the time, at least. Was it enough? Maybe it was like his grandmother once told him. She said there was a big difference between "religious" and "spiritual."

Enrique approached the bed, a look of pleading in his eyes. "Look, Sam, I could stand here for another week and try to make a case for you to help us, but I think you've got enough information. Perhaps your mind is already made up. I need to know, Sam. Events overseas indicate that the world is about to experience an event that will dictate the future of mankind. It may seem that demons operate independently, but I assure you, Legion has a master plan, and that plan is entering the final stages."

"Heh. So, you're saying the world is coming to an end? We're on the verge of Armageddon? That old song's about played out, don't you think?"

"You of all people should recognize the truth in that old song, Sam. You've seen firsthand what Legion is and what they can do. Look, do you recall what I said back in Casa Grande about getting back to Boston today? That something big was about to take place?"

"Yeah, vaguely."

Enrique paused for a moment and gave Falco a curious look. A look of total resignation. Turning back to Sam, he said, "Something has happened overseas, an event that leads us to believe the remaining Veils are in imminent danger. Sam, you're the only person who knows how to shut down a Veil. We've got to know . . . are you with us?"

So, it comes down to this. Help an enemy defeat an enemy. Aid the lesser of two evils. Then what? Don't they realize the closure of a Veil requires the blood of an Offspring? What'll happen when that bit of news becomes common knowledge? And what of Kat?

Sam was near penniless and Kat would require serious medical attention for an indefinite period of time. Of course, if he refused, it was all moot. The Hierarchy would either have him killed or imprisoned for the rest of his life. Sam decided it was time to test his bargaining power.

"The drugs are messing with my head, guys. Can't concentrate. Look, let me sleep it off. Just a couple of hours. Then come back and I'll give you my decision. I think you owe Kat and I that much."

Enrique frowned. Time was critical and he'd hoped to have Sam's answer before leaving the room. "But—"

"He's right," said Falco. We do owe them that much. And more." Falco looked at his watch, then said, "Two hours, Sam. When we come back, you'll have to give us an answer."

Enrique said, "I've got some calls to make, so if you'll excuse me." Falco waited until Enrique left the room, then looked at Sam. Before I go, I . . ."

"Yeah? What is it?"

Falco studied Sam for a long moment, then said, "How long have you known?"

"Known what?"

"C'mon, kid. The games are over. You spoke to me . . . in my head. You told me that's how Offspring communicated."

Sam grinned. "Oh, that. Yeah, this sorta puts the capital *I* in *irony*, doesn't it? I wondered when you would connect the dots. I knew it the night I pulled you off the roof."

Falco shook his head. "Why didn't you tell me?"

"Tell you what? You wouldn't have believed anything I said. You had to see it for yourself. Believe me, I know. Been there, done that."

For a long moment, neither spoke. Finally, Falco walked toward the door. Just before stepping out into the hallway, he turned and said, "When you're feeling up to it, maybe you can fill me in on how all this works. Three days ago, I was sure I had all the answers. Now I realize I don't even know the damn questions."

"Welcome to the club," said Sam. "Maybe we can figure out the questions and answers together. But later. Right now, let me get some rest, will you?"

chapter 24

A half-hour. No more. Malcolm poured himself a tall Scotch and tried to relax. If the plan succeeded, the Offspring would be dead. The Hierarchy would finally elevate Malcolm to the highest position in the Western hemisphere: Lord Protector. Such control would place Malcolm among the most powerful men in the free world, even if few outside the Watcher organization knew it. Legion would gain a tremendous advantage, with high-placed thralls, greater demons, and lords operating without fear of Watcher assassins. They would own the Americas within the year. All Watcher operatives would be exposed, hunted down, and executed. The Seventy-two would destroy the remaining Veils and the Nine Princes of Sitra Akhra would enter the Plane of Man. And for his service, Malcolm Reading would be exalted above all other humans.

If the plan failed, however, Malcolm would escape to Syria before midnight. *With a dozen Swords in hot pursuit, no doubt. Ah, well. No matter, that.* As a trusted agent, for that's how Malcolm saw himself, he'd have the protection of Legion during his flight. They must protect him. After all, he'd still have a critical role to play during the End of Days—few humans had Malcolm's resources and access to covert intelligence. With the Keys now in the hands of the demon lords, the beginning of the end was close. Legion would make great use of Malcolm's extensive connections and knowledge of Jerusalem. And once the Seventy-two were freed, the entity that shared Malcolm Reading's body and mind promised him, he would have wealth beyond imagination, position in the New Order, and dominion over entire worlds. Most important, it promised him an opportunity to strike back at a hypocritical, manipulative God. The same cruel God who had taken Malcolm's wife.

Four long years, Malcolm watched helplessly as his beloved wife succumbed to cancer. An illness very similar to that suffered by Gilbert. Yet while Gilbert had responded to what he termed "a harmonious blend of medical science and spiritual faith," Elizabeth had wasted away until there was little left. The disease spread throughout her body, eventually reaching her mind. Before death, the once brilliant, vivacious, and deeply spiritual woman was reduced to a babbling husk of humanity. All this despite the weeks and months Malcolm spent upon his face in supplication to an unhearing, uncaring God. *My life for hers. Please, heal her. Heal her!* His pleas went unanswered.

Once, Malcolm would have stormed the very gates of Heaven in order to take revenge upon God Almighty. Now he had Legion to do the deed for him.

The Scotch tasted flat, stale. He set aside the glass, and watched the wall clock's pendulum swing from side to side. With each pass, the plan grew nearer to success or failure. There was nothing more he could do to influence the outcome of tonight's events. Malcolm's "partner," the demon lord that shared his body and mind, had visited Elliott Glenn in yet another dream. Glenn was fully enthralled, eager to do his seducer's bidding. Not that it was a difficult task, enthralling the man. He had a natural inclination toward the darkness. That was the primary reason Malcolm had recruited him.

By now, Glenn, his mind clouded beyond reason by a powerful, malevolent spirit, was outfitted for his mission—weapons selected and checked, and route plotted. Minutes later, he'd use his newly acquired pass card to enter the security wing of the mansion. He'd kill the girl first, then her brother. Afterward, he'd activate an intruder alarm, then wait patiently for security staff to respond. They'd find the slain siblings and immediately notify Malcolm, who would in turn notify Falco and DeLorenzo. When the half-brothers rushed to the security wing, as they no doubt would, Elliott Glenn would be waiting.

If Elliott did his job, Malcolm would be made sole top-level Watcher on the North American continent. And if Falco and DeLorenzo somehow survived the ambush, well, Damascus was nice this time of year.

Fractured dreams ran in uneven sequences inside his exhausted mind. Running through wind-blown alleys . . . *step, shuffle* . . . hiding behind Dumpsters, trying to stay ahead of the white Lincoln . . . *step, shuffle* . . . atop a bridge over the Mississippi River, staring in horror at the approaching Trenchcoat . . . *step, shuffle* . . . huddled inside a cardboard fort with Mark and Janet while the Enemy searches . . . *step, shuffle* . . . watching helplessly as Michael Collier, dying, yet still filled with superhuman resolve, steps into the Eye of God . . . *step, shuffle* . . . gunfire followed by screams . . . Kat reaching out to him . . . Kat!

Sam came awake with a start. He arose from the bed, staggered, then gripped the IV pole for support. His body was sluggish and slow to respond, but his mind was sharp, focused. He rolled from the bed, paused for a moment to steady his legs, then made for the door.

Outside in the hall, he found a nurse lying in a growing pool of blood. The door to Kat's room was ajar. When Sam burst into the room, he found Elliott Glenn standing over Kat, pressing the barrel of his handgun to the side of her head. When Elliott saw Sam, a wide grin spread across his face.

"Excellent! Big brother rushes to the rescue just like he predicted."

"You don't want to do this, man. I don't know what the demon promised you, but it's all lies."

"Enough!" shouted Elliott. "You won't talk about him like that! He's all I've got! He's . . . he's the only one in this entire fucked-up world who knows me. Now turn around. I'll make this quick as long as you cooperate. If you fuck with me, I'll make it hard on little sister, I promise you."

"If you hurt her, I'll—"

"You'll what?" said Elliott as he raised the muzzle of the handgun and centered it on Sam's chest. "Boy, you don't get it. You've messed with something so much larger than yourself. Larger than all of us. You and your sister are already dead, but you're too stupid to know it. Say good-bye, kid." Elliott's finger tightened on the trigger.

A starburst of brilliant multicolored lights, painful in its intensity, exploded in front of Sam. He shielded his eyes, then felt himself thrown back against the door as a violent, swirling wind ripped through the windowless room. The fluorescent light fixture mounted above the center of the room shook loose from its anchors and crashed to the floor inches from Sam. Broken pieces of metal and plastic, along with paper debris and loose items of clothing and bedding, were sucked toward the middle of the floor where they were caught up and suspended by a spiraling, supernatural vortex.

Sam sagged to the floor, half-blinded by the light, covering his head with his arms against the flying debris. *Oh, God. He shot me! I'm dead!*

Above the roar of the miniature tornado that danced across the floor, a loud voice roared, "Harm not His servants!" Across the room, Elliott Glenn screamed once, then fell silent.

As his vision cleared, Sam made out the image of a large man standing at the foot of Kat's bed. A full head taller than Thomas Falco, the man's arms and face were covered in strange, glowing tattoos. Elliott Glenn, his head twisted at an odd angle, lay upon the floor at the man's feet.

"Do not be afraid, Sam Conner."

Sam shook his head. "Easy for you to say. Who are you?"

Nathan said, "I'm a friend of Uriel's. Or perhaps you'd prefer to think of him as Horace. I'm also a friend to you and your sister. I would have come sooner, but I didn't know your location or the exact extent of your current problems until Uriel contacted me and asked that I check on you."

Sam looked at Kat and whispered, "My sister. Will she be okay?"

The man walked to the head of the bed and laid a hand upon Kat's head. He gently stroked her hair and whispered something. Tears glistened in his eyes as he studied the girl. After a moment, he looked at Sam.

"She's suffered much for one so small, so young. But she will recover. I give you my word."

Sam walked to the side of the bed. The tortured expression was gone from Kat's face. She slept now, no longer tortured by the nightmares of Casa Grande.

"My brother hunts the one called Little Stevie, even now. The monster won't trouble you or yours again. You have my solemn oath. And Horace's."

Tears stung Sam's eyes. "There are other monsters out there. It'll never be safe for us, will it?"

"True, you still have enemies, little brother. Zynth and others like her, and humans like Malcolm Reading who've bowed before the Runner. But there will come a reckoning, this I swear. Even now, Legion prepares for a final battle. They've stolen an ancient text, sometimes called the Lesser Keys, that once allowed a king to imprison a horde of powerful demonic entities. The text can also be used to free them. The world cannot endure such an event.

"Very soon, you and others like you will have to make a decision. Join us in this final confrontation, or sit back and allow Legion to proceed unopposed.

"Once before, you and your kindred managed to close one of the Veils. Imagine, if you can, a world full of damaged portals, allowing countless demons to pour into this world from Sitra Akhra."

"How—how could that happen?"

"In another age, before God established the Law of Balance, great demons walked in number upon this world. These demons, seventy-two in number, were among the most powerful in all of Creation. The Creator knew that, in time, these demons would rival the Nine Princes of Sitra Akhra in terms of power and influence. Unopposed, these demons would have unraveled Time itself, thus destroying much of the Multiverse.

"In another age, the Creator spoke into existence certain Words of Power or 'Keys,' and He gave those Keys to a human king. He bade the king to use the Keys to bind the Seventy-two for eternity. For centuries, the Seventy-two have remained in an earthly prison, and the Keys were hidden on hallowed ground, beyond the reach of the corrupt—the Fallen and Legion alike. Or so we thought.

"The Keys have been stolen, Sam Conner. We don't know how, but we do know why. The bearer of the Keys can release the Seventy-two from bondage. Such an event will mark the End of Days. We must recover the Keys and restore the balance. Else mankind, those who survive, will endure a life not worth the living."

Sam shook his head slowly from side to side. "This is too much! I don't understand! Why doesn't God just . . . fix it?"

Nathan smiled. "The Creator has given us all the tools to do what is needed. We each must find the faith to take up those tools and do what is necessary. First, we must find the Keys. Then we must forever break the back of Legion.

"Know this, Sam Conner. Many innocent lives will be destroyed in the attempt. Perhaps even your own. As ever, the decision, the choice, is yours. You will know how to contact me with your answer once you have it.

"And in the meantime, you've acquired new friends and powerful allies. In fact, two of them are coming this way now. You can trust them, Sam. You must. Without one another, you have little hope for tomorrow. Remain strong and true to one another. Now I must go."

"Wait! Your name . . ."

"I am called Nathaniel. Or Nathan, if you prefer. Oh, yes. Both Joriel and Uriel send much love." And he was gone.

Sam sat down on the edge of Kat's bed and held her tiny hand in his. *He said you'll recover. God, if you're listening . . . thank you. Thank you.*

Sam was still holding her hand when Enrique and Thomas entered the room.

αUϮhΟR'S ΝΟϮε:
The "What If" Game

Not long ago, a close friend asked me if I thought *Offspring* was actually grounded in an element of truth. The person wanted to know if I believed "evil" roamed the earth, in both incorporeal and corporeal forms, with the capacity to influence human behavior or cause direct harm. And if I believed in demons, did I also believe in angels? My friend wasn't the first person to ask me that question. In fact, that issue surfaces during nearly every interview I participate in.

The answer is yes . . . and no. It requires no stretch of the imagination to believe in evil. One has only to read the newspaper or watch the evening news. And, as goes the ancient principle of Yin and Yang (equal opposites, i.e., black and white; soft and hard; left and right, etc.), if evil exists, so must its polar opposite, "good."

Now, having stated the above, please keep in mind I didn't write *Offspring* with the intent to make a moral statement. *Offspring* is a work of fiction with a decidedly supernatural theme. It's a tale constructed by playing the "what if" game, drawing from part and parcel of several religious belief systems, as well as various historical incidents.

For instance, I reference the Knights Templar in several scenes. The meteoric rise and fall of the Templars has been thoroughly chronicled by several prominent historians and scribes. Most historians agree that the first Templars, nine knights of noble birth, took up residence inside the Temple Mount in Jerusalem.

Most also agree that those knights embarked upon a massive excavation project beneath the temple. What they allegedly found in the catacombs (though it depends on which conspiracy theory you subscribe to) catapulted the group to a position of European prominence. Over the next couple of centuries, kings and popes alike found themselves financially indebted to the Templars, that once "poor band of brothers."

Again, depending on which version you choose to accept, the root cause of the Templars' demise may be traced to a greedy king of France and a corrupt, and some say fearful, Church. The knights were tried and convicted of numerous charges of heresy and debauchery. Others "confessed" (under extreme duress) their crimes and were spared execution, while still others were burned at the stake while proclaiming their innocence. The Order was disbanded and forever outlawed.

Some scholars believe a few members of the Templars did survive the purge, and much speculation has been raised about the post–Templar era activities of those men and their families. Modern-day descendants of the Templars were a perfect fit for *Offspring*. There's an awful lot of "what if" material in there.

The more recent, and tragic, May 1998 incident involving the murder of a Swiss Guard commander and his wife upon Vatican grounds also receives mention in *Offspring*. The conspiracy theories surrounding the crime are too numerous to list in this limited space. Love triangles, office politics, brain tumors, and yes, demonic influence, are but a few of the conspiracies I've read to date. Another prime opportunity for the "what if" game. And I assure you, I do not write about such real-life incidents with a callous attitude. I truly believe that buried in the quagmire of supposition, rumor, and innuendo, the truth does exist. Until that truth makes its way to the surface, we're stuck with "what if."

The Vatican, and more precisely, Pope Benedict XVI, also blended well into *Offspring*. In fact, I would have been hard-pressed to find a better papal fit for this story. The scene in *Off-spring* that describes events at the Our Lady of Akita Church, is based on numerous factual accounts, including news reports, Church archives, and testimony provided by more than five hundred Christian and non-Christian witnesses. After a lengthy investigation of the alleged miracles and ominous prophecies that occurred at Our Lady of Akita in Japan over a period of nearly fifteen years, Joseph Cardinal Ratzinger, Prefect, Congregation for the Doctrine of the Faith, issued a definitive judgment: He declared "those events and messages as reliable and worthy of belief."

Cardinal Ratzinger is now better known as Pope Benedict XVI. Benedict may also be forever known as the first pope ever to ordain a Vatican-operated educational institution that has only one mission: teaching the secret discipline of exorcisms. This is something of an odd turnabout from former papal attitudes in which exorcisms were considered a near-dead ritual. After all these many centuries, why would the arguably most influential and politically powerful religious institution on earth embark on such a course? Great material for playing the "what if" game, don't you agree?

Again, thank you for reading *Offspring*.

Liam Jackson

GLOSSARY OF TERMS

Angel. A souless, celestial entity, created by God and capable of taking ethereal or corporeal form in Heaven and upon Earth.

Archangel. One of three classes of angels found in the highest tier of Heaven. Michael, Raphael, Gabriel, and Uriel are the most well known of the Archangels, while Anael, Metatron, Ragual, Raziel, Remiel, and Sariel are commonly believed to be the remaining archangels who surround and protect the Throne of the Creator. Often incorrectly referred to as Guardian Angels, though they sometimes fulfill that function.

Authority. A class of angels found in the middle tier of Heaven, and occasionally upon Earth.

Brethren. Another name for fallen angels and much preferred by Lucifer over other, less flattering titles.

Cherubim. A class of angels found in the highest tier of Heaven. Very powerful.

Creator. God

Demon (Lesser Demons). The lowest form of sentient corruption, originating on the plane of Sitra Akhra. Lesser demons possess the ability to occasionally cross over into the world of men.

Demon Lord. An extremely powerful demon with limited access to the world of men.

Domination. A class of angel found in the middle tier of Heaven and occasionally, upon Earth.

Earthbound Host. The collective body of angelic entities, comprised of many classes, and assigned to various tasks upon Earth by the Creator. May take either corporeal or ethereal form. Often referred to as Guardian Angels.

Eye of God. A juxtaposition or joining of all the planes of existence at a single point. It is possible to travel among planes by entering the Eye of God.

Fallen. A name given to Lucifer and his followers. Angels cast out of Heaven during the First Great War.

Fury. A powerful demon charged with war and violence. May manifest in either ethereal or corporeal form.

Greater Demons. Demons of the Third Order. Very powerful and most often manifesting upon the plane of Man in ethereal form.

Herald. Angels from the lowest tier in Heaven.

Host. The collective body of angelic entities, comprised of all classes, and responsible for a multitude of tasks including the protection of Mankind and Heaven.

Kiv. An ancient weapon of tremendous elemental power, favored by angelic warriors.

Legion. The name given to the collective inhabitants of Sitra Akhra, or any group of demons.

Multiverse. Infinite planes of existence, also theorized in quantum physics as being comprised of as many as eleven dimensions.

Nephilim. Judeo-Christian Old Testament name given to angels who took human wives.

Offspring. The descendants of angels and humans. The only beings in all of Creation within whom flows the blood of both Divinity (angels) and Divine Creation (humans).

Power. A class of angel found upon the middle tier of Heaven and, occasionally, upon Earth.

Principality. A class of angel found upon the lowest tier of Heaven and, occasionally, upon Earth.

Reach/Reaching. An ability to mentally communicate over great distances. Sometimes *reaching* is a subconscious act, occurring during periods of great physical or mental stress.

Runner. The Runner is the leader of the fallen angels that reside on Earth. Many scholars believe he is of the Seraphim or Cherubim class, although some scholars maintain he is a fallen archangel. Regardless, it is an accepted notion by all parties that the Runner is one of the most powerful entities in all of Creation. Other names for the Runner are Satan, Lucifer, and Shaitan.

Seraphim. A class of angel found upon the highest tier of Heaven and, very rarely, upon Earth.

Seventh Law. The Seventh Law was instituted by the Creator. The intent was to prevent other, potentially dangerous entities from crossing over into the Plane of Man by restricting travel through the Eye of God (the Veils). According to this law, the more powerful the entity, the more difficult it is to navigate the Eye of God.

Sitra Akhra. The dwelling place of Legion. A foul plane of existence so far removed from Heaven, its inhabitants refuse to acknowledge the existence of God.

Soldier (demon). A lesser demon charged with protecting greater demons, or demon lords. Vicious and cruel in the extreme. Most commonly manifest in physical form upon Earth, but possess the ability to escape human notice.

Throne. A class of angel found upon the middle tier of Heaven and often, upon Earth. One of the classes commonly referred to as Guardian Angels.

Usurper. A new challenger has emerged to challenge God for the Throne of Heaven, much as Lucifer did in the early days of Creation. It is believed he commands between a third and half of all heavenly angels. His name and class is currently unknown.

Veils. The common name for the Eye of God.

Virtue. A class of angel found upon the lowest tier of Heaven and often upon Earth.

Void. An empty expanse, without any reference to time or space, and existing outside any known natural law. Some angels believe this place is the final resting place for their deceased kin.

Watchers. A modern-day militarist religious order with ancient roots, traced directly to the original Order of the Knights Templar. Oddly enough, these righteous warrior-priests took for themselves the name Watchers, as a reference to the Nephilim, a group of angels who had taken human wives in the early days of humanity, and thus fell out of favor with the Creator. The reason is unclear. The church outlawed the Order and demanded they disband in the fifteenth century. Modern descendants still carry on the highly secretive mission of the Order. The Watchers are believed to possess powerful religious artifacts taken from eleventh- and twelfth-century Jerusalem, and the latter-day French government, as well as the Vatican, is rumored to have a serious interest in recovering these artifacts.

Word of Power. Words spoken in the "tongue of angels" that allow these celestial beings to command vast elemental power.